the

CHARMER

Madeline Hunter

BANTAM BOOKS

THE CHARMER
A Bantam Book / December 2003

Published by
Bantam Dell
A Division of Random House, Inc.
New York, New York

ISBN 0-553-58591-6

Manufactured in the United States of America
Published simultaneously in Canada

OPM   10 9 8 7 6 5 4

*Journey back to an age of seductive danger,
passionate intrigue, and scandalous love as nationally
acclaimed author Madeline Hunter draws you into
the hearts of three irresistible men:*

THE SEDUCER

Daniel St. John Charismatic and mysterious,
this dangerously seductive man has survived a
treacherous revolution: a master at the arts of war
and intrigue, he knows the secrets of winning
a woman's heart . . . and body.

THE SAINT

Vergil Duclairc This dashing nobleman leads
a dangerous double life: beneath his perfect composure
and self-control is a sensual master whose mere touch
can tempt a woman to the wildest abandon.

THE CHARMER

Adrian Burchard This virile aristocrat
was used to having women at his command: darkly
handsome, sensuous, magnetic, he lived in a world
of mysteries and secrets . . . a man dangerous
to love, impossible to resist.

*Fighters, protectors, and lovers, they live in a dazzling
and treacherous world of glittering ballrooms and sinful
gaming halls, in a time of heart-stopping duels and
soul-searing passion.*

These are their stories . . .

And coming in January 2004,
THE SINNER, *Dante's story*

Also by Madeline Hunter

By Arrangement

By Possession

By Design

The Protector

Lord of a Thousand Nights

Stealing Heaven

The Seducer

The Saint

and coming soon

The Sinner

For my sister

ROSARY

whose serenity, grace, and

generosity create a quiet harbor

in life's storms.

the

CHARMER

chapter I

~ May 1831

Adrian crossed the drawing room's threshold and found himself in the middle of an Arab harem.

Women swathed in colorful pantaloons and veils lounged beside men dressed in flowing robes. A fortune in silk billowed down from the high, frescoed ceiling, forming a massive tent. Two tiger skins stretched over the pastel tapestry rugs, and bejeweled pillows and throws buried settees and chairs. An exotic, heavy scent drifted under those of incense and perfume. Hashish. In the darkest corners some men kissed and fondled their ladies, but no outright orgy had ensued.

Yet.

A man on a mission, with no interest in this type of diversion, Adrian walked slowly through the costumed bodies, looking for a female who fit the description of the Duchess of Everdon.

He noticed a canopied corner that appeared to be the place of honor. He aimed for it, ignoring the women who looked his way and smiled invitingly.

The canopy draped a small dais holding a chaise longue. A woman rested on it in a man's arms. Her eyes were closed, and the man was plying her with wine. Adrian's card had fallen ignobly to the floor from her lax fingers.

"I am grateful that you have finally received me, Duchess," he said, announcing his presence. Actually, she had not agreed to receive him at all. He had threatened and bluffed his way past the butler.

Her lids slit and she peered down her body at him. She wore a garment that swaddled her from breasts to bare feet, but which left her neck and arms uncovered, revealing pale, glowing skin. In the low light he could not judge her face well, but her hair was a mass of dark curls tamed by a gold band circling her head.

She looked very sensual with the red silk wrapping her curves and her armlets and anklets gleaming in the candlelight. The blond, bare-chested man who held her thought so too. Adrian half-expected him to take a bite out of her while he watched.

The duchess gave Adrian a frank assessment and he returned one of his own. The only living child of the last Duke of Everdon had attained instant importance with her father's unexpected death. For the last two weeks everyone who was anyone in England had been speculating about Sophia Raughley, and wondering what she had been up to during her long absence from England.

Adrian did not relish reporting the answer to the men who had sent him here. From the looks of things, the new duchess had occupied herself lo these last eight years in Paris with becoming a shameless libertine.

She twisted out of her lover's hold and stretched to

grope for the card, almost falling off the chaise longue. She appeared childishly clumsy suddenly, and a bit helpless, and Adrian experienced a pang of pity. He picked up the card and placed it in her fingers. She squinted, and gestured to her partner to bring a candle close.

"Mister Adrian Burchard," she read.

"At your service, Your Grace. If we could speak privately, please."

Gathering her drapery, she rose to her feet. With the breeding of centuries stiffening her posture, she faced him.

"I think that I know what service you offer, and you have wasted your journey. I am not going back with you."

Of course she was. "Again, I ask to speak with you privately."

"Come back tomorrow."

"I have come the last two days, and now tonight. It is time for you to hear what I have to say. It is time for you to face reality."

Anger flashed in her eyes. She advanced toward him. For a moment she appeared quite formidable. Then her foot caught in the flowing silk. She tripped and hurtled forward, right into his arms.

He grappled with the feminine onslaught, gripping her soft back and bottom. She wore no stays or petticoats under that red silk. No wonder her blond Arab gleamed with expectation.

She looked up in dazed shock, her green eyes glinting. Her smile of embarrassment broadened until he expected her ears to move out of the way.

She was drunk. Completely foxed.

Wonderful.

He set her upright and held her arm until she attained some balance.

"I do not much care for reality. If that is what you offer, go away." She sounded like a rebellious, petulant child, provoking the temptation in him to treat her like one. She waved around the drawing room. "This is real enough for me."

"Hardly real. Not even very accurate."

"My *seraglio* is most accurate. Stefan and I planned it for weeks. Delacroix himself designed the costumes."

"The costumes are correct, but you have created a European fantasy. A *seraglio* is nothing like this. In a true harem, except for the rare visitor, all the men are eunuchs."

She laughed and gave Stefan a playful poke. "Not so loud, Mister Burchard, or the men will run away. And the women? Did I get that right at least?"

"Not entirely. For one thing, an entire *seraglio* exists for the pleasure of one man, not many. For another..."

Stefan's expression distracted him. His smile revealed the conceit of a man who assumed that if only one sultan were to enjoy the pleasures of this particular harem, it went without dispute that it would be him.

Stefan was going to be a problem.

"For another, except for a few ornaments, the women in a harem are naked."

Suggestive laughter trickled to the dais from the onlookers. Bawdy shouts pierced the smoky shadows. As if his words had been a cue, a woman on the other side of the room rose up from her circle of admirers and unclasped a broach. Her diaphanous drape fluttered to the floor amidst shouts and clapping.

Another woman rose and stripped. The situation deteriorated rapidly. Garments flew through the air. The shadows filled with the swells of breasts and buttocks. Embraces became much more intimate.

The duchess's eyes widened. She appeared dismayed at the turn things had taken. Ridiculous, of course. She had just explained that she had planned it herself.

Stefan reached for her. "Come, Sophia, *moi skarb.*"

The duchess staggered back with his pull and fell onto his lap. Adrian watched, a forgotten presence. Stefan began caressing her arm while he held the goblet to her mouth.

Adrian turned to go. This promised to be a distasteful task. Still, it was essential for him to complete it. A lot was riding on this foolish, debauched woman. Quite possibly the future of England itself.

He glanced back to the chaise longue. Stefan had loosened her gown from one shoulder and now worked on the other. Her head lolled on his shoulder but her dull reaction did not deter Stefan in the least. She sat limply while the man undressed her.

Adrian stepped back onto the dais just as Stefan bared the duchess's pretty breasts.

"Perhaps in your amorous zeal you have not noticed, my friend, but the woman is no longer with you. She is out cold."

Stefan was pulling the canopy's drapes closed. "Mind your own affairs."

"Gentlemen rarely mind their own affairs when a lady is about to be raped. But then, you would not know how gentlemen react, would you?"

Stefan rose indignantly and the duchess slid away into

a half-naked heap on the chaise longue. "How dare you insinuate that I am not a gentleman. I will have you know that I am a prince of the royal house of Poland."

"Are you? What are you doing in Paris? With your countrymen fighting to throw out the Russians, shouldn't a prince be leading an army somewhere? Or are you one of those princes who doesn't like war much?"

"Now you call me a coward!"

"Only if you are really a prince, which I will wager you are not. I suspect that, in truth, you clawed your way out of the Warsaw gutters and have been living off women since you left home."

Stefan's eyes bugged with fury. Adrian casually dragged red silk discreetly over the duchess's naked breasts. "Exactly how do you employ yourself, Stefan? When you aren't whoring for rich women, that is, and helping them plan orgies?"

"I am a poet," Stefan snarled.

"Ahhh. A *poet*. Well, that makes all the difference, doesn't it? Women do not *keep* you, they *patronize* you."

Adrian bent and slid his arms under the duchess. "I am taking the duchess to where she can recover. Interfere, and I will kill you."

Stefan sputtered with indignation, but his expression quickly turned taunting and mean. As Adrian lifted his burden, Stefan moved to block their way.

"I am serious, Stefan. Stand aside or I will call you out and kill you. Since you are a scoundrel, it will not even ruin my day."

Stefan was almost drunk enough to ignore the threat, but, to Adrian's disappointment, not quite. With a scowl he moved away.

Adrian carried the duchess off the dais. Movement caused the loose garment to shift so that a breast peeked out of the red silk. Noting once more that her breasts were quite lovely, he bore the duchess out of the *seraglio* with as much dignity as he could muster for the two of them.

The old butler lurked in the corridor. Adrian called for the man to accompany him.

"Your name."

"Charles, sir. She insists that we all use our Christian names here. The French influence, I'm afraid."

The evidence that the duchess harbored some frivolous egalitarian notions was not welcome news. "Are any of the other servants English besides you, Charles?"

"Her maid, Jenny, that is all. The rest are French, and there is an assortment of Poles and Austrians and Bohemians feeding at the trough, but they are here to serve their own masters, who in turn are permanent guests, as it were."

"How many permanent guests?"

"Four at the moment."

"All men?"

Charles flushed to the top of his balding pate and nodded. "Artist types. Writers and whatnot. They are known in the city as Miss Raughley's Ensemble. All of them full of the high sensibility. My lady is a great patroness of the new romantic style in the arts." He looked at his mistress's lolling head with affection, and delicately reached to ease some silk over her bare breast. "I would like to say that this is not like her. Since hearing of her father's death, she has not been herself."

"Grief-stricken?"

"Terrified's more like it. Not much love between her and the duke. It's why we are here, isn't it? But the news affected her badly. It is as if she knows that she cannot hide anymore."

They had reached the grand staircase. "Show me her chambers, Charles, and call for Jenny and two other women whom you trust. Then I will give you instructions for packing. The duchess will be leaving Paris. If you have any doubts regarding my authority to initiate these plans while she is indisposed, I should tell you that I have a letter from King William himself summoning her home."

"The King!" The news rendered Charles suitably impressed until they reached the second landing. "I do not think it will be possible to affect a departure so quickly."

"If closing the house proves complicated, you will stay behind and do it. The duchess comes with me at once."

"I do not think she will agree to that."

Adrian had no intention of letting Sophia Raughley's lack of agreement interfere with his mission. Charles pointed him down a corridor and they stopped at a large double door. "Why will she want to delay, Charles? If it is because of Stefan, I will deal with that."

"I was not thinking of the Polish poet. It is the animals. She would never leave without them."

"A small matter. We can take them. I have a good hand with dogs."

Charles turned the doors' handles. "As it happens, not just dogs."

Adrian entered and stopped in his tracks. Dozens of inhuman eyes peered at him from around the chamber.

He had escaped the harem only to find himself in a menagerie.

"There are more," Charles said.

Of course there were. Adrian strolled around the opulent sitting room. The bright plumed birds had ceased their noise, but the little monkey was still throwing a tantrum because his mistress's arrival had not meant freedom from the cage. There was an odd-looking reptile in a glass case, and two large snakes in another. An ocelot skin stretched under the window. Unlike the pelts in the drawing room, this one still had the animal inside it.

And, of course, there were indeed dogs. Three of them. Mean-faced mastiffs. They posed like soldiers in front of the hearth and tensely eyed Adrian's neck. The feminine shrieks coming from the dressing room had put them on edge.

"The big ones are at the country house," Charles explained. "Well, one can hardly house a giraffe and a lion and such here in the city, can one?"

"Indeed not. I tried that once with my giraffe and lion and they destroyed the library." Adrian threw himself into a chair right in the middle of the mastiffs and proceeded to stare them down.

More screams sounded from the dressing room where three servants were bathing the duchess. With luck, at least half of her wits would return so he could explain what was going to happen.

Hopefully she would not remember the first few moments of her reawakening. Jenny had turned out to be a little thing, and the two French servants were even smaller. They could not lift the duchess, so he had been forced to carry her in when the bath was ready.

In the interests of modesty he had lowered her into the water still clothed, but the wet silk adhered like a second skin and created an image much more erotic than mere nudity. The duchess had thoroughly quashed his sexual reactions by regaining consciousness upon submersion. She half came to, absorbed her situation, and then awoke with a roar.

At which point she had gotten sick.

Yes, this was turning out to be quite a night.

Two of the mastiffs assumed positions of submission at his feet, but the third refused to budge, bow, or blink. Adrian intensified the contest while his memory perused the last hour's events, pausing longer than it should on various images of Sophia Raughley soaked, in *dishabille,* or bare-breasted.

The duchess's angry voice could be heard, threatening the sack to one and all. Charles shot Adrian a beseeching glance.

"You may leave. You know what to do," Adrian said.

The last hound broke and lowered his tail. Adrian permitted some friendly sniffing, then gestured for the animal to lie. He poured some of the wine brought in for his refreshment, stretched out his legs, and waited.

chapter 2

Sophia cradled her spinning head in her hands. She had drunk a glass or two more wine than normal tonight, but nothing to deserve this misery.

"Is he still there?"

Jenny cracked open the door and stuck her nose to it. "Yes, sitting by the hearth like he has a right to be here."

Sophia gestured to the two women mopping up the water around the tub. "Leave now and go to bed. The rest can wait until morning."

Lisette and Linette bustled to the door. As they slipped out, Sophia caught a glimpse of the man sitting amidst her hounds.

Adrian Burchard. She knew of the Burchards. Randall Burchard, the Earl of Dincaster, had been a friend of her father.

The only thing that she knew about this particular Burchard, however, was what she had learned from Jenny. He was here on an errand from the King, no less, to bring her back to England.

"Send him away."

"I do not think that he will go. He said that he would wait until you were well enough disposed to speak with him."

Sophia pushed Jenny aside and stuck her own nose to the crack. Adrian Burchard drank her wine, gazed at her fire, and scratched Yuri's ear. It was a wonder he had not removed his shoes. He cut a stunning figure with his dark tousled hair, dark eyes, and black evening dress. Many women would not mind finding him ensconced in their chambers.

He possessed a compelling presence that affected her even in her pitiful condition. Still, he struck her as somehow fraudulent. The cut of his clothes and the manner in which he lounged, announced his Englishness. He exuded an English aristocratic breeding that could not be faked. But . . . his face, yes, that was it. There was something suspiciously un-English about his face.

He did not resemble the fair-haired Earl of Dincaster. This man had thick, wavy, black hair, and very dark eyes, deep-set and shaped the way they are in Mediterranean countries. The contrast with his fair skin created a slightly unnatural appearance. There was something foreign about his mouth, too, a hard definition that gave it a cruel aspect.

She could not shake the impression that if he changed his clothes, demeanor, and a few physical details, Adrian Burchard could pass for a Spanish prince much more successfully than that rapscallion Stefan passed for a Polish one. Which was peculiar because while Stefan might not be a prince, he most certainly was Polish.

The more she peered, the more familiar Burchard

looked in ways that uncomfortably pricked at her recollections. She tried to brush aside the thick clouds that obscured the events of the night. It was extremely disconcerting to realize that several hours of your life had passed without your awareness of them.

Jenny held up some stays for her attention. "Will you be feeling well enough to dress now, my lady?"

"I have no intention of getting fully dressed again to greet him. Fetch my violet undressing gown, do something with my hair, and throw a shawl over my shoulders. If he is shocked, I do not care."

"Oh, I do not think you could shock him," Jenny mused while she pulled open doors of armoires. "After what he has already seen, it would be peculiar if he was scandalized by a perfectly respectable undressing gown, wouldn't it?"

Well, now, that depended upon what it was that he had already seen.

"What do you think of him, Jenny?"

Jenny glanced to the door. "He is very formidable. He does not frighten the way your father did, but there is something to him that makes one want to put things in his hands, because he is sure to make it come out as he intends. And he is every inch a gentleman. Charles said that while he carried you up here you were partly exposed, and not once did Mister Burchard look."

Sophia's unsettled stomach kicked in outrage. Through some bizarre misadventure, this stranger had seen her partly undressed.

"And he can be very gentle, my lady," Jenny continued while she tried to tame Sophia's curls with combs. "He carried you to the bath like a baby, and when you got sick he assisted and showed no dismay."

Sophia felt her face burn. Suddenly *that* memory broke through the mist. Sloshing water. Masculine hands holding her chin and forehead over a porcelain rim. Yards of ruined, soaked red silk.

Jenny pinned her curls back and encased them in a thin net. Sophia rose to don the violet satin sack gown.

Gathering the tattered shreds of her dignity around her, she made as grand an entrance into the next room as circumstances permitted.

The effect, if any, was wasted. Adrian was bent over Yuri's prostrate, panting form, giving a good scratch to the stomach slavishly begging for attention.

Sophia waited. He had heard her entrance but was pretending he had not. He planned to make this a contest. She really was not in the mood, even if his dark looks left her mouth dry.

He finally acknowledged her. Rising, he snapped his fingers and pointed Yuri back to his place by the hearth. Sophia did not miss the symbolism. *Your household is already mine to command,* the gesture said.

He gave her a sharp assessment with those wonderful eyes. His expression implied that he expected to find the next conquest quick work too.

He advanced and she presented her hand. He bowed over it. "Under the circumstances, perhaps we should start at the beginning and repeat the introduction, Duchess. I am Adrian Burchard. You are feeling better? I took the liberty to ask that some food be brought up. It will help if you eat something."

Tea and cakes waited atop a table. He guided her over,

sat her down, poured her tea, and settled himself several feet away. Masterfully.

"Please eat something." It wasn't a request. Not really.

She reached for a cake in spite of herself. She nibbled and drank a bit of tea under his watchful approval. A silly, still-inebriated part of her wanted to glow with delight that he was pleased.

A different, sensible part, the part that had developed a gargantuan headache, knew what he was doing. He was taking her in hand, as if she was some dimwit.

"You are one of the Earl of Dincaster's sons, are you not? I met your parents, years ago." She was amazed that she got the words out. He was so handsome that she couldn't concentrate. She had to force herself not to stare at his face. Close like this, she found it astonishing in its severe beauty.

He possessed a square jaw and defined cheekbones and his eyes positively glowed in the candlelight. His black hair fell carelessly about his forehead and face and collar, but not in the carefully mussed styles seen in drawing rooms these days. Rather it seemed to really grow that way because nature decreed it be a little wild.

Tell me, Mister Burchard, as I have always wondered. What is it like to be so beautiful that hearts skip when you pass by?

"I am his third son, after my brothers Gavin and Colin."

Third son. After the "heir and a spare." Lady Dincaster had been as fair as her husband, Sophia recalled. She examined Adrian's dark, foreign appearance with new interest.

"You have a letter for me, I believe," she said, barely

swallowing a tactless query regarding his legitimacy that wanted to blurt out.

He extricated a small missive from inside his frock coat. Sophia noted the royal seal.

"What does it say?"

"The King was surprised that you did not return to England upon your father's passing. He summons you at once. It would be his pleasure to welcome the newest peer to her position."

It appeared that they were going to talk about sad, complicated things. She found him a tad less attractive all of a sudden.

"My father was dead. Attending his funeral would not bridge the gulf that we found impossible to cross during his life. As to His Majesty, I expect that he wants his lords to enjoy the joke of a peeress in a country ruled by primo-geniture. Let them find their amusement elsewhere."

"Your situation is unusual, but it is not a joke. Nor will you be alone. As you know, there are other women who have benefited from traditions of inheritance in their families as you have."

"Two hundred years ago an ancestor convinced a king to permit a daughter to inherit his title, and I am now forced to play the duchess." She leaned toward him. "I do not want this. I will not do it. A steward can manage the estate. I intend to stay here in Paris."

"You must return. Certainly you know what is occurring in England. The French journals describe it, and English visitors surely report it."

"I do not associate with English visitors much, but yes, I am aware of what is occurring."

"Then you know that Parliament has been dissolved

and elections are being held. A movement to change the representation in the House of Commons has swept the country, pitting class against class. If an act of reform passes the next Parliament, it will change how England is governed as no war ever did."

"Perhaps it is time for some changes. I myself wouldn't know. I will let others decide."

His eyes flashed. Magnificently. Goodness, he was handsome.

"There are those who want revolution rather than reform. The power of Everdon cannot sit this out in France." He caught her gaze and held it with his compelling own. "I have come to bring you home, and if I have to carry you slung over my shoulder to the coast and across the channel, I will do so."

He maintained an utterly cool demeanor while he made his threat. No pomposity at which to laugh. No posturing to puncture. He laid out the facts in a quiet, firm voice. *This is how it is,* he said. *This is what will happen.*

"As a woman I cannot sit in Parliament. I inherited no political power along with the title and estate."

He examined her thoughtfully. "I cannot decide if you are truly as ignorant as you claim, or if you have adopted the pose in the vain hope that it will make a difference."

"You come very close to insult, Mister Burchard."

"Forgive me. Allow me to explain the situation in broad terms. As Duchess of Everdon you control twelve members of the Commons. They come from boroughs under your control in Devon and Cornwall."

"Rotten boroughs."

"Mostly. Your nomination is required to return them

to the Commons in this election. Your direction on their votes, once elected, will also be needed. Every vote will matter. So, while you cannot participate directly, you still hold significant power."

It was accepted tradition that hundreds of seats in the Commons were "owned" by peers sitting in the upper house. She had no idea that Everdon controlled so many, however.

Very suddenly she experienced complete, horrible sobriety. It was going to be much worse than she had feared. Her situation promised to be terribly precarious.

"You were sent by the King. Who else?"

A spark of approval flickered in his dark eyes. "The Duke of Wellington, and other men of influence in the Tory party."

"We both know that these men have no intention of leaving the power that you describe in my hands. They need to find a way to dictate to me, and the surest way to do that with a woman is through her husband. So I ask you, who is the man who has been chosen for me?"

His hard mouth quirked with quiet amusement. He appeared extremely charming like that. "If I had to venture a guess, I would say Mister Gerald Stidolph."

Oh, Lord, not Gerald. *Anyone* but Gerald.

Fury and fear flashed like lightning through her aching head. It sought a destination and Adrian Burchard was the closest one available.

"Why were you chosen to bring me back? Why did they send you instead of someone else?"

"I knew your father. I am the M.P. from Stockton in Devon. It is one of your boroughs."

"Don't you fear alienating me with your interference in

my life? Tell me, what would happen if I did not nominate you for this election?"

His lids lowered and he quirked another smile, less
amused and friendly this time. "I expect that the party
would find another seat for me to stand to. If not, I would
be forced to pursue my other interests."

"So you are an important member of the party, and not
just a back bencher."

"Not especially important, but useful."

"No wonder they sent you. You are not too beholden.
You serve me, but only to the extent it suits your true
masters. For this meeting to be complete, shouldn't you
be giving me something. A ring or seal?"

She said it to goad him. The last thing she expected
was for him to reach into his pocket and indeed withdraw
a ring. She recognized it as her father's, with the crest of
Everdon raised on its jewel.

He held his hand out for hers. She glared at that ring.
A chill shuddered through her, trembling out of time
and memory. He reached down and raised her hand from
her lap.

His hand holding hers felt incredibly comforting, so
much that she almost embarrassed them both by asking
him not to let go right away. He slid the circle of heavy
gold on her finger. It looked ridiculous on her.

His touch fell away and she was left to support the ring
alone.

"Since it was not clear how long you would be indisposed, I took the liberty of giving Charles instructions for
your journey." He looked at her impassively. She was a
problem to be managed, a difficulty to be cleaned up.

"Regarding my indisposition, Mister Burchard, I would like to clarify something."

"Yes, I expect that you would," he said dryly.

He expected excuses. She had intended to give some, but she abruptly changed tack. "My maid tells me that you accompanied me into the dressing room. If I had been alert I would have forbidden it, and I expect you to show more respect for my modesty in the future."

"I did not accompany you, I carried you. I needed you conscious and your maids could not manage it alone. I suggest that you replace them. If you intend to continue on your course of living, you will need women far more substantial to assist you." He rose. "Now, I think that you should sleep. You will need to direct the packing of your private things tomorrow, but I will see to the household for you, with Charles's assistance."

She stood as well. "Perhaps I did not make myself clear. I am not going."

"Yes, Duchess, you are. The morning next we depart. Bring whatever you need for your comfort. Bring your menageries and your artists. Bring your Arab silks and your hashish. Bring your orgies, for all I care. But believe me when I say to you, finally and definitely, that you will accompany me back to England."

She watched him leave with her mouth agape. Hashish and orgies, indeed. To accuse her of such things was insulting. Why, it was—

With horrible abruptness, memories lurched out of the fog. Bits of images pressed on her.

Perfumes and silk and laughter. Her *seraglio* a success, but a few of society's leading lights departing too early . . . the fantasy growing too real and too dreamlike at the same time ... colors becoming too vivid and sounds too far away.

More memories now, a flood of them ... A hand on her body and a thick accent in her ear ... Garments flying through the air ...

"Jenny."

Her maid scurried out of the dressing room.

"Jenny, tell Charles that I must speak with him in the morning as soon as I wake."

Scandalous visions, observed through a haze ... naked women and male flesh ... bodies entwining ...

"And Jenny, tell the footmen that they are to enter the drawing room and invite any remaining guests to leave. *At once.*"

chapter 3

Beginning at dawn, Adrian initiated preparations for Sophia Raughley's removal to her title's seat in Devon.

Long before noon he had arranged for the eventual transport of the menagerie, assigned caretaker duties to servants recommended by Charles, hired wagons to accompany them to the coast, and ordered the packing of valuables to be carted along. Things were well in hand by the time Miss Raughley's Ensemble came down from their chambers.

They all looked to be tousle-haired men of the world a few years out of university. That made them several years younger than the duchess herself, who was twenty-nine. Adrian, at thirty-four, thought they appeared unseasoned and untried and too contented by far.

He put aside the portfolio containing the letters of instructions that awaited the duchess's signature (or, if necessary, its forgery) and joined them at breakfast.

Charles had explained that membership in the Ensemble flowed and fluxed. Stefan was the most recent arrival, while a Greek had departed several months ago. The duchess had been maintaining guests for at least five years. She possessed a weakness for artists from countries torn by revolution and strife, but that was not a requirement for her patronage.

Adrian sat at the table while the artists looked him over.

"What are you doing here?" Stefan snarled.

"The duchess offered me her hospitality for a day or two," Adrian said. "At first I did not want to impose, but then I thought, What will one footloose man more or less matter?"

Everyone chuckled with self-deprecating humor.

Everyone except Stefan. "Who the hell are you? What are you?"

"Adrian Burchard. I am her countryman."

"A damned nuisance is what you are, and you don't look like one of her countrymen."

A dark, thickly built man with a heavy mustache at the other end of the table laughed heartily. "Ignore him, Mister Burchard. Stefan is always surly in the morning. I am Attila Toth, and you are welcome at our board."

"You are Attila Toth, the Hungarian composer?" Adrian asked, employing the information he had pumped out of Charles this morning regarding the permanent guests.

A smile of delight broke beneath the brush of mustache. "You know my music? I knew that my *Sonata Hongrois* was introduced in London at a small performance, but that you should have heard it and remembered my name overwhelms me."

He did look overwhelmed. So much that Adrian feared he might do something of embarrassingly high sensibility like cry or swoon. It had become fashionable for young men of creative dispositions to display their turbulent moods. The trend was the human counterpart to the strongly expressive dynamics in their music and art.

The composer retreated into his dreams of artistic grandeur, gazing out the window to the garden. Attila was a bit of a fool, but not a scoundrel like Stefan, Adrian decided. Possibly the Hungarian was the duchess's lover instead of the Pole. Hell, maybe they both were.

Actually, maybe they *all* were.

That notion raised an edgy irritation in him.

It went without saying that Stefan would not be coming to England, but he had been prepared to follow the duchess's wishes regarding the others. Now he abruptly decided that none of the Ensemble would make the trip back to Devon.

"Allow me to complete the introductions," the man closest to him said. "I am Jacques Delaroche, and this handsome rogue to my left is Dieter Wurzer."

Adrian dipped into Charles's coaching again. "It is my pleasure to meet such a talented poet, and also one of Prussia's leading young novelists."

Jacques, the French poet, was all sleek, fine-boned, dark elegance, the sort of man who would go hungry before he wore an unfashionable coat. Dieter, whose surname announced his humble origins, possessed a quiet blond nobility that Stefan, the would-be Polish Prince, would do well to emulate.

Two poets, a novelist, and a composer. Not an Englishman in the batch. Nor a painter, for that matter. This human menagerie was unbalanced and incomplete. Adrian considered that a mark in the duchess's favor. Spontaneous extravagance had the potential to be charming, while calculated self-indulgence promised no redemption whatsoever.

"Are you another artist?" Dieter asked.

"No."

The three of them eyed him more curiously. Attila still communed with nature.

"Would you happen to have anything to do with the sudden activity among the servants?" Jacques asked. "The confusion woke me."

"It looks as if they are turning the place out for a thorough cleaning," Dieter commented. "A footman intruded to remove the silver from my chamber."

"Not a thorough cleaning," Adrian explained. "A thorough move."

"To the countryside?" Attila asked with enthusiasm, his attention returning to the group.

"Yes."

Dieter cast Adrian a careful look. "How long before she leaves? For the country?"

"Tomorrow is the plan."

Adrian finished his breakfast and took his leave. It was time to make sure that the duchess was awake, aware, and packing. He strode to the staircase. Rapid footsteps alerted him to Jacques following.

"Dieter seems to think that Sophia will be traveling alone," he said, falling into step.

"I will accompany her."

"Dieter also thinks—he is very quiet but also most

observant—he also thinks that all of this activity means that this house is being closed."

"That is Her Grace's pleasure."

"She said nothing to us. The last anyone saw her was when you carried her away last night. I feel bound to ask if you have the right to make these arrangements in her name, especially since they affect us."

"If any man does, I do." Which meant nothing, of course, since no man did.

Jacques' face fell. "She told me once . . . but I just assumed the arrangement was . . . my apologies for questioning you, but I am sure that you will understand that my concern was for So—, for the duchess, whose heart is too generous, and whom some try to take advantage of, like Stefan, who I am sure will rue the day he was born when he learns who you are, especially since you caught him last night attempting such liberties. . . ."

The smooth, urbane Jacques blurted his endless sentence in a manner that implied he had concluded Adrian was someone who actually mattered.

Not daring to respond, Adrian merely smiled. Jacques' relief bordered on a swoon. The French poet aimed down the corridor and back into the breakfast room.

Jenny admitted Adrian to Sophia's apartment only to inform him that her lady had taken the ocelot, Camilla, to the garden.

He surveyed the preparations that had turned the dressing room into a disaster. He had never imagined that one woman could accumulate so many clothes. Dozens of gowns, a field of bonnets, stacks of gloves and shoes . . . It appeared that one of the duchess's favorite diversions was shopping.

"Two portmanteaus only for tomorrow. The rest must be sent later," he reminded Jenny. He then made his way to the garden to inform the lady of his own progress on her behalf.

She rested on a bench beneath a pear tree budding with new flowers. Camilla paced on a long lead, cautious and slit-eyed. The duchess wore the latest fashion, a wide-skirted, gargantuan-sleeved rose gown that revealed little form except a sashed waist and no skin except pale hands and neck.

Adrian disliked the new fashions for women, and remembered the softer, classical styles of his youth with nostalgia. The duchess was just a bit on the plumply curved side, and not very tall, and the style did not become her. Neither did the gown's color, although it was very beautiful. He pictured her falling in love with the hue and not caring whether it complemented her skin and eyes. An extravagant woman, perhaps, but not an overly vain one.

He advanced through the fertile spring smells filling the garden. This was the first decent look he had gotten of her, since last night's candles obscured more than they revealed.

He noticed now that her dark hair was as lustrous and jubilant in its curls as it had appeared on the dais, and that the cruel gown did not completely hide the pleasant feminine softness that he had briefly held in his arms. Her creamy complexion possessed a luminous quality.

He could see the duke's blood in her firm little chin and full lower lip and the fine, gently crooked bone of her nose. She was attractive, and even striking when she focused those green eyes on something. At the moment she did so, and the something was him.

Unfortunately, the way she appraised him indicated that she had not yet surrendered.

Time to take matters in hand.

chapter 4

He came to her through the low grass, bringing his aura of command and dark magnetism. She resented her tingling reaction to his slow smile.

Camilla paced over to block his path. Adrian had the good sense to halt. The ocelot was no larger than a medium-sized dog, but she could be dangerous.

"She has been with people since birth," the duchess reassured, calling Camilla aside. She noted Adrian's reaction. "You do not approve."

He shrugged. "The imprisonment of wild animals for educational purposes is one thing, but..."

"But the unnatural restriction of one to be a woman's plaything is another. I agree. Camilla belonged to a foreign diplomat who was marrying. His bride was afraid of Camilla, and he was going to have her shot. I took her instead." She scratched Camilla's ears and the big cat moved for more, just like a huge tabby.

He lounged with his shoulder against the tree, a

disturbingly attractive presence intruding on her peace. He felt closer than he actually was.

"Did all of the animals come to you that way? As strays and homeless petitioners?"

"The big ones came with the country chateau. The former owner had collected them. As for the rest, it just happened. One bird amuses you so you accept another. You agree to take a dog, and his brothers ask to come too."

"Certainly. It would be cruel to refuse." He stretched his hand toward Camilla. She ignored him with disdain.

"Unlike my servants and my hounds, Camilla is suspicious of you."

"I am a stranger. She does not know my scent. And unlike your dogs, she is female. They are often more cautious, but with patience and the proper handling, they usually come around."

"Is that why you were sent, Mister Burchard? Because you know how to make women come around?"

"I was speaking of four-legged females, not the human variety."

No, you were not.

"What were you told about me?" she asked.

"Very little."

"I take it that you are shocked by what you have found."

"Your tastes in diversions are not my concern. Getting you quickly and safely back to England is."

"You have been hard at work preparing for that. Charles tells me that you have accomplished in one morning a feat of organization that should take at least a week. Do you have some experience as a man of affairs or a military officer?"

"I have experience as neither, although as a young man I served as an assistant to the Foreign Secretary, and on occasion accompanied ambassadors who could not have found the right ship on their own, much less the correct country."

"And now you are sent to fetch errant duchesses who don't want to go home."

A chill trembled through her. Perhaps it was because the sun had moved and shade now covered her head. More likely it was the thought of going home and confronting the memories waiting there.

He noticed. Without a word he slipped off his frock coat and placed it around her shoulders.

It was the sort of thing that any gentleman would do. It didn't really mean anything other than simple courtesy. However, the protective gesture touched her so profoundly that her soul quaked. The greedy way her heart grasped at its insinuation of friendship laid bare how lonely she had been in this foreign city, despite all the animals and diversions and guests.

The May weather in Paris still carried a northern bite, but he appeared comfortable enough in his shirtsleeves and dark neckcloth and gray silk waistcoat. And devastatingly dashing. She rather suspected that he *had* been chosen because of the way he could handle women.

A part of her wished that she had it in her to make him demonstrate his skill. She would know some closeness then, for a while at least. She could probably lie to herself that it meant something. She had a bit of experience in doing that.

His presence was making her foolish and nostalgic. She had avoided the English community in Paris. She had forgotten how very pleasant it was to talk with someone who shared a common history and language. It created a flow of essential familiarity even though they did not know each other at all.

"Mister Burchard, there are reasons why I have not lived in England and why I do not even visit."

He sat on the far end of the bench, where he could see Camilla's face. "I respect that you have had your reasons, but they are not important enough anymore."

"That is an unbearably arrogant thing to say. Are you the kind of man who assumes that a woman's concerns must be frivolous?"

"No. I am a man who believes that there are times when the greater good is more important than any individual's preference."

"We must find another way to do this. I will give you letters saying whatever needs to be written. I will give you my father's ring so others can speak in my name."

"You must be seen in the boroughs, and your nominations known as your choice. There is no other way." He engaged Camilla's attention, and held out his hand to her. The ocelot sniffed warily. "If there were, I would gladly spare you, whatever your reasons for rejecting your family and homeland."

She thought that she heard an invitation to confide. It would be delicious to do so. But what could she tell? She had no tales of great injuries or insults. Her story was the age-old one of a woman who had discovered that she had been born only to be used.

Now this man had come to take her back, to be used again.

In the next moment he elegantly vanquished Camilla.

His hand turned, and one long finger lined up the cat's nose in a seductive scratch. With a rumble of pleasure, Camilla stretched for more. Up on her feet now, she rubbed against his leg, positioning her spine. With languid strokes, Adrian Burchard bound one female to him forever.

Sophia watched his hand move, mesmerized. Splaying through fur, rubbing along head, scratching near tail. For a moment that palm was on her, warming down her body in a confident, possessive caress. Her own visceral, silent purr joined Camilla's.

One more ally lost. He was good at this. By supper she would undoubtedly stand alone.

A small commotion near the house caught her attention.

Then again, maybe not totally alone.

Jacques, Dieter, Attila, and Stefan had entered the garden. They noticed her under the pear tree and headed her way.

"You told them," she said.

"Yes."

"I cannot just abandon them."

"You cannot step off the King's own ship with four acolytes in tow. Also, before they reach us I should warn you that Jacques has decided that I am someone of significance to you."

"Are you saying that you permitted Jacques to think that you are my lover?"

"He thinks that I am a man from your past. Whether I am supposed to be a lover from your past, I do not know."

Sophia examined the young men bearing down on her.

Their serious expressions suddenly made sense. They were afraid.

She beamed her best smile of welcome. Her friendliness counted for nothing, as Adrian's dark gaze brought them up short. They stopped thirty feet away to discuss the situation.

Adrian observed with fascination. "It would help if I know who they think I am."

"It was convenient for me while I lived here to invent events in my past in order to protect myself," she explained. "On occasion I would attract the attention of a man whom I wished to discourage. I discovered that the best way to do that was to have a husband."

"Except you never married. Even in France that would be well known about a woman of your birth."

"He is a secret husband. Someone thoroughly unsuitable, and very dangerous. He possesses a terrible temper. He has dueled five times and killed four men. If he ever learned that someone had pressed unwanted attentions on me, who knows what he might do."

"How did you explain why he isn't living here with you?"

"He is a spy for the English government and has been active in Turkey and the Balkans for years now."

He gave her a very peculiar look. "What an outlandish tale."

"Isn't it? In addition to his spying, my father never knew of the marriage, so he could not live with me openly anyway."

The artists had worked themselves into something approaching bravery. Attila had been elected standard-bearer.

"With your father dead, however . . ."

"Jacques must have concluded that my secret husband could come to claim me now." She sighed. "I had completely forgotten that I had told Jacques that secret when we first met."

Attila stepped up and performed an elaborate bow. "Mister Burchard, the other gentlemen and I would have a word with you."

Sophia rolled her eyes. "Leave this to me, Mister Burchard. I need to speak with my friends anyway about something else. I will explain the mistake."

Adrian looked down his nose at her. "The gentlemen wish to speak with me, not you, my dear. Also we should drop the formalities. I have made it clear that I am not prepared to continue the secret any longer."

She stared at him. *My dear? Secret?*

Oh, good heavens. He was taking up the role.

He turned his attention to Attila. Attila swallowed so hard that it was audible.

"Mister Burchard, we feel some necessity to clarify the arrangement here," Attila said. "Soph—your wife has, on occasion, been generous enough to extend her hospitality to poor artists who arrive in this magnificent city ill-provided for its expenses. Her salons are attended by the leading lights in the arts, and of course such introductions are invaluable as well. Currently, we four are fortunate to have the patronage of this great lady. We would not want you to wonder, however, whether our affections for her have ever been other than of the purest nature."

Sophia felt her face getting redder and redder. "Attila, there has been a ridiculous misunder—"

"Actually, it had never occurred to me that any of you

might have dishonored my wife, and through her me," Adrian interrupted. "Except for Prince Stefan, of course."

Three men exhaled in relief. Stefan struck a brave pose, but he appeared sickly.

"However, now that you mention it, I expect that I had better interrogate the lady herself and learn the truth."

Attila's eyes widened with horror. He dropped to his knee in front of Sophia. "Oh, *kedvesem,* we have made a bad business worse for you. We only sought to allay any suspicions that he might have because, you must admit, the situation here could be seen as a little peculiar by a husband not aware of your excess generosity."

"Except that he is not—"

" 'A little peculiar' puts it rather too finely. After I speak with the duchess, I'll be dealing with any man here who so much as suggested anything improper."

That was not good news. Stefan went pale, but all of them looked uncomfortable. At one time or another each had made a suggestion or two. It was to be expected. Part of being patronized was to make sure the patron was happy. When the largesse came from a woman, it behooved a young artist to explore just what sort of services were required.

Attila clutched her hand and pressed his lips to it. "*Istenem, istenem.* My sweet lady, if I had known. Jacques told us but this morning. That accepting your kindness might put you in danger like this fills me with guilt."

"Oh, for goodness sake, I keep trying to tell you that he is not—"

"She isn't in danger. You are," Adrian clarified. "Although, after all these years on her own, she forgets who is her master. I may have to discipline her, but nothing dangerous is in store."

Jacques had been holding back, but now he stepped forward boldly. "You speak like a rogue instead of a gentleman. It will be uncivilized if you touch her in anger. She confided that you were a cruel, vile man, but I never expected such harshness."

One dark eyebrow rose devilishly above one dark eye. "Is that what you called me to your lovers, my sweet? *A cruel, vile man?*"

She rose and forced Attila up as well. "Heaven's mercy, Burchard, look what you have done. Jacques, he isn't going to beat me. Nor is he going to hurt any of you." She slid his coat off her shoulders and threw it to him. "Are you enjoying yourself? Tell them that your wit got the better of you."

She faced her friends with her back to Adrian. "He is not my husband. I never saw him before last night. Stefan will tell you that I had to read his card to know his name."

"That was a standard ruse to hide our relationship," his voice countered from behind. "Repudiating me will do no good, my dear."

"He is lying and he has taken over this house without authority."

"If a husband does not have authority, who does, I ask you, gentlemen?"

"He thinks to force me to return to England. I have explained that I am not going, but it has occurred to me that a journey would be pleasant all the same. How would all of you like to join me? I have decided to make a long visit to Italy."

Like a *tableau vivant,* her Ensemble froze and looked at her in surprise.

After a stunned five count, Attila clasped his hands, happy again. "Italy?"

A voice, not happy at all, spoke right behind her head. *"Italy?"*

"Venice first, then we will make our way down the coast. Ravenna, then over to Rome and up to Florence. We will lease a villa in the Tuscan Hills. It will be grand. All you need to do—"

A masculine warmth along her back distracted her. Hands circled her waist possessively. "I must forbid this, my darling."

She tried in vain to squirm away. "All you need to do to make it happen, dear friends, is to get rid of this man who has intruded on my life against my will. Tie him up and put him on a slow boat back to England."

They considered it. She could see it in their eyes. Jacques wavered, with one foot already over the line.

"Italy," she cried brightly, reminding him of the prize.

"Death," Adrian said coolly, spelling out the cost.

Jacques threw up his arms in surrender, casting her a regretful smile and shrug. Her worthless Ensemble eased away.

"Not fair." She twisted around to face her adversary. "You are all bluff. You have no intention of hurting them."

"Would you prefer if I did? Now, smile at me sweetly or I will have to drive them out completely to make sure that they do not aid you in any foolish schemes you might have."

He still held her, his hands pressing her through sash

and gown and stays, keeping her in place despite her squirming resistance. He glanced to the circle of men who had moved off into the garden.

"They are just four more strays, aren't they? Like the animals in your sitting room."

Those hands and his closeness were making her feel horribly flighty and foolish and female. He could probably tell, which was even worse.

"Do not presume to know what they are to me. Furthermore, there have been others. I have lived here eight years."

His fingers pressed more obviously, as if he checked the feel of her and tested the fit of his hands. She arched away but he did not release her.

"Then on the chance that one of them is your lover and willing to risk all for you, I should convince him that, with my return, *none* of his services are required now."

He eased her closer. She realized his intention. Shocked, she tilted away. "Don't you dare. I am a peeress of the realm. There is probably some law against taking liberties with me. This is—"

His mouth silenced her.

It probably was not a long kiss, even though it seemed to last forever. He did not even embrace her, just controlled her with his hands on her waist. It began discreetly, like a kiss of farewell or welcome between friends. Hardly a passionate exchange. A mild liberty, that was all, to discourage Jacques and the others.

But its tenderness stunned her. The taste of sweet connection pierced her heart with nostalgia and yearning, and she could not fight him as she had planned. She submitted, limp and dazed, her skirt crushed against his legs. Maybe she even softened in a way that might be construed as kissing him back.

He lingered. One hand rose to caress her face and hold it to a brief, warm exploration of the boundaries of discretion. Emotions long ignored and denied stirred within her, a frightening rumble that almost made her gasp.

He stopped but he still held her, with that warm palm against her cheek. His touch was so gentle that she could not feel indignant like she wanted to. She sensed that he saw everything during the few moments his dark gaze looked into her eyes. All of it. That kiss was dangerously seductive in ways that had nothing to do with sex.

He moved away and looked to the Ensemble. She blushed when she saw Attila's grin and Jacques' roguish expression.

"Make what arrangements you will for them. Let them follow in a month or so, if you insist. But not Stefan."

"No, not Stefan."

"You remember, then? That he drugged you last night?"

"Drugged me!"

"Your memory loss suggests it, as does your rapid fall into unconsciousness. Your Polish prince intended to have you without bothering to plead for your consent. To what end, I cannot imagine. Blackmail?"

"I confess that I have regained some memories that made me wonder what occurred with him. If it was as you say, I owe you my gratitude. I had planned to request his departure, and will be sure to do so now."

"There is no need, really, since *you* depart in the morning."

He seemed very confident of that. He spoke with a

quiet authority that said further resistance was futile. That piqued her annoyance. He probably thought that kiss had thoroughly established his dominance.

He took a few steps toward the house. "Have you eaten? Come and have something now. I do not want to risk your getting sick on the crossing."

"I will come later. I want to speak with them."

"I must insist that you do so in my presence. Also, I will stay in your house tonight, to ensure that all is ready at dawn. If you give me your word that you will not try to sneak away for Italy or elsewhere, I could find a room and not lie across the threshold to your chambers."

Camilla cried for release. Sophia untied the lead from the tree branch. The ocelot trotted to Adrian's side, where she made delicate pivots in order to rub his legs with her head.

Adrian waited. Sophia joined him and Camilla and they all strolled toward the house.

She would let him think he had won. Tomorrow morning, however, she would not be leaving for England with him.

chapter 5

Sophia gazed down at the activity in the street below. Servants tucked items into a wagon laden with portmanteaus, boxes, and cages. Her coach stood at the ready.

Adrian Burchard strolled past it all, calmly surveying the results of his high-handed interference in her life. He appeared contented and confident. The relaxed ease of his gait irritated her.

She welcomed the vexation. Anger was soothing compared to the nauseous hollow in her stomach that had plagued her since rising.

"Are you ready, my lady?" Jenny asked.

Sophia turned. Trunks filled the wardrobe, waiting their turn to make the voyage to England. Gowns and dresses and slippers and trinkets nestled inside them.

"Mister Burchard is amazing," Jenny said, with what Sophia considered traitorous admiration. "All of this so quickly arranged."

"Yes. He managed to pack up my whole life in two days. Since the substance of that life consists of little more than the objects I purchase, however, it was not such a difficult feat."

"That is not true. Your life is full and wonderful. You will be much missed. Paris will mourn your departure."

She doubted that Paris would give much notice. This city had lost better than her and survived the gap with ease.

"I do not want to do this," Sophia said. "He has no right to force it on me."

Jenny beamed an encouraging smile. "It will not be so bad, you will see. You are the duchess now. Your father is gone. It will not be as it was before."

Sophia wanted to believe that. The emptiness inside her knew differently, however. For one thing, her father was not really gone. He lived on in the estate and the title and the duties. Worse, he survived in the way he shadowed her soul.

Jenny tried again. "Shall we go down now?"

Without responding, Sophia walked past her. Going down was the easy part. It was what came after that sickened her.

She marched forward, forcing herself not to look at the familiar furniture and appointments of the house. She was determined not to get weepy and nostalgic. She was not a child. Besides, it was not what she left that grieved her, but what she returned to.

Sadness and fear, that was what she carried down the grand staircase. The sadness and fear of a desperate young woman running away from a life she could no longer live.

The girl she had been in England had resurrected during the night as she lay in bed, trying to find a way to thwart Burchard. With the growing realization that she could not abort his plans, that he would indeed drag her back to England, all the old, unhappy emotions had started to drown her.

They flooded again as she stood on the bottom step and looked out the open door. Its lines framed Burchard as he stood with his back to her, supervising the last of the packing.

It wasn't his fault that she fought a losing war against all the bad memories. He knew nothing about her life and was only obeying his masters.

Admitting that did not help. What was left of her spirit began a simmering rebellion against this man who was making her return to a world that she hated.

Jenny looked around. "Where are your artists? I expected them to be here."

"Mister Burchard made sure I was alone this morning. He bought off my guests by saying they could stay in the house until it was closed if they remained in their chambers this morning. We said our farewells last night. Perhaps it was just as well, since Attila cried so much."

"Well, I never cared for long leave-takings anyway." Jenny walked forward a few paces and looked back at her expectantly. "Shall we go?"

Adrian heard. He turned, then stepped aside two paces to indicate all was ready and they could leave the house.

Sophia gazed past him to the waiting coach. It would take her to the coast and to a ship that would carry her to England where another coach would transport her to Marleigh, the country seat of her family and title.

Adrian Burchard thought he was taking her home.

Not a normal home. Not a place that one longed to see

and remembered with fondness. Ghosts waited for her there. So did her own weakness and humiliation.

The little rebellion grew. She grabbed it as a raft of support amidst the chaos swimming in her head and heart.

Early this morning she had resigned herself to this journey as inevitable. She had decided to wear a sophisticated mask to hide her panic and melancholy.

Now, facing that coach, she knew that stepping out the door would destroy what little contentment she had built in her life.

She ignored Jenny's expression of encouragement.

She did not move.

Adrian stepped back to his old place and faced her over the threshold. "We are prepared to depart, Your Grace."

"Then all who are prepared should indeed depart, Mister Burchard. I regret that I cannot be counted among you."

If a body could sigh, his did.

He walked into the house.

A few servants lingered at the top of the stairs to the lower level. With the subtlest of gestures, he told them to leave. They scurried down.

Sophia resented the docility he could command from everyone. She narrowed her eyes on the cool, dark figure of Adrian Burchard.

"Jenny, wait in the coach. The duchess will join you shortly," he said.

Jenny hesitated, looking at Sophia helplessly. With an expression of apology and surrender, she left the house.

Sophia and Adrian faced each other. He did not say anything for a while. During that brief span, the lights in his eyes changed. His expression grew less stern and annoyed and even a little sympathetic.

"There is no choice," he said.

Did he mean for her, or for him? "Only because you do not give me one."

"Since there is none, let us do this with the dignity that befits your position."

"That is the odd fate of women, isn't it? Being a dignified adult means submission and surrender. Resistance to the whims of men makes one an obstinate child. You must forgive me, but I think the world has that backwards."

"You may be correct. Today, however, there is still no choice."

She hated the confident way he announced his control of her life.

He held out his hand, beckoning her forward. "It is time to go, Duchess."

A vivid memory came to her, of entering port after her flight from home. She had taken a deep breath when her foot landed on French soil. In that instant she had experienced a profound sense of deliverance and safety.

The relief had been so physical that she might have just survived a drowning or strangulation. She felt as if she had not been able to breathe for years and suddenly she could.

Entering the coach meant gasping for air again.

She would not embrace that fate willingly.

She ignored his offer of an escort. Instead she sank down and sat on the bottom step of the grand staircase and stared straight ahead.

He did not speak. He did not move. She refused to acknowledge him. She knew she was acting childish and spoiled, but she did not care. Every speck of her screamed against taking another step.

Suddenly he was standing right in front of her and she gazed only at his hips. That embarrassed her enough that she looked up.

She expected to see exasperation. Instead he looked down with a warmth that surprised her. He was not angry at all, only resigned.

In that instant she knew that he understood. Some of it, at least.

"As I said yesterday, I would spare you if I could," he said.

But he could not, so he would not.

"I said that I would carry you if I have to, and I will."

She looked away, swallowing hot tears. She would not accept this, but it was going to happen anyway.

"My sincere apologies, Duchess."

He reached down and lifted her to her feet. When she did not stand on her own, he dipped, grasped, and rose.

She found herself facing his back, slung over his shoulder, with his arms wrapped around her legs.

Carrying her like a carpet, he forced her to begin the journey back to England.

She stood at the railing of the ship and let the wind do its worst. It dismantled the careful style in which Jenny had fixed her hair. Its spray wet the mantle that she clutched to her body. She faced the gray expanse, and imagined the coast that would come into view soon.

A presence warmed her side and she glanced over. Adrian Burchard had joined her.

"You keep hovering nearby," she said. "Do you fear I will jump over? I assure you that I lack both the despair and the courage. I almost drowned once when I was a girl, and I would never ask for such terror again."

"I am more concerned that the damp will make you ill."

"I am dry beneath my mantle."

If he had inclinations to order her away from the railing, he did not speak them. Instead he leaned his forearms against the railing himself and looked to the sea with her.

"Where will we put in?" she asked.

"Portsmouth. Is that the port that you used when you left England?"

"Yes."

The sea appeared endless. Only it was not. She kept watching the horizon for evidence of land. Watching too hard.

"I rode there, on my horse. I carried only a bunch of jewels in my reticule. No clothing, nothing else at all."

"It sounds very bold and daring."

"I was not the least bit bold. I was terrified, but other emotions were stronger than fear and so I did it, much to my own amazement."

She did not know why she told him. He was the enemy. Something about him, however, offered a peculiar solace and a vague friendship. His eyes still contained that soft comprehension that she had been in the house. She wished they did not. She could hate him if not for that glimmer of understanding.

"My father was in London, but I knew the Parliament would end soon," she said. "I was not happy at Marleigh, but I could tolerate it when he was not there. When the letter came, announcing his imminent return, I knew that I could not bear his presence every day. So I ran." She laughed at the memory of her astonishing recklessness. "I had no idea what I was doing. I even had to ask other travelers for the way to Portsmouth. I kept worrying that he would catch me at an inn if I rested the horse, so I did so in the fields and woods. It was all very dramatic."

"Since he did not catch you, perhaps your caution was wise."

"It was unnecessary. He did not follow. I learned later that he made no attempt to catch me. He wrote to me in Paris and explained that the Duke of Everdon does not tear after a headstrong daughter who is determined to court scandal and ruin. The story would be too undignified."

"He simply washed his hands of you?"

"I was not that fortunate. I was his heir. If his young wife had borne him a son, I would have been free of him, but she did not."

Her steady gaze locked on a shadow in the distance. The smallest ridge had appeared on the horizon. She squinted, hoping it was just the distant mist, but her heart fell because she knew it was not.

Adrian must have seen it too. "We will stay in Portsmouth for the night, and then begin our journey to Marleigh in the morning."

"How long will I have before I must go to Court and meet with the King?"

"He will be traveling to Marleigh to see you there."

She turned her gaze from the horizon to him. She no longer needed to look to the distance. The landfall would grow in her head without her watching it. Her soul would tick off the time until this ship pulled into port.

"You did not tell me that my trials would begin so quickly, Mister Burchard. I assumed that I would have some time to accommodate myself before the worst of this ordeal started."

"I did not make the arrangements. Others did."

And those others had not worried whether their arrangements were considerate of her. She really did not matter. It was the power of Everdon that they waited for. It was only the bad luck of fate that made her the vessel in which that power now rested.

Heartsickness and agitation began sneaking into her again. She instinctively let go of her mantle and crossed her arms over her stomach.

The wind caught the edge of her wrap and whipped it back until it flew behind her.

Adrian caught it and gently tucked it around her again. His polite protection touched her battered spirit.

She looked in his eyes. She guessed that this man could be very hard if he needed to be, but he was not now. He gazed back with a familiarity not at all appropriate, but undeniably compelling. Once more she had the sensation that he examined her heart and soul until he knew her better than she knew herself.

Oddly enough, she saw no criticism in his eyes. They reflected none of the harsh judgments that she expected, considering what he had learned of her during their brief association. The depths of those dark pools contained determination and confidence, but not of a type to threaten her.

And maybe, just possibly, she saw lights of genuine concern.

Her spirit calmed. It seemed as if the wind did, too, until they were standing in a tiny spot of serenity. His quiet strength provoked a latent courage in her. It was almost as if he willed a transference of fortitude as he looked at her.

The ship clearly turned, commanding her attention. With a start she saw that the land loomed far closer than she expected.

That confused her. How long had they been connected by that naked gaze? The ship's progress suggested it had been much longer than she thought.

"England," she said, narrowing her eyes on the buildings and ships growing with each moment.

"Home," he said softly.

"That home was my prison, Mister Burchard. Do not expect me to meekly surrender to its chains again."

chapter 6

He created a mild disturbance wherever he walked. Like a pebble skimming the surface of a placid lake, his stroll around the periphery of the guests caused ripples of attention.

Even men glanced his way, but the women actually repositioned themselves to get a better view. Several trailed behind him at a distance, as if hooked on invisible lines that he had cast their way.

Sophia watched from the highest terrace at Marleigh, Everdon's country estate. Below her two more landings stepped down to where the garden spread out in its spring splendor. Officially the guests were not here for entertainment. That would be unthinkable with the recent demise of the duke, not to mention the month left in the year of mourning for the last king. All the same, despite their somber colors, the throng of notables drinking punch bore a remarkable resemblance to a garden party.

They had called en masse to welcome her return and to express their sympathies. Their collective descent on

Marleigh had been arranged by Celine, her father's second wife and widow. A house cramped with curious aristocrats was the last thing that Sophia wanted to endure. She suspected that Celine had planned it specifically to discomfort her.

This should have occurred four days after her return, but demonstrating mobs had necessitated a circuitous route from Portsmouth, so she had only arrived last night. Despite such hazards of travel, it looked as if half of the House of Lords and their ladies had made the trek to Devon. They probably thought the danger and inconvenience well worth it. After all, the King had come, Sophia promised to be grist for the rumor mill, and this was the closest thing to a decent assembly to occur in almost a year.

She knew that the real point of the day was not to welcome her home. The lords' interest and the royal favor had a purpose. Time was of the essence. It was imperative to cajole the sacrificial lamb to the altar.

Recognizing one's fate does not mean that one must run to it with open arms. Sophia had slept late, dawdled in dressing, and delayed making her entrance. Upon finally emerging from her chambers, dressed in a black gown that was ten years old, she had looked for the one man who was not a stranger. It had not been difficult to locate him in the crowd.

He did not seem to realize how women reacted. Secretly watching him, Sophia marveled at how oblivious he appeared to most of it, and how indifferent he was to what he did see.

"He is a bit too dramatic-looking, don't you think?" a voice asked. Celine stepped up close and tilted her black parasol at an angle over her blonde curls, providing a bit of shade for Sophia too. Anyone watching would think they were old friends seeking solace in their grief, which was hardly the case. Although Celine was actually a year younger than Sophia and might indeed have become a friend, the two had never liked each other.

"Of whom do you speak?"

"As if you do not know. The stallion down there, creating so much heat in the herd, of course. Your escort, Burchard."

"Is he dramatic-looking? I had not noticed." She actually said it with a straight face.

Celine gave a sardonic smirk, as opposed to one of her other ones. She had perfected a whole repertoire of them. One of the great beauties of society since she had left the schoolroom, she assumed that her reactions should be of interest to everyone. Her face left men stammering in ways no one had ever reacted to Sophia, and Sophia admitted that her dislike of Celine contained a big dose of jealousy. Right now she thought it highly unfair that even black crepe flattered the young dowager duchess.

Celine's eyes narrowed as she examined the strolling Adrian. "What do you think? Italian? I have a friend who says Persian. He is a mongrel bastard, of course. It is so embarrassingly obvious, and to his credit that he does not try to grasp for full acceptance. You would think that if the Countess of Dincaster was going to bolt the corral, that she would at least have picked up with one of her own."

Perhaps it was exhaustion from the trip, but this critique of Adrian incited a vivid flash of anger. "Is that how it is done, Celine? Discretion now means choosing a man with the same nationality and coloring as your husband? Perhaps Lady Dincaster's heart did not understand the rules governing infidelity as well as you do."

Celine's lids lowered. "I can see that you have not changed much, Sophia."

Actually I have changed a lot. So much that I do not belong here anymore. So much that sometimes I do not even know who I am.

Her presence on the terrace had unfortunately been noticed. A footman wearing royal livery began the long climb up the stone stairs toward her.

Celine watched resentfully. The royal welcome waiting inside would change her life as surely as Sophia's. "You are glad that he is dead, aren't you? You have been waiting for it."

"I am not glad, Celine. He was my father. Nor do I want what his death brings me."

"Liar. It is all yours, despite your willfulness and disobedience. It sickened him to know that it would all go to you, after everything you had done."

"I do not know why you speak as though I am to blame. You were the one who was supposed to guarantee that this day never came to pass."

Celine flushed. "The least you can do is finally respect his wishes."

"I was counting on your solving the problem for us all by providing him with another son to replace my brother Brandon. Now the only wishes that I intend to respect are my own."

The footman had reached their level. Sophia listened to the formal request for her presence by King William. She stared Celine down until the dowager duchess retreated. Then she stepped closer to the footman and gave him new instructions.

Adrian strolled through the copse of trees bordering the water garden, wondering how the duchess was managing. Their delayed arrival meant she had not had much time to rest before this ordeal. The ride from Portsmouth had been slow and tiring, with him sitting with pistols at the ready atop the carriage. The extreme tension in England rarely exploded into deadly violence, but it only took one radical or one displaced farmer to hurt a woman.

She had grown quiet upon their landing. Her withdrawal had troubled him. She did not castigate or accuse, she barely seemed to notice him at all, but by the time he had deposited her here at Marleigh last night, he had begun to feel guilty for crimes unnamed.

A crunch on the path behind him broke through his thoughts. A delicate cough demanded his attention. He pretended he had not heard either announcement. The Dowager Duchess of Everdon had been stalking him all day. In a manner of speaking, she had been stalking him for years.

As an unmarried ingenue named Miss Celine Lacey, the duchess had not given serious consideration to the Earl of Dincaster's third son. The vain mind inside her pretty head did not seem to grasp that she had insulted him later by offering her favors in adultery. Nor had it ever concerned her that he was beholden to her husband in ways that would make an affair especially dishonorable.

Still, some men might have ruthlessly accepted the

opportunity. He had strongly suspected, however, that no matter what his motivations in bedding the willing Celine, he would have ended up feeling like an exotic animal permitted into the lady's boudoir, to be petted and admired as a trophy.

A bit like the animals in Sophia Raughley's menagerie, come to think of it.

Speaking of Sophia Raughley . . . He glanced through the trees to the terraces rising up against the beautiful classical palace. Things must be underway now.

The crunches sounded closer and faster. Adrian quickened his pace and cut toward the garden. His brother Colin and his Aunt Dorothy rounded the pond and hailed him just as he exited the copse.

"There you are. Everyone is singing your praises in getting the duchess back so quickly," Colin said.

Adrian greeted his brother and kissed Dorothy Burchard, the earl's maiden sister. With his mother dead, she and Colin were the only two people whom he really considered family. "Good to see you, Dot. It has been some weeks."

Colin glanced slyly to his left, where Celine had retreated to study some new buds on a bush. "Thought you looked on the run and could use a rescue, although why you would ignore her I'll never know. The duke won't mind now."

Dorothy swatted Colin with her fan. "Disgraceful, that's what it is. The man is barely cold and she is casting enough lines to empty the Thames of fish."

"Dowager duchesses are not for me, Colin, any more than the Celine Laceys were," Adrian said.

"This dowager does not want to marry you, Adrian," Colin said, only to get swatted by Dorothy's fan again.

Precisely.

Colin kicked up gravel with his casual gait. "Is Gavin in with Father?"

"Yes, Gavin is with the earl and the King. So is half of the House of Lords."

"Not very sporting of them," Dorothy said. "She is only one woman."

"I was just thinking the same thing. One would assume that Wellington could defeat her with only the King and one or two earls to help."

"What is she like? There have been rumors about her life in Paris. Did you find the den of decadence that some whisper about?"

"Is that what is said, Dot? I wish you had told me. I would have girded myself with more moral outrage in preparation."

They had circled the small pond. Celine had not and now awaited his approach.

He had kissed her once over ten years ago during her first season. It had been a long embrace on a dark terrace the night before she became engaged to the Duke of Everdon. There had been others like her, girls who stuck one toe into the lake of audacity by permitting him small liberties.

Later the liberties became less small and the females less innocent, but the game remained the same. Eventually he had refused to play the role of the safely English foreigner whom every sophisticated girl should try at least once.

He acknowledged Celine as blandly as possible, but it

looked as though he would not escape. Dorothy separated from their group, bore down on Celine with outstretched arms, and engaged the widow in effusive expressions of sorrow. Spared by the generous diversion, Adrian and Colin continued toward the great house.

"So, what is the duchess like?" Colin prodded.

"Trouble."

"Is she? What fun."

"I know that you have no interest in politics, but this is no laughing matter."

Colin frowned. "She isn't going to boot you out of your Commons seat, is she?"

"She may withhold the nomination just to get back at me. She truly did not want to return to England."

"Any problems there?"

"When it came down to it she refused to budge and I had to make good on an earlier threat and carry her out of her house, slung over my shoulder."

Colin cocked an eyebrow and half a smile. "You jest."

"Damned if I do. She wears at least ten petticoats, and all I could think was that if a strong wind should whip under her skirt, we might both take to flight like one of those big air balloons."

Colin laughed. "With all the revolutions on the Continent, who knows where you might have been shot down. Then to find all of that trouble on the road from Portsmouth."

"I have exaggerated that somewhat. Part of our delay came when we landed in Portsmouth itself. The monkey climbed to the top of the ship's main mast and it took half a day to get him down. I am sure that she deliberately let Prinny out of his cage."

"Prinny? She named a monkey after the late king?"

"He was alive when she named her monkey after him. It gets worse. She and I had an interesting conversation during the crossing. We discussed last summer's *petite revolution* in France, and the deposition of King Charles in favor of Louis Philippe. The duchess thought it a splendid drama. Her exact words, and I quote, were 'helping the citizens of Paris man the ramparts last July was the most exciting and worthwhile thing I have ever done in my life.' "

"Now, that *is* trouble. Have you told Wellington about this?"

"Do I look like a man who wants to die?"

They had reached the second terrace. Their reflections sparkled sharply in the new plate glass that had recently been installed in the windows and French doors. All over England the great houses were embracing the new, costly, large planes, and all over England mobs were smashing them. Even Wellington's Apsley House in London had seen all of its new glass destroyed a month earlier by a rampaging mob after dissolution of the last Parliament had killed the first Reform Bill.

The glass produced an eerie effect that was very different from deliberately gazing in a mirror. It caught casual vignettes and poses and showed one in the world as others saw one. Now it displayed the contradictory appearance of Adrian and his brother. Colin was all fair and blond, with an angelic face of perfect features. Adrian looked like night to his day, Satan to his saint.

He did not resemble the earl or Gavin, either, but the contrast was greatest with Colin. Colin never seemed to have noticed, or at least acted as if he had not, except during those fights at school when he had stood by Adrian's shoulder to defend the honor of their mother. Gavin always seemed to be away on the playing field whenever that happened.

A footman approached them and informed Adrian that the duchess requested his attendance in her sitting room.

"It sounds as though it is over," Adrian said after the footman left.

"What do you suppose she wants?"

"Perhaps she thinks that her new position permits her to order my execution."

He entered the drawing room, walked through the immense house, found Charles serving as underbutler, and followed his balding head up to Sophia's chambers.

The doors stood open. She paced the sitting room with Yuri and the other two mastiffs on short leads and Camilla following behind. Prinny the Monkey climbed up and down a chair.

Black did not become the duchess. With her dark curls and pale skin and strained expression, she looked like death itself. Annoyance and worry formed faint lines that framed her mouth. Her hair was pulled into an unattractive style that caused curls to spring out from under a silly little bonnet. Her old-fashioned bombazine dress covered fewer petticoats and showed less fullness than current styles, but she could not have looked less attractive if she had tried.

Which probably meant that she *had* tried. Adrian wondered how Gerald Stidolph had reacted upon seeing his intended after eight years.

"I trust that the King and lords are satisfied now," he

said after her greeting. "Confess, it was not nearly as bad as you anticipated."

"I wouldn't know. I haven't met with them yet."

"Are you saying that you have kept the King waiting over two hours?"

"I was indisposed. However, he has summoned me again, so it cannot be avoided any longer."

"You left it to His Majesty to summon you *twice* to greet him in your own house? King William may be generous about this, but I assure you that Wellington will not find it amusing."

She yanked the dogs to a halt. "Let me guess. He is your hero. You have regretted all your life that you were too young to fight at Waterloo. As a schoolboy you idolized the general and dreamed of sharing his glory."

"He has the King's ear and is a force to be reckoned with. You do not want him as an enemy. I advise that you present yourself to the King at once."

She gathered the leads tighter, pulling the hounds closer. They circled her, their heads rising to her elbows. Camilla took up position by her side. Prinny happily climbed onto her shoulder and clutched the little black bonnet.

She presented a positively bizarre picture.

Which, God help him, he actually found endearing in addition to exasperating.

"I intend to go down now. You will escort me," she announced. "I am ready."

"Don't you want to drape the snakes around your bosom? If the point is to convince them that you are a madwoman, why not tuck the iguana under your arm?" He walked over, grabbed a squealing Prinny, dumped him in his cage, and slammed the door. "Camilla stays here too."

"I will not go unguarded."

"A passion for dogs is a respectably English eccentricity. They may accompany you, but you need no guards at the audience."

"I suppose not, since you are coming."

"I was not called. I cannot go in."

She pierced him with an accusing glare. "You forced me to come back here. Dragged me out of my home, abducted me for all intents and purposes, and subjected me to unknown dangers and possible death."

"At no time was your life in danger."

"You cut me off from my dearest friends and dumped me here, where I know almost no one and do not much like the ones whom I know. There is an army waiting for me in the study, Mister Burchard, led by the great Wellington himself. You are no ally of mine, and one of them, but I will be damned if I will enter their camp totally alone. Either you come with me or I do not go."

He considered refusing. It would cause an ungodly stir. And he could not help her. What was going to happen was inevitable.

The glint of obstinacy in her eyes gave way to one of distress. It flickered and burned, deepening their color. She did not look at him, but at Yuri and his brothers. "Please accompany me." The words came low, as if making the request strangled her. "It will be my *faux pas*, not yours."

He had glimpsed her vulnerability several times since meeting her, and it always twisted something inside him. It was probably why her bouts of resistance about coming back had made him more concerned than angry. His role in this had made him responsible for her, in a way.

He stepped to her side and offered his arm. "I promised to deliver you, and if I take my words too literally no one can blame me for it, I suppose."

chapter 7

Steeling her strength, Sophia accepted his escort down to where the meeting would be held. The hounds behaved magnificently since Adrian's commanding eye watched.

"You will not bring them in," Adrian insisted at the study's door, prying the leads from her fingers and handing them to a footman.

As it turned out, the whole army did not await her. Most of the lords had arrayed themselves in the library and corridors. Only ten men sat in the study itself.

They rose upon her entry, forming a masculine wall. The breadth of nobility was as daunting as their number. Besides the King she counted two dukes, two earls, a marquess, and an assortment of minor titles. Adrian's father, the Earl of Dincaster, sat by the window with his eldest son Gavin.

She made her bow to the elderly, rotund King. At his royal gesture she sat in a chair facing him, smack in the middle of the room like a curiosity on display.

"Well, now, my dear, it is good to see you again," hailed King William after all the introductions had been made. His gray head inclined her way and he favored her with an avuncular smile.

"And I you, Your Majesty. Your presence honors us."

"My pleasure. Came to settle things. Delightful house. Near the sea too. Old navy man myself. Glad to come. We need to settle this, don't we? Ill winds blowing and all that. Need to settle things."

A man with gray hair and bright eyes and a hooked nose caught her attention and smiled. "What His Majesty is trying to say, is that we need to settle things."

She knew this man. His presence did not bode well for her, even if he invited her to join him in a speck of disrespectful wit. She might be able to outsmart the new King known as "Silly Billy," but not the famous Duke of Wellington.

Having made his official welcome, the old King grew distracted. From the far wall Gerald Stidolph caught her eye and smiled with warm recognition. She hadn't expected him to be here. Even more than the phalanx of lords, even more than the dominating presence of Wellington, she resented the assumptions that had invited Gerald to participate.

Adrian had retreated against the wall closest to her. His magnetism created an intensification of gravity where he stood. Sophia half-expected the lords seated by the window to slide across the floor, right into the hearth.

Did no one else notice but her?

At least one other person did. The Earl of Dincaster's pink-tinted skin flushed a deeper hue. "My youngest son's errand ended with your arrival, Duchess."

"Mister Adrian Burchard is present at my request."

"This is a matter for the upper House, and not—"

"If the duchess wants him to stay, he stays," Wellington snapped.

King Willian jolted alert at the sharp military tone. "Quite. Let us move along." He pressed his hands on his thick knees. "Now, my dear, here you finally are. Should have come home on your own as soon as you heard. Odd choice not to, but we are not here to talk of that. There's work to be done, and quickly. Ill winds blowing and we need every man on deck. The problem is, you're not a man, are you?"

"It would appear not, Your Majesty."

"Only one thing for it, of course. If the captain can't take the helm, his first officer is sent instead."

"What His Majesty is saying," Wellington clarified, "is that, while at another time your inheritance might not cause problems, at this particular moment it does. Revolution threatens. These elections are crucial to the future of the nation."

The King slapped his hand on his knee. "Duty. Duty. That is what it is about for the likes of us. Marriage, Duchess. That is what it must be. Nothing else for it. Your father favored your cousin Stidolph over there, didn't he? Good man. Only right to make the match now."

She summoned every speck of courage that she could. "I could not possibly consider marriage while I mourn my father. Perhaps next summer."

"Normally such restraint would be expected, of course," Wellington said, his gaze sharpening on her in a way that said he immediately saw her game. "You honor your father more, however, by doing his will, and the situation in the country cannot permit such delay."

"It is more than my grief. My cousin and I have become strangers to each other. It may be that we do not suit each other. I will not take such an important step so impetuously." She got it all out, but her voice sounded awfully small.

Wellington rose. He instantly dominated the King, the study, and her. He looked down his hooked nose at her much as he must have examined the lowest of his soldiers.

"Gentlemen, if you would."

His brittle tone left no room for argument. The lords bobbed toward the door in obedient formation.

"I must insist that Mister Burchard remain," she said.

"Of course," Wellington agreed unctuously. He gave Adrian a glance that said, *Why not? After all, he is my man.*

Seeing that Adrian had not budged, Dincaster kept his seat too. Wellington stared at him until the earl's face was red with outrage, but still the father would not move if the third son stayed. Finally only Adrian, the Earl of Dincaster, the King, and Wellington remained.

Except that the King had fallen asleep, so he wasn't with them in truth.

"Now, Duchess, let us speak frankly," the Iron Duke said, pinning her in place with an eagle's stare. "I am aware that you are a woman of the world, so I will be plain. If marriage to your cousin does not appeal to you, that is unfortunate but hardly a major problem. Produce an heir and then do as you will."

"I am not such a woman of the world that my views are as practical as yours."

"This is not about you. It is about Britain. It is about responsibility. Furthermore, there are other matters at work. We did not want to frighten you, but you should marry for your own sake too. There is some possibility that you are in danger, and a husband would be protection."

In some danger. The words sucked the wind out of her gathering storm of indignation. A seed of raw fear and sickening guilt that had been planted upon hearing of her father's death suddenly shot out stems and roots.

"What do you mean, *danger*? What sort of danger?" Adrian asked.

The Iron Duke looked at her as if requesting permission to speak of it. The branching fear made her nauseous and she suddenly did not care what was said or done.

"As a girl the duchess had a friendship with a young radical who operated in this area and the midlands. He called himself Captain Brutus. Her father learned of it, laid a trap for the man, and got him transported. That was almost nine years ago, but it appears that Captain Brutus is back. Broadsides have been found with calls to action over his name." The duke paused. "Under the circumstances, the Duke of Everdon's death while hunting is somewhat suspicious. Those of us who know about the tie between Captain Brutus and this family think that caution is in order."

"If what you say is true, wouldn't the duchess have been safer in France?" Adrian's icy tone made her twist and look up. He stood closely now, next to her shoulder.

"If she is in danger, it was just a matter of time before the man learned she was there. Better the war be fought on ground she knows, where there are those who want to protect her."

"We are speaking of one woman's safety, damn it, not the deployment of an army."

"See here, Adrian . . ." the forgotten earl began severely.

"That is where you are wrong, Burchard," Wellington countered. He turned back to her. "I am sure that you see the rightness of the solution. It is in everyone's interest, including yours, for this marriage to happen. Gerald Stidolph was in the army, and will both see to your protection and to the proper exercise of Everdon's considerable political influence."

Wellington's formidable presence, his very size and demeanor, demanded submission.

She raised her chin until she looked the most famous man in England squarely in the face. There was only one thing to do if she did not want to be browbeaten into agreement.

"I am sorry. I will not marry," she said. "I cannot. You see, I already have a husband."

Somehow Adrian got the duchess out of that study and away from the shock that greeted her announcement and story.

With perfect poise she allowed him to collect the dogs and make a retreating processional past all those lords, and up to the third level where her apartment sprawled. Once there he banished Jenny and closed the doors of the sitting room.

He pried the gripping hand that revealed her true emotions off his arm and stepped back. "I cannot believe that you told the King that bald lie."

Her bland expression broke, but she did not appear dismayed. She looked pleased with herself.

"I did not tell the King any lies. He was snoring. I fibbed a bit with Wellington, but since he was trying to force me to marry Gerald, I don't feel guilty."

"Fibbed a bit? You told him the whole ridiculous tale. He probably thinks that you married Captain Brutus and that Everdon is now at the mercy of a man who encourages insurrection."

She propped herself on a chair. "I made it very clear that it is not Captain Brutus because, God forbid he really has come back, I certainly do not want to be stuck proving that he *isn't* my husband. Nor did I tell the whole tale. I never mentioned about my husband being a spy for the government, for example . . ."

And thank God for that.

". . . because Wellington would probably know all the spies and would be able to figure out who it was, or rather who it wasn't, which is all of them. I decided that I had to keep it mysterious. Using that excuse was brilliant, if I do say so myself. He doesn't believe me, but he cannot prove that I am lying."

She appeared happier than she had since he met her. "I have you to thank. When you faced the duke down like that, I realized that he was just another man. The way you were not intimidated gave me strength. I could never have stood my ground without your help."

He supposed that it was incumbent upon him to give the plan one last try, not that he had much stomach left for it.

"The news about Captain Brutus appeared to frighten

you. If there is the chance that he is a danger, it really may be best if—"

"The man I knew would not be a danger to me."

"Men change, especially if they are embittered."

"Possibly. I knew his seven years were up, of course. I have wondered if he would come back, and if he would blame me. If he has, perhaps I deserve it."

"You must take care, just in case."

She quirked a trembling grin at him. "I will keep the dogs nearby." He could see her force her mind to other business. "Please bring Wellington a message from me. Tell him that I will accept his advice in exercising Everdon's power. Tell him that I am prepared to nominate the men recommended to me, and will send his selections to the new Parliament."

Adrian had no trouble recognizing what she offered, and what she withheld. The elections were imminent, and she would submit to the Tory leadership for them, but she made no other promises. Those twelve seats would remain twelve question marks when anyone tried to anticipate voting.

Her green eyes met his in frank acknowledgment that she had survived a crucial battle and found the victory exhilarating.

When he had told Colin that she was trouble, he had not known just how much.

He went in search of Wellington, thankful that his part was done and that he was out of it.

"You have to stay on."

Wellington gave the order upon receiving Sophia's

message. "Offer to help her settle her father's affairs. She probably has no head for that herself and will be glad to have advice. I doubt that she trusts the old duke's lawyers and stewards, since she trusts no one in England, from what I can tell. Except you, a bit." He stood beside the study window, enjoying a cigar. The King and the earl had departed and Adrian and Wellington were alone.

"Find someone else."

"Who? She will refuse. She is not sure of you, either, but you at least are the devil she knows."

"Tell Stidolph to take care of it."

"I am sure he will try, but having met her, I don't have much faith in Stidolph anymore. I think that he exaggerated their affection for each other, and her claim of being married closes that door until she recants. Even if he should win her, I doubt that he can control her."

"Then you do it."

"My good man, I am the enemy. You are only the ambassador."

"No, I am the man who forced her to return here even though doing so places her in danger." He had been finding their use of her increasingly distasteful. The realization that they had been using him, too, was thoroughly unpalatable. "Damn it, I should have been told."

"From your reaction, I am glad that you were not. She had to come back. As to Captain Brutus, I meant what I said. She is no safer in France if the man is determined. If you are feeling responsible, all the more reason to stay close to her."

First duty, now guilt. First for England, now for his conscience. The Iron Duke was very good at this, but then he would have to be, wouldn't he? You couldn't get thousands to die at your command unless you were.

"Stay and keep an eye on her," Wellington continued. "While you do, reason with her. With some influence and persuasion, she'll see what needs to be done. She just wants it to be her decision. Should have expected that. Willful blood in the family. Do you believe that story about a husband?"

"It is a fiction she invented in Paris and told to selected men."

"Clever woman. Damned shrewd. You are hard-pressed to prove someone *isn't* married if they want to claim they are. I convinced Dincaster to keep quiet about it. If word got out, she might be tangled in her own lie. Anyway, I leave her to you. Get her to the boroughs for the nominations and get her in line for the Commons vote. Shouldn't be hard. You've managed Serbs and Turks, one woman should be easy."

Not so easy, and not at all the same. This mission had a face and a name and a troubled sadness.

He would do what the Iron Duke wanted. He would take her to the boroughs and he would even reason with her. But his priority in staying nearby would be to make sure that she came to no harm because he had forced her to leave Paris.

"Take care of it, Burchard. Hell, seduce her if that is what it takes. Just make sure that she delivers those damn votes."

chapter **8**

Marleigh's chambers were apportioned out according to precedence that night, which meant that Adrian slept at a nearby inn. The next morning he returned and went looking for the duchess.

He found her in the duke's study. She sat on the floor in a black riding habit behind the huge desk, immersed in a mountain of paper. She had caused a mess that would take several days for someone to reorganize.

"I can't find it," she muttered when she saw him. "The will. I can't find it."

"He probably kept it in a safer place than his desk. Besides, his solicitor has a copy. Why do you want it now?"

"I was hoping he added a codicil and found some way to keep me from inheriting *this.*" She raised her arms in reference to the house and the rest. Papers flew.

"It was not in his power to prevent your inheriting most of it, and you know it." He waded in and lifted her up.

"Oh, dear, I have made a shambles of it." Her

black-covered backside curved up to him while she bent to gather documents into a useless stack. He experienced contradictory urges to both swat that bottom and caress it.

The events in Paris had breached some fundamental formalities between them, so he did not contemplate his action much before circling her waist with one arm and carrying her, derriere first, away from the documents before she did anymore damage.

She squirmed until he released her. "You go too far, Mister Burchard."

"Your secretary will need salts when he sees this."

"I have no secretary. I released my father's last evening. I think that I will change solicitors too. Papa's caused me a lot of trouble when I wanted to have my income from Mother's portion sent to me in Paris."

Adrian gestured to the mountain of documents. "May I suggest that you wait on either change until that is dealt with?"

"I am sure that you will take care of it neatly. Didn't you come here this morning to offer your help in such things? I just assumed that Wellington would want someone spying on me and would realize that you are his best chance."

She did not look at all sly, but Adrian suspected that the duchess had just revealed a depth of perception that would make everything about this business more difficult.

"The Duke of Wellington does not set spies on British citizens."

She looked at the Mont Blanc of parchment. "Oh, dear.

Then I did that for nothing. I wanted to see how quickly you could fix it all."

"Wellington did, however, express concerns for your safety, and thought that you might accept my continued presence on that count."

She settled herself on a chair and lounged with a pose more relaxed than was proper. It was probably one more example of the inappropriate behavior that she had adopted in Paris. That behavior, and just how inappropriate it might have been, had been on his mind quite a bit. The musings had been part of very male speculations regarding the duchess, Parisian freedom, and provocative memories of soft curves and soaked red silk.

"I do not expect to be in danger, and I have a dozen strapping footmen if I should be, so a position as a guard is overdoing it. However, if you are going to be underfoot, we have to find something for you to do."

She made a display of contemplating hard. Her attitude provoked the devil in him.

"I don't suppose you play the pianoforte or violin?" she asked.

"Not well enough to be your entertainment."

"Hmmm. Do you write poetry?"

"Sorry."

"Then I am afraid that we are back to the documents."

"Actually, Wellington suggested a different role for me. He thought it would be convenient if I became your lover." He said it to retrieve the upper hand, but he waited for her reaction with interest.

"Considering your proven efficiency, you should make quick work of it," she said, gesturing to the mess, simply ignoring his last comment.

"Not too quick. I'm sure we both want it done right."

"A few days should get it all suitably arranged, I would think." She spoke blandly, but a blush betrayed that she recognized the double meaning of the exchange.

"Only if you cooperate."

Redder now, she persevered. "I will leave it to you, Burchard. I have no competence with such matters."

He really shouldn't . . . "Women always say that, and then often prove amazingly adept at the business. It is really just a matter of proceeding with care and attention until one is satisfied."

Her eyes widened. He gestured innocently to the mound of papers. "We will work at it together and I will teach you. We will get right to it after you nominate your candidates."

The abrupt change in subject confused her. "Candidates?"

"The election. You must visit the boroughs at once. We will leave tomorrow. Jenny is already packing."

"Oh, no, you don't. Not again. *I* will make the arrangements for this circuit and I will complete the journey alone. You just write down where I need to go."

"The locations of the boroughs are often obscure. I will map out the general route for your planning purposes, but you will never find them without a guide."

Her brow puckered peevishly. "Very well. If I need a guide, it may as well be you. You can come, but only for that purpose. You are not to give a single order, least of all to me." She rose and headed for the door. "Now, please excuse me. I need to leave this house. It oppresses me even more than I thought it would."

He followed her into the marble corridor, and gestured to her habit. "You are going riding?"

"Since my guests will not come down for at least an hour, I decided to take the opportunity."

"May I join you?"

"I do not need a guardian angel. I am in no danger on Everdon's lands."

She had not really refused his company, so he followed her to the stables and called for his horse. Her confidence in her safety was misplaced. The duke had died on Everdon lands.

However, as he watched the duchess settle on her saddle, he admitted that the idea of a long, private ride with this errant daughter of the nobility appealed to him for other reasons besides protecting her.

They walked their horses through the formal gardens and park behind the house. She stopped atop a rise and looked down its hill to where the family graveyard hugged one side of a little chapel. A freshly built small marble building dominated the sculpted memorials.

"My apologies," he said. "I should have guessed that you might want to visit there."

"I did not come out today to say prayers at my father's grave."

She kept looking at the sepulcher. Adrian backed his horse away. She may not be saying prayers, but whatever worked through her mind absorbed her just as completely.

He watched her serious expression from his short distance, wondering what she tried to reconcile. He noticed that, as with her other mourning ensembles, her riding habit was old-fashioned and girlish for her age. They must all be costumes made when her brother Brandon died.

He remembered the accumulation of clothing tumbled around her dressing room in Paris. That extravagance spoke of a woman who would never be seen in dated fashions, no matter what the situation. He would have expected her to have modistes stay up all night sewing and altering to make sure she was turned out appropriately.

She didn't really care about it, he realized. Shopping was just a diversion, like her salons and parties. All of her behavior in Paris had been a means of distracting herself from something. What had Charles said that first night, about her reaction to the duke's death? *It is as if she knows that she cannot hide anymore.*

A complex woman. An interesting one, with a compelling combination of strength and vulnerability. Pain hid behind the studied gaiety. A mask of frivolity deliberately obscured intriguing layers.

She turned her horse abruptly and broke into a gallop. Adrian pursued.

She rode away from the house as if devils drove her from its shadow. When they entered a wooded section of park that hid the palace from view, she finally reined in beside a large rock and used it to dismount. Adrian swung off his horse and they strolled together along the sun-dappled path. Rich, earthy odors of spring filled the air around them.

Slowly, her self-absorption lifted. "You think me heartless not to visit his grave."

"You were estranged from him. Death does not always resolve that."

"Especially because he is not dead. His body lies in that stone monument, but I am under his thumb more surely now than I was a year ago." She smiled ruefully. "I was counting on his fathering another son. I never gave up hope for that. Nor did he. However, it appears that he let others know about his plans for Gerald and me, just in case."

"It is typical for fathers to try and influence their children's matches, especially if the child will become a duchess."

"I doubt that Gerald sees me as a duchess. To him I will always be Alistair's difficult little girl."

"You, difficult? I can't imagine that."

She laughed, in frank admission that she had been little else since they met.

"How long have you known Stidolph?" he asked.

"Ever since his mother married my late uncle, my father's brother. It was her second marriage. I was ten then. Gerald was at Oxford. He entered the army for a few years after and I never saw him much, but once he sold out his commission, he always seemed to be around. Papa favored him. He became like another son to him. Rather like Wellington and you."

"Wellington hardly thinks of me as a son. I am useful to him, that is all. Did you go to Paris to avoid the match?"

"That is one of the reasons I went."

"Why didn't you just marry someone else?"

"There was no one else. Papa could be very discouraging. I was isolated too. I was presented, but I never came out. My mother died when I was seventeen, so we were in mourning the season I should have done it, and other circumstances interfered later. I think that Papa was glad. He did not approve of marriages based on *tendres* with men met at London balls. The choice should be his, as with every other detail in my life."

"I knew your father only through politics, but I suppose I can see how his sense of order might have appeared harsh to his family."

"My father was an autocratic, cold man, too aware of his power. He treated my mother with little warmth. My brother and I were opportunities to be exploited and responsibilities to be managed. He forced Brandon into his own mold, and then harped when bits and pieces of my brother's nature bulged out of the container. He could be unbelievably cruel."

She blurted it out with piercing bitterness. Her whole body tensed, as if she braced an invisible shield against the memory of the man. Even her hands tightened on the reins that led her horse.

"Men are what they are, Duchess. Their basic natures rarely change, even if they wish they might. Your father probably thought that he was doing what was best for his family."

"He thought that he was doing what was best for Everdon. But then, I would expect you to defend him. You were his man."

"I was his M.P., a position negotiated by Wellington."

"I am well aware of where your first loyalty lies, Mister Burchard. As to my father, his family should have had more than a peer of the realm in their midst. There should have been some consideration of our dreams, and some love along with the lectures and criticism."

Her resentful words speared his heart. He understood her bitterness more than he wanted to admit. Understood it at the visceral level that only a shared experience can evoke. He had long ago come to terms with that child-hood misery, but that did not mean that her unhappiness moved him any less.

In spitting out her memories about Alistair, she also gave voice to his own about Dincaster. His attempt to soothe her had been an articulation of the boyhood ex-cuses that he had used to assuage his own pain.

"Should there have been some love? I expect so," he said.

She paused in her stroll and those green eyes turned on him with naked perception. He suddenly felt exposed, so complete was the comprehension in her expression. She knew that he understood, and she knew why.

An emotional bridge instantly formed between them. The empathy made something long-buried within him suddenly real again, and raw.

The silent, mutual acknowledgment that they had both lived with that void touched him profoundly. The urge to pull her into his arms flashed through him. He would carry her off to a private meadow and show her how embracing the present could free one from the past.

"Do you plan to live your whole life getting back at him? Will you let that consume your heart and rule your nature? If so, it will be a terrible waste, and his greatest victory."

She glanced about desperately, as if he had cor-nered her.

"I cannot imagine why it should matter to you."

He reached over and brushed at an errant curl, grazing her temple with his touch. Her eyes widened in surprise. The intimacy born of her revelations pulsed harder between them. "It matters to me, and you do know why."

He may never have made his interest explicit, or at least not so soon. He might have continued expressing it through light flirtation unless she encouraged something more. But the mood of the moment not only permitted this, it demanded it, and also much, much more.

He laid his palm against her cheek and kissed her without deciding to. It was an impulse born of the urge to soothe her distress and acknowledge their little bond. He also wanted to taste again the trembling lips he had kissed in her Parisian garden, and feel once more her pliant surrender.

She responded. He could feel it in her rapidly fading shock and hear it on her quick breaths.

He began to embrace her so he could lead her to the exploration waiting.

When his hands touched her body, she jumped back and turned her face away. She appeared frightened and tragically vulnerable. "I suppose that I do know why it matters to you. If revenge against my father drives me, it will make me more predictable. Easier to manage."

He smiled at her attempt to pretend that she did not comprehend what had just happened. "Just as long as you understand my intentions, Duchess."

Her blush revealed that she indeed understood them. She gathered her reins clumsily and pulled her horse closer. "I think that I will go visit some of the farms."

He helped her to mount, more charmed than disappointed by how flustered she had become. Surely she had learned in Paris that ignoring a bridge was not the same as burning it. This one would remain there, connecting their two islands, whether they ever acknowledged it again or not.

He would have to cross over now. He was curious about what lay on the other side.

She did not hate all of her inheritance. She loved the land and the distant sound of the sea. The parks and farms and hills had been her refuge as a girl. If she could be rid of the ghosts and memories, she would welcome this part of the legacy. She could probably even reconcile herself to the duties and restrictions if her heart could find peace with the past.

She aimed toward the closest village, too aware of the exciting man riding beside her. He always made her jumpy and alert. She wondered if she would ever learn to ignore his presence. After what had just occurred, probably not.

That worried her. She knew how to handle flirtatious wit and flippant innuendoes. That was a game with certain rules. This kiss had been different, and much more dangerous.

It had disarmed her, coming as it had during that spell of deep empathy. She still struggled to control her reactions. The appeal of what he might be offering shook her soul. A reflexive yearning gushed, frightening her with its force. It had been foolish to get drawn into that discussion of Alistair. She had revealed much more than she ever had to anyone before.

His quiet strength had encouraged that. It still beckoned, as surely as a hand reaching toward her, offering to make everything better.

They turned onto a dirt road and a little village appeared on the horizon. Its low, small buildings clustered picturesquely in the distance. A cart lumbered toward them, pulled by a woman and a youth. Three children walked alongside it.

She recognized the woman. Her name was Sarah, and she was the wife of Henry Johnson, a farmer. Both Sarah's and Henry's families had lived for generations on the estate as tenants.

The boy paused as she approached, more from fatigue than deference. He and his mother set down the cart's arms. Sophia noticed the cloth sacks that each of the children carried, and the pack sashed to Sarah's back.

"Your Grace," Sarah said, bobbing her head. Eight years had aged her tremendously. Sophia remembered a bright-eyed young mother, not this pale, tired matron.

"Sarah, it is good to meet a familiar face. I see that your brood has increased since I left. And your husband, Henry, how does he fare?"

The boy gestured to the cart with his head. "See for yourself."

She paced her horse around. Henry lay barely conscious inside the cart, wedged among pans and household goods. His pallor and labored breathing marked him as a very sick man.

"Mister Burchard, will you help me down, please."

He was with her at once, lowering her from the sidesaddle. Together they considered Henry's condition.

"He is dying," Adrian muttered.

"Sarah, what is ailing him?"

"Don't know, Your Grace. He's been poorly for months, just getting worse."

"What did the physician say?" Adrian asked.

"No money for a physician. Old woman Cooper gave us some potion, but it didn't help much."

Sophia surveyed the family, noticing again the cloth sacks. "Where are you going?"

Her son glared insolently. "Crops didn't get planted, did they? Steward knows no rent will be paid, so we are out."

"But your father..."

"Out of his head now. Won't know where he dies." He turned away, dismissing her interest. He bent to lift the cart's arms again, placing his young body where a donkey or ox should be.

"Turn the cart around, young man," she ordered. "Mister Burchard, will you help Sarah onto my horse? It is a long way back to the village, and she is exhausted."

Sarah looked confused and frightened. "Your Grace, the steward, he will——"

"You can remain in your home, Sarah. Marleigh is mine now. If I say that you can stay, that is how it will be."

Adrian lifted an astonished Sarah onto his horse, instead, and then settled two of the children on Sophia's. "I will help the boy," he said, taking the cart's other arm.

As they drew closer to the village, its details became clearer. The picturesque vignette turned into one of creeping decay. Adrian and the boy pulled the cart down a lane of graying wood and rotting plaster until they stopped in front of a sad little cottage. Adrian set down the cart's arm, carried Henry into the cottage, and then returned to lift the children and Sarah from the horses.

Sarah clasped Sophia's hand. "Your Grace, this is so generous. It will ease his passing so. We will be on our way afterwards, I promise you."

"Nonsense. I will have a physician sent, and perhaps Henry can be helped. If not, you will stay anyway, Sarah. Your son will be strong enough in a few years to manage the fields, and your other boy will be old enough to help him. I will see to your keep until then. Now, go and make Henry comfortable."

The family disappeared into the cottage. Adrian helped her onto her horse, his firm hands grasping her waist and his strong arms slowly lifting her. His closeness made her heady.

She surveyed the village as they rode out. "I do not remember it looking so poor."

"The cottages show little recent improvement."

"I cannot believe my father let things get to this state. He most likely never saw it. Tenants were just a source of income to him. It was my mother who knew their names and visited the sick. She probably badgered my father to make improvements. When she died, I suppose his conscience did too."

"It is your own conscience that will matter now. Such decisions are yours."

They were, weren't they? One word from her and this tired village could look once more as it did when she and Brandon would ride over to play with the tenants' children.

"I suppose that I can plan some improvements and establish some new policies before I leave."

He reached over and grabbed her horse's bridle, stopping her. "Leave?"

"Of course. I will nominate the candidates as agreed, but then I am returning to France."

"I do not think so. If you leave, I will probably be sent to drag you home again."

She jerked her horse from his grasp, and kept moving. "If I decide to go back, you cannot stop me."

"Try it and see whether I can or not," he said. "You have duties here. You just accepted that in helping that family. You cannot set policies and then leave the realm. Your stewards and managers will do things in the old ways if you are not here to oversee them."

"If I stay, those duties will form a yoke around my neck. They will control my life, and Alistair's ghost will be the teamster with the whip, driving me for the rest of my days."

His expression softened. "It will not go away. You cannot pretend it hasn't happened. And you have been given the power to do good too."

"Helping one family and improving a few cottages is easy. Managing all of it, that is different."

"Do you doubt that you can do it? I don't."

It was a simple statement, and not spoken in flattery. Just there, in his quiet, firm way.

Her heart lurched at the calm affirmation. It provoked that sense of empathy again. For a moment she tasted once more an intimacy such as she had not experienced in many years.

He assumed that she was better and stronger than she could ever be. She was going to disappoint him if he got to know her better.

She wanted badly to explain why she could not stay. Some things burned too deeply for her to confide, however, so she only broached the reason easiest to understand.

"If I accept the duties, the most important will be to preserve Everdon by giving birth to the next duke. When I marry, my own competence will no longer matter. I will be reduced to a figurehead. At least if I direct a steward from Paris, I will own him and not him own me. I cannot bear the notion of being chained to Gerald that way."

"It need not be Gerald."

"If I accept that part of it, it will not make any difference who the man is. It will be Everdon he marries, not Sophia Raughley."

"Until that day, it is yours as surely as if you were a man. You can use your position until you hand the reins to a husband. Why not take them up yourself for a while? Why not see whether being the Duchess of Everdon is in you?"

She almost laughed. She had made it a point never to discover what was in her.

His challenge prodded at her on the ride back to the house. It was strange to have someone who hardly knew her express belief in her abilities. Her own father had seen nothing but deficiencies.

The royal coach was waiting by the house when they arrived. The King would be leaving soon. She would have to run and change so that she could see him off.

She dismounted and faced Adrian under the eaves of the stable. "I think that you may be right. While I am in England, I should take up those reins."

"Your tenants will be glad for it."

"I do not think I should just attend to the lands. That is only one rein. If I am going to use this power for a while, I should try and do it right. My members of Parliament, for example."

His lids lowered. "What about them?"

"If I am expected to direct their votes after the election, I think that I should start learning all that I can about the issues."

From the expression on his face as she turned away, Sophia suspected that Adrian had not fully considered the implications before he encouraged her to take Everdon's power in hand.

chapter 9

She suffered the slow departure of guests, mentally urging them on. She had no history with these people. Since she had never come out, she had never enjoyed a London season. Everyone knew everyone else, but she knew almost no one at all.

The ghosts of Marleigh watched. She could feel their presence in the chambers and corridors. Her father and mother. Brandon, and the sister who had died as a baby. Even old servants from her childhood seemed to have left some of their essence in the building. The whole time she talked and sat and moved, she saw them in filmy pageants as memories distracted her. It only took an object or a smell to call them forth.

Finally only one guest remained. Gerald Stidolph had disappeared everytime a group departed, adroitly ducking below the current whenever the flow threatened to carry him out.

She found him in the drawing room after seeing off the last carriage. He stood near the terrace doors, gazing out to the garden, the image of a man determined to have his say.

She did not dislike Gerald exactly. He was very decent. He possessed no bad habits that she knew of. He stood tall and strong, his early years in the army still stiffening his posture. His face was composed of pleasant features and a strong jaw, and his sedate dress and short brown hair spoke of the temperance of his habits and tastes.

There wasn't anything specifically wrong with him. He was a little dull and a little too formal and a bit too enamored of power and wealth, but many women would consider him an appealing match.

So why had the very notion of marriage to Gerald always turned her blood cold? She contemplated him from the threshold and an eerie familiarity nudged at her. Suddenly she knew the answer. Marrying Gerald would be like marrying her father.

He stood like him. He walked like him. Now that she thought about it, he had adopted the duke's manner of speaking. The thoughtful pauses. The judgmental sarcasm that could shred even while it amused. Of all the people with whom Gerald had labored to ingratiate himself, the duke had been the primary target.

He had succeeded magnificently. In some ways, Gerald had become more the duke's offspring than even Brandon, and definitely more so than herself. Gerald had methodically modeled himself after the duke until, when the duke looked at him, he saw a younger version of himself. Small wonder her father had favored him, and had wanted him to have Everdon's power through her. It would be a form of life after death.

She walked toward him and he turned on the sound of

her step. He hesitated, as if deciding how to deal with her. Would he have the good sense to play the petitioning admirer, and not the reincarnation of Alistair Raughley?

"I have overlooked much, Sophia, but your refusal to speak privately with me until now piques my annoyance."

"I had guests to attend to, Gerald."

"You managed to ignore them often enough when it suited you."

"True, but ignoring them in order to have an argument with you did not suit me."

"As willful as ever, I see. No doubt your time in Paris only reinforced those inclinations. It does you no credit."

"Circumstances mean that it is a duchess's will that I exert now. I am rather enjoying that."

"You made that abundantly clear yesterday with His Majesty. Your stubbornness was an embarrassment."

"Gerald, in the last half-minute you have criticized me three times. Is it any wonder that I grew obstinate at the King's suggestion that we marry?"

His censorious expression softened. "Forgive me. My surprise at your attitude has made me forget myself."

"No, it has interfered with your hiding yourself, and I am glad for it. I cannot imagine why my attitude should surprise you. I resented how Father tried to browbeat me into marriage when he was alive. Do not expect me to tolerate such handling from you and Wellington now that he is dead."

He held out his hands beseechingly and smiled. "I have blundered it badly, haven't I? This has gotten off to a bad start."

"I think it has gotten off to a splendid start. I had feared we might spend hours pretending first."

He evidently decided that petitioning admirer would be the better tack after all. He gestured to a settee. "Please sit with me, Sophia. I wish to learn how you have been."

She considered refusing to be diverted from the confrontation that needed to be finished. Years of training in civility won out, however, and she perched herself on the settee's edge.

Gerald eased beside her. His sharp brown eyes had grown hard with the years, but his expression of appeasement dulled their harshness a little.

"You are looking very lovely. Maturity suits you," he offered.

She looked terrible and she knew it. In fact, she had worked at it, and just for him too. He had never found her very lovely, not even when youth had given her some claim to it. She had overheard him once, when she was sixteen, frankly discussing her lack of beauty with a friend.

"By maturity you mean age. You think that I make an attractive spinster?"

He feigned a fluster. "I am heartened and grateful that you never married."

She considered telling him the lie about the secret husband. It would make mercifully quick work of this for the time being. Her pride resisted it. She had not needed the story of a violent husband to fend off Gerald when she was young and vulnerable. She certainly would not rely on a hoax to do so now.

"While in Paris I learned the sweet life available to a single woman of wealth. In comparison, marriage has little to recommend it."

"I have been told that you were a leading light in the arts circles there. It must have been fascinating."

"Yes, fascinating. And educational. And exciting. And sometimes, deliciously naughty. Paris was always freer than England, of course, but among the artistic community a whole separate code of behavior reigns."

She saw a scold begin forming, but he restrained himself. "Well, you are back home now at last. What is in the past is done with."

"Goodness, Gerald, do I hear absolution? You will forgive and ignore any indiscretions?"

"Of course, my dear."

"We wipe the slate clean? Any excesses are forgotten?"

"Certainly."

"And my young artists, Gerald, are you prepared to ignore them too? Father knew all about Paris. Certainly he told you."

This time the fluster was not feigned. "He did warn that you might come to our marriage with more experience than one might prefer."

"How nicely put. When did you plan to raise the problem with me, and conduct your interrogation?"

He flushed to his receding hairline. "I assumed that we would never speak of it. It is indelicate to do so."

"But you contemplate marriage. Would you never wonder? Never be jealous? For the rest of our lives, you intend to never ask about Paris, or throw your suspicions in my face? My father would never have restrained himself thus, nor, I think, would you. I suspect that there are men who could, but you are not one of them."

"I can understand that you might fear my anger about it. Is that the reason for your refusal yesterday? I promise you now, Sophia, that I will never ask about your lovers, or upbraid you for past liaisons."

"Yes, with a life interest in Everdon's wealth and a seat in the House of Lords as my dowry, I expect that you could forgive me just about anything."

"You insult me. My wish to marry you is not grounded in avarice and ambition."

"In what, then? Affection?"

"Of course."

"Please, let us at least keep this honest. Whatever you have convinced yourself, this is all about ambition. It always was. I do not begrudge you that. After Brandon died, I knew that no man could ever look at me again without seeing the map of this estate engraved on my face. Nor was it my concern about your reactions to my past that gave me reason for refusing you yesterday. I will not marry you, because I do not want to. You are too much like him, Gerald. Too much like Alistair. I went to Paris to escape him. I will hardly bind myself to him for life now."

"You speak nonsense. I am not Alistair."

"You imitated him for so long that you even look a bit like him now."

Signs of annoyance quivered through his face. What a battle it must be for him not to let loose the biting sarcasm that would establish his dominance.

"It was wrong of me to force this today. You are still tired from your journey. We will discuss this in a few days when you have reaccustomed yourself to where you are and who you are."

"I do not think so. For one thing, you will be back home by then."

"You are inviting me to leave?"

"I am accepting with regret your desire to depart in the morning."

He rose and paced away, as if composure were impossible if he remained beside her. "You need someone to take care of you, Sophia."

"I did well enough on my own in France. I am not a girl anymore, as you so ungenerously noted."

"It is not only that. I do not know if anyone has told you, but you may be in some danger."

"I know all about Captain Brutus, and the suspicions regarding my father's death. Even so, there is no point in your staying now. As it happens, I must leave at once to nominate my candidates."

This explanation for his dismissal relieved him. "Yes, of course. That must be done at once. I will arrange it, and accompany you."

"That is not necessary. I already have assistance. In fact, I already have a guardian for my safety. Wellington saw to everything."

He started, as if someone had poked him in the ribs. "I do not understand. Surely the duke would have consulted me. Who is this guardian who assists you?"

"Adrian Burchard."

"He will accompany you? It will not be proper."

"No less proper than if you did, since I share as much blood with him as I do you. Besides, I think it is safe to say that if Mister Burchard seeks a liaison with some woman, he can do better than me."

He had the good sense not to concur outright, but his expression cleared in agreement. That hurt more than she wanted to admit. For an instant she truly hated Gerald.

"I don't know why Wellington patronizes Burchard so much," he muttered.

"Maybe he sees something of himself in Mister Burchard. Older men often favor the young who possess similar traits. But then, you would know about that better than I."

"He more than favors him. Wellington has promoted Burchard in the party. He intends for him to get a position in the Treasury in the next government, with an income in the thousands. A rather large prize, no matter what services Burchard has performed or what talent he possesses. Even Dincaster thinks it excessive."

A thick fullness suddenly pressed inside her chest, choking her breath. So, Adrian had personal reasons for wanting this election to go a certain way. His bright political future, as mapped out by the great Wellington, depended upon it.

No wonder he was displaying such tenacity about staying with her. She had rather hoped . . . what had she hoped? Maybe that he really was motivated by concern for her safety. Maybe that something like friendship drove him.

It had been a mistake to agree he could accompany her to the boroughs. He was not doing it to protect her, but to manage her. As to what had happened this morning—well, a man who looked like Adrian Burchard probably knew all kinds of ways to make women come around.

Humiliation at her reaction to that kiss seeped through her, making her feel like a fool. She knew that he was Wellington's man, but she had not understood how ruthlessly he would exploit every opportunity to achieve his master's goals. But then, he had warned her, hadn't he? *Wellington thinks it would be convenient if I became your lover.*

An astonishing disappointment throbbed beneath her embarrassment. For an instant Gerald became Alistair, cruelly forcing her to face unpleasant realities. *He only uses you, Sophia. You are nothing but a means to an end for him.*

Not if she had anything to say about it. She had no intention of being used by any of them, least of all Adrian Burchard. She would make that very clear to him. She would sever the connections that had been stringing between them since that first night in Paris.

Foolish connections. Tempting and delicious too. Disillusionment stabbed sharply, penetrating her heart with wistful regret.

She pushed to her feet, suddenly exhausted to the bone. "Please forgive me, but I must rest now. I will leave early in the morning."

He took her hand between his two, making a little stack. How icy his skin felt, compared to Adrian's warmth. A false warmth. At least with Gerald, one knew what one had.

"I will come and see you when you return."

"Come when you will. This house has been more your home than mine for years. However, I will not change my mind about the marriage, Gerald. I will never get so reaccustomed to being home that I agree to that."

T he sun peeked over the park's horizon at Marleigh. It illu-minated a confusion of activity in front of the house.

Obscured by the deep shadows in the woods that flanked the drive, a man watched the preparations for the duchess's journey. Servants ran out of the house with baggage that others stacked into a large wagon and tied to the huge coach that displayed Everdon's crest. A tall, somewhat foreign-looking gentleman lounged serenely against an open carriage as the chaos rained down around him.

The watcher narrowed his eyes on the waiting gentleman and a vicious annoyance spiked through his mind. He had not ex-pected the duchess to arrange that kind of special protection. His own plans would have to change now.

He calmed himself by considering how this might be a blessing in disguise. Someone charged with protecting the duchess would recognize danger in ways the duchess might not herself, and help her to see her vulnerability. She was not strong, and would be more pliable if she was afraid. The sooner she felt helpless, the *better. That had been the whole point of announcing with those broadsides that Captain Brutus was back, after all.*

A groom exited the house with three large dogs on leads, accompanied by stable boys bearing cages. The servants who had just tied down everything in the wagon took one look at the new arrivals, made pantomimes of exasperation, and began untying the whole lot again.

A small figure dressed in black strode out of the house, waving her hand, calling for attention. A few feminine orders drifted on the breeze to the woods. A footman tried to speak to the duchess, but she marched to her coach.

From his dark spot in the trees, he watched the imperious display. It was not the first time he had seen little Sophia play the duchess since her return. He had witnessed it, from his hidden shadows, at the dock in Portsmouth and on the road as she traveled to Marleigh and even the day all those lords had descended. Yes, Sophia could appear quite formidable if she tried.

It would not matter. He knew her very well, in ways no one else did. He would have his way with her. She would do what he wanted.

He had known she would come back once her father died. Come back to him, to aid his quest. How convenient that her brother was gone too. Now she would help him achieve what was necessary, whether she wanted to or not. He would have justice and an accounting, and she would pay the old debt she owed.

The coach rolled. The open carriage, now filled with servants, followed. The wagon took up the rear. With an entourage like that, the duchess would make slow progress and be easy to find.

He walked through the woods to where he had left his horse. It was time for Sophia to learn exactly what coming home really meant.

"I need to tell them where I stand. I'll like as get lynched if I don't." Frustration tinged James Hawkins' emphatic statement.

He echoed the concerns of the three other Cornwall M.P.'s whom Sophia had nominated this day.

The duchess gave Hawkins a sympathetic smile. Adrian noted that it had been one of the few to crack her face all day. She had been in a prickly mood ever since leaving Marleigh.

The departure itself had been a confused affair. Adrian knew that she did not travel light, but the parade of grand coach, servants' carriage, and wagons loaded with animal cages and portmanteaus proved she had little experience with logistics. By the time she had finally emerged from the house and abruptly ordered them all off, he was very sure she had lost track of what and whom had been packed. Since she had insisted that he not interfere, he had not felt obliged to mention several glaring omissions.

It had been afternoon before it all rolled into Lyburgh. Determined to hold to her schedule, the duchess had left the servants and wagons in the town and continued immediately on to the nearby boroughs.

Now, instead of retiring to rest for tomorrow's journey, she had invited Hawkins to join her for an evening supper at the inn in Lyburgh, where her entourage had been left earlier. She had not even visited her chamber first, so she did not know about the surprise that awaited her there.

The youthful, blond, handsome M.P. had been awed and delighted that his patroness had honored him. He now picked at his lamb and bubbled with earnestness. For twenty minutes he had been regaling the duchess with breathless stories regarding the tense mood of the population.

She sat across the table from Hawkins in the private room where they all ate, giving the callow young man her attention.

All of it.

Adrian bristled. Her attitude toward him had been cool and distant all day. Their hours in the coach had been very silent. They might have never taken that ride and built that bridge.

Hawkins himself further pricked Adrian's annoyance. The young man was about the same age as Ensemble members present and past. At best, a year or two out of university, he was the son of a local gentry family and no doubt expected to be Prime Minister one day.

"You will have to explain that you are assessing the various positions on reform and will exercise judgment in due time," Sophia said with a sweet smile.

"Not sure that will work, Your Grace."

"It will have to. It is the truth, isn't it?"

Hawkins looked confused by the question, as well he might. His own judgment had nothing to do with it.

"What *is* your view on all of this so far, Mister Hawkins?" she asked. "I value it, since you have been in the thick of things while I have been abroad. No, do not look to Mister Burchard for permission to speak your mind. I am sincerely interested in what you have to say, and it will not be held against you."

Hawkins flushed and debated his answer.

Adrian waited for him to choose the wrong one, which of course he did.

"Well, Your Grace, I'm not sure it can be avoided. Reapportionment, that is. I've actually got an opponent in the election. He has come out solidly for reform and he may win."

"Nonsense," Adrian interrupted. "There are only thirty voters in your borough, and twenty of those men farm lands on lease from Everdon. Your seat is secure."

"That is how it is supposed to work, but there's been lots of talk here in town, and broadsides flying." Hawkins fished in his pocket and withdrew a stack of folded papers. "They have a way of inflaming people."

Sophia unfolded the three pages and perused them with a puckered brow. She halted over the second one. Adrian noticed its signatory name. Captain Brutus.

He plucked it up along with the others, from under her suddenly frozen expression. "More nonsense," he said, stuffing them in his coat. "Your borough will vote you in. Unless you plan to exercise unseemly independence once seated, your position will remain secure. As to any consideration which you may have given to such a move, I remind you that during the last Parliament your seat was one of those slated for abolishment."

The young M.P. actually had the brass to work up some indignation. "To be sure, Burchard. Still, a man has a brain and a soul, no matter what his debts. There are times when the greater good—"

"Let others with more experience judge the greater good."

"Enough, gentlemen," Sophia said. "Straddle the fence for now, Mister Hawkins. I must still educate myself on this issue and have not yet decided how my M.P.'s should vote."

She turned a melting smile on Hawkins. "Let us be done with politics. Tell me about yourself. Have you any special interests besides government?" She reached over and patted his arm.

Hawkins' gaze slid to the informal gesture. Suddenly he looked very much a man and not at all a lad. Possibilities instantly loomed behind his clear blue eyes.

"I have a great passion for the literary arts, Your Grace."

"A scholarly interest?"

"I confess that I dabble myself. Poetry."

Sophia's face lit with admiration. Hawkins drank it in. Adrian could practically hear the young man calculating that the duchess was an attractive, worldly woman with whom an affair would be appealing and advantageous.

"You must let me read some of your poetry. When we go up to London for the sessions, I expect you to visit and bring them," she said. "What form do you prefer? Sonnets? Epics?"

They embarked on a spirited dialogue of poets and poetry, of rhymes and meter. Adrian drank his wine, watching like an intruding chaperon. Sophia forgot Adrian existed, but Hawkins did not. He glanced over on occasion. *Time to remove yourself, old man,* those darting looks said. *You know how it goes.*

Yes, he did. He read Hawkins like an open book, and could see Sophia's familiarity turning vague speculation into bold decision. The belief that he might become the lover of the Duchess of Everdon before morning glimmered in the sparkling looks Hawkins gave her.

The hell you will, boy.

The three mastiffs dozed by the hearth. Adrian dropped his arm and quietly snapped his fingers. Suddenly awake, they rose in formation. They began circling the table, eyeing its scraps.

The canine entourage interrupted a lengthy discussion about Coleridge. Sophia scolded the dogs to no avail.

"It appears they want to go out," Adrian said. At the last word they pranced over to her with excitement. "They have been away from you all day and are acting jealous. I would take them, but I don't think it will pacify them."

Her frown broke as her demanding children drooled delight at her attention. With a mother's sigh she rose. "Mister Burchard is right, you must excuse me, Mister Hawkins. I always give them a brief walk in the evening. There is still a bit of light, so I had best do it now." She fetched their leads from a bench near the hearth. "Only down the street and back, Yuri. Feel free to smoke, gentlemen."

With hounds straining for freedom, she tripped out of the chamber.

He knew which chamber was hers. While her entourage had unpacked and settled into the inn, he had joined them, one more anonymous body moving about in the confusion, with hat pulled low and boots scuffed with dirt. The inn servants had assumed he was with the duchess, and the duchess's servants thought him with the inn, and no one had given him more than a passing glance.

He stood beneath the side eaves of the stable, waiting in the gathering dusk. Through a lower window he could see her face at the table, and the profiles of two men.

She should retire soon.

His boot tapped the sack on the ground. Time for Sophia to learn that the man with first claims on her heart and soul was very close by.

A movement caught his eye. Sophia had risen and left the table. He waited for her companions to do the same.

The inn's door opened, and Sophia stepped out into the twilight. She was not alone. Three huge dogs lunged ahead, straining on their leads, pulling her into the lane.

The temptation to follow entered his head. She would be alone and vulnerable.

His better sense rejected the idea. So did the presence of those dogs. No, he would wait, and take this in the small steps he had planned. The unseen watcher was more unnerving than the assailant. Fear would give him more power than any attack ever could, and his ultimate goal was not really about her at all. He had to remember to keep those things separate.

He settled against the stable wall to wait, but the impulse to follow did not die. He pictured her tripping down the silent lanes, and saw himself following and dragging her into an alley and releasing all the fury against her that had built in him over the long years.

The possibilities titillated him, tempting him to give in to the cold anger in his blood. Bitterness beckoned him to forget the bigger game in favor of some personal satisfaction.

Hawkins lit a cigar and assumed the demeanor of a contented man biding his time.

"I expect the duchess will be gone longer than she

thinks. The dogs will expect a good walk," Adrian advised.

"There is a moon if I need to ride back after dark falls."

Adrian poured them both some port. "I admire your self-confidence. At your age I would have been less at ease with the notion."

Hawkins drew on his cigar in a cocky manner. "Well, I have had a lot of experience."

"I envy your precocity. I was a few years older than you before I even had my first affair with a Frenchwoman, let alone sufficient experience that would let me face the next few hours with the *savoir faire* that you are showing."

"Frenchwoman? The duchess is not French."

"Officially not, but she has lived in Paris for eight years."

The smallest frown marred Hawkins' perfect brow.

Adrian stretched out his legs and gestured with his cigar through their cloud of smoke. "The first time was a shock for me. Claudette, her name was. An angel in the drawing room. Who would have thought she could be such a taskmaster in bed? But then, you know all about that, eh? I say that their French lovers have spoiled them, don't you agree?"

"Um, well . . ."

"Nothing but demands. I didn't even know what she was after half the time. The really discomfiting part was being compared. One always suspects that with a woman of experience, but at least English ladies are discreet and don't *tsk* and sigh about it."

Hawkins fidgeted.

"Of course, Claudette really was French and her imperfect English might have had something to do with her bluntness. Presumably a woman who was fluent in our language would be able to express her disappointment with more tact."

Hawkins smiled weakly. "No doubt."

"Yes, I admire your aplomb, especially since you will be dealing with the duchess long-term. I remember untold relief when Claudette's family was called back to France. I am thoroughly impressed, Hawkins. I had no idea you were such a man of the world." He fished in his pocket and withdrew the broadsides. "Now, tell me about this sheet here. The one signed Captain Brutus."

Hawkins blinked away whatever worries distracted him while he perused the paper.

"A new name. I doubt it is a local," he said, handing it back. "More virulent than the others. The last line caused a lot of talk. *If the aristocrats will not share the power, it must be seized from them.* Damned revolutionary sounding, isn't it? I hear that up north there are a lot of such calls, but not in Cornwall."

"True, but then Cornwall has more than its share of boroughs. What kind of talk did it raise?"

"More agreement than one would like. Emotions are running high here. The whole country is a tinderbox."

"When did this appear?"

"Some boys were posting it around the town today. They said a man called them into an alley and offered them three pence each."

"*Today?*"

Captain Brutus had been in this town this very day.

Cursing himself, Adrian leapt out of his chair.

He was halfway to the door when it opened. Sophia stumbled in, dragged by Yuri and his jubilant brothers.

Slowly, very slowly, Adrian's heart returned to a normal beat.

"I fear that took longer than I expected," she said, pulling the dogs in line. "I should bring them upstairs to my chamber where the cages are. Finish your cigar, Mister Hawkins. We can continue momentarily." She disappeared again.

Adrian gritted his teeth. She had actually invited Hawkins to stay. Right in front of him.

"If you will excuse me, I will retire," he said.

"Don't!...that is, don't you think it would be improper? If she is returning..."

He was damned if he would watch this unfold. "I leave you a clear field. However, if you take uninvited liberties, I will make you wish you had never been born."

The warning came out a tad too pointedly.

Hawkins flushed. "I should take my leave. Not all that much moon tonight, and what with those broadsides, there could be trouble on the road later."

Seeing that his sabre had found its mark, Adrian could not resist twisting it. "They have no argument with you. Besides, if all unfolds as you expect, you will be busy until dawn."

"*Dawn?* Oh, yes, all the same, I wouldn't want to wear out my welcome."

"No fear of that. The duchess invited you to stay." He clamped a firm grasp on Hawkins' shoulder. "Do England proud, my man."

Hawkins edged toward the door. "She should rest, what with the other boroughs to be visited. You will give her my farewell, won't you?"

He hurried out of the room.

Adrian awaited Sophia's return. No matter what her intentions with Hawkins, she would be back. For one thing, right about now she was discovering the surprise up in her chamber.

In short order the quiet inn sounded with stomping feminine feet descending the stairs. The door flew open and a furious column of black crepe trembled in the threshold. She looked absolutely stunning when her green eyes flashed like that.

She nailed him with an accusing glare. "Where is Jenny?"

"Where you left her, I expect."

"I left her here this afternoon with the other carriage and the wagon. But she is not in my chamber, and nothing has been prepared. Camilla's cage is empty, too, but if she had taken her out I would have seen them when I walked the dogs."

"You indeed left her, but not here. She is back at Marleigh."

"Do not be absurd. She was with the footmen in the other carriage when we departed."

"I am sure she was not. She had gone up to fetch Camilla and you ordered your entourage off before she returned."

Her brow puckered while she searched her memory. She strode over and stuck her face up at him. "You *knew.* Why didn't you say something?"

"You made it explicitly clear that I was not to interfere. When one of your footmen tried to explain and you wouldn't listen, I assumed you had decided at the last moment not to take Jenny and Camilla." His pique about Hawkins got the better of him. "After all, you could hardly initiate a liaison with a man if Jenny slept in your chamber."

"You dared to manipulate it so that I would not have my maid with me?"

She had misunderstood. She thought that he referred to a liaison with himself, not Hawkins.

On the other hand, she had misunderstood nothing. He had considered the provocative possibilities presented by this journey.

The evidence that she also had recognized them raised a sensual edge in his annoyance with her. She had never intended to take Hawkins as a lover. She had only been using the young M.P., much as she had used her brittle mood all day, to create a shield.

He held her wary gaze with his own, letting her see that he understood, enjoying her growing discomfort more than was fair. This special vulnerability hardly incited the protective response that he often felt for her. Very different inclinations took over, and he did nothing to suppress them.

They had just crossed a line, and he would not pretend they had not.

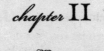

chapter II

She knew as soon as she blurted it out that she had made a mistake. His gaze sharpened with a heart-stopping expression that made it very clear that he was a man and that she was a woman who thought he wanted to sleep with her. It had been a huge error to make that explicit. She had stupidly kicked open a door and he did not look inclined to let her shut it again.

His eyes burned with a frank warmth. "When I spoke of a liaison, I referred to our junior M.P., not myself."

She walked away with a scalding face. It felt as if her body were iron that she had to yank from a magnet. "No matter whom you meant, it was extremely presumptuous of you to let me travel without my maid."

"Since presumptuous was the earl's favorite rebuke in my youth, I dislike the word intensely. Do not use it with me again unless you want to see just how presumptuous I can be."

The subtle threat sent a dismaying streak of excitement down her core. "You have been overbold from the start, and much more so this evening. It must be the port."

"Having just watched you with Hawkins, I have concluded that I have been far too timid."

She whirled around at him. "Your insinuation is insulting. I was holding a simple conversation."

"He pursued more than a conversation, and you know it."

"Why shouldn't I enjoy his attention? Do you think he forced himself to flatter me merely out of his own self-interest?" *Like you.*

"Every man's pursuit of a woman contains an essential self-interest, and I do not think that Hawkins had to force himself at all. I have thought from the first that making love to you would be very pleasant. I daresay he reached the same conclusion. With your encouragement."

The announcement of his thoughts was cast out straightforwardly. From the start he had always spoken to her with a disconcerting man-to-woman tenor, but tonight the casual wit had been dropped.

"Where is he?" She felt a need for the protection of another person. Anyone would do.

"He felt obliged to leave."

"What did you say to him?"

"Nothing to hasten his departure. Rather the opposite."

"What did you say?"

"I reminded him that you had asked him to stay. Oh, yes, I recall that I also admonished him to do England proud."

"To do England proud?"

"Considering the international flavor of your diversions

in Paris, we wouldn't want you disappointed in your own countryman."

He strolled toward her. She almost jumped out of her skin.

"What is this fascination that you have with boys barely out of school, Duchess? Do they seem safe to you? Controllable? You can dole out only what you choose to bestow and they are too callow to comprehend what you withhold?"

The room moved. No, she did. She instinctively backed away. She bumped into a stool and almost fell. He reached to help her but she righted herself and scurried far out of the way.

He reacted to her clumsy distress with a devastating smile. She pulled herself into some semblance of dignity while she edged away from his meandering approach. "My fascinations are my own business. Or do you intend to manage my love life now too?"

"That is exactly what I intend."

Now, that was blunt. Her flirtation with Hawkins had probably forced his hand.

She dug in her heels and stood her ground. He advanced until only an inch separated them and she could smell the soap that he used. Stubbornness stiffened her straight.

"Now you truly are being presumptuous."

"Despite my warning, you provoke me again with that accusation, when my behavior thus far has been anything but presumptuous."

"You can say that with a straight face? Since the moment that you stepped into my house in Paris you have engulfed me in a wave of high-handed, tyrannical, *presumptuous* interference."

"I have been a citadel of restraint in the things that matter."

"You don't think that where I live matters? You don't think that being carried out of my home like a carpet matters?"

"I think that we are really speaking about other things. For example, true presumption would be taking you in my arms right now and kissing you again."

Her eyes narrowed. "Don't you dare." The words came out one by one in flat enunciation.

"After a challenge like that, I think that I must."

She could have gotten away. He hesitated just long enough for her to stop it, but she decided that the only way to end his dishonorable game was to let him kiss her again and show absolutely no reaction.

That was the plan, at least.

Strength and warmth encompassed her. Fingers stretched into her hair, to position her head. The decisive pressure of his lips and the command of his embrace took control.

This was not the kiss in the garden, or even the one in the park. Masterfully, deliberately, he drew passion from wherever it hid in her. With a greed that stunned her, the void of loneliness accepted the offer of intimacy, heedless of the cost. Her soul groaned with relief, as if a long thirst was being quenched. Her secure understanding of his motivations quickly dimmed, eclipsed by the marvelous glow of pleasure sparkling in brilliant rays.

Within instants she possessed no control over any of it. She neither encouraged nor denied, but she definitely reacted. When the kiss deepened and he demanded more, her limp will acquiesced. She permitted the startling, invasive joining that meant she could never lie about this kiss in the future.

If it could have gone on just like that, she might have welcomed the connection forever. To surrender to such innocent happiness, to breathe in another's essence and bask in another's light, created a bliss that blotted out all unpleasant memories and realities. To be wanted at all, for whatever reason, soothed the oldest hungers in ways that overwhelmed her.

He broke the kiss but pulled her closer. With palm on her cheek and thumb caressing her lips, he looked down with a breath-stopping warmth. If he kissed her again, she would have no strength to stop him.

"An even greater presumption would be for me to escort you to your chamber and not leave you at the door as I had intended."

The warning was really an oblique request. In demanding that she choose, he threw a lifeline into the turbulent river of her emotions. Gratefully, regretfully, she grabbed it. "A good thing that you are not a presumptuous man, then."

His lips brushed hers gently. "That was not the answer I hoped for."

"It is the one that I have to give."

"Pity. I had hoped to discover what was underneath all those layers."

"Just an average body. You have undoubtedly known better."

"I did not refer to layers of petticoats. I have already seen what is under them." He released her. "If you are determined to thwart my great conquest, we had better get you some sleep. Tomorrow will be a long day."

For a man who had just been rejected, he was taking it awfully well. Better than she was.

He held out his hand in that commanding way of his. She forced her body not to tremble while she let him lead her from the chamber and hand her up the stairs of the silent, sleeping inn.

They stopped in front of her door. She almost crumbled with relief when he made no move to enter. At least she told herself that the emotion that sagged down to her toes was relief, even if it felt a bit like disappointment too. She nervously jimmied the key in the lock.

"It seems that with Jenny's absence we have finally found a role for me in your entourage."

She froze with renewed caution. "It is bad form for you to pursue this. We will not be lovers. Wellington will have to be disappointed."

"I meant the role of lady's maid."

"I will find an inn servant to help."

"They have all gone to bed."

"I can manage on my own."

"If so, you are the only woman who can." He firmly turned her to face the door. Nimble fingers found the closure of her gown, and the black fabric loosened.

"I said that I can manage," she repeated desperately, twisting to escape. He pressed her back in place until she hugged the door's oak planks.

Level by level, with excruciating slowness, he unlaced her stays. The warmth of his hands permeated the thin chemise underneath. She tried to give voice to indignation, but vibrating sensations full of forbidden desires and anticipation trapped her voice in her throat.

Finally the gown and stays gaped loosely down her back to her hips. She reached behind and tried to clutch them closed.

"So now you see what is beneath the layers," she said nervously, fumbling at the door key with her other hand.

A sly caress snaked up her spine. "I never forgot the soft pale skin, or the pleasant curves in my arms."

She trembled so badly it seemed as if the corridor had shaken. The damn key was sticking. "You have the advantage on me again, since I was unconscious."

"You aren't unconscious now."

That was an understatement. She was awkwardly, embarrassingly, unnaturally alert. Her back felt him as if he pressed against her even though space separated them.

He stepped closer and the space became very tiny. He slid her gown down her shoulder and bent to kiss the exposed flesh. The heat of his lips seared right into her blood. Only his commanding hold on her arms kept her upright.

He turned his mouth to her neck. Mesmerizing pleasure shot through her in hot little streaks. His magnetic aura lured her, waiting an inch away. The temptation to sink back into his confident strength almost defeated her.

She closed her eyes and savored the glory for a moment, then gritted her teeth and bent away, twisting and turning so that she faced him. "Unconscious or not, you still have the advantage and it is not fair to press it. What if someone comes out of another chamber and sees me like this?"

"Then open your door and go inside."

"The key is stuck."

He took it from her and poked the lock. Of course it turned at once. He pushed the door open.

"You will not come in," she said. "I do not want you to." A lie, that. A pitiful lie.

"I have never had much patience with the games that accompany these things. For whatever reason, you will not let me make love to you tonight. But you do want me to, maybe almost as much as I want to."

"Your self-confidence is extremely presumptuous."

"At least I am a presumptuous man and not a presumptuous boy. We will have to find a way to overcome your fear of that."

He stepped aside. Forcing her heart down out of her throat, she backed in, clutching her gaping gown and stays to her back.

Humiliation suffused her as soon as the door closed. So much for the sophisticated woman of the world. Instead of putting him in his place, she had fumbled and stumbled and melted like a schoolgirl.

But, heaven help her, she had not known that he would be so bold. Or so merciless. Nor that her attraction to him would make her so weak.

This was not like her flirtations in Paris. This man created cravings that she had never expected to know. The excitement obscured reality and reason. The pleasure even submerged her resentments of why he pursued her.

Nothing but disillusionment waited if he succeeded. She could not let this happen again, that much was certain.

There was only one way to make sure it would not.

chapter 12

They made love on white sand at the edge of the surf. Red silk formed the sea, lapping lightly against them, as if air created its swells. A turquoise tent of sky stretched above, framing Sophia's face. Clouds of gold drifted overhead.

Pleasure moistened her eyes, and joy softened her mouth. She eased forward so he could lick the tips of her breasts. Her sighs of anxious desire came in a rapid rhythm that matched the speed of his thrusts. He caressed up the thighs straddling his hips. Grabbing her waist he pressed her body close and careened toward the end. Her scream pierced the bliss, and shattered the world. . . .

Adrian's eyes snapped open. An aggressive chorus of dog barks assaulted his disoriented senses.

The scream had been real. A scream of shock, not ecstasy.

He shot out of bed and dragged on trousers and shirt and boots. He threw open the door and instantly faced the backs of two footmen dressed in Everdon's livery. The hounds' vicious snarls behind Sophia's door discouraged any investigation.

"We heard glass break and her scream," one explained. "Someone should go in, don't you think?" He stepped aside, making clear who he thought the someone should not be.

One of the inn's maids fretted near the stairs. "She came for me to fix her gown, then sent me to wake the coachman and footmen," she said. "I didn't see no one about, sir."

Adrian shoved open the door and strode into Sophia's chamber. The mastiffs were halfway to his throat before they caught his scent. They quieted immediately and crowded his legs, demanding orders to kill someone.

An open portmanteau stood beneath a broken window whose remaining shards hung like teeth. Splintered glass littered the floor. Sophia sat on the bed in last night's black gown, holding a wad of cloth to her arm. She turned wide, terrified eyes on him.

He went over and moved her hand away. With a firm rip he tore her sleeve apart. Blood oozed freely from a cut near her shoulder. He wiped it away with the cloth, and then pressed against the wound.

"You are understandably frightened, but you are safe now. For all the blood, it is not a bad cut. Tell me what happened."

She gestured toward the corner of the chamber. A good-sized rock rested there. "Someone hurled it through the window. It missed me. I was cut by a piece of flying glass."

A mixture of anger and worry clapped through him. "You could have been seriously injured. Had you been leaning over that portmanteau, the glass would have showered you. If you had been in bed as you should be at this hour, you wouldn't have been hurt at all."

"Well, I wasn't in bed."

"No, you were up and packing at three o'clock in the morning. Your footmen are dressed for travel, as are you."

"I could not sleep. Since there is a moon, I decided to make good use of the time."

"So you roused your whole retinue. Except me."

"Weren't you told? Goodness, that was a terrible oversight."

"The oversight was deliberate, and we both know it."

She glared at him, pushed his hand away, and took the cloth from him. She blanched when she saw how much blood it had absorbed.

"It looks worse than it is," he reassured again. He let her tend to herself for the time being, and walked over to the rock.

There was a folded paper tied to it. A letter. He scanned down to the signature. Captain Brutus.

The note carried a familiar tone. Its writer urged the duchess to see the light, and cajoled her to support not just Parliamentary reform but also universal suffrage. He scolded her for hesitating to use her new power for the greater good. He addressed her as "Sweet Sophia," closed with unseemly affection, and claimed to presume the communication because of their "old friendship."

Nowhere did it contain any threats, but Captain Brutus was letting the duchess know that he was back, that he was watching, and that hurting her would be easy.

He gave her the letter. "I doubt that your attacker is still about, but I will go and check to be sure."

He made an inspection of the streets nearby, but

Lyburgh slept silently. No evidence of Captain Brutus could be found.

He returned to the inn's carriage yard. Everdon's grand coach stood ready, with its horses in rein. The coachman lounged at its open door.

"Where is the other carriage? And the wagon?" Adrian asked.

The coachman groaned. "Will she be wanting them, too, now? If so, it will delay us. Just so's she knows that."

"Actually, she will not be wanting any of them. The duchess has changed her mind and will wait until morning."

Shaking his head at the inconstancy of women, the coachman lumbered to the lead horses and began undoing all of his labor.

Inside the inn, Adrian found the two footmen cooling their heels in the public room.

"You will be relieved to know that Her Grace was not badly hurt," he said. "Where are the others?"

"We were all the inn maid came and got. Just to be us, she made that very clear. Tom and Harry are still asleep, unless the noise woke them," one explained.

One carriage and only two footmen. Free of the slower vehicles, that coach could make good speed. He doubted she had planned to aim for the next borough.

"I expect that her change in plans surprised you."

"Not for us to question, is it? If the duchess wants to leave at night instead of morning, if she wants to go to Portsmouth instead of Devon, we do it."

"The plans have changed again. Her Grace has thought better of this night journey."

Adrian headed for the bedchambers. The maid still

huddled on the top stair. He sent her for some warm water and salves, then returned to Sophia.

The letter had fallen to the floor by her feet. Blood smears on the paper said she had read it.

He took over with the cloth again. "I had hoped the suspicions about Captain Brutus were wrong, but that letter says not. I apologize for prying, but now I need you to tell me about him. What is his real name?"

"I do not know. He was sentenced to New South Wales as John Brutus."

"Would you recognize him?"

"He was an educated young man. Golden-haired. Of middle height and stature. Eyes ablaze with purpose. I do not know if I would recognize him. Seven years of servitude probably wrought some changes."

Her expression had softened with a wistful sadness. A pulse of jealousy beat quietly in Adrian's head.

"How did you know him?"

"I chanced upon him one day by accident. I rode deep into the woods that edge the estate. Suddenly I entered a clearing and there he was with five other young men, like a Robin Hood. They were preparing to go on one of their raids that night, to burn threshing machines. The whole county had been in an uproar about him for weeks. I was not alone in finding his growing legend very exciting and romantic."

"You are lucky that you left that clearing alive."

"He only asked for my oath of silence. Two days later a note came for me, unsigned, asking me to come to the woods' edge that afternoon. I knew it was from him. Mother had died recently and my life was terribly vacant.

I went. Five times over the next month we spent the afternoon together."

"Your father found out?"

She nodded. "He never confronted me. He never asked me to betray him, but he arranged for the betrayal anyway. He let me learn that a trap was being set one night. Of course I ran to tell Captain Brutus. But I was the trap. Papa and some others followed me. I never forgave my father for using me like that. He in turn produced evidence that Brutus had been learning the movements of the landowners from me, so that he could plan his raids. My Robin Hood had a reason for listening to my girlish social gossip. I guess I never forgave my father for laying that out so brutally either. The lesson of the episode was not lost on me."

He did not doubt that. Two men who claimed to care for her had used her to their own ends most ignobly.

"When he went before the Assize court, my father demanded that I bring witness. I refused. Papa tried to break me the way you might a horse. He browbeat me endlessly." She shrugged. "When that did not work, he beat me literally."

Adrian bit back a curse, but a breath of it sounded anyway.

He pictured Alistair Raughley, self-righteous in his sense of civic duty, taking strap or cane to her. Outrage scorched at the image, flaming higher from memories of his own beatings at the hands of the earl. During his youth he had been the family whipping boy, receiving the punishment no matter who instigated the transgressions.

The idea that she had experienced the same brutality wrenched something inside him. Whippings could be the least of it, of course. A father's coldness could lash in a thousand ways without a hand being raised.

A pained expression flickered, cracking her composure. "You are wondering if it worked. It did. I brought witness at the court against that young man, about what I had seen in that clearing and what he had told me."

"He was a criminal and Alistair was your father. To anyone's mind, your choice was clear."

"I sent him to hell, Burchard."

The maid entered with the water. He instructed her to place it on the washstand and go and wait outside the door. He removed the cloth and checked the cut. "It does not look as if it needs sewing. The maid can get it cleaned and bandaged. I do not think you need a surgeon."

"I am relieved to hear it. I would not like to be delayed by it."

"If you still think to leave tonight, you are mistaken. I have told your coachman that you will not be departing until morning after all."

"You had no right to do that."

"You can hardly travel with that wound still fresh, and you should rest."

"I will wait until morning to depart, but I intend to be off at dawn."

"Dawn it will be. There will be one other change, however. You will not go to Portsmouth so you can sail back to France. I am keeping you in England, where I have some control over your safety."

Reference to her safety checked her argument. Either that or acceptance that her plan had failed.

"You will sleep in my chamber," he said.

"I will not." She pointedly looked him over, reminding him that he was dressed informally, to say the least.

"This is not a contrivance to spend the night with you. You will use my chamber and I will take this one. Whoever did this knew which window was yours. I do not think that we will see any more drama tonight, but we will not take the chance."

She began to protest, but thought better of it. Her shoulders sagged. "You think that I am a coward."

It wasn't clear if she meant because she had intended to run away, or because she refused to share a chamber. The notion that the two were related occurred to him.

"You said at Marleigh that you would try taking up the reins. Why did you decide to flee to France?"

"I changed my mind. Frivolous women like me do that all the time." She spoke flippantly, but her gaze met his eyes and then slowly descended. It lingered for a moment on the gape in his shirt that exposed his chest. For one delicious moment he expected her to lay her hand on his skin.

She looked away. "I will have the maid clean up the glass. It is dangerous."

Her retreat into practicalities did not fool him. He understood why she had decided to flee. It had not been the act of a frivolous woman, because she was not frivolous, despite the mask that she often showed the world.

She was frightened of him, and of what had started. Nor was she indifferent. She would not have to run away if she were.

"Would you prefer if I separated from your entourage? Will this duty be easier if I am not with you?" The words were harder to say than he expected.

She thoughtfully toed at the letter on the floor. "If something happened to me, Wellington would have your head. Also, it appears that I may need some protection after all. Under the circumstances, it may be best if you come along."

"Will you promise that I will not wake one morning to find you have taken the coach to a seaport?"

"I will see this part of it through. Leaving was a foolish impulse. The enormity of it all overwhelmed me suddenly, that is all. I will manage it in the future."

She shot him a glance that clarified her declaration. *I will manage you in the future.*

The carriages and wagon lumbered back into Devon. Each mile took them closer to a storm.

Heavy black clouds announced the oncoming tempest, but it was not a spring rain that kept Adrian alert. Other signs of a different kind of storm claimed his attention, and, on occasion, his intervention. The *thud* of a clod of dirt against the carriage. The curse of a wagoner when he saw the ducal crest. The milling of farmers along the fields' edges, and the hateful shouts that they yelled at the passing noble.

There had been trouble on the way from Portsmouth to Marleigh, but this was more consistent. It was as if someone had guessed the duchess's route and was riling the people deliberately.

Adrian knew who that person undoubtedly was.

The last stop of the day was Haford. This was not a rotten borough, but a largely populated one in the shadow of one of Everdon's coastal manors, Staverly.

A steady rain greeted their arrival. The whole country-side seemed to have congregated in the town. Silent tension quivered off the congested streets in a way that made the earlier demonstrations seem benign.

Harvey Douglas, the M.P., appeared oblivious to both rain and danger. He met the carriage with a broad-toothed smile parting his tawny mustache and beard. It turned out that the duchess knew him.

"It is good to see you, Mister Douglas. When I saw the list of candidates, I was delighted to recognize at least one name."

He helped Adrian guide her to the local inn. Already the wagons were being unloaded there. "Saved enough as your father's steward at Staverly to buy some property, I did. Was proud as a man can be when he offered me the seat. I'd like to think that I've done the job as well as any man could."

He grinned at Adrian for confirmation. Douglas had indeed been the consummate puppet M.P. He never expressed an opinion and probably did not possess any. Other "owned" members of the Commons sometimes chafed at their obligations, but Douglas thrived on them because politics did not interest him at all. His position gained him entrée into drawing rooms otherwise closed to him, and he got to play the big man at county assemblies. He was understandably grateful to the dead duke for the gift of social elevation.

And also grateful to Gerald Stidolph. Adrian remembered that it had been Stidolph who had recommended Douglas for the seat when its last occupant passed on five years ago. Stidolph's influence in the matter had made his own position in the duke's favor very clear to everyone.

"The town is unusually busy considering it is not market day," Adrian observed as they all shook off the rain.

"They're curious. Haven't seen the duchess in years. It's all Everdon land around here. I had the husting put up near the church. I expected a crowd, what with the duchess returning, and thought they would want to see it. I hadn't thought it to rain, of course."

"We will go to the church shortly," Adrian instructed. "I will tell you now that the duchess is making no formal statement regarding reform."

"I don't understand. The duke—"

"It is for the duchess to decide now."

"But I've already let it be known how we stand. He made it very clear on the last bill how we were to vote. You know that, Burchard. You are the one who gave us the word."

Sophia cocked her head. "It was not for you to let it be known without my saying so, Mister Douglas."

"Of course, Your Grace. But people have been asking, and Mister Stidolph explained that Everdon would stand against any new bill as it did the last one."

She stood, assuming the formidability that she could summon unexpectedly. "Do not assume that Mister Stidolph, or anyone else, knows Everdon's mind now. No one will give you the word on this except me. Until I do, you are not to speak in my name. Now, if you understand that, I am ready."

The main coach had already been taken away, but the servants' open carriage still stood outside the inn. Adrian requisitioned it from the groom and handed Sophia in. He took reins in hand and trotted quickly to the church.

The farmers and townspeople formed a river behind them.

By the time they had all taken their places on the platform, at least three hundred men and women had gathered to hear their landlord speak. Adrian wished they were not so quiet.

Douglas introduced the duchess with a long speech that extolled her father's benign rule in the region.

Sophia stepped forward to speak. Silence fell until only the splattering rain could be heard. She launched into her standard nomination.

She never got past the third sentence. The tension in the crowd snapped, releasing a barrage of emotion.

It was as if someone had given a signal.

"Support reform!" a man called.

"We want our due!"

"Go back to France!"

Sophia persevered, finishing the brief announcement while the crowd transformed into a mob. Political sentiments of every color mixed freely with personal grievances in the uproar. Some yelled at landowners, some at the government, some at reformers, and some at Sophia Raughley herself. She stood straight as a rod, letting the swells of anger crash against her.

Adrian stepped close to her. "Time to go."

She ignored him and raised an arm against the tide. "My good people. This is no way to settle differences or to influence events."

"*Now,* Your Grace."

"Only rational discourse will help us find common ground." Her voice barely penetrated the uproar.

The agitation grew physical. The crowd milled and

surged. Fights broke out. Sweating with fear, Douglas bobbed his respects and disappeared.

"My apologies, Duchess." Circling her waist with his arm, Adrian pulled her to the stairs. Amidst the increasing roar of resentment, he hauled one indignant, squirming duchess away.

He pushed her into the carriage and jumped up to take the reins, cursing Douglas for being too stupid to fathom what had been brewing right under his nose.

He moved the horses, aiming for the closest edge of town. Most of the crowd peeled away, but some bolder men clutched at the reins. He whipped them off. A scream from Sophia shot his head around. Hands were grabbing for her.

"Up here," he ordered.

She furiously slapped off the dragging arms. Half-crawling, half-tumbling, she managed to climb over the seat. Adrian grasped her arm firmly with one hand while he maneuvered the horses with the other. When she had all her limbs beside him, he slammed her down where he could keep an eye on her. He whipped the horses into a gallop, trusting Providence to move people out of the way.

He careened past the church and onto the northern road while rain poured down on the huddle of black cloth, white face, and flaming eyes beside him.

A mile out of town he pulled the horses to a stop.

She rose, the drenched bow of her bonnet sagging over one of her livid eyes. "I had things well in hand back there. They were coming around. Now there will probably be a riot and all of England will hear that I was run out of a town on my own property."

"The riot was underway before you left. That is what we call a crowd of three hundred fighting in the streets here in England. I need to walk the horses, so sit down."

"Where do you get the notion that you can manhandle me whenever you feel like it? I will not have you picking me up and carting me about at will, especially not in front of all those people. Paris was bad enough, but this was inexcusable."

"None of those people noticed or cared. Now, sit or you will fall." He grabbed her arm and pulled her down.

He got the horses moving. She sniffed with indignation, still beautifully angry. Drops of water dripped off her bonnet's edge, right onto her nose.

"How are those people ever to take me seriously after what you did?" she fumed. "It was extremely presum—"

"Don't say it," he warned.

They drove past sodden fields for a few more miles.

"Turn around now. I am sure that things have calmed down," she said.

"The hell I will, and the hell they have. When a mob gets its blood up like that, it doesn't calm for hours, unless the yeomanry enforces order. With any luck it has been called up."

"If you are not returning to Haford, where are you going?"

"Someplace dry and safe. I am taking you to Staverly."

"No. I forbid it. I will not go there. As the Duchess of Everdon I order you to turn this carriage around."

"For someone who claims not to want the position, you throw out ducal orders easily enough when it suits you. I don't care about your noble prerogatives right now. I suspect that your Captain Brutus was on that street, managing the whole thing. Staverly is the closest place where you will be safe and that is where I am taking you."

The road met the coast and curved east along its edge. The rhythm of crashing waves joined the faster beat of pounding rain. Sophia retreated into a simmering anger, ignoring the downpour that had drenched them both to the bone.

The gates to Staverly were closed, but a man stepped out of the gatehouse upon their approach.

"No one goes in here," he announced as Adrian pulled up the horses.

"This is the Duchess of Everdon."

The old man peered beneath the bonnet. "Miss Raughley! I got no word you would be visiting, Your Grace."

"It was a sudden decision, and not mine, Martin."

Martin looked down the road. "Are the others following? None to do for you here, Your Grace. You know how the duke left it."

"We are alone," Adrian explained. "There was trouble in Haford. Are you saying the house is closed? There are no servants here?"

"Just me, as Her Grace could have told ye."

"Then we will have to make do. Close and lock the gate behind us, then go to a nearby farm and buy some provisions." He handed over some shillings. "You are to sleep here tonight. If anyone tries to enter, come and get me."

The drive wound through a quarter mile of overgrown park before stopping in front of an old Tudor manor. Chipping plaster and high weeds announced that no one had tended the estate in years. The sea roared louder here, and Adrian surmised that the cliffs began not far from the garden doors.

He handed Sophia down. An overhang waited five steps away, but she remained in the rain, gazing up at the half-timbered facade.

"We used to come here every summer when I was a girl."

"It is a charming property. Why did your father let it go to ruin?"

Gathering her drenched skirts, she headed to the door.

"It is a wonder that he did not burn it down. This is where it happened. This is where my brother Brandon died."

She supposed that she always knew that she would have to come back to Staverly. Perhaps it was fitting that it would be on the day when she had made such a magnificent failure of being Alistair's heir.

She paced around the library, pulling covers from the furniture. Puffs of dust rose like specters following her progress.

Adrian lit a fire to burn off some of the damp that had claimed the house years ago.

"We should see if there are some dry clothes for you," he said, poking at the coals.

"And you too. Follow me."

She led the way up to the bedchambers, grateful that Adrian was much larger than Brandon and she would not have to go into the room her brother had used.

"You will find that this is not a very large house. Mother would not let Father add to it. She wanted it reserved for family life."

A few items remained in the duke's wardrobe. They

reeked of Alistair. The whole house did. Marleigh was so large that one could find places where he had never gone much, but that was not the case here.

"You can sleep here. Martin has kept it clean, in case my father should ever come. You should build a fire here as well. This chamber was always cold, even in the hottest summers."

She left him and entered her mother's old room through the dressing chamber. Unlike Marleigh, where Celine had methodically obliterated the memory of the first duchess, nothing had been changed here.

Nostalgia squeezed her heart while she rummaged through the personal items still imbued with that gentle woman's scent. Finding a high-waisted muslin gown and some underclothes and slippers, she scurried out as fast as she could and sought her own small chamber.

Memories bombarded her. She gazed out the small northern window. Every summer she had played in the garden below. When she was seven she had learned to swim in the surf. She could spot the rocks near the sea that her imagination had transformed into a castle.

She remembered starlit nights sitting at this open window, dreaming about a pure and passionate love.

A shelf held the items collected in the course of twenty summers. They contained the story of the girl she had been once. She had left them all when she and her father hurriedly departed that last summer, just as she had left behind the girl herself.

She opened the wardrobe and tossed them all into it. The tokens of play with Brandon. The book of romantic poems written her fifteenth summer. The radical tracts toted here the season before Captain Brutus, when the idealism of youth had excited her intellect much as her Robin Hood would soon excite her womanhood.

She slammed the door closed, as if she could silence the memories if she hid their remnants. She began peeling off the black weeds.

The old-fashioned, scoop-necked muslin gown would not cover her stays, so she stripped naked and then slipped it on over only her mother's chemise. The damp had turned her hair to ringlets. She gathered most of them into a topknot and let the rest hang around her face. Turning to the long oval mirror, she surveyed the results.

A ghost stared back at her. Long and willowy, wearing this same high-waisted white gown with its scattered violets, it approached with a gentle smile and comforting arms. She could not remember why her mother had come to her that afternoon, but suddenly it might have been yesterday.

She had never realized how much she resembled her mother. The nose and chin were Alistair's, but the rest, the eyes and hair and face, were not.

She suddenly realized that she could not run away from the ghosts. They did not exist in objects and places that she could avoid. They were in her, all of them, waiting to be recognized. Good ones had been ignored along with the ones that brought pain.

She ran to her mother's chamber again and grabbed a long fringed shawl. Passing the main bedchamber she saw through the open door that Adrian had built the fire.

She found him bending to the old hearth in the kitchen. Pails of water had been brought from the nearby pump house and he had wiped the dust off a table where some cheese and ham waited.

"You have not changed your clothes," she said.

He rose and combed his damp locks back off his forehead with his fingers. "I took care of the horses."

"You had better take care of yourself now."

He gestured absently to the food, began to speak, then stopped. He looked her way with a serious expression. "I apologize for making you come here. I did not know what this place meant to you."

"You could not know. Your decision was sounder than my denial."

"The rain looks to be stopping and there is at least an hour before dusk. I will ride back to Haford and see how things stand. If it has calmed, I will come and get you. I know the road now and once the clouds break there will be some moon, so it will be safe enough even at night."

She found a knife on a shelf and wiped it with the damp cloth. She sliced a bit of cheese and nibbled. As soon as she tasted, she knew which farm Martin had gone to.

"It will be dawn before all those trips are made. Do not look so worried. I am not going to turn into a madwoman on you. I never thought to return here for many more years, but now I wonder if it was a good thing to come. There is a sweetness to the sadness. Also, I had forgotten how beautiful it is here."

She fetched some crockery cups and poured the home-brewed ale that had arrived with the food.

"You are sure that it will not distress you?"

"No, but it occurs to me that if I am not going to live my whole life getting back at him, as you put it in the park, this is a good place to start. Besides, the ghosts will come whether you are here or not. I'd rather not face them entirely alone."

The rain had stopped, and rays from the low sun peeked golden light through the clouds. Sophia opened the door to the kitchen garden so the fresh breeze could enter. Through the growth she spied the roof of the Chinese gazebo that perched on the cliff at the end of the gardens. One could see the sea and rocks of the whole cove from it.

Not yet. She would enjoy the good memories first.

She inhaled the clean scent of a newly washed world and admired the sparkling droplets on the high grass before turning back to the table.

She looked beautiful standing near the open door. The breeze fluttered the tendrils around her face and the late sun bathed her pale skin in hazy gold.

The dress must be at least twenty years old, but it suited her perfectly. The low neckline displayed delicate bones and the thin muslin curved around her soft breasts, emphasizing them with its cinched high waist. The ethereal rays made the cloth vaguely transparent, showing her legs and the absence of any petticoat underneath. Adrian had seen her in black so much that he had forgotten how fresh and vibrant and youthful she could appear.

She took her seat. "What will you do first? Eat or get out of those wet clothes?"

"I had thought to eat, but if Your Grace demands the latter, I will oblige." He teased even though she had not asked him to stay for lovemaking. The request had been much more flattering than that.

He broke some bread and cut some ham.

"I have been thinking," she mused as she munched more cheese. "Mister Hawkins may be right. From what we have witnessed, reapportionment may be inevitable."

"Do you want the people who attacked you today to make English law? Did they strike you as suited to the task?"

"You must admit that the way things stand is unfair."

"Much in life and government is, but the system works well with its checks and balances. It is not clear that the alternative would."

"The French and the Americans have fairer systems."

"The French system gave the world Napoleon and a generation of war. The American system permits the continuation of slavery. The influence that the upper house exerts on the lower one here maintains stability and avoids governance by the mob."

"It does more than that. We both know it preserves privilege too."

"Your privilege, Duchess. Even so, there have been some reforms that were not in the lords' interest. Voices for change are heard."

"So you really believe it should be stopped? If you would neither win anything nor lose anything by your vote, would you vote reform down?"

He met her frank gaze. "What are you asking me?"

"I am asking what you really believe about this. And I suppose I am asking just how thoroughly you are Wellington's man."

"In other words, am I a toadying sycophant? I regret to say that those of us who must make our own way are, to one degree or another."

She looked down quickly. "I am sorry."

"Do not be. It was a fair question. I did not form my opinions and persona in order to gain a powerful man's favor. Wellington would see right through that, for one thing. I do not always agree with him or the ministers, and I present my own arguments. However, if you are asking if I have ever cast a vote for a position with which I did not agree, the answer is yes. Politics always involves compromise. And if you are asking if my general agreement with the party leadership has benefited me, again the answer is yes."

He spoke more sharply than he wanted, for reasons he did not care to explore. She grew subdued while she watched him. He had the sensation that he had revealed more than he knew, and that she was comprehending something he did not fully grasp himself.

"You must think I am insufferably spoiled," she said. "Childish and self-absorbed and resentful about a life that most would kill for. How unfair it must seem to you that a woman who knows only parties and gowns should be given the kind of power that belongs to Everdon."

"I do not judge its fairness at all. I do not think that you know only parties and gowns, and I only find you a little spoiled, and not much at all when it comes to the things that truly matter. As to your self-absorption, I think that you are salving wounds that I cannot know about."

"Can't you? I look at you and find myself thinking that if I had been required to make my own way, the achievement of doing so might have healed those wounds, or at least made them less significant."

The quiet observation unsettled him. He had not expected the ghosts confronted here to be any from his own life.

He rose. "I will go and change now. If when you next see me I am too informal, you must forgive me. It remains to be discovered what of the duke's wardrobe will fit."

She laughed and picked at her muslin skirt. "At least your garments won't be twenty years out of date."

He lifted two buckets and paused to look at her. He memorized the image of her smiling, with bright eyes and the hint of sadness behind that glitter, and the shadows of her feminine curves still visible in the last of beautiful light.

"It is a lovely gown," he said, turning away. "And you look beguiling in it."

She was gone when he came back down. Dark had fallen, and he guessed that she had sought solitude in her chamber, perhaps to sleep after the day's tumult, perhaps to hide because of last night's advances. He had thought it would be pleasant to spend the evening with her, and so he entered the empty library with some disappointment.

The shelves mostly held popular novels and the lightest of poetry, the kinds of things one might read during a holiday by the sea. He tried to pass the time with one of Humboldt's travel portfolios, but the exotic engravings could not hold his attention. He wondered if the ghosts were upstairs now, and how Sophia was dealing with them.

Putting aside the portfolio, he made his way to the whitewashed kitchen and out to the gardens. The night sky was perfectly clear and a refreshing breeze blew through the shirt that he wore without coats. He headed toward the cliffs.

The sloping roof of a Chinese gazebo loomed against the star-speckled sky. He began to walk around it when he noticed a shadow move inside. Sophia rocked back and forth against the balustrade as a child might, stretching away on extended arms and then pulling forward until her head stuck up toward the sky.

She stopped suddenly, bending out. "Burchard?"

He stepped onto the planked floor. "I did not intend to disturb you. I assumed that you had retired."

"I decided to come out here first and look at the sea." She pointed down at dark masses. "Even at night you can see all the way around the little cove. That big shadow is a point of land marking its eastern curve. The water near the land is very placid, except over there. We used to swim every day. Everyone except Father."

"You came to visit the memories?"

"I suppose so."

"Good ones, I hope."

"Not entirely."

He could not see her face, but he knew that distracted tone. "Do you want me to leave?"

"I think that I was hoping you would come." She resumed rocking, angling back and then pulling forward until her hips hit the balustrade. He pictured her doing that over the years, learning each summer that the wood hit differently on her growing body.

"Do you know what Jenny said about you that first night? That you were the sort of man one wants to hand things to because you will make it all come out right in the end. That is why the Foreign Secretary found you useful, and why Wellington depends on you, isn't it? It was rude of me to suggest otherwise today."

He should probably tell her that foreign missions and political plans were one thing, and the hidden pain of a woman was another. He had no idea at all how to manage that.

"What would you have done?" she asked. "If I had not nominated you? You said in Paris that you would have occupied yourself with your other interests."

He suspected that she posed the question only to avoid something else.

"I have been asked on occasion to manage other than ambassadors, M.P.'s, and duchesses."

"Businesses?"

"Sometimes. More appealing have been the offers to accompany scientific and archeological expeditions. The latter in particular require extensive organization, much like a military campaign. They make use of native workers, and in my travels for the Foreign Secretary I learned how to be accepted by them."

"Then perhaps you would make a good ambassador, if you are sympathetic to foreigners and their ways."

"Ambassadors are too visible. They must be Britain personified. For important posts, they are always drawn from the nobility and mostly serve a ceremonial role. It is left to their staffs to conduct the more subtle work."

"Were you good at being less visible and more subtle?"

"My appearance helped with the first."

"I hadn't thought about that, but I imagine that it did."

The fact that she did not think about that, and had never found him especially exotic, was one of her appeals.

After Greeks and Hungarians, a half-breed Englishman would not be very distinctive.

"The Foreign Secretaries were lucky to have you. Do you still do that sometimes?"

"On occasion, when Parliament is not in session. Since taking my seat in the Commons, I mostly just serve as a fancy messenger boy."

She seemed to accept that. She turned back to the sea.

Abruptly, as if some inner decision had been made, she pointed to the east. "He drowned there, where the rocks make the water churn badly. He was twenty years old. We were twins."

He could sense her fragile hold on her emotions, and wished that he could do more than stand like a silent witness. Whatever ghost she had decided to face here was bigger than his protection. In the things that mattered, he was worthless to her.

"It was my fault," she breathed the words so low the crashing surf almost submerged them. "I swam too close to the eastern edge, and got into trouble. I almost died. I remember fighting the water with a ghastly panic and then losing consciousness. I came to on the shore. Gerald was here, and he and the steward saw me washed up and pulled me out of the surf. Brandon must have seen me going down and came in to help. They found his body a few hours later on the other side of that promontory."

"It was not your fault."

"It was. In this one judgment my father was right. I was angry and hurt that day and I swam like a madwoman, not caring where I went. It was my brother's misfortune to be walking on the rocks where he could see me struggling."

"You would have tried to help him, too, I have no doubt."

"It was my carelessness."

Her body swooned subtly. Her battle against the anguish twisted his heart.

"The wrong child died," she said, her voice strangling on a swallowed sob.

Those were Alistair's words. He just knew it. Anger blazed at the realization that the man had been so cruel as to actually say that, no matter what was thought. He pictured the duke, stern and accusatory and unforgiving. No comfort had been given to her that day, or later.

She pressed her hands to her eyes. "This is so embarrassing. I'm sorry. When I asked you to stay I did not expect to get like this. I think it would be better if you left after all."

He did not move. He could not leave her like this, balanced on the brink.

With deep breaths and a rigid stance she fought valiantly for composure. "I realize now that I never mourned him. Not properly. I could not. Thinking about it at all made me feel as if I were being physically torn into pieces."

He reached for her and pulled her into his arms. "Then mourn him now, Sophia. I will hold you together."

She struggled but he held tighter. Her fingers stretched and twisted into the fabric of his shirt.

With a moan of defeat, she gave up.

He had never seen a woman cry as she did then. Soul-wrenching, groaning sobs racked her, sapping her strength until only his arms kept her upright, clutched to his chest. The shredding pain that she feared tore through her, and into him. Throat and chest burning, he buried his face in her hair and prayed that she would not emerge shattered forever.

Slowly, her explosive grief calmed to a quieter sorrow. Her clawing fingers relaxed against his chest and she lay against him, weeping gently. He kept her wrapped in his arms, giving what feeble comfort he could, hoping this confrontation with the past had helped her.

After it passed she stayed resting in his arms, her spent breath warming his body between her flat palms. He fought a swelling awareness of her soft femininity beneath his hands. A flowing sensuality bathed the poignant intimacy that her emotional outburst had created.

He angled his head and kissed her brow, telling himself that he intended no more than a single gesture of friendship and solace. She tilted her face up and suddenly his good intentions came undone. A soul-shaking desire flared. His lips tasted the salty tears on her cheek and then met her mouth.

She accepted his kiss with an assenting sigh that obliterated good sense. Hoping that he gave as well as took, he lost himself in the taste of her mouth, the scent of her body, the signs of her climbing arousal. Her palms caressed up his chest to encircle his neck, their pressing paths inciting a ferocious hunger.

He knew how to manage a woman's pleasure and mindless passion led him to exploit hers. His caresses brought her closer, trembling against his length, gasping with helplessness. No stays or petticoats interfered. His hands explored soft curves of hips and back and thighs, pressing, feeling, and stroking her to a needful delirium that left her rising up into his body until his erection buried in her stomach.

His mind was already taking her in the damp grass outside, against the post of the gazebo, on the wood floor beneath their feet. His imagination already had her naked, pliant, accepting him any way he wanted her. His body responded to the expectation with an eager fire. Easing his knee between her thighs he caressed up to her breast and stroked the erect nipple straining against the muslin.

Arm around her waist, he lifted and carried her to a nearby bench and pulled her onto his lap. He trailed kisses down her neck and found the rapid pulse that throbbed in time with the one pounding in his head. He tasted the smooth warmth of her skin down to the gown's low neckline.

He caressed her breast and she melted. Kissing her again, claiming and exploring her mouth the way he planned to learn all of her, he released the two tapes on the back of her gown.

She straightened and gazed at him in the dark. For a few seconds she did not move. He waited for whatever she was deciding while her short, shallow breaths prodded his desire so high that he thought he would burn if she pulled away.

Then she surprised him in the unpredictable way that she had. She removed her arms from his shoulders and he thought that she intended to leave. Instead her hands bent to the shoulders of her gown, and then slid down as she lowered the bodice.

He peeled off her chemise and took her lovely breast in his hand. As he had wanted to do since that first night in

Paris, he dipped to kiss it while gently palming the hard nipple. Her head lolled against his neck. Her desperate kisses heated his skin while her gasps of pleasure scorched his brain.

He took his time, caressing those full swells and teasing at the hard tips until she grew impatient and the gasps turned to cries. The sound of her need sent his own arousal soaring. Taking a breast in his mouth, he licked and drew. He caressed down the length of her flexing, rocking body and then retraced the path under her skirt.

Again she paused, as if he had confused her with an unexpected question. He kept his hand on her legs, stroking ever higher, his mind blank to any thought but of soon following the path of his fingers with his lips. He took her breast again and this time she held it to him. He did not wait for a sign of assent this time, but moved up her thigh and slid his hand to his goal.

He stroked the secret, soft flesh. A tremor shivered through her, into him, shaking his control. She suddenly went as limp as she had been in her grief. A low, melodic cry of submissive passion broke the breezy night.

Its desperate, helpless note touched him. It resonated with the night's earlier defenseless emotions.

A spot of lucidity reemerged. He lifted his head and stilled his hand.

Her mouth sought his impatiently, almost angrily. "Don't stop," she gasped, pressing him down to her breast and moving her hips against his hand.

"Sophia—"

"Don't. Please don't."

He pulled his hand away from her undulating body, cursing the chivalry that was asserting itself. "This will go too far." With the fevered, biting kisses they kept giving each other, he barely got the words out.

"You said that you wanted me. Last night . . ."

"I do want you. Too much to start it like this."

"But I want this."

"For the wrong reasons. This is not the way to bury your pain. You are vulnerable and if I take advantage of that you will hate me for it, with good cause."

She stopped showering kisses on him. Her body stilled and her forehead sank against his shoulder. "Damn it, Burchard. Why couldn't you just use me like you were supposed to? For once I wouldn't have minded."

"I do not want to use you at all."

She sat upright and turned her face away. "Yes, you do." She sighed deeply. "All men do. I do not mind so much anymore. In Paris I learned how to manage all of that."

That provoked an edgy resentment. He had just rejected an offer his body did not thank him for refusing, and she had responded by lumping him in the same group as the duke and Captain Brutus and those artists.

Furthermore, she implied that she managed a man's use of her now, which meant that in reality she used the man. She insinuated that tonight had not been under his control, and out of hers, quite the way he thought.

Still, he would have gladly held her in his embrace all night, but he sensed her retreating emotionally. As with her recent child's game at the balustrade, she kept swinging into intimacy and then pulling back. This time, however, he suspected that he knew why.

She scrambled off his lap and hurriedly drew up her garments. She would have bolted immediately but he rose and blocked her escape. Turning her, he fixed the gown's tapes.

"I should thank you for being so honorable. And for before, when I spoke of Brandon," she said.

"I do not want your thanks."

"Then what do you want?"

"I want you. I can offer you nothing but affection and pleasure, but when the ghosts do not interfere as they do today, I want to make love to you. If I can make it happen, I will."

She turned to him. "Then you should have done so while you had me at a disadvantage, because now it will not happen. You see, I know that is not all you want. I know why you are here."

"Sophia, politics is the last thing on my mind this evening."

"No, it isn't. I know what you stand to gain. I know about the Treasury position. It is a stepping stone, isn't it? To a ministry someday."

"Are you convincing yourself that this was about my career? Do you assume every man is only moved by self-interest?"

She stiffened at the accusations. "I did not like this. I will not let it happen again."

"You liked it. Too well. That frightens you, doesn't it? It complicates the game of who uses whom that you worked out so neatly in Paris. Keep control, keep it shallow, and there are no risks. That is how you want things with men, isn't it?"

"That is right. That is how I want it."

"Sorry, darling. I am not one of your boys looking for a frivolous friendship, or an artist offering the great lady amusement in return for a chamber. It will not be that way with us, even if you prefer the safety of it."

"It will not be any way with us."

"The hell it won't."

A renewed, pounding desire ached to show her how it would be, right now, and to hell with the restraint provoked by her grief.

He forced himself to turn away so that he would not act on the impulse. "Return to the house now. I will wait until you have retired before I follow."

She had the good sense to obey. She ran away, up the garden path.

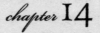

S uch a pity that you have to wear weeds all through the summer," Dorothy said. "Although I think that an argument can be made that you should attend the coronation ball come September. After all, you are Everdon. Don't you agree, Adrian?"

"If the duchess seeks a rationale, I am sure that we can devise one."

Adrian strolled beside his willowy aunt, and glanced past her cloud of white hair to Sophia. The duchess's broad bonnet, laden with black sweeping feathers, obscured his view, so that only her nose and chin were visible.

Adrian had invited his aunt on this walk, knowing that they would most likely meet Sophia, since she took a morning stroll in the park each day at this time. He was reduced to these machinations because Sophia had been avoiding him. She had dismissed him at the end of the journey to nominate her candidates. Since coming up to

London three weeks ago she had arranged that someone else was always present if she received him.

Sophia managed to engage Dot in a conversation that did not include him. The two of them pulled ahead by a few steps, and the Earl of Dincaster paced alongside them. That the earl had tagged along this morning was, Adrian suspected, not good news.

Adrian turned his attention to the other members of their party. Daniel St. John and his wife, Diane, had also taken a morning stroll, and Adrian had introduced them to the duchess upon meeting them in the park.

"She seemed to recognize both of you," he said to Daniel.

"We have been introduced before, several years ago, while we visited our home in Paris."

"Then you know something of her life there."

"Miss Raughley and her Ensemble were well-known in Paris." St. John's voice carried no censure or sarcasm. "She built another life there. Another identity. Pity she could not hold on to it if she preferred it to the one here."

Adrian knew that St. John spoke from experience. Daniel St. John himself now lived a different identity than the one to which he had been born. Adrian was one of the few people in England who knew that secret and why the mystery had been created. He was not entirely sure why St. John persisted in the deception when the reasons for it had long ago been resolved.

"She appears very tired," Diane St. John said, her soulful eyes fixed on the duchess's black dress. "I expect coming home has been a trial."

"Yes, and coming to London has made it worse. A steady stream of visitors has been calling on her. Every woman in society wants to conduct an independent inspection before agreeing with the growing consensus that Sophia Raughley really isn't very suitable for her position."

"Let me guess. They also think that the right husband would go far to redeeming her, and she would be much improved if she just married the visitor's perfect son, brother, or nephew," St. John said.

"Undoubtedly. I arranged this accidental meeting with Dot because she could use a friend who is formidable enough to protect her through the next few months of social hell."

"That was thoughtful of you, since she has no family to help her. She must do this all alone," Diane said. "Perhaps she could also use some friends who are not a part of that particular hell. I will call on her, to reminisce about Paris, if you think it would help. Unless you think she would find us beneath her."

"I think it would help enormously. Nor does the duchess hold strict notions about who is suitable for her circle, as she proved in Paris." Nor would the friendship of Daniel and Diane St. John be much of a step down. St. John had become incredibly wealthy through shipping and finance, and could buy most of the peers of the realm.

"Then I will make the overtures and see if she is amenable." Diane lengthened her stride just enough to fall into step beside Dot.

As she did so, the earl slowed enough to trail the ladies a bit.

St. John noticed. "It appears he wants some conversation with you."

"There is no other explanation for his presence here

this morning. I don't think he has seen this much exercise in months."

"I will make myself scarce, then." St. John joined his wife and extricated her from the ladies. The two of them turned and retraced their steps.

That left Adrian walking with the earl, who sidled up closely.

"Is it done, then?" he asked, slowing even more so the ladies could not hear.

"They were all elected and are arriving for the Parliament even as we speak."

Sophia's candidates had been voted in, but not enough other Tories had won. Whigs elected on a mandate of reform firmly controlled the lower house by a huge margin.

Wellington and Peel and the other Tory leaders now faced a delicate situation. The goal would be to see that the bill was very moderate at worst, and that the vote was very close so that the House of Lords could kill it without too much public outrage.

Which meant that Sophia's twelve votes still mattered, and that Everdon's empty seat in the upper house had become more critical.

"Heard talk out of Cornwall. Seems she didn't tell them how to vote."

"That is her choice for now."

"Heard she started a riot."

"A very small riot."

"Damn it, you were supposed to manage it, keep her in hand, control the ribbons."

"She is not a horse to be steered by a bridle."

"No, she is a woman to be steered by a husband. Stidolph still doesn't know, although I think someone should tell him. Thinks he still has first claim, when in fact the filly is tethered in someone else's corral. Hell of a situation. Why couldn't Everdon have sired a nice, demure, obedient colt?"

"Maybe he did, but pulled too hard on the bit and ruined her mouth. Now, don't you think that we have butchered the horse metaphor enough?"

It was the lengthiest conversation they had suffered in years, and Adrian waited for the rest. What had been broached thus far was not important enough to force the earl to arrange for it.

Suddenly the earl pivoted, placing his body in front of Adrian, forcing him to stop.

Adrian squarely met the gray eyes so different from his own. The earl's pale skin had flushed from the unaccustomed exercise. His swept-back white hair, once fair like Colin's and Gavin's, poked out the back beneath his hat. The face, once angular, and the chest, once fit and strong like his sons', had gone soft and puffy from too much indulgence. As had the mind.

Adrian considered that if the House of Lords were made up entirely of Earls of Dincaster, he would vote for reform in an instant.

"She went to a radicals' meeting last night," the earl confided.

"Did she?" Adrian was amused that the earl thought this would be news. He could himself recite where she had gone everytime she had left her house these last weeks. He could relate what she ate every day. He could tell that she had embarked on a frenzy of extravagance that had modistes all over the city elated.

He could report that she had received two more letters

from Captain Brutus, and had not called for Adrian to discuss them.

"Laclere gave a speech. The duchess met with him afterwards. She's to visit his house tomorrow."

The Viscount Laclere was one of the few Tory peers supporting reform. He was also a member of a circle of Adrian's friends that included St. John and a few others, men with whom he had experienced events that forged bonds that transcended social rank or politics. When young they had dubbed themselves the Hampstead Dueling Society, and they still congregated on occasion at the Chevalier Corbet's fencing academy, to spar with sabres.

It was, in essential ways, the only social circle where he had ever really been accepted, and to which he ever truly belonged.

"Laclere's wife is an artist," Adrian said. "The duchess is probably more interested in that than Laclere's political views."

"Artist! Hell, the woman is an opera singer. American at that. Laclere used to be solid, but she's ruined him. Everyone knows that he dabbles in trade now too. I think that you should find a way to go tomorrow, to keep an eye on things and make sure the duchess doesn't get bamboozled."

Adrian forced an expression of agreement. Wellington had already made this suggestion, and seen that an invitation had arrived the past evening.

"There is something else," the earl began, looking uncomfortable but determined.

Adrian almost didn't hear him because he became distracted by activity seen out of the corner of his eye. In the distance behind them on the carriage path a curricle approached, careening back and forth from inexpert handling. A dark figure stood in it beside the driver, wobbling off balance, waving its arms. A shout just barely made it to them on the breeze.

Sophia.

"Whatever else you need to say, let us discuss it while we catch up with the ladies," Adrian said.

"It is best discussed in privacy."

Sooo . . . pheee . . . aaaa.

The Earl cocked his head. "Did you hear something?"

"Not at all. Now, what is this other matter?"

"I could have sworn . . . It has to do with the duchess as well. Stidolph spoke with me. Thinks that you have been attending on her far too much. Won't do, will it?"

Oh, sweet Sophia, my lady.

"First you instruct me to keep an eye on things, and now you say to stay away."

"See here, Adrian, you know what I am saying."

They were almost alongside Dot and Sophia. Adrian glanced back and watched the curricle weave precariously. The waving figure tumbled into the seat.

"I am not sure that I do know. Perhaps you had better say it more clearly."

The gray eyes turned to flint and the puffy face found some angles. "It won't do. A liaison would be scandalous."

"Any liaison, or just one with me?"

"I do not want my family to be the entertainment of the summer gossips."

"In other words, you want me to remain as invisible as possible. That has never been very easy."

The earl scanned his face with a cold appraisal that

Adrian had resented since he was old enough to understand what was reflected in his mirror. No response came
to his oblique reference to what his face revealed, however. None ever had.

He caught up with the ladies and herded them away
from the carriage path toward some trees. He could hear
the curricle bearing down on them, but its noise broke
and obscured the continued shouts.

Soph . . . stop . . .

"There is a lovely pond back here," Adrian said. "There
are swans, and one is black. You really must see it."

"I have seen it already and none of the swans are
black," Sophia said. "Why are we hurrying? I will ruin
my skirt if you do not slow—"

Wait. Come back.

"What was that?" She glanced around.

"The black swan must have been hiding the day you
visited. Come along."

"I am sure that I heard . . ."

Sophia! Kedvesem, wait!

She pivoted. "Attila! Look, Burchard, it's Attila and
Jacques."

"By Zeus, so it is."

She ran the seventy yards back to the carriage path.
Adrian followed with Dorothy and the earl in tow. By the
time they arrived, a display of hugging and kissing was
underway. Dorothy watched with a curious smile. The
earl's face puffed.

"*Kedvesem!* Oh, it is so good to see you again," Attila
cried. "Jacques and I were so worried about you. There we
were, sitting around Paris, talking about our wonderful
Sophia, and then inspiration struck. Why not go and

visit? When we went to your house this morning Jacques cajoled Charles into telling us where to find you." He bowed to give her hand another big kiss, then turned to Adrian. "Mister Burchard, we meet again. I hope that you do not mind. Jacques said that you might want more time alone with Sophia after all those years . . ."

Hell.

". . . but I said you would not mind old friends coming to make sure that she was happy in all her new responsibilities, not only to her country but to you and that . . ."

Fortunately Sophia interrupted the effervescent flow to make introductions, and neither Dot nor the earl noticed the odd references to Adrian.

"Is it just you two? Where is Dieter?" Sophia asked.

"Dieter got word that a countess back home will pay to have his latest novel printed, so of course he had to return for that," Jacques explained. "Stefan just disappeared one day. A new composer arrived in Paris from Poland. His name is Chopin, and he really *is* of their nobility, so of course things got a little warm for poor Stefan."

"Did you just disembark?"

"Yesterday. Jacques found us a charming little inn for last night, and we came looking for you at once this morning."

"An inn? I will not hear of it. We will send for your things at once. There is plenty of room at Everdon House."

Attila grinned with delight. "Wonderful. It will be just like old times."

Jacques smiled smoothly. "We would be honored, dear lady. Of course, that is if Monsieur Burchard does not mind."

"Burchard?" Sophia frowned. Adrian watched the potential disaster dawn on her. She glanced askance at Dorothy and the earl. *"Oh."*

"The duchess is more generous than prudent," Adrian said. "We would not want to affect her position, especially since she is so recently returned, would we, gentlemen?"

"I cannot countenance having my friends stay in some inn with flea-bitten beds." Sophia was getting that formidable, determined, the-world-be-damned look about her.

The last thing Adrian wanted was the Ensemble living with her again. "May my aunt offer you both accommodations? Dincaster's town house is on the same square as Everdon's."

"Yes," Dorothy said. "You must both stay with us."

The earl absorbed that his hospitality had just been extended to these two foreign persons. "I say . . ." he blustered, but Attila moved in with a flow of gratitude that submerged his objections. Overwhelmed, the earl inched away, mumbled about an engagement, and headed down the path.

Jacques eased next to Adrian and tilted his head conspiratorially. *"Pardon,* but am I correct in surmising that you do not live at this Everdon House and that the marriage is still a secret here?" he muttered.

"Yes."

"But why? Surely now . . ."

"Politics."

Jacques' expression cleared. "Ahhh, *bien.* Politics. Of course." He nodded knowingly.

"We will go to my house and send for your things at once," Sophia announced. She let Jacques hand her up into the curricle before he settled in and retook the reins. Attila climbed onto a footboard in the rear and bent to pour an enthusiastic description of their crossing into her ear.

"I will send a carriage in the afternoon to collect you," Dorothy called after them.

"I love England already. What warm and wonderful people," Attila effused as the wheels rolled. "See, Jacques? We should have come sooner."

"Thank you, Dot," Adrian said after they had driven off.

She raised her eyebrows. "Who are they?"

"Artist friends. Try to keep them away from the earl, will you?"

"I suspect he will take his dinners at his clubs while they are in residence."

"That will not be necessary. She will probably insist that they dine with her."

Dot looked to the shrinking curricle. "You did not want them staying with her, and I do not think it was only concern about the harpies' gossip."

"Not entirely."

"Am I correct in assuming that you will not join us at the house to help me entertain them, but remain at your private chambers?"

"The earl would prefer that, don't you think?"

"How much do you want me to divert them so that you can be alone with her?"

He smiled at Dorothy's perception. "That remains to be seen."

She slipped her arm in his and they continued their walk. "I do not think she is as sophisticated as her Parisian *savoir faire* suggests. Having witnessed you work your charm before, I daresay she does not stand a chance if you are determined. I would admonish you to be discreet, but I know that is not necessary."

"No, that is not necessary."

She narrowed her eyes on the tiny, disappearing speck that was Sophia's bonnet. "I trust that you will be kind too. For all her brave front, she is very frightened. Of you?"

"Partly."

"Then perhaps you should retreat. After all, she must marry and you may only make it harder for her."

Perhaps he should retreat. Sophia obviously had, with determination. But he would not. He had spent years sensibly doing that. He had spent a lifetime being the discreet, as-invisible-as-possible third son of the Earl of Dincaster, but this was different.

He wanted Sophia Raughley. He wanted her in his arms and in his bed. He wanted to slay the ghosts and soothe her quiet sadness and protect and take care of her for as long as their world would let him.

Mostly, however, he wanted what she was afraid of. Unfortunately, he suspected that she would never again trust any man enough for that.

"When she decides to marry, I will retreat, Dot. I will not make it harder on her."

chapter 15

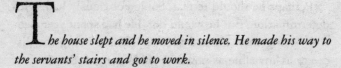

The house slept and he moved in silence. He made his way to the servants' stairs and got to work.

Sophia was proving more resilient than he had expected. She was not acting like the little mouse he remembered.

She knew he was watching and what he was demanding. He had made that very clear. Even if she had not realized he had been in Haford, her protector surely had. She was not reacting the way he wanted, however. He kept waiting for a sign that he had won, that she had broken, but she remained ambiguous about the vote and everything else.

Perhaps she thought he was bluffing. Well, she would learn differently tonight.

He pulled some of his broadsheets from his coat, crushed them in his fist, and piled them on the bottom step. He slipped to the kitchen hearth and lifted some glowing coals on a small shovel. Toting them through the dark, he mounted the stairs again, and slid them into the bed of paper.

Lines of hot orange slowly formed around the coals.

Charles opened the door just enough for Adrian to slip in out of the night. With a finger to his lips and a criminal's glance over his shoulder, the butler gestured for Adrian to follow. They stole their way through the sleeping house to Charles' chambers off the silver pantry.

His sitting room was tiny but comfortably appointed. Adrian settled into a chair and held out his hand expectantly.

Charles hesitated. "Still doesn't seem right, sir. Telling you what she's been doing doesn't seem as much a betrayal, since she isn't doing much at all. This is different, and I'm of two minds, I am."

Charles' unease pricked at Adrian's own. He was unaccustomed to using such subterfuge in England. "It is different and it isn't right and under any other circumstance I would never ask it. However, I did not lie when I said she might be in danger. If she is being threatened, I want to know."

Charles debated, then extracted two papers from his Bible and handed them over. "She'll release me if she finds out."

"You can return them shortly to her desk."

Adrian held the sheets near a brace of candles. Like the first letter from Captain Brutus, these were neatly printed in anonymous block letters. However, they contained much less restraint than the other, and bore an accusatory, demanding tone.

The first called on her to support the most radical of the proposed reform plans. It ended with a reminder of their "intimacy" years ago, and a demand that she not display the weakness again that she had so ignobly shown during that episode.

The most recent one was more explicit. "You have the chance to expiate your betrayals and crimes, Your Grace. What you did to me is nothing compared to the blow you struck at the hopes of the people, the hopes that I embodied. My own life is nothing in this. Nor is yours. History calls, and it is time for you to rectify what occurred. I must call in the debt, and you must pay it. One way or the other."

That the next paragraph read like a lover's appeal, remembering her "soft warmth" and "kind heart" and "generous affection," did not dilute the implied threat. Adrian reread those endearments more often than he needed to.

Why hadn't she shown him, or anyone else, these letters? Were the overtures of affection touching her more than the warnings were frightening her?

"Do you have any reason to think that she has met with him?" he asked Charles. "Have any men visited, whom you wondered about?"

"None that I saw. But she does go out, doesn't she? On those walks alone. And last night she went to that political meeting."

"It was a meeting of reform supporters, but not of Captain Brutus' ilk. The Viscount Laclere does not associate with revolutionaries."

He quizzed Charles more specifically on the callers, but only learned that they were all well-known members of society. The park was busy enough in the mornings that he doubted she would arrange an assignation there.

He read again the most recent letter. The mind that

wrote it couldn't decide if it wanted Sophia for revenge, for love, or for political advantage.

He rose. He would have to have a firm talk with the duchess.

Charles ducked around to open the sitting room door. He escorted Adrian through the silver pantry and out into the corridor.

Almost immediately they both stopped short.

Charles cocked his head. Adrian sniffed.

"Sir, do you? . . ." Charles began warily.

The sting in Adrian's eyes told him for sure. He ran to the stairwell. Puffs of smoke billowed up from the lower level. "Rouse the footmen to fight it, then go and raise the cry in the neighborhood," he ordered.

Already the smoke was thickening. Turning on his heel, Adrian headed for the chambers above.

He ran right into Gerald Stidolph, who was exiting the library.

"What the hell are you doing here, Stidolph?"

"*My* presence is not at all irregular. I visited with Sophia and paused for a glass of port after she retired."

"Making yourself at home prematurely, aren't you?"

"I do not care for your impertinence."

Adrian brushed past him and started up the stairs at a run. "No time for this, Stidolph. Follow me. There is a fire below."

"A fire! My God, Sophia . . ." Gerald was at his heels in an instant.

"Go above and alert the servants," Adrian ordered.

Gerald pulled at Adrian's arm. "The hell I will. You go up. I will save Sophia, not you." He slammed Adrian against the wall, almost making him topple.

Cursing Stidolph's determination to be heroic, Adrian followed to the third level and saw him aim for Sophia's chambers. Flying now, because acrid smoke already wafted through the house, Adrian continued up to the attic chambers.

Sophia stared around her dark chamber. This house still felt foreign to her, and the shadows' shapes unsettled her. She reached down beside her bed and let her fingers drift along Camilla's fur and pretended that she was back in Paris.

Near the hearth Yuri and his brothers snorted in their dreams, and she could make out Prinny snoozing in his wooden cage near the settee. The presence of her animal friends provided some comfort of the familiar, just as the arrival of Attila and Jacques today had created a welcome distraction from the silent turmoil that she carried inside her.

Her emotions were at war about many things, including Captain Brutus and the elections and Gerald and so much else. However, all of those pressures had become secondary to the battle that her heart waged over Adrian Burchard. Her loneliness so badly desired the comfort that he offered that yearning perpetually stung like a new burn.

She wanted desperately to lie to herself and embrace the closeness for whatever it was worth. But that night at Staverly had proven that she could not control things with him the way that she needed in order to be safe from scathing disappointment, so she had been hiding from the intimacy entirely.

Which only left her more alone at a time when she could use his friendship and advice very badly.

She drowsily considered the last weeks of false smiles and critical eyes and threatening letters. Everyone was waiting for her to make choices she did not want to face. Wellington had called and obliquely broached the issue of her marriage, letting her know he did not believe the story of the husband. It would not be long before he and others ceased being subtle.

The image of Gerald entering this house this evening, of him sitting in the drawing room as if it were his own, and loitering in the library later, too comfortable by far, began intruding.

Her mind took refuge by drifting off to sleep. A mild commotion from below barely penetrated. She became drowsily aware of her chamber door opening.

It was Prinny's squeal that snapped her alert. And Yuri's growl. And the sudden rise of Camilla's back under her fingers.

A tall presence loomed beside her bed.

"Gerald? How *dare* you."

"Wake up, Sophia. You must leave at once. There is a fire."

"A fire!"

With one hand he hauled her out of bed. With the other he grabbed her dressing robe off a nearby chair. She heard running footsteps on the boards above her head, and shouts from below.

"Do not worry, my dear. I will save you." He pushed her toward the door.

"The dogs . . ."

"There is no time."

"Prinny..."

He pressed a hand on her back and shoved. "Move quickly, down to the front door."

She could hear servants pouring down from the upper levels with shouts and screams. Frightened and agitated, the dogs howled and Prinny squealed. "I cannot leave them."

"The fire is in the lower stairwell and if it isn't contained it will shoot right up to the attic."

"Just let me go and—"

"No!" Gripping her arm, he dragged her to the door.

She dug in her heels and yanked free. "Go, if you must. I will be right behind you." Currents of smoke stung her eyes shut. She bumped into the dogs' cages and bent to open them. She groped her way back toward Prinny.

Gerald opened the door and smoke billowed in. "Sophia, there is no time!"

She felt for the cage's latch.

"Sophia!" His shadow took one step toward her, but the sound of wood crashing below stopped him. His head turned to the chaotic sounds of a terrified household and the obscuring smoke, then back to her.

He ran, swallowed by the darkness.

She frantically reached for the monkey, but he lunged past her, over to the window. Calling to him, she felt for the dogs' leads. Yuri and his brothers paced in the dim light by the windows, barking at the danger they sensed all too well.

Her chest burned. The upper levels of the house grew quiet but the street below her window had filled with noise. She began to panic. She grabbed for Prinny but he jumped away.

Suddenly the door closed. The air cleared a little. She startled as an arm encircled her waist.

"Burchard." Relief swept her. "The animals...they will not obey and come."

"That is because you indulge them too much, as I do you." Releasing her, he called sharply for the dogs and Camilla. Silenced, they all filed forward.

He brought them to the door. "Out. Run," he commanded, opening it. The dark line lunged with a fast patter of paws. He slammed the door after them.

He took Sophia's arm and guided her to the window. "They are fast and will be in the street within moments. You, however, cannot go that way now. The smoke is too thick."

She had already guessed that. Despite the closed door, she could smell it. Feel it. Her chest began constricting again, both from smoke and from fear. She stuck her face to the fresh air and gazed into the torch-lit street.

The fire had drawn the whole neighborhood and men of all classes worked the water line. She made out the forms of the dogs and ocelot pouring out the building, into the arms of Attila and Jacques.

Dincaster's house was also on St. James Square and the news of the fire had brought the whole household. The Burchard family craned inspecting gazes up at the building. Colin noticed her and Adrian at the window, and tore toward the entrance.

Adrian bent out and yelled for his brother to stop, then ducked back in. He grabbed a heavy chair. "Stand back," he ordered. He shouted the same command to the people below and then crashed the chair into the window. Glass and wood splintered and flew. He battered the remnants away until a large hole gaped.

"You expect to go out this way? If we jump it will kill us."

He strode over to her bed and began tearing it apart. "I will climb down and you will hold on." He began tying the bed cloths together.

"This is not going to work."

"Of course it is. I've done it before."

He sounded so confident. Her terror retreated a little, and she helped him shove the heavy bed over near the window and tie the escape line to its base.

"Up on the chair. Arms around my neck and legs around my waist."

"You are sure that you know what you are doing?" she asked, assuming the embarrassing position.

"Absolutely. Hold tight now."

He threw down the line of sheets. A cry went up from the onlookers.

"At least we will give London some entertainment tonight." He backed her out of the window and climbed out legs first.

Night air sucked at her and suddenly she was clinging to his dangling body forty feet above the street. A squeal tore her attention from her precarious hold to a desperate little face peering out above her.

"Prinny! Adrian . . ."

"God forbid we should leave His Majesty behind." Twisting one arm in the sheets, he plucked the monkey and threw him onto her head. Prinny screamed and grabbed her, much as Sophia clutched Burchard.

They began to descend. Very slowly.

"You are sure that you have done this before?" she whispered.

"Well, the last time there was no woman and no monkey. And it was a rope, not sheets."

"No woman . . . you do not know for sure that this will work, do you?"

"Of course I do. We have made it at least five feet closer to the ground already."

He bumped against the facade with each lowered hand hold, skinning her legs against the stone. Swallowing a fear that wanted to suffocate her, she clutched tighter and hitched her legs more snugly.

Adrian paused. "Move your right leg just a bit."

"It is all I can do to hold on at all."

"If you do not move your leg, I will be the one to let go. We would like all of my concentration and strength centered in my arms."

She realized with a jolt what he meant. Under her lower calf a ridge of hardness had emerged. "Really, this is not the time or the place."

"I am all too aware of that. Now, try and move your leg. Please."

Burning with humiliation, she tried. She managed something of a rub instead of a move.

"Hell," he muttered. They just hung there, supported only by his strained arms.

"We are both going to die if you don't get hold of yourself. Think of something else, Burchard."

"Why don't you distract me by promising to repay the debt you are incurring by having your life saved?"

She ventured a peek to the distant street below. The

height made her head swim. "What prize would instill the resolve to hold onto those sheets?"

"You know what I want."

"It is yours. I will direct my M.P.'s to vote against all reform bills unless directed otherwise by the Tory leadership."

Hand over hand he continued his descent. Each move jerked them precariously. He wound his legs in the sheets and that seemed to stabilize them a little.

Their slow progress made the crowd restless. Encouragement and advice shot up through the night.

"Halfway, Adrian," Colin called.

"Good heavens, Adrian, couldn't you have found a simpler..."

"Oh, Jacques, look at our poor Sophia. Do not worry, my lady. We will catch you."

Finally the rusticated stone of the house's first level moved into view. Then a window. Finally came the heavenly sensation of feeling Adrian's weight land on the ground.

Gerald was the first of the closing crowd to reach them. He helped Sophia off Adrian's back. "Awfully dramatic, don't you think, Burchard?"

"Less so than a funeral," Sophia snapped. "If you had helped me with the animals and not run away—"

A huge hug from Attila separated her from Gerald's seething reaction. "Oh, my lady, we saw the smoke and came, never knowing it was your house. Thank God that Mister Burchard was staying with you tonight."

The closest onlookers, the Burchard family and Gerald, inhaled a collective breath. Colin and Dorothy exhaled exclamations and congratulations to blunt the absorption of Attila's insinuation.

The *faux pas* pricked Sophia's mind. How had Adrian come to be in the house to save her?

The crowd milled and pressed, sorry that the spectacle was over. Adrian plucked Prinny from her shoulders and handed him to the earl. The monkey embraced his neck and settled into the crook of his arm. The earl, flustering with indignation, was left holding him like a child.

"Don't let Prinny get away or we will spend all night scouring London for him," Adrian said.

"Prinny? By Jove, that is treasonous."

Prinny smiled up beatifically. The earl froze. "What the hell is he . . . the damn ape has . . . My coat is ruined!"

Adrian shook off his frock coat and threw it around Sophia's naked shoulders.

"The fire is contained and almost out," Colin reported. "The damage was significant and the building is still filled with smoke. That was a close call, Duchess. Bravo, Adrian."

Adrian dusted himself off. Sophia sensed that he would brush off the attention if he could. "You had better take the duchess home with you, Dot."

"Of course. You will stay with us, my dear, until things can be assessed. Will you escort us, Adrian?"

"Colin, would you do it? I need to see about some things here. I will speak with you tomorrow, Duchess. We have some things to discuss."

"We certainly do." Including what Adrian had been up to tonight in her home.

A man from the water line pushed through to Adrian.

He handed over a charred scrap of paper. "It was found where the fire started."

"What is it?" Sophia asked.

"Part of a broadside used to start the flames," Adrian said quietly. "Robin Hood's calling card."

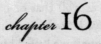

chapter 16

Adrian knew how to blend in with the night. After learning what he could from the charred evidence at Everdon House, he disappeared into the shadows of London's streets for several hours.

He poured ale down the throats of talkative men and paid barmaids and whores to tell what they knew. He ventured into a house across the river that served as a lair for smugglers and petty thieves. The denizens accepted him because two of their members had once made his acquaintance when they were acting as privateers in the eastern Mediterranean. Finally, in the hours before dawn he called on the shabby home of a political radical with whom he periodically shared arguments and wine.

None of them could point him toward Captain Brutus. The man was only a name to them. They had never met him, nor heard talk of whom he hired to distribute his broadsides and do the more criminal work such as the fire.

Adrian headed home frustrated. Normally London's netherworld was rife with rumors. Captain Brutus must be very intelligent and careful to remain so obscure. He decided it was just as well that he had not tracked down the man tonight. With Sophia's mortal danger still fresh in his mind, he might have killed him.

He let himself into the building where he lived and went up to the rooms he leased on the second floor. This had been his home since the day fifteen years ago when he had endured his last big row with the earl.

It occurred soon after he left Oxford and a month after his mother died. Summoned like a retainer, he had received the announcement that the earl had procured a position for him with the East India Company. The earl was severing all financial responsibility for him, but had arranged this, ostensibly so he would be provided for.

If he had been a normal son he might have been grateful, but he knew that this was really the earl's way of removing his presence from society. This employment would render him invisible. Banished to the other side of the globe. It had been the final, blatant example of the repudiation that he had suffered in countless ways over the years.

Boiling with resentments only exaggerated by his mother's death, and determined to take no gifts from the man, he had refused.

Anticipating that, the earl had then offered an army commission. As a boy Adrian had dreamed of redeeming the accident of his birth on the battlefield, but he could see no point in being an army officer if there were no wars in which to demonstrate valor and patriotism. He did not doubt that the earl would see that he was assigned to a unit in some distant colony too.

Again he refused. So the earl had fallen back on a third

alternative that would at least demand periodic long absences from England. He offered to intercede to procure for Adrian a minor post with the Foreign Secretary's office.

This time he had accepted. It had been a chance for travel and a small role in government. He soon discovered that it also provided opportunities to prove his loyalty to England. His countrymen might find his face vaguely foreign, but much of the world found it very familiar. His natural disguise allowed him to blend into countries in ways he had never been able to at home.

It never bothered him that his risks and successes remained a secret, never to be publicly celebrated like the great battle victories he had dreamed about in his youth. The men who mattered knew all about what occurred on those missions.

Using his salary and the income from the portion left to him by his mother, he had removed himself from Dincaster's homes and all but the most formal relationship with the earl. He had taken these rooms. He had never felt the urge to move to more expansive and fashionable quarters. If he conducted an affair with a lady of society, he did so elsewhere.

And so, when he stepped into the sitting room of the masculine, comfortable chambers, he was surprised to find a duchess waiting for him.

Not the one he wanted to see.

The Dowager Duchess of Everdon barely acknowledged his arrival while she surveyed the items on his shelves.

"How did you get in?" He poured himself a glass of sack. She had already helped herself to one.

"Your manservant did not want me lounging around the entrance."

No doubt Celine had played the grand lady to the hilt. His manservant could hardly stand against that.

He did not bother to ask why she had come. The way she held herself, and the way that she looked at him, and the way that she made the black gown sway when she strolled, told him the answer to that. The real question was, why now?

"I heard about your daring rescue tonight. Very heroic. I wanted to make sure that you had not been harmed."

"How considerate." He wondered who had gone to Celine in the dead of night with the story.

"You do not sound as if you appreciate my concern. Perhaps if I was helpless and lost I could provoke more interest. Maybe if I was too stupid to leave a burning building and thus precipitated a public spectacle..."

Gerald must have visited her. He knew about Sophia staying behind for the animals.

"You have decided to visit London during the summer sessions?" he asked.

"I may live here permanently. I do not care for that Cornwall manor that is my dowager property. Sophia made me leave, I'm sure you know. Sent me away from Marleigh." Something between a girlish pout and a very calculating glare played over her lovely face. "It was insulting for her to do that. Marleigh is large enough for us both."

"I seriously doubt that."

"She did it to diminish me. To set me down."

"I doubt that as well."

"It is mine too! I gave up quite a lot to have it."

"Yes, I expect that you did. Your youth. Your chance for love. Certainly you gave up whatever softness was once in you. But Alistair is dead and Sophia is duchess. If you have come for advice, I can only offer that it is time to move on."

"I did not come for advice."

He already knew that. She strolled around the chamber, examining and fingering the oddities brought back from his travels. She acted very absorbed in the Greek icon and Turkish bronze, and studied the primitive African carving with its distorted features and jutting breasts. Every move, every tilt of the head and pose of the body, was intended to entrance a man.

"Since you did not come for advice, perhaps you should explain why you are here."

Swishing across the room like it was a stage, she took a chair and he sat in another. "I am told that you have some influence over her."

"You were told wrong."

"You have a friendship."

"A very formal one."

"Still, you could speak with her. Explain that she could use a friend and companion to help her at Marleigh. I could be a great aid to her."

"Everyone can use a friend. If you propose to be hers, your actions will speak louder than my words. However, anything less than sincerity will be a waste of your time. The duchess is very sensitive about people using her."

She did not like the insinuation. She glared with a defensive smirk. It passed quickly. She relaxed into the chair.

"I went to great risk to come here. If anyone finds out, my reputation will be ruined."

"Since your husband is barely cold, that is probably true. In fact, it would be best if you left."

She kept her blue eyes locked on him. She was beautiful enough to affect any man, and he was not completely untouched. Ten years ago he had been thoroughly bedazzled. Age begets some wisdom, however, and in him that was especially true about the Celine Laceys of the world. His reaction now was a thin, superficial thing that he could easily contain and ignore.

"I will never forget the time you kissed me. It was a wonderful kiss."

"If I had known that you were to become engaged to Everdon the next day, it never would have happened."

"He was a duke, Adrian. *A duke.* And you were..." she caught herself and smiled apologetically.

"Yes." He usually did not resent that anymore, but he did now. Not because of Celine, but because of another duchess and what it implied about the limits of his relationship with her. The flare of annoyance provoked a bluntness that normally he would have suppressed. "Tell me, when did you conclude that you were unable to have children?"

Her face fell. "What an extraordinary thing to ask. I am not—"

"When you began taking lovers I assumed it was the duke, and that you sought another way to provide the son that he could not sire. I suspect it began that way."

"I did not take lovers."

"I know about Laclere's brother Dante. And a few others." *Stidolph?*

She did not even blush. "Alistair was old. I knew after two years that he would never get me with child. If there were lovers, I was not the first wife to solve the problem thus."

"Except that after a few more years, you realized it was not him, but you."

"You are determined to insult me."

"There is no insult in it. I know because the pattern was obvious. Dante and the others were fair or brown-haired. Their bastards could have passed muster. When you offered yourself to me it was clear that you knew there was no danger of a child. You would hardly risk presenting Everdon with a son who had my eyes and hair."

She rose and began her stroll again. "I wish I had known at once. Before you became his M.P. and felt honor-bound to him."

"If it is any consolation, I would not have been any more agreeable earlier."

He might have slapped her in the face, so immediate was the reaction of shock. Evidently Celine had never faced the notion that any man would not succumb.

Unfortunately, shock turned into determination. She smiled as if a gauntlet had been thrown. "That is a blatant lie. You wanted me."

"Once I did. It passed quickly."

"Such things do not pass."

"You are a lovely woman and you can incite a physical reaction in any man. It has been many years since I *wanted* you, however."

Sharp of eye and sensuous of smile, she eased toward him until she stood close to his shoulder. "You think that you *want* her now?"

He did not answer.

"You see what she can do for you, that is all, but she is just prickly enough to resent your expectations that she advance you. I, on the other hand, understand such things perfectly. It is the least that a lover can do." She reached down and stroked one fingernail gently along his jaw. "I know many powerful men. They owe me. In a year we will not even have to be very discreet anymore."

He grasped her hand and pulled it away from his face. She twisted her wrist until she held his hand instead. Looking down like an angel, she placed his palm on her breast.

He met her eyes and let her see his indifference. He removed his hand and stood. He walked to the door and opened it.

"As you said, you risk your reputation coming here. You should leave now."

Unlike Sophia, Celine did not appear at all beautiful when she was angry. The emotion distorted her face into something brittle and ugly and dangerous.

"You dare to dismiss me?"

"I worry for your reputation, as you should. He is no longer alive to blunt the talk. You should be more discreet now that your circumstances have changed."

She collected her shawl and breezed past. "Do not lecture me, Burchard. My circumstances have changed but my position is unassailable, and I did not become Everdon's duchess by being stupid."

He closed the door on her beauty and fury and returned to his sack.

What the devil had all of that really been about?

"It is early to be calling, Gerald," Sophia said as she entered Dincaster's morning room to greet her guest.

"The events of last night render propriety unimportant, to my mind."

"Gerald, you are the sort of man for whom the approach of an invading army would not render proprieties unimportant. So, to what do I owe the pleasure of this unseemly visit at ten o'clock?"

"We need to speak, frankly and directly. Please sit."

She perched on a chair. He paced around her, giving her a hard gaze like one would to a naughty child.

"That spectacle last night was beyond the pale."

"Do you think so? Now that I have had some sleep, I am beginning to see it as quite humorous." That wasn't true. With the passage of shock had come an insistent fear and a helpless confusion about how to protect herself.

"Climbing down that building, dangling like that, you barely clothed . . . it is all over town. The entire episode is highly embarrassing."

"I would rather endure an embarrassing rescue than a discreet death. I am grateful that Mister Burchard chose to risk his own neck in order to help me save mine. I daresay that he could have been on the ground in a minute without me on his back."

"If you had not been so willful about those stupid animals—"

"You would have gotten me out. I do not blame you for running when I refused to obey. It was the sensible course. I have told no one, if that is your real reason for coming. Society will not brand you the coward in contrast to Adrian's hero."

His flush revealed that that had indeed been one of his concerns, and that he resented her articulating it so baldly. A defensive sneer twisted his mouth. "What was he doing in your house?"

"Not visiting me, as you well know. You were present when I left the library and retired. You found me alone in my chamber. I assume that he was passing the house and noticed some smoke and found a way in."

"That strange walrus of a man, the Bohemian, assumed otherwise."

"Attila is Hungarian. Unfortunately, his mouth runs ahead of his brain. Considering that Adrian was lowering us both from my chamber window, his assumption is understandable even if it is incorrect."

"Only if he knows you for a woman who takes lovers. Who is this Attila, anyway, and what is he doing here?"

"He is a friend from Paris. He and Jacques have come to visit me."

"Are you saying that you have imported your lovers? Is it your goal to humiliate me before the whole country?"

"Really, Gerald. I have no intention of answering any more of your impertinent questions."

"My future bride is the center of a public spectacle that will be the tattle of drawing rooms for weeks, she has her virtue publicly compromised by the indiscreet yapping of a hairy foreigner, and you call my concern impertinent?"

"I call your concern self-centered. You have expressed no interest in my health or disposition after last night's shock, but only in how things affect *you*. However, your continued assumption that we will marry is indeed impertinent."

Anger brought out something icy and hard in Gerald. He stopped his pacing and looked her over with his best Alistair inspection, instantly giving that ghost physical substance. The similarity sucked the strength right out of her. She barely suppressed a tremble. *So this is what I am left with,* that expression said. *And a sad specimen it is too.*

"Harvey Douglas has come up for the sessions. He said that you visited Staverly."

"He no doubt also told you why I took refuge there."

"Another spectacle. They follow you wherever you go, don't they? I would not have expected you to ever go back to Staverly, let alone so soon after your return."

She knew that he could see that broaching this subject made her composure wobble. He was glad for it. "It was not as difficult as I expected."

"Wasn't it? Are you that heartless? I would think that being there would overwhelm you with guilt."

She could only glare at him while her heart filled again with the dismay she had felt in the gazebo.

Unlike Adrian, he did not seek to comfort her, but cruelly pressed his advantage. "You accuse me of impertinence for assuming we will marry, but Everdon was everything to Alistair. With the succession secured by Brandon, he knew some peace. You robbed him of that."

"I did not."

"Have you blocked the memories that well? You killed him. Your willfulness and rebelliousness killed him. Call it an accident if you want, but you were the direct cause of his death, and the death of your father's dreams."

The way he ruthlessly spelled out her guilt, giving

voice to her own horrible thoughts, left her boneless and nauseous.

"The notion that you would be the heir distressed him to no end. Your behavior in Paris only confirmed his fears. In your childish, extravagant hands, Everdon's status would be ruined in a generation. So he gave you to me. Not to some earl or marquess, but to me. He did not want the power of Everdon to be swallowed by being joined to another great title. I would be its caretaker until your son could assume his position. The legacy would continue whole, just delayed by a generation."

"I do not care why he did it. It was not my choice."

"Your choice? How like you to think only of yourself. It has always been like that. Your shocking friendship with a revolutionary ruined your reputation. Your recklessness killed your brother. Your father sought a way to rectify the disasters, and all you could think about was whether he had pampered your childish sensibilities by giving you a choice."

The relentless picking at the scab of those memories was driving her close to tears.

"You owe it to him, Sophia. You owe it to him, and to Brandon, to obey him in this. For once in your frivolous, intemperate, and thoughtless life you must do his will. There will be no peace about your brother's death until you expiate the damage that you caused."

She was beyond defending herself. The browbeating had worn her down, just as Alistair's always did. There was too much truth in what he was saying. She could not even look him in the eyes anymore.

He picked up his hat and walked to the door.

"One more thing. I would not put too much faith in

Burchard's friendship. I heard a rumor that he had a visitor at his chambers last night. Celine. He was one of her suitors before she married your father, you know." He opened the door and threw out his last punch with a vicious smile. "As you once said, if he is interested in a pleasurable liaison with a woman, he can do better than you."

She did not move for a long while after he left. She felt as if she had been pummeled by fists. The final blow, the information about Celine, had knocked the life right out of her.

Maybe Gerald was right. If she married him, she might bury the ghosts and the guilt. With Everdon's power transferred to her husband, probably Captain Brutus would lose interest in her and the letters and danger would cease. There might be some peace. Finally.

She pictured a life as Gerald's wife. The images left her queasy. They might make an arrangement, of course. One that permitted her to go back to France. She had him at a disadvantage and he would most likely agree. But would he honor that solution once he had her? The husband of Everdon would be much diminished if Everdon was in Paris.

With a weary sigh she pushed to her feet. The coercions would only increase. In a few days the Parliament would start, and the demands that she choose her political course would get more insistent. The calls for her to marry would mount. All the time that she tried to discover the right decisions, Captain Brutus would be watching and waiting.

What had been his intention with that fire? To frighten the duchess into obeying his political demands? Or to harm the woman who had betrayed him years ago?

His letters implied that he might not know for sure which he desired more badly.

She wanted desperately to hand this all over to someone else. Someone who would manage it for her and make it come out good in the end. Someone like Adrian.

She had woken this morning much softened toward him. Last night had moved her to reconsider the judgments that she had formed. She had even decided to show him those letters and ask his advice.

How stupid of her to read genuine affection into that rescue. How very childish to grasp at the excuse it offered to make a fool of herself. How ridiculous to experience this excruciating disappointment on hearing how he had spent last night.

Do not put too much faith in Burchard's friendship. It had been weak of her to ever do so. He had been managing her to his own ends from the start. He had tried to make love to her even while he cast his lure for Celine.

She coldly looked into the future of demands and expectations and threats and confusion. It was unfair that her life should have been disrupted like this. She wanted none of it. By what right did all these people, these *men,* pull her in several directions like a criminal to be quartered?

Simmering annoyance gave her back some spine. She left the drawing room and headed in search of the only two friends she had in England.

She remembered that first conversation with Adrian. *I am nothing in this.* How true. It was Everdon that they wanted to control, not her.

Well, damn it, let them have it.

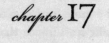

chapter 17

The gathering at Laclere's house in late afternoon was a political meeting, which was how Sophia justified attending despite being in mourning. Fortunately, the conversation did not completely revolve around Parliamentary reform.

Perhaps that was because Laclere's wife had invited some friends who were not in the government. Maybe it was because Sophia herself did not encourage the few overtures to political discussions that wafted her way. Most likely, however, it was because many of the guests had an interest in the arts and found that topic more pleasant.

She attached herself to a group that did. It included the St. Johns, whom she had met the day before in the park, and members of Laclere's family.

The viscount's handsome younger brother, Dante Duclairc, began charming her after their introduction. Dante displayed absolutely no interest in politics, which she found refreshing. He was also handsome as sin, with thick brown hair and heavily lashed, beautiful eyes.

"I had expected a more formal gathering," she said to him when he sought reassurance that she was enjoying herself.

"Would that have pleased Your Grace?"

"Not at all. I have been spared formalities for years, and do not relish living with them again."

"Then you have come to the right place. My brother's wife possesses a spirit that undermines most social rituals through her mere presence. No matter what my brother's intentions in this gathering, Bianca will not permit it to be boring."

"We will be spared speeches, then?"

The Viscount Laclere's sister, the Countess of Glasbury, had joined their conversation. She now glanced at Laclere. "No speeches. If you notice, however, my brother is speaking quietly with the M.P.'s present who straddle the fence."

Sophia had noticed those private chats. The tall, imposing lord with his harsh good looks and piercing blue eyes was using the assembly to work his persuasion individually and subtly.

She wondered when he would make his way around to her.

"I apologize that I have not called on you, Your Grace. I thought it best to be introduced first," the countess said.

"I hope that you will call now. Your interest in the arts matches my own, and it would be a joy to have friends with similar sympathies. I count on you to introduce me to others of like mind."

Sophia felt guilty making the overture, since it was

unlikely that friendship would have a chance to blossom. Still, she understood the unspoken allusion in the countess's comment, and wanted to reassure her that the new Duchess of Everdon did not judge women as harshly as others might.

The countess appeared surprised and grateful for the invitation. With a smile, she allowed her attention to be claimed by Diane St. John.

"That was kind of you," Dante said.

"You mean, because she is separated from the earl?" Sophia had been pointedly educated by several imposing and annoying arbiters of society on how that scandal had affected the countess's social status.

"Penelope did not want to risk criticism because of it."

"Such things are common in France, and I do not hold them against a woman."

"Not criticism from you. *Of* you."

"I daresay that with all of the criticism *of* me filling the drawing rooms these days, any I might receive for receiving your sister would be the least of it."

Dante laughed lightly, and gave a warm look that indicated he found some of that criticism both interesting and intriguing.

Any inclination he had to explore how intriguing was thwarted by a new presence in their midst. Adrian Burchard had arrived, and was suddenly standing right beside Sophia in a manner that crowded Dante away.

Adrian looked tousle-haired and a little tired and handsome as the devil. He managed to separate her totally from the group. She could not tell if he eased her away or if the others retreated, but suddenly it was just the two of them talking alone.

"I see that you have met Laclere's family," he said.

"The countess is very sweet, and his brother is very charming."

"You are not the first woman to think that of Dante Duclairc. Do not even consider adding him to your Ensemble, however. Dante has no artistic pretensions, and prefers married women."

"He spoke earlier as if you are his friend, but you do not sound like one."

"He is a very good friend, as are Laclere and St. John. That is another reason why you should not consider him for your Ensemble." His scrutiny snapped from Dante to her. "You appear none the worse for last night's adventure. I am relieved to see that you have recovered so well."

"I slept soundly and woke much refreshed. And you, Mister Burchard? Did you sleep well?"

"Passably."

"That is good news. After such strenuous activity, the wise course is to rest. However, I am told that some men seek more exertions after such occurrences, as if their blood does not know how to calm."

"That is true, but considering your shock, it did not seem polite to pursue further exertions last night."

He had a lot of brass to make such insinuations after exerting himself all night with Celine. His quiet, slow tone lacked the playful flirting of their earliest exchanges. It caused an unwelcome sensation to tingle through her, despite her pique.

"I assume that you managed to solve the dilemma," she said.

"Again, passably."

Really!

"I will escort you home after this, Sophia."

"My coach will be waiting, so I must decline."

"I will escort you. The fire was deliberately set and your danger is no longer in question."

"Again, I must decline. However, I want to say that I am grateful for your help last night. I truly am. Although I have come to wonder how you were in my house when the fire began."

"Are you implying that I may have started it?"

The question astonished her. "In no way did I intend to suggest that, although someone other than Captain Brutus could be responsible, of course. I am merely curious about your timely presence. What were you doing in my house last night?"

"Reading the letters that you have received from Captain Brutus." He did not so much as blink.

"You dared to intrude on my privacy in such a dishonorable way?"

He studied her with sharp deliberation, standing too closely, towering above her in a very male manner. "I found them interesting, and I find your willingness to believe he was not responsible for the fire astonishing. The threats in those letters were unmistakable. Maybe you did not absorb the danger because you were distracted by his references to your past intimacy with him. He writes to you as a lover, and now you consider excusing him from this criminal attack on you. It is enough to make one wonder if you welcome his return into your life."

"You cannot seriously believe that."

"I can think of no other reason for your keeping those letters to yourself."

"Perhaps to share them would embarrass me. How did

I come to be making the explanations? You are the one who stole into my house and read my private correspondence."

"You can voice your displeasure about that on the way back to Dincaster House. No matter what your feelings toward this man, you should not be about alone, considering your apparent danger from him."

"Why do you assume that I will be alone? Every woman in society is intent on throwing eligible men my way. If I need an escort, I daresay I can find another one. I would not dream of delaying you from pursuing whatever pleasures and diversions await you this evening."

His jaw tightened at her crisp tone. At least she hoped it sounded crisp, and not shrewish and hurt. "In the best of circumstances you are a vexing woman. It has its charm, but your demeanor today does not amuse me. I must demand your company for the evening. You and I have some matters to discuss."

"I do not think that we have anything to discuss."

"Of course we do. Captain Brutus, for one thing. The way that you have been hiding from me, for another."

"I have not been hiding from you. I have been discouraging you."

He began to respond, but stopped because their hostess approached. Lady Laclere bore down on them with a tall, dark, brooding man in tow.

"I see Julian Hampton is here," Adrian muttered dryly. "Do not consider recruiting him to your Ensemble, either. He is far too old, and is a lawyer despite his poetic appearance."

The viscount's wife, Bianca, possessed a distinctive face that managed to combine youthful innocence and worldly sensuality in its wide blue eyes and full lips and firm little chin. "There you are, Duchess. I want to introduce Mister Hampton. He is a dear friend of our family, and has served as solicitor to the St. Johns as well."

Sophia was relieved by the interruption, and delighted to meet the solicitor. His presence reminded her that she had not taken care of a few details about her inheritance. It was past time to rectify the oversight.

"Mister Hampton, are you willing to consider new clients?" she asked after a few pleasantries had been exchanged. "I ask because I have relieved my father's lawyer of his duties."

Julian Hampton appeared vaguely surprised by the question, but if he thought it in bad taste to broach the matter at this assembly he did not allow his expression to show it. "I would be happy to discuss the matter at your convenience, Your Grace."

"That would be right now, I'm afraid. It will not do to have the estate matters left drifting. Would you meet with the previous solicitor and procure the documents and such? I will contact you soon regarding anything that needs my attention."

Julian Hampton took it in stride, and Lady Laclere appeared delighted that her introduction had borne fruit so quickly. Adrian, however, gave Sophia a very peculiar look.

Mister Hampton requested some conversation with Adrian, and the two men wandered off. That left Sophia with Lady Laclere.

In no time the viscount found them. Sophia suspected it had all been planned, and that Mister Hampton had been asked to get Adrian out of the way.

"I am sorry to hear about the damage to your home, Duchess," Laclere offered. "There is a rumor that it was deliberately started. I trust that is not true."

"There is evidence to that, but I hope that you will help me to quash talk of it."

"Do you think it was politically motivated?" Lady Laclere asked.

"It may have been."

Laclere sighed with annoyance. "The more impatient radicals do not understand the fruitlessness of violence, I am afraid. Nothing will be accomplished through intimidation. Rather the opposite."

Sophia could not agree. She was feeling thoroughly intimidated on many fronts, and it had definitely borne fruit.

"I risk being overbold, but how is it that Adrian Burchard attends this meeting?" she asked. "He is firmly in the antireform camp."

Laclere glanced to where Adrian and Hampton spoke near a window. "Burchard is an old friend of mine. He is also an intelligent man. I am hopeful where he is concerned."

"Vergil is quite the optimist," Lady Laclere said.

"Decidedly, my dear. Those of us who support reform are optimists who think that men are capable of understanding issues and acting in the common good. Those who oppose assume that the general population is weak-minded, just so many children to be led by their parents."

"I think that your optimism is misplaced where Mister Burchard is concerned," Sophia said. "He did not attend today to listen to reason, did he? Nor did you invite him in the hopes that he would."

"As I said, I am hopeful. But no, his attendance was arranged by certain ministers in my party. Because of you?"

"Probably."

"For romantic reasons, or because they feared that I would corrupt you?"

"They think that I am one of those children, to be led by my parents."

"Just like men," Lady Laclere said, "to assume that a woman is incapable of determining the right course on her own."

The viscount eyed her more sharply. "Have you been able to determine your own course, Duchess? Despite the overbearing influences that certain powerful men are trying to exert?"

"Yes." And she had. Not the course that Laclere meant. Nor the one that Adrian tried to manage. She had most definitely decided her own course, however, and it was time to act on it.

The viscount chatted a bit about Paris and then excused himself. Sophia turned to her hostess.

"That was very mild. I expected more exhortations."

"My husband is too clever for that. It is enough that you know that there are men of principle with other points of view. He assumes that you will seek him out if you need him."

"His restraint is welcome, I assure you."

Lady Laclere examined her with a naked interest. As if making a decision, she guided her over to sit side by side on a bench. "Vergil says that they are exhorting you to marry."

"Yes."

"Not the man whom you want, I assume. It never is."

"I suspect that they would welcome any man who agrees with them. I would prefer to remain unmarried, however. I know that sounds odd."

"You will receive no censure from me. If not for falling in love with Laclere, I expect that I would still be unmarried. Without love, marriage has little to recommend it if a woman can provide for herself through property or employment."

The viscountess spoke with a familiarity that Sophia had rarely shared with a woman. She warmed to this young American woman who did not seem to know how to dissemble.

"I am told that you are an opera singer," Sophia said. "That must be very exciting."

"Thus far the roles have been in theaters in England, but I have been offered a major one in Italy next year." She gazed toward her husband. "Laclere married someone quite unsuitable. Not only an American, but a performer. You cannot get much more unsuitable than that."

She stated it matter-of-factly. Sophia surmised that here was a young woman who dealt with society on her own terms, and who had found a man who did as well. The Viscount Laclere rose significantly in her estimation.

"Has it mattered?"

"Of course. You learn who your friends are, and who the fools are. It has not been as bad as it might have been. Vergil is seen as a bit eccentric and that makes me almost interesting, like an outrageous extravagance."

Their conversation had been refreshingly frank, the sort out of which true friendships are sewn. Sophia risked pushing the intimacy further. "I have a peculiar request to make of you. I would like you to occupy Mister Burchard when I depart."

"You do not welcome your rescuer's attendance? After my husband, he is the most handsome man in the room, and from the way he was watching you earlier I assumed that he was in love."

The offhand observation startled her. "His attendance would be intrusive this evening, and it is his management that I do not welcome."

"Yes, he has that tendency, much as my Vergil does. It can be comforting and charming sometimes, but..." Lady Laclere patted her arm conspiratorially. "When you take your leave, I will see that Mister Burchard is distracted. He will not impose, not that the attention of a man who looks like that is ever a complete imposition."

How in blazes had she left without his noticing?

Had it been when Lady Laclere engaged him in that private conversation that probed none too subtly about his affections for the duchess? Or when Laclere cornered him to conduct a quick assessment of his true sympathies in the upcoming political debate? Both exchanges distracted him, and it was only after Laclere walked away that he realized Sophia was no longer in the house.

He commandeered his curricle and snapped the horses toward Dincaster House. Sophia might prefer to avoid talking about Captain Brutus, but it needed to be done.

The way she had given him the slip darkened his mood, which had been shadowed enough from her attitude earlier. He had not realized until their exchange just how jealous he had become of the elusive Captain Brutus.

He arrived at Dincaster House just as the earl was exiting the dining room. "A fortuitous visit, Adrian. I was just about to send for you."

Adrian did not welcome the distraction, but the earl appeared purse-mouthed and serious and he had no choice but to follow him to the study.

The earl settled in the chair behind an elaborate desk that had not been the site of any serious study for decades. Adrian sat across its polished, inlaid expanse.

The earl tossed a scandal sheet across to him. "Have you seen it?"

Adrian perused the only story that could have possibly interested the earl. It described the famous rescue of the Duchess of Everdon last night, only the building was higher (five stories), the descent more precarious (sheets shredding from the weight), the hero more romantic (a dark, brooding, man of the world), and the duchess more naked (barely covered by tattered silk). Three times it mentioned that the window had been that of her bedchamber.

"It was inevitable, I suppose."

"Damned embarrassing."

"I could have let her roast and spared you this. It was inconsiderate of me not to do so."

"Your flippancy is not amusing. What the hell were you doing there?"

"Stealing a look at her correspondence."

"Her correspondence! See here—"

"I will not be lectured by you about my behavior. I apologize for the attention that last night has directed at me. I know how much you dislike anything that reminds the world of our relationship. Short of letting the duchess stay in that burning house, this spectacle could not be avoided, however."

The earl did not like his tone, but Adrian had not liked the earl's tone for most of his life, so he did not care.

"You are not without your debts to me, Adrian," the earl said, suddenly flinty-eyed.

"I am *fully* aware of *exactly* what I owe to *whomever* I am indebted."

The earl blinked surprise at the emphasis, and retreated. "Yes, well, that story is not the actual subject that I want to discuss. I had a most peculiar conversation with that Frenchman today."

Any conversation between the earl and Jacques was not good news. Only being informed of a chat between the earl and Attila would be worse. "I hope that you found it enjoyable."

"Not bad, not bad. If you can get that Hun out of the way, the Frenchman can be almost presentable. He is very curious about our ways and our government. Can't hurt to educate 'em to the superior culture here, that's what I say. If the whole world were English, it would be a damn sight easier to manage."

"Definitely. On what points did you educate Jacques?"

"That was the odd part. It began normally enough, but then he asked some questions about the peerage. Very detailed. Wanted to know if we could marry without the Crown's consent, and if we did if the marriage would stand. The more I thought about it later, the more it struck me that he knows about the duchess being married. Maybe he knows who the man is."

He would kill Jacques. "It may have only been a passing

curiosity because he knows the King wants her to marry Stidolph."

"Possibly, possibly. Then he quizzed me about marital rights here. Asked how marriages could be ended."

"Again, just curiosity, I am sure."

"Then he asked what would happen to someone who helped a woman to leave her husband. Whether they could be jailed if caught. I explained that the biggest danger came from the husband, and that the French may think nothing of absconding with another man's wife but that we take a much dimmer view of such behavior here." He said it forcefully, as if to emphasize a moral rule.

Adrian ignored the lesson. His mind had completely focused on the implications of Jacques' last question. *He would hang Jacques by the...* He rose to leave.

"Then he asked the most peculiar question of all," the earl continued, stopping him. "He inquired if you were a spy."

"A spy?"

"A spy. An agent provocateur."

"What did you say?"

"That it was preposterous, of course. The very notion. I explained that when you go abroad you are nothing more than a secretary or clerk. Good heavens, a *spy*." The earl chortled at the idiocy of the idea.

"What did Jacques say to that?"

His brow puckered while he searched his memory. "He muttered something about assuming that I would know, which of course I would, and we spoke a bit about the weather and then he removed himself." He leaned over the desk. "The point is, I think he knows who the husband is. We should try and get it out of him. Whomever she married is probably influencing her, and not to the good. Perhaps we should think about getting the husband out of the way if he is about, for the time being that is."

The "we" part of this made Adrian uncomfortable. Almost as uncomfortable as the various revelations embedded in Jacques' questions. Adrian experienced a profound gratitude that the earl had long ago given up the habit of deep thought and calculation.

"An excellent idea. Leave it to me. It would be best if you do not broach the subject with him. It might warn him off. I know the man quite well and will worm it out of him quickly."

"Thought that you would want a go at it. It will give you a chance to fix things. Haven't been too successful with getting her in line, have you?"

"I am grateful for the opportunity to redeem myself."

He strode down the corridor to the dining room. He found Colin there, smoking a cigar.

"Glad you came, Adrian. Join me." He pushed a box toward him. "Just me and Father for dinner tonight, and your company will help me recover from the tedium."

"The duchess was not here? Nor her guests?"

"Just the two of us."

"Have you seen her at all in the last few hours?"

"Her carriage went to Laclere's sometime ago to fetch her. Jacques and Attila rode along to escort her home. She should return shortly, I expect."

Adrian swore and slammed a chair hard against the table. "She will not. She has bolted, I am sure of it, and those damn artists are helping her."

"Bolted? To where?"

"She could be headed to India for all I know."

"Not by ship. The tide won't be right until the morning."

Adrian turned to go. "I will have to check the docks."

Colin laid down his cigar. "That could take hours. I will help. It will spare me the boredom of listening to political yammering in my club. I think that I can find some friends to join us. It sounds like a splendid diversion. We will have a duchess hunt."

"I welcome your aid, Colin. However, when we run this particular fox to ground and trophies are being claimed, her tail is *mine*."

chapter 18

Y ou should rest, Sophia. Go to your cabin and sleep. This boat does not leave until close to dawn. We will wake you after the crossing," Attila said.

Sophia peered up at the starlit sky. Jacques and Attila flanked her, leaning against the railing of the small ship that would take her to France. "I will retire shortly. Thank you again for helping me."

"It was Jacques who found these berths for hire. I am only sorry that the tide meant we could not depart at once."

"A few hours will not matter too much." She did not add that now that she was here, waiting to leave, she welcomed the delay.

A melancholy filled her. It was ridiculous, but she could not shake it. They had spent the last hours laughing about her great escape and anticipating the wonderful times waiting on the Continent. She had already planned the next year full of balls and diversions and a long sojourn in Italy. It would be like old times. But her merriment had been a facade to hide an inexplicable heartsickness. She should be excited and relieved, not aching and sad. This mood made no sense at all. She hated England.

"You do not think that he will interfere?" Jacques asked.

She knew who "he" was. The same "he" who intruded on her thoughts while she gazed into the night sky. Without even knowing what she was up to, "he" had already managed to interfere. Although Attila had agreed to this plan after a little cajoling, Jacques had resisted, because to his mind they would be stealing her from her husband, which could have dire consequences.

She had explained again and again that she and Adrian were not married, but neither artist believed her. Adrian's performance in Paris had been too effective, and the old lie about a husband had come back to haunt her when she asked for their assistance this morning. In desperation she had pled horrible unhappiness and had even, she recalled guiltily, made a few ambiguous accusations about Adrian being the cause of it. That had finally swayed Jacques, which was just as well. She doubted that Attila could have managed this on his own.

"I am worried about Camilla and Yuri and the others," Attila said. "You do not think that he will take vengeance against them or hold them hostage? Such a man might."

The lie's details about her husband's vile temper had not made this any easier. "He is kind to animals, and will see to their care. When I write and ask for them, they will be sent, along with Charles and Jenny."

"Just like an Englishman to be more kind to dogs than to a woman," Jacques said.

"He was not actually unkind to me."

"Do not speak of it, Sophia. It is an indelicate matter, but I understood you well enough. I was hesitant to help you escape, but when I comprehended your situation it became a matter of honor for me to see that he does not touch you again."

"It is not as if he hurt me. I hope that you do not think that."

"There are deeper wounds than those inflicted by a fist or weapons. Like all women, you are resilient about such things, but you are free of him now. The clumsy, selfish brute did not deserve you."

Adrian, clumsy and selfish? She was quite sure that she had never said that about him. She scoured her memory to remember exactly what she *had* said.

Jacques' relaxed body suddenly tightened. "What is that?" he asked, cocking his head. "Do you hear that? There. At the far dock." He pointed.

They all turned to the rail and bent over to watch. Torches danced in the night around two carriages over-laden with passengers. Bodies began pouring off their sides and tops and out of their compartments. Soon a raucous crowd milled around a distant dock.

"Good heavens, not another demonstration," Sophia said. "It is the middle of the night."

"Maybe they plan to burn all the boats," Attila said. "Maybe a revolution has begun, and they want to make sure the aristocrats cannot escape the country. It would be the perfect time, with all the government here for Par-liament."

"It does not look like a revolution to me and I should know, having just been in one," Jacques said. He squinted at the crowd, which had moved to the next nearest dock. "More like a group of drunks looking for some sport."

That dock ceased to amuse them, and the crowd milled to the next one. Sophia could make out some details now. They were apparently in high spirits, playing some game. Flames briefly illuminated bits of them. Some wore army uniforms and others evening clothes. They swarmed over the piers onto the boats, disappeared for a spell, then swarmed back onto the dock.

"You should go to your cabin, *kedvesem*," Attila warned.

She barely heard him. One of the men had gone onto a small ship alone and spoken with someone there.

Her gaze locked on that man. He was no more than a dark blotch amidst the jumping torch flames, but . . .

They were only three docks away now and it was clear what was happening. They were searching the ships.

The merry crowd jostled forward. The uniforms became distinct. The officers among them were not common army, but Royal Guardsmen.

The dark blotch strode in front of them all. He suddenly took distinct form.

"*Merde*," Jacques hissed.

"It is *him*. And he is wearing a sabre." Attila gulped. "We are dead, Jacques."

Jacques narrowed his eyes. "Go to your cabin, Sophia."

"Once he sees you he will know I am here anyway. Let me handle this. He must listen to reason."

"There is no reason in such matters."

The crowd approached their dock. The gangway was down and they could not board. Sophia recognized Colin, carrying one of the torches, and a few other gentlemen to whom she had been introduced during the last few weeks, including Dante Duclairc. Unmarried, all of them, and right now totally foxed.

Except Adrian, who stood front and center. He appeared completely sober. And furious.

They collected in front of her on the wharf.

"There she is! At the railing!"

"Run to ground in two hours. By Jove, we're better than hounds."

"Two men with her, Adrian. Do we lynch them?"

Attila frowned. "Lynch? Lynch? What is this lynch?"

"Hang," Jacques said.

"Hang!"

"They are not going to hurt you," Sophia said, not entirely convinced of that herself. Adrian, for one, looked fit to kill.

The noise brought the captain from his cabin. Well into his night gin, he staggered forward and peered over the rail.

"What the hell is this about?" the captain yelled.

"Raise the gangway," Adrian called. "The woman desires to disembark."

"I do not," Sophia countered. "Do not permit them to board, Captain."

The poor man shook his head, as if he tried to clear it. "You've Royal Guardsmen with you. Were you sent by His Majesty?"

"Of course he wasn't."

Adrian muttered something and the officers tried to line up neatly and look steady. "Would these officers be with me otherwise?"

"He is tricking you. He collected them out of taverns and brothels, and not at the King's command. I have paid for this ship, and I demand that you not raise the gang-way. I order you to cast off at once."

"I can't cast off. Nowhere's to go, and night is no time to be navigating down river, not to mention the crew ain't on board."

"Just drift for an hour or something, as long as you get me away. I will pay you double."

That made him pause. He faced Adrian. "What do you want with this woman?"

"She is the Duchess of Everdon and the King requires that she remain in England."

The Captain debated and sighed. "Damned situation. See here, Your Grace, if that is who you are, better you go and settle this with the gentleman and the King. Tide is at five if you will still be wanting this ship, but I don't take any passenger against the Crown's pleasure, no mat-ter how good the silver." He lumbered over to the winch and began raising the gangway.

Adrian waited patiently, glaring at her. The officers tried to maintain an official stance, but kept wobbling and giggling like the besotted fools they were. Colin and the other gentlemen joked and enjoyed the spectacle.

Sophia seethed.

With the gangway in place, the captain ambled away. One very annoyed third son of an earl strode onto the ship.

He marched right up to her. She instinctively took a step back before she dug in her heels.

"Going somewhere?" he asked coolly.

"Yes."

"Not tonight, you aren't." He turned to Jacques and

Attila. "I am left to conclude that you two only came to England in order to abduct the duchess."

"Abduct?" Attila cried.

"Worse, you have dishonorably taken advantage of my family's hospitality even while you plotted against the realm."

"Plotted against the realm? Oh, no, Mister Burchard, there has been no plotting. Why, Jacques and I would not know how to plot, would we, Jacques?"

"Speak for yourself. I am weary of being threatened by this man. The English win one little war and they think they are masters of the world. As to how we came to accompany Sophia, that is none of your concern."

"It is very much my concern."

"She is a free citizen. Even a husband's rights do not nullify that. She does not want you anymore. Her decision to leave makes that clear. I cannot say that I blame her. She does not belong in England, or with you. After experiencing the glory that is France, she could never be happy again on this provincial island, or with one of its men sharing her bed."

A very tense silence fell. Adrian's stance relaxed. Somehow it made him seem more dangerous.

"What do you mean by that?" he asked ever so calmly.

"Nothing," Sophia inserted quickly.

"Please, M'sieur. We broach a topic best left alone, don't you agree?" Jacques' finely hewn face pursed into a bored, knowing smirk.

"Yes," Sophia said. "Especially with a lady present."

"I am interested in broaching it. Compelled, actually."

Jacques sighed with exasperation. "It is well-known that Englishmen do not know how to handle women."

"Is it?"

"Oh, yes." Attila concurred apologetically. "Jacques is too frank, but what he says is true. The rest of the world does not throw it in your face because that would be impolite."

Adrian glanced to the crowd of Englishmen on the wharf. "And dangerous."

Jacques ignored the warning. He made a disdainful gesture. "The English have no great art, no great music, so it is not surprising that their imagination fails in love. A woman is like a new rose, beckoning all the senses. An Englishman sees it, plucks it, and then crushes it."

Sophia felt her face burning. This was no time for Jacques to wax poetic.

"This is fascinating," Adrian said.

"Eh, *bien*? Listen and learn. The right way to enjoy that rose is to gently sniff. To carefully peel the petals apart. To caress and nibble its velvet layers and lick its nectar."

"I am entranced, Jacques. Although I would like to interrupt here and say that if I ever learn that you attend the duchess in the hopes of licking her nectar, I will kill you."

Sophia rushed in. "I assure you, neither Jacques nor Attila has ever licked . . . that is to say . . ."

Jacques threw up his hands. "You are hopeless. What did I tell you, Attila? I generously try to help this Englishman by imparting the secrets of my heritage, and all I get is threats. You do not deserve her, and unless you plan to use that sword, we will not let you force her to return."

"Then I will have to use the sword."

"If you use it with the skill that she says you deploy with your other weapon, we are safe."

Utter silence this time. Not a sound, not a movement. The air stilled around them. Sophia tried to speak, but her wide-open mouth would not move.

Finally Adrian shifted his weight and scratched his brow, as if checking to be sure that he was really standing on this ship and had just heard correctly.

"Are you saying that Sophia told you that she is leaving because I am a poor lover?"

Jacques struck a brave pose and made a shrug that answered more eloquently than words.

Attila tried desperately to smooth things. "We hesitated helping her. To come between a husband and wife is a serious offense. She repudiated you as she did in Paris, and we could see her unhappiness and desperation, but of course we knew that when she said again that you were not married, that she was lying to enlist our assistance. I even tried to intercede on your behalf. It was then that she blurted the truth."

"Did she?" Adrian asked silkenly. "What did she say?"

"Nothing!" Sophia's voice returned so abruptly that the cry startled her.

"I insist that you tell me, Attila, so that I can correct my ways."

Attila missed the ominous undertones. He looked relieved that Adrian was being reasonable. "She said that you are domineering, too aggressive, and that you only manage her to your own interest and pleasure, and that you manhandle her almost daily." He smiled sympathetically. "We do not blame you. As an Englishman you cannot help being prone to the quick, crushing style that in reality most woman only enjoy every now and then. It is your misfortune that in your absence she went to Paris and discovered that love can be pleasurable. There were all those years apart."

"And all those artists to teach her."

Attila coughed nervously. "Our hearts went out to her to have to suffer such clumsiness, and we could not leave our sweet Sophia in such a situation, since it had so distressed her."

She wanted to die. She would grab Adrian's sword and fall on it and that would be that.

He looked down at her. "Well, my dear, I stand admonished. I can see that I will have to endeavor to do better in the future."

"See, Sophia, he is contrite. I suggested this morning that you speak honestly to him, did I not?"

"Gentlemen, the duchess will not be staying on this ship tonight. I will see that she is back by sailing time. There is a second carriage that will take you two back to Dincaster House if you choose, or you can stay here. You can all sail to France in the morning, if you like. In fact, you can sail to hell, for all I care."

"We will accompany Sophia back to Dincaster House," Jacques said.

"She will be coming in another carriage with me."

"I will not leave this ship," Sophia said. "You have no authority here, and no right to interfere. Collect that rabble down there and be on your way."

"Foolish of me to think that you would obey so that we could do this with some dignity." He stepped up to her. "Time to go, Duchess."

With a quick move he bent and embraced her legs.

The world flipped and she was facing his back, slung over his shoulder as she had been in Paris. He strode down the gangway, and Colin and the others went wild.

"I will have you drawn and quartered," she said, thumping his back.

The young men made the most of it by hooting and cheering. The Royal Guardsmen stood smartly as they passed.

Adrian toted her to the first carriage and set her down at its open door. Burning with mortification, she considered refusing to enter. One look at the dark eyes glaring at her said that he would bodily throw her in, if necessary.

She surveyed the little mob with her best ducal stare. That quelled them a little. Turning away with what poise she could muster, she entered the carriage with her head high, determined to give Adrian a piece of her mind.

"That was inexcusable," she snapped as he stepped in behind her.

"You left me no choice."

"Do not act as if some mandate from God required you to interfere. Coming after me was *presumptuous*." She emphasized the hated word.

"Probably, but I am in one hell of a presumptuous mood. Who knows where it could lead if you do not behave."

They headed away from the wharf with the second carriage close behind. Adrian sat across from her, his dark mood filling the compartment. She decided it might be wise to wait a few minutes before continuing to upbraid him.

His silence became a thick cloud that the night breeze could not penetrate. She got the sense that she was the one being scolded, and he wasn't even speaking.

He was probably brooding about Jacques and Attila's little misunderstanding.

It might be best to explain her innocence.

"I want you to know that Jacques completely mistook what I said to him this morning. About you. I never... that is, I couldn't criticize... after all, we haven't..."

He didn't respond.

"I may have mentioned something about your managing me and manhandling me, which, of course, you have just done again, but it had nothing to do with... well, that."

He just watched her.

"I want to make that clear, since we took this carriage in order to discuss matters that require privacy, and that is definitely one of them."

"It certainly is, but we will not discuss that or the other matters here."

"We are unlikely to find more privacy at Dincaster House."

"I never said that I was taking you to Dincaster House."

As if to emphasize that, the sounds of the second carriage peeled away.

"Are you abducting me?" She laughed nervously.

"I am collecting on your debt."

Of course he would not want to risk losing the great prize. She should have thought of that. "There was no need for tonight's dramatics. You have removed me from my ship for no reason. As I promised last night, I have directed my votes the way that you want. I left letters with Jenny that give my M.P.'s the word."

"Very honorable. Only that was not the payment that I referred to last night."

"It certainly was."

"You offered anything in your power to bestow. You assumed it would be the votes, but I never agreed to that payment."

"You did not disagree either."

"I was preoccupied."

Their isolation on the silent streets suddenly pressed on her. "Where are you taking me?"

"To my home."

"Exactly what payment did you have in mind, Mister Burchard?"

No reply.

"You are a scoundrel."

"Considering the insults that I endured from your Ensemble, I am barely resisting the temptation to be one. Right now. In the quick, crushing style preferred by clumsy Englishmen. Provoke me and I may lose the battle."

His tone suggested the threat was real, but her outrage knew no prudence. "You intend to take advantage of something I said while facing the jaws of death, while dangling thirty feet above a street?"

"You offered me whatever I wanted, after I had specifically told you on two occasions what that was. Your assumption that I would claim those damn votes instead of you is charming. Maybe you really convinced yourself that I only wanted you in order to get the votes."

"Do you really intend to hold me to this debt? Do you think that I will agree to make love with you under such a condition?"

"If I require it, you are bound by honor to do so. The devil of it is, I cannot convince myself to be enough of a scoundrel to press my advantage that far. So I only demand an hour of your company for some conversation, and one kiss."

"Some conversation, and one kiss?"

"That is all."

"After this conversation and kiss, you will allow me to return to the ship and leave England?"

"I will even arrange that your Ensemble, your servants, and your animals join you."

That seemed awfully fair. Suspiciously so. Still, if he promised, he would abide by it. She would be off to the Continent as she had planned, with only this brief diversion.

Some conversation with him was probably in order too. It had saddened her to leave without saying good-bye.

The only snag was the kiss. She remembered his kisses too well. The dangerous but compelling intimacy they offered. The potential they embodied. It would tear her heart to experience that again, only this time in final parting.

It might be best to manage that part of the debt her own way.

Clutching the door, she pulled herself up and bent over him. She quickly pecked him on the lips and then plopped back into her seat. "Now we have only to deal with the conversation."

He leaned forward and took her chin in his warm

hand. "The kiss is mine to collect, when I want, how I want. I will choose the time and place." His fingers caressed her jaw and chin before releasing her, leaving her tingling from the contact. He might have embraced her whole body, so thorough was her reaction.

The carriage stopped on a street of large houses on the edge of Mayfair. Adrian escorted her up the four stone steps to the door of one of them. Her stomach did a strange lurch as they passed the threshold and climbed the long marble staircase to the second level.

Every instinct told her to balk. He appeared as relaxed and coolly elegant as ever, but his eyes held an expression that was sharper and deeper than normal. He looked as if he had accepted something as inevitable. Her departure and the failure of his mission?

Just one kiss. She wasn't a complete fool where he was concerned. She could handle that.

He ushered her into a sitting room. It struck her as deliciously comfortable. Good chairs for reading and a large hearth for fires. Dark patterns and dark wood everywhere. A polished desk in one corner. A shelf of exotic oddities.

"So this is where you bring your women."

"This is where I live. I bring my women elsewhere."

"This conversation will probably be our last. I think that we should be honest, or there is little point to it. I know that you bring Celine here. Gerald told me."

"It appears that Stidolph gives no quarter and takes no prisoners. That is good to know." He came up behind her and lifted her shawl from her shoulders. "I did not bring Celine here. She came on her own."

"Well, goodness, that makes all the difference."

"I threw her out."

"You expect me to believe that you rejected one of the most beautiful women in England?"

"Celine's celebrated beauty is a superficial thing. Unlike you, she possesses very few layers, and they barely conceal her selfish vanity."

A manservant appeared and Adrian sent him for some wine.

They sat in chairs across from each other.

Seeing him in his home created an unexpected intimacy. It occurred to her that she had never ventured into a man's private spaces before. Her Ensemble were always the guests and intruders, not her.

"Your hour is ticking away," she said.

"If I choose to spend it only looking at you, that is my prerogative."

An hour of being looked at by those dark eyes would be more than she could bear.

She was grateful when the wine came. She was more than happy to have someone else in the room for a few minutes. But the little ritual of pouring and presenting ended quickly, and then they were alone again.

"Why are you running away?" Adrian asked.

"I am not running away. I am returning to my life."

"You are returning to the place where you hid for eight years."

"I did not hide. Everyone knew where I was."

"You hid from yourself there."

The comment dismayed her. Its insight pierced her like a shaft of light. She retreated from its illumination.

"If I am running away, I think that I can be excused. Someone did try to kill me yesterday."

"Someone tried to frighten you yesterday. If the goal had been your murder, there were more efficient ways to affect it. Captain Brutus counted on that fire being discovered before you came to harm. You are of no use to him dead." He glanced at her over the rim of his glass. "Did you enter into a secret marriage with him?"

"No."

"Were you his lover?"

"Our intimacy did not go that far."

"Has your affection survived all these years, or been rekindled with his return?"

"You ask because I did not show anyone those letters?"

"I ask because I want to know if he owns your heart."

"It was not his reminders of our affection that touched me. It was the rest."

"His threats? Surely you know that I would have seen to your protection if I had known."

"Not the threats. It was his reminders of my sympathy for his cause. When I was younger, I believed and cared about such things. I confess that those letters, coming from him, called forth the idealistic girl."

"Which only made your situation here more difficult. So you are running away from having to make a real decision about reform. Leaving those letters to your M.P.'s, but only in payment of a debt, absolved you of that responsibility."

"You make it sound as if I slyly construct excuses for myself. I am not that clever."

"You are very clever. I had not realized until now just how clever you have been in finding ways to run and hide."

His frankness made her uncomfortable. "I cannot decide if I have just been complimented or insulted."

"What else are you running from? Stidolph?"

"I do not choose to talk about Gerald. Spend your hour elsewhere, what is left of it."

"He has been intimidating you, hasn't he?"

"I can manage Gerald's calls to duty and responsibility."

He studied her as though he sought to read her soul. "My mention now of his name disturbed you, and simple calls to duty would not affect you like that. He has been using the past to get to you, hasn't he? Brandon and the rest."

When she had suggested that they be honest tonight, she had not expected it to go this far. His perception astonished her. The mention of Gerald had indeed disturbed her, and summoned again the horrible confusion she had experienced during that conversation this morning.

"He says there will be no peace until I rectify what happened by fulfilling my father's wishes about Everdon's future. That peace would be a delicious thing to know. It may be worth any price, I think sometimes."

"So you ran away from the temptation to pay the price, because you know that you would only exchange one hell for another."

She resented the way he kept peeling away, exposing her heart. "You seem to know my mind better than I do. If I ran from that, it was a sensible course. I am not very strong. Not like you."

"I think that you are one of the strongest women I have ever met."

"Then your knowledge of women is pitiful. Those memories leave me weak. You have seen it yourself. Gerald came and threw my guilt at me this morning and within moments I had no will. Yes, damn you, I am running away. From him and the ghosts and Everdon and Captain Brutus."

He set down his glass. "Aren't you forgetting something?"

"I think that you have forced me to thoroughly admit my cowardice. What more is there?"

"You are also running away from me."

She struggled to phrase an offhanded denial, but the truth of his comment flowed like a thick current between them. The air was full of him suddenly, as if he physically reached across to her.

Trembling, she shot to her feet and paced to a window to break the effect. It didn't help much. He rose, too, relaxed and confident. She could feel him watching her, calmly waiting for a response.

"I trust that you do not intend to force a discussion of that now too," she said.

"I had, but I have changed my mind."

"That is generous of you, and probably very wise."

"Not generous or wise. It is selfish and calculating. We will talk about it later."

She turned in surprise. "Not much later. Your hour is almost passed."

He removed his frock coat and laid it on the chair. "Later. After I have made love to you. Surely you know that is why I brought you here."

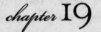

chapter 19

He strolled around the chairs and leaned against the back of one with his arms folded over his chest. He reminded her of how he had looked that first night in Paris. *This is how it will be,* his expression said. *This is what will happen.*

His aura of calm decision contrasted starkly with her own demeanor. Her heart had grown into a heavy weight whose deep pulse shook her body.

He looked so splendid with his dark hair mussed over his brow. Long lines angled from his broad shoulders to his hips. And those eyes. His gaze practically scorched.

Running away might be a good idea at that.

"You said only one kiss."

"Only one kiss as payment of your debt. I would not enjoy it if you felt obligated about the rest."

"There will not be any of 'the rest.'" She tried to adopt an authoritative tone, but it came out tremorously.

"If you are determined, that is how it will be. I am hardly going to force you."

He pushed off from the chair and came to her until he stood just inches away. His masculinity assaulted her like a force, pinning her against the window. A primitive response inside her reveled in the power he projected. Sensual expectation fluttered through her body.

He gently took hold of her shoulders with firm, exploring caresses. She shuddered from the warm pressure of those splaying fingers. So appealing. So unnerving.

He tilted his head to see her face. "You are afraid."

"I am not." But she was afraid. Afraid of that kiss and where it might lead. Frightened of the vulnerability that the passion would create. Fearful of discovering that this was just a more dishonorable way of manipulating her.

"You still worry that I only want you as a way to gain something else."

He possessed a second sight tonight. "You do seek a way to gain something else. Do not deny it."

"You would prefer it if I did, but I told you it would not be that way with us." He eyed her bonnet for pins, and pulled them out. "That hiding place is denied you. I could have gone and fetched those letters once you told me about them. Now you can destroy them. You can even write others, directing us to vote for reform, before you leave on that ship."

He lifted off the bonnet and set it aside. Night air from the window cooled her head. She felt that she had just been deprived of an essential piece of armor.

He tilted her chin up with one finger. "What happens here has nothing to do with controlling Everdon's power, nor will I ever speak to you about those damn votes again. This is only about you and me."

"I think it best if you do not do this."

"If I do not do it now, I may never get to."

"I do not know why you persist in this."

"Yes, you do. That is what really frightens you."

He stretched his fingers into her hair along her nape. He guided her head toward him. "I will have that kiss now."

It was a kiss of a lifetime, full of slowly ascending demand. Deliberate and determined and merciless. She did not begin to know how to defend against what it did to her. Cradling her head, arching her into his embrace, he turned that "one kiss" into a long exploration of arousal that left her alight with shivery, spiraling sensations. The loneliness groaned with gratitude that he possessed the skill to make capitulation almost inevitable.

He ended it with a tender bite on her lower lip. Caressing her face, he looked down at her. "Another? I must warn you that it is the last time I will ask. After this you are on your own to express your will."

Decision time. She knew what she risked. She would be giving this man the power to use her and hurt her as none other had. The disillusionments of her youth could one day pale in light of what might await her with him. But maybe he was right. She had been running and hiding from that danger for too long.

She neither agreed nor disagreed. His mouth suddenly fascinated her. Maybe one more. She reached up and grazed her fingertips along his lips.

He clutched her hand and held it there, kissing her palm and inner wrist.

His tight expression enthralled and dismayed her. His reaction to her gesture left her light-headed and confused.

He pulled her back to him and the river of her emotions flowed with renewed turbulence.

He had lied.

He had said that he had no ulterior motive for seducing her, but he did. He had implied that they would share one night before she left for France, but he had no intention of bringing her to that ship for its dawn sailing.

He planned to bind her to England. Not because of Everdon or the promise of a Treasury position. He would do it for the simple reason that he could not let her go, and wanted much more than one night.

She felt so good in his arms. Soft and feminine and trembling with her touching hesitation. He kissed her again until the last of the stiff caution melted, caressing through the black gown and rigid stays, seeking the curves of her body. Angling his head, he tasted the sweet skin of her neck. The shortening rasp of her breath flurried against his ear, a melody of desire that instantly drowned out his own inner chant that exhorted control.

The hunger that had been building for weeks suddenly roared for release. He barely suppressed the urge to take her at once against the wall. Pulling her tightly so he could feel her along his length, he kissed her again with a devouring mouth as impatience overwhelmed him.

Her arms slid around his body in a shy embrace. Her tongue darted in play with his, but retreated at his demanding reaction. Both responses possessed a caution that checked him. Her body might be bowed into his, and his caresses might be raising gasps of pleasure, but she was surprised and frightened.

He wrapped her in his arms and nuzzled her hair and forced some restraint. He did not need Jacques' lessons to know that this was no way to make love to a woman the first time.

When he kissed her again he did so carefully, slowly luring her. She joined him in her tentative way. He reveled in her soft curves as she grew relaxed and pliant beneath his hands again, but arousal still surged and retreated, as if she feared the sensations and kept forcing control on them. Something inside her resisted knowing again the abandon she had experienced in the gazebo.

Her breasts, hardened with passion, pressed against his chest. He drew his hand forward and smoothed at their fullness. A deep sigh breathed from her, a lovely sound, and her whole body trembled. He set her away from him against the wall and cradled both breasts in his hands. When he rubbed their hard tips with his thumbs, she grasped at his arms as if to steady herself.

He watched the soulful battle as she alternately gloried in the pleasure and fought it. Her clutching fingers on his arms both held him to her and pressed him away. His own need burned fiercely at the image she presented, liquid-eyed and beautiful, tottering on the brink of ecstasy.

Dipping his head, he kissed her breast. He slid his hands to her back and released the closures of her gown. Her heavy lids rose with renewed alertness.

If she was going to change her mind, it would be now.

He knew how to stop that from happening. He slid the gown's bodice down, determined to subdue any misgivings with his hands and mouth.

The relief in her expression stopped him.

He realized that it was what she expected and wanted. Defeat instead of surrender.

They faced each other, their breaths the only sounds, both resisting for their own reasons the pull of desire. They held each others' arms in an odd, distant embrace. Her gown hung around her hips and her lovely breasts strained against the thin fabric of her chemise. Their swells peeked erotically over the hard encasement of her stays.

He traced one finger along the neckline of her undergarment. "Remove it. Offer yourself to me as you did at Staverly."

Surprise flashed in her eyes. She glanced away in embarrassment. He fought the urge to trail his hand lower and provide the excuse of seduction she wanted.

She looked back. With the charming awkwardness that claimed her at times, she pushed the straps of her chemise down her arms.

The small cooperation ended her fragile resistance. When he caressed this time, skin on skin, her head lolled back against the wall with a sensual sigh of acceptance.

He took her hands and placed them behind her neck so that her bent elbows flanked her head and her lovely breasts rose to him. He caressed and licked them, teasing at the hard tips, drawing out her passion. She arched against the wall in growing delirium, and finally stroked one hand into his hair to encourage him to draw more aggressively.

His thoughts blurred to everything but the smell and taste and sounds of her. Chaotic need crashed through him. He stroked to her thighs but the armor of petticoats interfered. Exploring ineffectively but unable to keep his hands off her, he took her mouth in another kiss.

She rose to it with an eagerness that equaled his own. They sparred with biting, impatient mouths. He grasped her head steady and tamed her cascading kisses with a deep joining that eased his burning even while it stoked it.

He broke away and took a step back. She looked wonderfully wild and dishevelled. Her eyes gleamed with the primitive sensuality of her arousal.

Taking her hand, he eased her forward. "Come to bed."

Her slight pull of resistance surprised him. She was long past retreat. He knew that even if she did not.

He released her hand and opened his arm. She stepped into it. Lifting a brace of candles from a nearby table, he brought her to the bedchamber.

She walked within that guiding arm, against his warm strength, almost tripping over her hanging skirts in her clumsy breathlessness. Electrifying emotions gave their progress an unreal quality.

Decorated like the sitting room, the bedchamber spoke of comfort created by a man with no one to accommodate but himself. The carved, draped bed impressed her as incredibly inviting. And frightening.

He explored her neck with kisses while he loosened the fastenings to her gown and petticoats. Acres of fabric billowed down to the floor.

He knelt to lift her feet out of the heaping fabric. "So many layers. Unlike the ones reflected in your eyes, these are a nuisance."

"You see more in my eyes than what is there."

He slid off her hose with tantalizing palms. "They are there, and they are intriguing."

Their talk barely distracted her from the shocking reality that she was down to her stays and underclothes. "Perhaps more intriguing than what is under them."

"I already know what is under them. You are the one who does not."

He stood and embraced her in a long kiss, then parted and began to loosen the sleeves of his shirt.

She tried to be a bold lover. She plucked loose the tie of his cravat and fumbled at the buttons of his waistcoat. He watched with warm amusement and did not seem surprised when her shaking hands stopped. He shed his waistcoat and shirt on his own.

Which left her standing with her nose an inch away from his bare chest.

His hewn beauty left her mouth dry. She laid her hand on the tautness and warmth. Her fingers stretched up a chiseled muscle and a sensual stirring purred through her. She had never thought that seeing a man's body could be so engrossing.

She looked up. Searing eyes watched her tentative explorations. Self-conscious suddenly, she let her hand fall away.

He sat in a chair, removed his boots, and began on the trousers that she had been too cowardly to deal with. Flustered and excited, she turned away and tried to unlace her stays.

"I will do it." Strong hands grasped her waist and guided her back until she sat on his knees. His bare knees, she realized with a jolt. He was naked.

She balanced awkwardly on his legs, facing away from him. Flush after flush tingled her skin while his hands released and removed the stays. She looked down at the thin fabric of her drawers and the chemise falling around her hips. Her naked legs dangled along his shins.

She made to scoot off but he pulled her back, into the astounding physicality of his arms and body. The sensation of his nakedness shocked her. It was also wickedly exciting.

Not as wicked as his hands. Slow, languid caresses raised waves of sensuality that drowned her embarrassment. She relaxed into him, her head against his shoulder and her face turned toward his handsome profile. His gaze wandered down her at will, while his strong hands traced delicious lines of pleasure around her breasts.

"How beautiful you are," he said. "Your skin is so luminous and your form so feminine. I could look at you for hours."

She watched him look at her. His hands moved and circled her breasts with trails of excruciating anticipation. He touched the tips in ways that forced cries to rise to her throat and her body to arch for more.

His head turned to kiss her while he gently rubbed and palmed. Anxious hunger churned through her, down deeply, pulsing with excitement. The craving pleasure created by his slow, patient hands was driving her mad.

A groan passed from her mouth into his. "That's right, darling. Let me know what you like," he whispered.

One hand pressed lower to her hips and thighs. With smooth slides he removed what was left of her clothing, leaving her atop him completely naked.

He parted her legs until she straddled his lap. The

change left his phallus nestled erotically against the cleft of her bottom. He lifted one of her knees and hitched it over the chair's arm, spreading her into an exposed position.

Punishing her mouth with a savage kiss, he stroked the soft flesh of her raised thigh while his other hand continued arousing her breast. Desire veered into a screaming need for him to explore her open vulnerability. Her entire consciousness focused on how badly she wanted him to touch her down there.

He did, and she arched and cried from the magnificent shock of it. He kept his hand to her, exploring her reactions, arousing astonishing pleasure and tension. His voice spoke lowly, praising the beauty of her abandon, but she barely heard him through the primal sounds springing from her primitive essence. Every gasping breath came out a moan or a cry. Her hips rose and fell, shamelessly begging.

He moved the caresses to a specific spot of sensitivity. She shot to an unworldly height of pleasure, a frightening place of excitement so sharp that it was almost painful. She tried to retreat and grabbed his hand to push it away.

He would not let her. "You do not run away tonight, darling. Not from me," he said with his mouth pressed to her temple.

She could not fight the intensity. With a helpless groan she surrendered and with a throaty scream she died. Only the death was a blissful moment, full of pure pleasure and heavenly release.

He carried her to the bed and laid her down. His body came over hers and she clutched him, joyed to finally embrace him and grateful to hold on to his reality amidst the unworldly sensuality in which she floated.

He was as careful and gentle as one could expect, but not careful and gentle enough.

She winced at the quick stretching. A burning tear brought her back from the edges of paradise.

He froze. Her gaze drifted up the naked chest suddenly motionless above her on taut arms. She ventured a glance at his face.

"You should have told me."

"Perhaps you should not have assumed otherwise."

"I can be excused, I think."

"Would it have made a difference? Would you have gone all honorable on me?"

"I don't know."

She caressed his chest. "Are you angry?" He looked it, a little.

He dipped to kiss her. "No. I am flattered." He moved. "I will try not to hurt you more."

He didn't hurt her at all. He entranced her, enthralled her, and mesmerized her. The physical joining astonished her heart and soul even more than his hands had amazed her body. Something beckoned to her much like the release had. Something spiritual and glorious and promising heaven. It stirred in her emotions and whispered in rhythm to his body. *Give yourself. Lose yourself. Believe. Trust.*

Toward the end, she knew astonishing pleasure again. Not with the physical fracture of before, but instead with an emotion-drenched joy that reveled in absorbing his demanding need and accepting his erupting passion and finally enfolding his spent strength.

He moved off her and pulled her into an embrace that connected their whole bodies. She savored the eloquent silence, and marveled at the new awareness of herself and him that had just been born.

He had lied. He *was* angry. Not at her, but at what she was and how that framed the implications of what had just happened.

He brushed damp curls away from her face and tucked her closer. He had not been nearly as surprised as he should have been. Maybe he secretly had not assumed otherwise at all. The truth fit with what he knew of her life and saw in her depths. But admitting the possibility would have made tonight impossible, and so he had chosen to accept her pose of worldly sophistication.

He rose on one arm and looked down at her serene contentment. "Why me?"

"Maybe I trusted you to do England proud." She smiled impishly, but her eyes met his with a silent request that he not insist that she search her heart for a serious answer.

"All those years. All those permanent guests and French gentlemen. Did nary a one touch your heart?"

"One or two. I would have never given them such a hold on me, however. It was not me they wanted. Not really. It was always something else."

Yes, she would assume that. Her own father had used her as a way to get something else. She would take it for granted that anyone's attention had ulterior motives.

It pained him that she had lived so many years with the loneliness that must have created. What must it be like to accept that every offer of friendship or love was really an attempt to procure your wealth or patronage or even Everdon itself? She had gone to France convinced that she had no value except for those things.

She may have finally accepted that was not the case with him. He would have to be very careful not to disillusion her.

Which restricted his reaction to tonight as surely as her position as the Duchess of Everdon did. It was that which angered him.

With any other woman he would be honor-bound to offer marriage now. The bastard son of an earl's wife did not propose to a duchess in her own right, however, even if he had just taken her innocence. Nor could Adrian Burchard do the right thing by Sophia Raughley, because the prize of Everdon would taint the purity of his motives.

She nestled snugly, her expression one of utter peace. He tightened his embrace on her soft body and kissed her cheek. "You are a beautiful, magnificent woman."

She blinked surprise, then smiled skeptically. "It is gallant of you to say so."

"Not gallant. Stay in England and I will say it again, often, until you believe me. Until you see your own worth and understand who you really are."

She looked troubled, as if facing who she really was must surely lead to disappointment. He would have gladly killed Alistair right then if the man was not already blessedly gone.

"Are you offering me a liaison, Adrian?"

"Yes. And affection and friendship and help, if you want them." He could not include more, nor could she accept it.

"You can do better than me."

"There is no one better, and no one else I want. I am not just being gallant, but if you think I am, humor me for a few weeks at least. You can always leave later if you doubt my affection, or decide an affair is not worth the risks."

Or decide to choose an appropriate consort for the Duchess of Everdon. No, in that event, he would be the one to leave. He had told Dot that he would not make it difficult for her, and he wouldn't.

She turned in his arms and clung to him. "Maybe I am magnificent when I am with you. I feel as if I might be."

"You surely are."

She nestled her face into the crook of his neck and breathed deeply. "Show me again, Adrian. Make love to me again. Can we?"

He could. With his body he showed her just how beautiful and magnificent she was to him. With more emotion than he had ever known before, he called forth her glorious passion from beneath the layers and then lost himself in it.

Afterwards he watched the contented peace reclaim her as she believed in herself for a while once more.

She did not make the tide. When the ships in port set sail, she was nestled asleep in his arms.

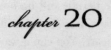

chapter 20

I have been thinking about the Marquess of North-ford," Dot said. White wisps blew around her head from the little gale raised by her snapping fan.

"For what reason?" Adrian asked, appreciating the bit of breeze wafting to him. Parliament had adjourned early and he had ridden over to Dincaster House in search of Colin, only to find him visiting Dorothy in her dainty private sitting room. He had joined them, and at Dot's generous invitation had stripped down to shirt and trousers like Colin, so as not to swelter on this unbearably hot August day.

"For Sophia. Surely you saw the letter in today's gazette, calling on the lords to gird for battle to slay the dragon of mob rule. It pointedly referred to a certain peeress who needs to ensure that a certain seat in the House of Lords is filled soon, in case a Reform Bill passes the Commons."

"Why the marquess?" Colin asked. "In case you don't know, Dot, he's—"

"Exactly. He has not even done his duty to his family line and the succession. If he ever married, he would accept that his wife had a lover."

Silence greeted this casual observation.

"It is one solution, is all that I am saying. Not an ideal one, I will admit, but not unheard of."

"I think that we should let the duchess manage her own affairs," Colin said.

Adrian agreed. In fact, Sophia was proving adept at managing her affairs. She had arranged her two-month affair with him with fastidious discretion.

She had moved to a leased house while Everdon House was being repaired. She had chosen one several streets from his chambers, and made sure that it was small enough to require only Jenny and Charles and a few servants whom Charles assured would be discreet. Besides those retainers, only Colin and Dot knew that many nights Adrian walked down an alley and through a walled back garden and into Sophia's arms.

It was often midnight when he slipped into bed beside her. Night debates at the Commons kept him late. Endless, raucous debates. Traditional alliances had begun to crumble. Demonstrating crowds daily reminded him and his colleagues that they held the fate of a great nation in their hands. One misstep might plunge the country into massive bloodshed.

The knowledge that Sophia carefully studied all the speeches as reported in the newspapers had something to do with his new willingness to listen to the other side.

He would have liked to talk to her about it. Conversation might help him to work out his chaotic ideas. He had promised never to do so, however, because she might think that he was not seeking a sympathetic ear, but instead trying to influence her. She might then conclude that he had seduced her only to continue his old mission.

It was one of the sore points that kept their affair from being perfect. Another was the pressure on her to marry. Those exhortations had now become public. More worrisome was the concern that their lovemaking invited a pregnancy that would make her future precarious.

He hoped that they would dodge that. If they didn't, the only way to avoid horrible scandal would be for her to negotiate a quick marriage to a man appropriate to her position. Eventually that would be inevitable, but he had no desire to hasten the day when they had to part.

"If it came to it, Northford might be a solution," he said, thinking aloud.

"And you would become the intimate family friend?" Colin asked. "It would be a humiliating arrangement for everyone. You deserve better. In fact, I don't see why you don't marry her yourself. You are far better equipped to exercise Everdon's power than the Marquess of Northford, or the other men being shoved at her."

"You know it isn't possible," Dot soothed.

"The reasons why are stupid ones. What could anyone do? Burn her at the stake? As to Adrian's birth, Father did not repudiate him. In the eyes of the law, Adrian is an earl's son."

"In the eyes of the law, but not in the eyes of the world," Adrian said.

"To hell with the world."

It was the retort of a man who owned the world, and so could easily dismiss its importance. The security to do that was the only thing about his brother's superior fortune in life that Adrian envied.

Dot changed the subject by asking about the day's debate. Adrian regaled them with a description of the outbreak of fisticuffs that had led to Parliament's early dismissal.

After a half hour, he and Colin took their leave. They went to Colin's chambers to fetch fresh cravats and make themselves presentable.

"I came to ask some favors of you," Adrian said.

Colin tied his neckpiece while he gazed in the mirror. "Something time-consuming, I hope. Aside from the fun when the new London Bridge opened, this summer has been boring. I'd go down to the country, but everyone is here."

"The first favor will only occupy one night. I would like you to escort Sophia to the coronation ball." King William was due to be crowned in several weeks, now that mourning for the last King had ended.

"I think that you should, not me."

"I expect to be unwell that day."

"I do not agree with how you are handling this. She is not some child. If an affair is suspected, it will not be the undoing of either of you. Besides, there is no declaration in merely walking her into a ballroom."

Adrian went to work on his own cravat. "My request has nothing to do with what is between Sophia and me."

Colin frowned in perplexity, then his brow suddenly cleared. "Is he coming? For the coronation?"

"I received word from the embassy that he is."

"Doesn't seem fair that you should miss the ball."

"The palace is planning a modest affair, so there will

not be that much to miss. I can hardly be in the same room with him. Despite his age and beard, the resemblance might be noticed if we are seen together, and a coronation ball is the last place where I would want to reinflame that scandal. Our mother asked that I never embarrass the earl and you and Gavin."

"That promise has proven a stranglehold on you, and it was unfair of her to demand it."

"It was part of her agreement with the earl, made while she carried me. To refuse to honor it after her death would be selfish and inexcusable."

"That agreement was for my sake and Gavin's. So that she would stay and we would have our mother."

"And mine. So that I could stay and have *my* mother."

"Still, we are all grown now, and she is gone."

"I do not owe the earl much, Colin, but I do owe him this. I will not invite speculation about either my birth or my relationship with the duchess by attending with her on my arm while a man with my eyes stands among the foreign dignitaries. You know that my choice is the right one."

"Probably so, but I do not understand your equanimity about either situation. Your feelings for the duchess are very obvious to me. I would like you to have some happiness, and how happy can you be if you conduct an affair of the heart assuming that it will end?"

Happier than I have ever been in my life, Adrian thought. As happy as the situation will permit. However, Colin had touched the biggest sore point in the affair, and one that Adrian carefully avoided pressing, because doing so might destroy the joy.

Although it was certainly an affair of the heart, she was

not in love with him. She needed him and trusted him and felt great affection. In her own careful way, maybe she even loved him, but she was not *in love*. She would not let herself take that final step.

Sometimes when they embraced he could sense it in her, like something fighting against restraints, but she was too afraid to let it free.

Just as well. It could not last. Sooner or later something would convince her of that. Then he would retreat as he had sworn to himself that he would. Doing so would be difficult, however, because he *had* fallen in love with her.

Colin broke into his thoughts. "There was another favor?"

"One that will give you something to do. I want you to look for Captain Brutus. I do not have the time, and it is vital to track him down."

"An investigation? Sounds almost as diverting as our duchess hunt. I will take up the charge with enthusiasm."

"I will explain what little I have learned, then, and hope that you can do better."

It was all Burchard's fault. Her protector was giving her more confidence in her safety than she had any right to have. The man had become an unacceptable interference. The solution was obvious. Get rid of him, and she would be helpless.

He considered that as he slipped into the garden and crept toward the duchess's house. Beside him another figure crept too. He had thought long and hard before getting help this time, but he would need someone keeping watch. This house was not so

*large as the other, and there would be no place to hide if a cry
was raised while he was inside.*

*Still, he preferred acting alone. No one knew better than he
did what could happen if another person knew one's secrets and
plans. Betrayal was always a possibility. He had no intention of
being vulnerable again if he could help it.*

*His companion felt the door's latch, and made a gesture to in-
dicate it was unbolted. Now, that was convenient. And irritat-
ing. Sophia acted as if Captain Brutus represented no threat at
all. By now she should know better.*

*He pulled a letter out of his coat. Well, this missive would
make it explicit, even if the fire had not.*

He began to turn the latch.

Adrian slipped through the portal of Sophia's garden well
past midnight. The Commons had sat very late, due to an
upcoming adjournment because of the coronation festivities.

The hour had made him contemplate not coming. She
would be asleep, and it would be selfish to disturb her.
But he needed to find some peace in her arms. Holding
her would soothe the inner turmoil churned up by the
day's events.

Three Tories had moved to the reform camp this afternoon. Two of them held seats sure to be abolished if reform passed. One was a protégé of Peel. He had watched
them cross the aisle, knowing as well as they that the act
was political suicide. He should have been furious with
their defections. Instead he had admired their independence and adherence to principle.

As he ambled through the garden to the house, he contemplated that unexpected reaction. His thoughts occupied most of his mind, but an essential, primitive part remained aware of his surroundings.

It was that part that made him abruptly halt halfway to the house.

Something shifted in the dark up ahead. A shadow moved near the building. His blood instantly pounded with alarm for Sophia. Easing over near the wall, he slid forward.

A man crouched near the door. Adrian could barely make out his shape, but it appeared he was trying to enter.

The black fury that he had known after the fire broke again. He rushed forward, determined to catch the culprit. With any luck it would be Captain Brutus himself. Even if it was only a minion, he would at least have a lead to the elusive radical.

He lunged at the shadow and grappled him to the ground. They sprawled and fought in a melee of confusion. Quickly getting the upper hand, he forced the intruder onto his stomach and pressed his knee into his back while he twisted and imprisoned one arm.

The air stirred behind him. His instincts snapped alert, but it was already too late. A hissed curse floated to his ear just as something slammed into his head and the dark night swallowed him.

A gentle yank pulled Sophia out of her dreams. Blinking, she looked up to see Jenny and Charles flanking her bed.

"You had better come downstairs, Your Grace," Charles said.

His gentle tone had her wide-awake in an instant. It was the voice one used for bad news. She knew immediately that it was about Adrian. She reached to the empty place where she expected him to be sleeping and her heart dropped into her stomach.

Tears flowed down Jenny's face while she held up a wrap. "Oh, my lady, he is badly hurt. Cook found him this morning outside the garden door."

She jumped out of bed and thrust on the wrap. Not bothering with shoes, she ran down to the kitchen with Charles and Jenny in her wake. The garden door stood open and she plunged into the dawn's soft light.

He still lay on the ground. Someone had fetched a blanket to cover him. Servants stood around helplessly.

"We dared not move him," Charles said. "He has been badly beaten. I thought him dead at first."

He did look dead. Pale and lifeless and eerily at peace.

Dread choked her. She sank to her knees and used the edge of her wrap to wipe some thick blood off his brow.

"We found this by the door," a footman said.

He handed her a folded paper. She opened it and scanned down its threats. Captain Brutus.

She crushed the letter in her fist. Eyes blurring, she bent and kissed Adrian.

She had caused this. Her recklessness and willfulness had hurt him.

She should have given Captain Brutus what he wanted. She should have kept Adrian at a distance, so he would not become a target of that man's twisted plans.

Stupid, vain woman. It had been madness to think she might have any use in this world besides being a means to an end.

She caressed his face and battled an anguish that threatened to unhinge her. He had only tried to give her friendship and protection, and now he might die because of her.

Just like Brandon.

"We cannot leave him here," she said. "The damp will do more harm than the blows. Two of you find something firm to put him on. Take down a door if you have to. Charles, send to Dincaster House for Colin Burchard, and get a physician here at once."

They moved him to one of the footmen's chambers on the lower level. With Charles's help she stripped off his clothes. Horrible bruises covered his chest and stomach, as if he had neglected to defend himself. His breath rasped lowly and she worried that they had worsened his injuries by lifting him.

Weeping at her helplessness, she washed the blood from his head and placed cold towels on the worst of his blows and prayed desperately that he had not been mortally harmed.

Colin arrived alongside the physician. So did Daniel St. John.

"Do not worry. St. John knows how to keep secrets," Colin reassured her. "We were about to ride out to Hampstead when your servant came for me."

"Adrian and I have an old friendship, and I am in his debt, Your Grace," St. John said. "I welcome the chance to aid him, if you will permit it."

She did not really care who knew what now. She only cared about Adrian.

They watched the initial examination and heard the

ambiguous description of Adrian's wounds. The physician then ordered everyone but Charles from the chamber.

Colin and St. John brought Sophia up to the library. Colin poured her some sherry. The little crystal glass seemed terribly heavy in her hand.

"Drink it. You look ready to swoon."

"It is my fault," she said. "He was coming here. Someone must have followed him, or been waiting."

"It may have only been a thief."

She withdrew the letter from where she had tucked it away. "This was near the door."

Colin read the missive. His face hardened when he got to the part that specifically spoke of Adrian as a Tory pawn and warned that her intimacy with him would not be tolerated.

"I will kill this man when I find him," Colin said.

"He knows about us. He must have been following Adrian, or watching this house. When Adrian arrived last night, he must have been hiding and overcame him."

"No one follows Adrian without his realizing it, and no one hides from him either," St. John said. He spoke with authority, as if he knew Adrian's abilities in this area very well. "More likely this letter was being left, and Adrian chanced upon the situation. This was hardly written in the dead of night while Adrian lay on the ground."

"I do not see that it matters how it happened. He is lying below, terribly battered. Maybe dying. Because of me."

"Do not blame yourself," St. John said gently. "It would wound him even more to know that you did. If he confronted those men, it was his choice. The only blame here lies with the animals who would do that to a man after he was down."

It took her a moment to hear him through the guilt fogging her perceptions. "Men?"

"There had to be at least two. One man could never succeed in rendering Adrian defenseless."

They stayed with her until the physician came up to make his report.

"Two broken ribs, undoubtedly a concussion, and possibly some internal bleeding," the man said while he adjusted his frock coat. "It should be worse. He should be dead. I gave the servants instructions for his care."

Colin's eyes asked the question that Sophia could not bring herself to voice.

The physician flipped his hand in the air. "Impossible to say. If an organ was badly damaged . . . but my impression is that he will recover."

A tentative relief flooded her, but the guilt still rippled, a current waiting to sweep her away.

"I brought him around. He asked for you, Your Grace."

She ran out of the room while Colin began a quiet explanation of the need for discretion.

Charles slipped out of the chamber as soon as Sophia entered. Adrian's smile of greeting was a valiant, incomplete effort.

She sat in a chair beside the bed and took his hand in hers. "The physician thinks that you will be well soon."

"It is not my first fight, so I can assess the damage. A few days and I will be up and about."

She ventured a light caress on his face. "Are you in pain?"

"My chest is bound so tightly that I can barely breathe, but aside from that it isn't bad." He glanced down her body. "They pulled you out of bed. You look beautiful. Very provocative. I feel better already."

Tears puddled in her eyes. It was such a typically Adrian thing to say. It sounded so normal, and so out of place in the mood of dread that had fallen on the house.

His attempt at levity had the opposite effect. The fear and guilt rose so quickly that she could not control them. Keeling forward, she buried his hand between her face and the bed and wept into it.

He spoke words of reassurance while the worst of it poured out of her. Eventually she managed to stifle the sobs with ragged breaths. She rubbed her tear-soaked face against the rough skin of his palm, grateful that he had not been taken from her.

Sliding his hand from beneath her head, he stroked her hair with the gentlest caresses. Calmed by the soothing tranquility of that hand, she told him about the letter.

"St. John is right," he said. "No one laid in wait for me. My untimely arrival caused this. And my carelessness. I should have suspected another man might be there, keeping watch."

"Your friendship with me caused it. The letter is very explicit. He threatens to remove you and your influence. He found the chance last night and tried to kill you. He may have only failed to do so because in the dark he did not know you still breathed. Next time—"

"There will be no next time. I will be on my guard."

She gritted her teeth and clutched the bed cloths beneath her cheek. She struggled for the strength to do what needed to be done.

Regret tore and burned her heart. She had been given a few weeks of happiness, but had not been brave enough to use them very well. How would she manage without him? How would she live with that void again?

How like you to think only about yourself. It has always been like that. The condemnation pierced her memory. Alistair's words? No. Gerald's.

She could do this. For Adrian she could do it.

Her voice came out on shaking, broken breaths. "I cannot risk you. I could not live with the guilt if I caused more harm. I think that we——"

"No."

She rose up on her arms and looked at him. His severe expression had nothing to do with pain.

"He wants to kill you."

"Then he missed his only chance. We do not end it because of this. I will not accept that."

She verged on weeping again. "Adrian, think . . ."

"No." He had that look in his eyes. *This is what will happen. This is how it will be.*

She had never been able to defeat that determination. She suspected that no one else had either.

He took her hand and pulled her forward. "Now, sit here with me. I may as well enjoy my infirmity by having you dote on me."

She found a spot up near the bed board. Bent around him, half-reclining, she nestled his head gently with her breasts and stomach. Stroking his brow, she tried to give back some of the comfort that she so frequently took from him.

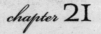

chapter 21

T he evening was a success?" Adrian asked. He lay propped up on his bed, still enduring the three weeks of immobile boredom to which the physician had condemned him.

Colin gestured to the hose and pumps and short breeches that he had worn to the coronation ball. "Except that we all looked like actors in a play from the last century. It really is time for Court dress to accommodate the changing fashions."

Adrian laughed, which did not hurt nearly as much as it had a few days ago. He had been back in his chambers for two weeks now. As much as he had enjoyed Sophia's unflagging attention, he would not compromise her by remaining at her house. Nor would he risk her safety if Captain Brutus had decided to make "the Tory pawn" his new target.

"Your duchess was lovely," Colin said. "Her pale grays were a welcome rest for the eyes in that sea of jewels and bright plumage. She could not dance, of course, so she sat in elegant nobility to the side. The other women looked like cyprians in comparison."

Adrian shifted uncomfortably. His infirmity had begun to annoy, a sure sign that he was practically healed. "You personally escorted her home?"

"Of course. Before you ask, let me assure you that the men whom you hired to protect her continue to make their watch very discreetly."

"That is more than I can say about the men whom *you* hired to protect *me*."

"Damn it, how—"

"I saw them from the window. They lounge in the same spots all the time. I certainly hope that my men are being more professional."

"You are supposed to be staying in bed, not spying out windows."

"Call them off. I can take care of myself."

"The men outside are not hired. They are friends of yours. Julian Hampton, Dante Duclairc, and some others. Even Laclere has taken watches. St. John is in command and told them to be visible, so it is obvious you have protection. I doubt that I *can* call them off. You are stuck with them."

"Do they know what happened?"

"Your absence from society was noticed, so St. John and I came up with an excuse. We told a select few that you were waylaid in a dark street. Some of the chaps who suspect about your missions concluded that it must have been agents of some unfriendly government seeking revenge."

"That is preposterous."

"I cannot account for the vivid imagination of others.

Your pride will have to swallow it. Besides, that pistol you have under the sheet will hardly help you if there is another fire." He held out his hand. "Give it here. It could go off accidentally in your sleep."

"I am never that careless." All the same, Adrian extracted the pistol and gave it to his brother. Just then the sounds of a carriage stopping at the building blew in the window on the night breeze.

Colin peered out. "It is the duchess. No wonder she wanted to leave the ball early. She is still in her ball gown."

"You should have told her there were men watching."

"Hell, most of them were all at the docks that night. Besides, when it is really necessary, we all know how to be silent."

Colin left the bedchamber, to let Sophia in. Adrian heard the mumble of their brief conversation and then the light *swish* of petticoats approaching through the sitting room.

His heart leaped at the sight of her. Her silvery gray gown of raw silk barely reflected the light and cast off the most subtle of shimmers. Three discreet plumes in dark gray adorned her hair, but he could imagine how she had looked in the ducal coronet. She wore no jewels, but the fashionably cut ball gown showed off her luminous, beautiful skin. The Duchess of Everdon had turned the restraint required by mourning into an opportunity to enhance her subtle beauty.

She bent to kiss him. He captured her head so it lasted a long time. They had only been apart two weeks, but he had missed her badly.

"You should not have come, but I am grateful that you

did. Colin said that you made the other women look like courtesans on parade and I can see what he meant."

"Dot advised me on the color and fabric. We think that I am sufficiently subdued, although there were many who questioned the appropriateness of my going at all. Attending the coronation was one thing, but showing up at the ball was quite another. The Queen greeted me warmly, however, so that was that."

"The ladies were just jealous that even subdued you could outshine them." He patted the bed beside him. "Sit here and tell me all about it."

She perched carefully. He inhaled her perfume and the underlying scent of Sophia the woman. His body responded to her closeness in a way that announced he definitely had almost healed.

She described the night, focusing on amusing confrontations and detailed menus, with occasional digressions about outstanding jewels and gowns. The tale animated her. While he watched her bright expression and excited giggles, his heart kept rising with delight and falling with foreboding.

She had finally taken her elevated place as a duchess in her own right. She had held her own among the highest of the high, and she knew it. He could practically see her spirit assessing what it all meant to her life.

Suddenly he wanted her. Desperately.

"Of all of the women besides the royals, I was introduced first to the visiting princes and dignitaries, of course. I confess that I enjoyed taking precedence, after all of the critical scrutiny these last months. Was it too naughty of me?"

"Not at all."

"I could not have pulled it off without Dot. She has spent the last week exhorting me to flex my power a little, and to use this opportunity to put certain ladies in their place."

That certain other ladies had learned their place would be good for her. That she was beginning to learn her own worried him. Not that he would change things. He was glad that the day had been a triumph. Glad for her, that was. Not necessarily for himself.

She darted him a pointed glance. "There were dignitaries from all over. Several from the Ottoman Court in Turkey. They wore magnificent robes. When I met them I almost giggled, because all I could think of was my silly *seraglio* in Paris."

"It must have been very colorful."

"One spoke with me, beyond the usual polite exchange. I gather he is an important member of the Sultan's government. His English is fluent. He told me that he has been here several times before, on embassies." She spoke casually while she drew little patterns on the back of his hand. Inflaming, torturous designs.

"That would be my father."

"I saw a resemblance. The same eyes. I expected to have to worm it out of you."

"About a dozen people at the ball knew. You may as well too."

"Have you always known about him?"

He lined his fingertips up her bare arm, entranced by her skin's glow in the candlelight. "My mother told me when I turned eighteen. She should have done so earlier. I had only to look in the mirror to know that I was not the earl's. His coldness to me told the tale as well."

He let his fingers trail higher and lower, enjoying the sensation of her skin. Its texture and warmth were acutely tangible tonight. It affected him as if he used his lips. "When my father learned that my mother carried me, he went to the earl and offered to buy her. Fifty horses, I think it was, and ten thousand pounds."

"I can imagine Dincaster's reaction to that."

"There was no way he would let my mother leave. The humiliation would have been insurmountable."

"Did she want to go away?"

"I think she considered it, but Gavin and Colin would be lost to her. So she forged an agreement with the earl that guaranteed I would not be repudiated and that he would accept me as his own before the world and the law."

His gaze and light caress traveled over her shoulder to the skin exposed by the flaring top of her gown. It felt so soothing to touch her. She subtly angled for more, like a cat encouraging petting.

"He did not really accept you and give you a father's love, did he? Even now he does not treat you like a son."

"His generosity did not extend that far. In return for being allowed to keep me, my mother agreed to stay. And, of course, she gave up her lover."

His touching had raised a lovely tint on her cheeks, but she kept to the subject. "Have you met him?"

"The first time I was in that part of the world, he made himself known to me. I have spent some time with him."

"I am glad for that, Adrian. It saddens me to think of you as a boy, receiving only sneers from the earl."

"It was not as with you and Alistair. Dincaster had his reason, and it was a good one. I will not say that I was not wounded, but knowing there was a reason made it easier."

She looked distracted and sad. He slid his hand along her back. "Now, I do not want to talk about it anymore. Actually, I discover that I do not want to talk at all." He found the gown's fastenings beneath a flap of silk and released them.

She straightened with a start. "You are in no condition."

"I am in superb condition. Astounding condition. In fact, I am astonished at the heroic proportion of my condition."

"I am sure it is not advisable."

He laughed. "It is damn close to being essential."

He reached for her and she scooted away. "Heroic condition or not, you know it is not wise. Besides, I want to talk even if you do not. I need to tell you something."

"Tell me while you get undressed."

"After I tell you, you may not want me to stay."

His playful mood drained away. "What is it, then?"

She bit her lower lip. "I have decided to leave London for a while."

"If you are running away to France, I will stop you as I did the last time," he warned.

"Not to France. I have decided to visit Marleigh. I am leaving in two days."

"Wait a few more. I should be able to travel soon."

"In a few days Parliament will begin sessions again, and you must be there."

"I can miss a week of debate."

"You do not understand. I do not want you to come."

She grimaced when she said it, as if she expected him to react badly. That was exactly what he began to do, but her expression checked him.

"I do not like it. It could be dangerous. We do not know that Captain Brutus has fully turned his attention on me."

"I will take an escort of four footmen as guards, and Jacques and Attila will ride in the coach with me. Jacques is very good with a pistol."

"I still do not like it."

She moved until she sat very close to him. She took his face in her hands and touched her cheek to his. "Do not be angry with me. This is something that I have to do. It is time to face it all, and make some decisions, and find out who I am and who I will be." She kissed him. "It is only because of you that I can do it. You have carried me halfway down the road. Now I must walk the rest of the way myself."

She was right, but he resisted accepting it. She might not know what she would find when she looked for herself, but he did. He had seen it from the start, beneath all of those layers.

He doubted that the woman who returned from Marleigh would have any need of him. Once she came to terms with Everdon, she would *be* Everdon, and duty to Everdon would rule her life.

Hadn't he brought her back from Paris so it would be so?

He stroked his hands into her hair and gazed into her eyes. So many interesting shadows played in their glow. He held her head to a deep kiss and tried to keep her from sensing the apprehension of loss that drenched his climbing passion.

This might be their last night.

He lowered his hands to her shoulders and slid her
gown down. "Get undressed."

"Adrian..."

"I want you to lie here with me. You can hardly do so
in these clothes." He turned her so he could unlace her
stays and release the petticoats. She glanced over her
shoulder to begin a protest, but he gave her a look that
warned her not to bother.

She got off the bed and slid the gown lower. "I suppose
if you just intend us to lie beside each other..."

He said nothing to that, but watched as she stepped
out of the gown and petticoats and shed the stays. She had
been beautiful in the luxurious gray silk, but he drank in
the sight of her feminine form emerging. The low light
hinted at her curves beneath the chemise.

He memorized every inch of her, and every move she
made while she carried the gown and laid it over a chair.

He let her climb in beside him still wearing her under-
garments and hose, because to order them off would only
set her scolding.

She snuggled under his arm and gingerly rested her
head on his shoulder and her hand on his chest.

"I thought about you constantly through all these days
of coronation festivities. I wished you were with me today," she said. "However, this makes up for it. This is very
nice."

It would be nicer soon, but he needed to know something first. "No more letters from our Captain?"

"None at all. Maybe what happened frightened him.
Did you think I would not tell you?"

"That is exactly what I thought, since you insist on
treating me like an invalid."

"I am only worried about you. The physician said three weeks of quiet bed rest."

"The physician is an ass. As I said earlier, I am practically good as new and am in fine condition." He closed his hand on her breast. "I'll prove it."

He silenced her startled objection with his mouth and conquered her brief resistance with his caress. She melted and her pliant body curved into him.

"That is wickedly wonderful," she whispered as he played at her through the thin fabric. "But if you exert yourself we will probably have to call the physician again."

"I do not plan to move much at all. All of the exertion will be yours." He went to work on her ear. "I will tell you what to do. As a beginning, curl up facing me so I do not have to twist like this."

That made it easier for him to kiss her properly and to reach her whole body, to finish undressing her. He plunged into the bliss of pure sensation and expectant hunger. Her arousal escalated beautifully, until she was with him kiss for kiss and breath for breath in their private world of emotion and pleasure.

He wanted, he wanted . . . all of her. All that he had known with her and all that he hadn't and all that he might never know again. The images of what he desired sent him veering toward the breaking point. He took her in a gentle, exploring kiss while he forced some control. Her mouth smiled against his.

"My need amuses you?" he asked.

"No more than mine does. No, that kiss made me remember Jacques' lessons in love on the boat. I will have to tell him that you are not at all clumsy and crushing when you peel apart a rose's petals and lick its nectar."

"Jacques' metaphor was not about a woman's mouth, Sophia."

She went still for a moment. He sensed her working out what it *was* about.

"Do you want that?"

"Yes."

Another moment of stillness.

"Tell me what to do."

He told her. After he had brought her to a thunderous climax he slid from between her kneeling legs and came up behind her and took her while she hung limply against the bed board.

It destroyed whatever restraints still existed between them. He did not leave the exertions to her after all. All night long he made love to her, oblivious to his healing ribs and bruises. He molded her recurrent arousals to his explorations while a ferocious, aching hunger tried to have enough of her to last a lifetime.

chapter 22

"Such an impressive palace." Attila's cry echoed from where he stood gaping in the middle of the immense ballroom. The room's dimensions turned his bearish form into a diminutive spot of astonishment. "Your home is as big as the Louvre."

"As always, our friend exaggerates," Jacques said while he strolled beside Sophia, inspecting the luxurious appointments. They had arrived an hour earlier and she was giving them a tour. "However, you are more important than I ever imagined. Everdon must be one of your country's great titles."

"Let us just say that if it had been a French title forty years ago, the likes of you would have sent me to the guillotine in the first wave."

"It appears that your countrymen seek to cut off some heads of their own now, only the weapon will be this new law instead of a blade. The result will be a half-measure, and incomplete."

Sophia could tell that, like all young men of radical

disposition, Jacques found half-measures unpalatable. Captain Brutus had been like that.

"Perhaps we are fortunate that you are French and not English," she teased.

"The condition of men anywhere is everyone's concern."

"I hope that you have not been instigating riots while you are here." She made it a mock scold, but admitted the possibility of outside interference that she had never considered before.

"I would never misuse your hospitality that way. However, it is inevitable that men have come here from other countries to use the turmoil to their own ends. Your husband, I think, can tell you how it works."

"What do you mean by that?"

"You told me yourself that your husband is a spy and agent provocateur. A dangerous man."

"I made that up, Jacques. It was a silly tale."

"Silly tale or not, I think that you touched the truth. Perhaps your heart suspected." Jacques fingered a gilt candelabra. "Magnificent. All of it. How many chambers, did you say? Eighty-four?"

"You disapprove."

"I prefer your house in London, and your *maison* in Paris. This is majestic, but empty. Cold, and full of echoes. Perhaps when you and Monsieur Burchard fill it with children it will be different."

She had come here to settle things for herself. A good first step would be to set Jacques and Attila straight about her relationship with Adrian.

She stopped his stroll and looked him in the eyes. "As I told you before, I am not married. Not to Adrian, or to anyone else. I lied to you about that, just like the part about my husband being a spy. Adrian exploited the lies so you would not interfere when he came to bring me back to England. I had never seen him before that night of my *seraglio*."

Attila joined them in time to overhear the last few words. "You plan another *seraglio*? Here? The cost of the silks for the ceiling would be exorbitant. Perhaps the east drawing room would be better. Much more intimate."

"Sophia is not planning another *seraglio*," Jacques said. "She is explaining again that she is not married to Monsieur Burchard. This time I find myself believing her."

Attila's happy expression fell. "It is so? You have been playing a very dangerous game. When your true husband learns what has transpired with Burchard, it could be very ugly."

"There is no husband at all," she said.

"No husband? But Jacques said that you told him . . ."

"She lied to me."

"And a few others," Sophia admitted.

"You lied to Jacques? But why? I will admit that I was wounded to learn that you took him into your confidence and not me, too, but if it was a lie, you only insulted him."

"She lied to me and others to discourage us."

Attila turned on Jacques with wide eyes. "Discourage you? Are you saying that you tried . . . ?"

Jacques responded with one of his shrugs.

"I am speechless, Jacques."

"I doubt that I will be so blessed."

"To think that you would take advantage of our sweet lady's generosity. Have the French no shame? To have pressed her to the point where she took refuge in a lie . . ."

Sophia slipped away while Attila continued his harangue. Jacques bore it patiently, looking to the ceiling with resignation while the lecture poured down on him.

She had debated all the way to Marleigh just when to do it. By the time she arrived she had laid out a schedule that would not require confronting the ghosts until a few days had passed. Therefore it surprised her when a fit of cold resolve gripped her as she left the ballroom.

Why not just face it now? It was why she had come. Best to get it over with. Delay would not make it easier, and might give her too much time to lose her courage.

Steeling herself, she wound through the house's chambers and up its grand staircase. At the third landing she looked at the door to Alistair's suite of rooms.

Sickening dread made her turn away. She would face a gentler ghost first, even though it would probably be more painful.

She made her way to Brandon's chamber. A mellow sadness swelled with each step. She could only contemplate this because she had already faced the worst of it at Staverly. She had only succeeded in that because Adrian had helped her.

Adrian. She wished he were here to hold her together again. But she knew, she just knew, that it was important to do this on her own.

She thought about the man whose passion could make her feel beautiful and magnificent. The thought of him pierced her heart with regret. She was not giving him everything like she wanted to. She loved him, but the deepest level of her spirit held back. Was there a sadder pain in the world than aching to believe and trust and love without question, and discovering that you are incapable of it?

That was why she was here. To reclaim the part of her soul that had learned to hide too well. There was a danger in the quest. She could discover that it was not hiding, but was dead.

She turned the latch and stepped inside the chamber. Its starkness startled her. Fury split her mind.

Nothing of her brother remained. She had always assumed that Alistair had left it as it stood on that summer day. Instead he had wiped it clean of Brandon's life.

He had done it on purpose. He had known that one day she would want to feel Brandon's presence again, and he had deliberately robbed her of it. He wanted to make sure she could never reconcile what had happened. He needed her to wallow in guilt.

Scathing resentment maddened her thoughts, turning them harsh. *I can do the same, Papa. I can go into that suite and wipe out your years there. I can burn the clothes and furniture and sell all the items that you used. I can even refuse to have a child. I can obliterate you.*

She stiffened with sudden self-awareness. The ugliness of her rage shocked her. The internal voice had sounded horribly familiar. Its cruelty reminded her of Alistair himself.

She forced some calm and blocked out the thought of him. Not yet.

She sat on the bed and closed her eyes and pictured this chamber as it had once been.

The image that came to her was from childhood, during the years when she and her twin lived one life. They used to make a fort out of a velvet quilt and bounce a ball down the chamber's long length. It was how she remembered this room best. After they had begun to mature, she had rarely ventured in here.

Memories flew by, and she embraced them all. Heartrending nostalgia made tears drip down her cheeks. She saw him as a little boy and as a young man. She had forgotten how much he looked like their mother, brighteyed and dark-haired and quick to smile. There had been little of Alistair in him, much to their father's annoyance. Too soft. Too kind. *Weak,* Papa had called him.

Not weak. Thoughtful and sensitive and giving, but not weak. A good person, full of their mother's quiet strength. No, there had been little of Alistair in him. Unlike her.

Brandon's childish face suddenly froze in one of those memories. He was looking at her after learning that she had gotten him into trouble for something he had not done. She forgot the crime now, but remembered the lie. She had implicated him because she did not want to face their father alone.

His eyes focused on her, gazing with a wisdom beyond his years. In them she saw understanding. And forgiveness.

The image held. Her eyes and throat burned. Then the memory was gone.

She looked around the vacant chamber. A peaceful elation moved her. She had not needed his clothes or books or toys. Opening this door to the past had brought more comfort than pain. She should have known that it would.

She walked to the door and glanced back at the emptiness. Maybe Alistair had not erased Brandon's history

because of her, but for himself. Perhaps he had feared remembering even more than she had.

There would have been no images of happiness and
forgiveness waiting on the other side of the door if it ever
blew open for him. He probably knew that.

She did not need clothes or objects in Alistair's chambers
either. They were all there, of course. Not even Celine
would dare to erase the late Duke of Everdon from his
home. Sophia had rarely seen him in this inner sanctum,
however, and its contents held no special meaning for her.

That disappointed her. She had counted on it just happening when she walked in the door.

She sat in a chair near the cold hearth. She would have
to do it on her own. Of course she would. None of this
really had to do with Marleigh's chambers. It was all inside her.

She let the memories come, steeling her composure to
face them.

Alistair critical and harsh and cutting.

A thousand little hurts when she was too young to understand anything but that Papa was busy or angry.

The nagging suspicion as she got older that it was not
just his manner.

The eventual admission that he really did not love
them much at all.

The more recent ones were harder, and she cringed
against their cruelty. She watched his triumph when he
captured Captain Brutus. She relived his blunt satisfaction in throwing the truth of all that in her face. She mentally turned away from his expression during the fierce

browbeatings and terrible whipping that he had used to force her to speak at the trial.

Finally, she called forth the steely coldness with which he treated her after Brandon died, as if he would gladly exchange her for the body in the grave.

She did not cry. Alistair never evoked that response. It had always been something much worse. He killed her confidence and joy. He made her feel worthless and insignificant. He sucked the strength and life out of her.

It was vital not to let him do that today. She battled to hold on to the woman Adrian had helped her to begin discovering.

"They say you were a good duke," she said aloud to the memory.

I executed my duties better than most.

"Did it consume you? Is that why there was nothing left for us?"

I did my duty to you too.

"I am not speaking of duty."

You have always been sentimental and emotional, Sophia. It does you no credit. Such things are not for the likes of us. You must learn to control those tendencies, and your willfulness and impetuousness and extravagance and...

"I am well aware of my deficiencies. You cataloged them for me often enough. Did you not love us at all? Were we only duties?"

I cared for you in that way, to the extent that I was capable.

"Which is your way of saying very little. Did Everdon make you that way, or were you born thus?"

Your question is impertinent. Another failing that requires self-discipline.

"The question is important to me. You see, I have

come back. It is mine now. I want to know what goes with the power and precedence and wealth."

You are unsuitable and will fail. A duke is born to the title, but his sense of duty is molded. I educated your brother for it, not you. He was too soft, but I had him shaping up. That you are all who is left...

"I am not afraid of the duties. I will not fail if I accept them. But will they turn me into what you were? Or was your inability to love a part of your nature?"

Which answer would you prefer?

"The first, I suppose. I can always run away from Marleigh. I can never get rid of the other legacy, the part of you that is in me."

Running away. You are good at that. It took your half-breed lover to get you to admit it.

"Do not insult him. Adrian is good for me. He sees wonderful things in me."

It is in his interest to do so.

"That is not true."

So he gives you affection and pleasure and asks no more in return? A rare man, considering your position. Except that you do not truly believe that. Which is why you cannot love him.

Her jaw clenched against the accusation.

Ah. So that is what this is about. All of this talk of love. I dared to hope for a moment that we were having an intelligent conversation. Listen carefully. I only bother because you are all who is left. You are Everdon now, and Everdon is a power to be used. Others will want to control it, and will try to use you in order do so. You know that. It has already happened. There is no place for sentimentality in any of it. You must be nimble, clever, and sometimes ruthless. Love will only leave you vulnerable.

Imagine how much more I would have been disappointed in you if I had loved you.

"So it was Everdon that made you what you were."

I was molded to become Everdon, but I was bred to be a duke. Since you do not understand, I will answer in a way you might comprehend. I was born unusually free of the sentiment you call love, and that helped me become a strong Duke of Everdon.

"I think that is sad."

You would. Because there is much of me in you, and you were hoping for a different answer. However, I have never held with telling people what they want to hear instead of the truth.

"Then hear some truth from me. You were not a good man. You were cold and hard. That is not strength. I will show you how it can be done another way. I will be nimble and clever, but never ruthless. Nor will I permit duty to turn me to stone."

Then I must watch the deterioration of the prestige and power built over centuries.

"Your confidence, as always, gives me heart."

I am finished with you. I had hoped these last few months had taught you something.

"There is one more thing, Papa."

What is that?

"I forgive you."

There is nothing for you to forgive.

"There is much to forgive."

Have it your way. But, Sophia, never forget. I do not forgive you.

"I did not expect you to. But I will forget. I intend to start forgetting today."

.   .   .

The next day after breakfast Sophia found two men cooling their heels outside the study. One was her new solicitor, Julian Hampton.

"Mister Hampton, I am glad that you could arrange to come. Have you been examining the papers?"

"I have, Your Grace. With Mister Carson's aid, we should know the state of things very quickly."

She turned to the other man. Aging and gray, he appeared ill at ease. He smiled cautiously while he made a bow. "Your Grace."

She led the way into the study. "Mister Hampton has convinced me that perhaps I was too rash in releasing you, Mister Carson. After all, you have been my father's secretary for over twenty years. Are you content to live off the bequest he left you, or are you interested in continuing your duties here?"

"The bequest was generous, but service to Everdon has been my life. I would prefer to serve until my abilities fail me."

She paced along the wall lined with mahogany shelves holding registers and portfolios of documents. Other walls displayed sedate oil landscapes. Some fox tails and other trophies of the hunt were tacked between the long windows. Besides some plain wooden chairs, the huge dark desk and smaller secretary were the only furnishings.

A man's study, and very much Alistair's. Alistair the Duke, not the father, and the part of him contained here did not disturb her too much. Still, she flung open the windows so the sultry summer air could decimate the vague scent of him.

"This is what I propose, Mister Carson. The three of us will go through my father's correspondence from the last two years and you will explain what every letter was about and what my father's plans and intentions were. If I perceive that you are forthright and honest, I will consider keeping you on. If you are not, you will never cross this threshold again."

"That is acceptable to me, Your Grace."

"Is it? We will be looking at his letters to me and about me, too, I should warn you."

"I can see where that could be awkward, but I will do my duty."

"Then let us get started."

They spent the next three days sequestered in the study while Jacques and Attila made free with the luxury of Marleigh. Her friends went riding and played tennis, while she pored over contracts and leases. Attila began composing a new sonata on the pianoforte, while she learned about Everdon's investments. After dinner the second night, Jacques read a new love poem. It employed the rose metaphor. Sophia barely heard it. Her mind was on items of unfinished business that Mister Hampton had brought to her attention.

The last day she discovered a thick green portfolio tied with red ribbon.

"That contains copies of the duke's private letters, Your Grace," Mister Carson explained. "The ones he wrote himself, and that I never saw."

"It might be prudent just to burn it," Mister Hampton advised.

Probably. That would be the wise choice.

She pulled at the tie of the ribbon. "Occupy yourselves. I will review this alone."

The portfolio spanned Alistair's adult life. She began

with the oldest letters and worked her way through the years. There were notes to old friends and a series of political missives. She discovered epistles of instruction to Brandon at school. Most of their contents were as distant and cold as the duke himself.

Early on she began finding some personal letters of a different tone, however. Love letters. Not to her mother. The Duke of Everdon had enjoyed a series of mistresses. There were few names on them, just salutations of "my dear."

She skipped their contents, but could not ignore the periodic flurry of them that indicated a new affair, and then the eventual silence that said that woman was history.

It surprised her how much they saddened her. She had assumed that she was beyond such a reaction where Alistair was concerned. Maybe she had hoped that with their mother at least . . .

She flipped quickly until she got to the most recent letters. Near the top, among the correspondence written the month before he died, she found the only letter addressed to Gerald Stidolph. Her cousin stayed so close to Everdon that most communication could be verbal.

When she read the letter she understood why Alistair would have wanted to convey its news from a distance.

In it the Duke of Everdon admitted that he was getting concerned about his age and the succession. He had concluded that his daughter would never be agreeable to marrying Stidolph. He was pursuing alternate matches in the hopes of luring her home to do her duty.

Then, at the end, he confessed that their plan to make her wed Gerald had grown distasteful to him, in any case.

She focused on that line, and read it again and again. It was the only evidence that she had ever had that her father had considered her feelings in anything.

Gerald's disapproving expression filled her mind. She remembered how he had been harping on her need to satisfy her father's wishes. The abusive way that he had played on her guilt had even been more insidious than Alistair's.

She removed the letter from the portfolio and folded it. This one would return to London with her. After Alistair's death, Gerald had conveniently forgotten that it had been written.

Mister Carson stacked some portfolios and carried them back to the shelves. Those endless documents represented an important part of Everdon's power and most of its wealth. The lessons of the last few days had not overwhelmed her. She could do it. She could make the myriad decisions if she chose to.

Only she did not want to. She did not want to spend her days deciding what the rents should be next year, and whether to hold or sell the investment in those canals. She possessed the head for it, but not the nature. She would much prefer to hand it all over to someone else who would manage it for her.

If she accepted Everdon, she would have to decide who that someone should be. There were important decisions and duties waiting, besides those filed on that shelf. Foremost was the one to produce an heir, and she wasn't getting any younger.

The spirit of the house suddenly saturated her. The dukes down through time clamored for attention. She sighed at their silent demands.

She had come to decide what to do, but of course there had never really been any choice. Hadn't Adrian warned her of that the first night in Paris?

But I will do it my way, not Alistair's way and not yours, she said to the house.

While dressing for the coronation, Dot had ceremoniously placed the ducal coronet on her head. Now Sophia mentally repeated the action, using her own hands.

She closed the green portfolio and finally laid the previous Duke of Everdon to rest.

Well, maybe not to rest. She suspected that before she was done, he would turn in his grave.

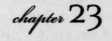

chapter 23

The invitation to share tea arrived in the morning post. It was inscribed on the finest cream-laid stock and bore the ducal crest. Sophia had not written it. Adrian recognized the hand as that of Carson, Alistair's secretary.

Tea? *Tea?* She had quietly returned to London three days earlier, had not contacted him, had moved out of the small house nearby, and now she had sent a formal invitation to share *tea?*

The message could not have been clearer if she had given him pearls as a parting gift.

Time had been fanning a slow burn since he had learned from his runners that she was back. Now it flared into scorching resentment.

He had been creating pitiful excuses to avoid facing the truth. He had rationalized that of course she would want to move back to Everdon House now that it was repaired. He had almost convinced himself that once she had resettled herself he would hear from her.

Hell, he had been right about that part.

Crushing the paper in his left hand, he scratched out an equally formal note of regret and sent it off.

He barely heard the debates in the Commons that afternoon. Since he was due to give a speech the next day, he knew that he should pay more attention, but his mind was full of Sophia. A thick, melancholic regret clouded his perceptions. Sometimes spikes of caustic rage penetrated it, but little else. Certainly not the histrionics of his fellow Tories, valiantly fighting a losing battle.

Which was why James Hawkins had to nudge his arm to get his attention after the session adjourned.

"Shall we go together?"

Adrian was in the middle of a mental lecture in which he was accusing Sophia of cowardice in letting a grand passion simply fade away. At the very least he had the right to a dramatic confrontation and clean break.

"Go where?"

"To call on the duchess. Surely you received the summons. We all did."

The slow burn instantly turned to white heat. "Are you saying that *all* of her M.P.'s were invited this afternoon?"

Hawkins backed up a bit. "Don't know why you are angry. Makes sense, doesn't it? Past time for us to get off the fence. Especially you, what with your speech planned for tomorrow."

Adrian came close to punching Hawkins merely because he was the nearest target.

"Of course I am going. Hell, I wouldn't think of missing it. It would not do to insult my patroness, would it? We will take my carriage." He grabbed Hawkins by the shoulder of his coat and hauled him away.

"I say," Hawkins muttered, stumbling to keep up. "This is most undignified."

"We must hurry. Don't want to be the last there, do we? She may think we don't have the proper respect. She may surmise that we take her damn favor the hell for granted. She may even conclude that we mistook her for a soft and caring woman instead of the great Duchess of Everdon."

Hawkins tripped along, more aghast with each step. By the time they claimed the carriage, he looked like he feared he had fallen into the hands of a madman.

"You seem out of sorts, Burchard. I heard that you had been conched on the head a while back. Perhaps you should beg off and get some rest."

"Get in."

"By Jove, the afternoon is fair, isn't it? I think that a walk would be very pleasant after—"

"Get in. Duty calls, Hawkins. Lesson number one in being an owned man is that Power should never be kept waiting. I trust that you brought some of your poetry to read in case the duchess wants to pretend that this is a social engagement."

Hawkins reluctantly climbed into the curricle. "Actually, I do have a few sonnets with me."

"That will be a rare treat for us all."

They were not the first to arrive. Harvey Douglas already fawned over the duchess in the drawing room when Adrian and Hawkins were announced.

Adrian almost forgot his annoyance upon seeing Sophia. She had dropped the mourning. She wore a pale green gown with a rose sash and its broad neckline exposed her shoulders. A discreet necklace of gold filigree lay on her luminous skin. She appeared serene and happy and at peace.

He knew at once that the visit to Marleigh had been good for her. She had accomplished what she set out to do. He had never doubted that she would. Hadn't he told her that she was one of the strongest women whom he had ever met?

Pride swelled in him, making an odd mix with his resentment. She had discovered who she was. The implications for her love affair with Adrian Burchard had been inescapable.

Still, she should have done it differently. Now he would always wonder if he had imagined the best parts.

She rose and came toward him. "I am grateful that you were able to attend after all, Mister Burchard."

"I was able to rearrange my appointments." He briefly took her hand and made a formal bow. She looked startled at the gesture. He glanced into her eyes and let her see his resentment.

Her gaze turned frosty. He still saw the depths and layers, but self-confidence had replaced the flickering guilt and fear.

She greeted Hawkins and then foisted him on Douglas before easing Adrian away.

"Where have you been?" she hissed.

"Where I always am."

"Why haven't you come to see me?"

"I received no request to do so."

"Since when do you wait on a request?"

"When you have left the city and I have no way of knowing that you are back."

"Of course you knew. Those men you had secretly

watching my house saw me return. I waited up that whole first night, expecting you. I needed to speak with you and tell you what I planned to do."

Two other guests were announced just then. "It appears that I will learn with everyone else."

"I am not speaking only of politics and you know it. Why are you so cold? Are you that unsympathetic a friend?"

"I am not amused by the circumstances of our reunion."

"It is your own fault. You should have come. What was I to think when you did not?" She glanced to where her guests waited expectantly. "I need to explain things to you."

"This is hardly the place for it."

"Stay after the others leave."

He felt his jaw stiffen. He looked away so anyone watching would think their exchange a casual one. "Ask sweetly and I will consider it."

"You came here determined to vex me."

"I came here because I was obligated to do so. I am not obligated to stay when this is over. If you have accepted your position, I am glad for you. If you are feeling your oats, that is understandable. But I am the man who has possessed you and who knows your body better than you do, and you *will not* command that man to attend on you."

She flushed so red that everyone must have noticed. "My apologies, Mister Burchard. *Please* stay after the others leave." She bit out the request before sweeping away to her backed-up arrivals.

He wasn't sure that he would. He suddenly realized

that he did not want a dramatic confrontation after all. He did not want to endure the regretful explanation.

The drawing room filled. Tea was served. They spent an hour pretending that it was mere coincidence that the duchess had invited her twelve M.P.'s to her house on the same afternoon.

Hawkins read his sonnets. They weren't half-bad, which made them barely half-good. The last was a flowery tribute to the duchess. Sophia beamed appreciation and Hawkins began looking roguishly hopeful again. The other men felt obliged to praise and discuss the poems for a quarter hour.

Finally, Sophia got down to business. "I know that all of you have been waiting for my word on the bill being discussed in the Commons. I expect that you are being pressed by your colleagues for your position."

"Hardly pressed, Your Grace," Douglas said. "Rumors have been about all summer that we will be with Wellington and Peel and the Tories."

"I trust that you are not behind those rumors, Mister Douglas. I made very clear at Haford that only I would give the word."

"Not me. I heard that Wellington himself has been counting us in. Some say he got reassurances, and I just assumed you had spoken with him."

Eleven heads nodded. Sophia's glare came to rest on the one that did not.

Adrian sipped some tea. She should have known that he was lying to Wellington when the Iron Duke didn't press her.

"Not that it will matter much," Hawkins said. "A bill is sure to pass soon."

"We still need your official word, of course," Douglas said. "The closer the vote, the easier it will be for the House of Lords to hold the line and kill it."

Sophia's gaze scanned the room. Talk dribbled off. Everyone knew that a ducal announcement was coming.

"I called you here to let you know what I have decided. I have thought long and hard about this, and I suspect that some of you will not agree with me, but it is how I choose to go."

Bodies angled toward her. Silence reigned. Her dramatic pause stretched.

Adrian succumbed to a childish urge to ruin the show. He set his cup down, very noisily. It wobbled and tinged and clattered, distracting the audience.

He had a thousand things to resent today, but the evidence that she had decided this without once discussing it with him was the last straw.

"Your decision, Duchess?" he asked.

"It is very simple. I have decided not to decide."

"Excuse me for stating the obvious, but deciding not to decide is not a decision."

Hawkin's perfect brow puckered. "He has a point there."

"The implication is obvious, if you will only consider it. I will not decide. You will. Each of you, according to his conscience. There will be no word from me. There will be no block of twelve votes."

The M.P.'s reacted with shock. Douglas's mouth gaped so wide that his tawny beard hit his chest.

Adrian stared in astonishment. She was throwing it away. She had accepted Everdon's power only to destroy it.

"There is something else that all of you should know," she said. "Your votes will not affect your relationship with me in any way, no matter how you go. In the future, Everdon will no longer be nominating candidates and requiring its tenants to support them."

Stunned amazement greeted this final surprise. It held for a solid minute while everyone absorbed the full implications.

Then chaos erupted.

The M.P.'s broke into noisy groups. One converged on the duchess to explain with strained politeness how this simply would not do. Adrian strolled over to the windows to contemplate the astounding development.

He was furious with her. Livid. Explaining this to Wellington would be nigh impossible. No man would understand why the duchess had just diminished a power carefully accumulated over generations. The Iron Duke would have apoplexy when he learned just how badly she had been managed.

He looked to where she calmly deflected the exhortations heaped on her. She had given them a freedom that they did not want.

Adrian realized that he did not want it either. He had been counting on her making a decision that he did not want to make himself. The choice would not really be his, and no one would really hold him responsible. His conscience would be clear, and his political future still bright.

Hawkins hustled over. "Hell of a thing. You brought her to the boroughs in May. Go explain how things work."

"It appears that they will work differently now."

"Easy for you to say. Stockton is a solid borough. I'm in a damnable situation. If I go with the bill, I vote to abolish my own seat."

"Then vote against it."

"Don't know if I can. She's gone and left it to me now, hasn't she? Changes things, doesn't it?"

It certainly did. Damn it.

"There are other boroughs."

"Not for a Tory who sides with the opposition, nor is there much need for a Whig whose friends are all Tories."

Adrian agreed. Solid borough or not, there was little political influence for an M.P. of those colors. She had put all of them in a hellish situation. Especially Adrian Burchard.

The crowd around her had gotten thicker. He strolled over and interrupted. "Gentlemen, it is clear that the duchess is resolved. May I suggest that we assess our squandered fortunes elsewhere."

He exited the drawing room first but did not leave. After instructions to Charles to send his carriage down the square, he nipped up the staircase before anyone else got away.

His entrance into her sitting room sent the animals into throes of excitement. He wasn't in the mood to play. After greetings and scratches, he ordered the dogs, Camilla, and Prinny to their cages.

It took her a half hour to follow. She finally slipped in, catching him pacing with impatience.

"From your expression, I gather that we will not be falling into each other's arms," she said. "I do not believe I have ever seen you so angry."

"The hell of it is, I cannot decide which angers me

more. Being summoned here like the lady's serf, or learning that I have been freed of my bondage."

"You were not summoned. The others were, but not you. If you had not been so stubborn, you would have known about the vote three nights ago. And my decision to cease nominations. And about the rest."

"Whatever the rest is, let it wait. You have given me enough to swallow for one day."

"Seeing your mood, I may let it wait forever." She strolled to a chair and arranged her skirts to sit. "Why didn't you come?"

"Why did you move out of the other house?"

"It was time for me to come back here. I would have explained if you had visited that first night."

"I could not visit without your requesting it. You know that."

"I know nothing of the kind."

"Sophia, you went to Marleigh for a reason. We both knew what it was. We both knew what it may mean about us."

"I did not know. If I had, I might not have gone."

"But you did go. And I am right, aren't I? You are Everdon now, of your own choosing. You must marry, and soon."

She looked to her lap. After a pause, she nodded.

So there it was. Ended. Finished. A sick weight filled his chest.

Her gaze rose and met his directly. She did not even look very sad about it.

That sliced him to his core. He had concluded that she was not in love with him, but he had thought there was more than that calm acceptance suggested.

"Do not blame me for foreseeing the end and avoiding the indignity of learning about it after sneaking in your garden door."

"And do not blame me for being who I am."

"I do not blame you. I love who you are. Runaway or duchess, fearful or strong. However, right now I am infuriated by how thoroughly you have disrupted my life."

"You are speaking of the vote now, and not us."

"I am speaking of both. I apologize if I cannot match your own noble equanimity."

"That is not fair. You misinterpret my mood and my feelings, but I do not think that today you will hear anything that I say about that. As to my announcement downstairs, I do not understand how I have disrupted anything for you. You are free to vote against the bill, as you have always wanted to."

He turned away in exasperation.

Her skirts rustled. She came up behind him. "Oh."

"Yes. Oh."

"You never indicated..."

"How could I? To have brought up the subject would have left you wondering if I still tried to manage you. Influence you. *Use you.* Nor did you seek discussion or advice. I never imagined that you were deciding not to decide, as you put it. Or that you were contemplating throwing the futures of twelve men to the winds."

"If it means anything at all, I did not choose this course until I was at Marleigh. Then I just knew what I had to do. It is not right, my controlling those seats. There are few enough votes among the people without my stealing the voices of so many. Please try to understand."

He turned to see her worried frown. The ducal facade had cracked. She looked earnest and concerned. And absolutely beautiful. His duchess. His Sophia.

"I understand. A damn sight more than I would like to at the moment."

Tilting her chin up, he kissed her. He intended it to be brief and light, a small gesture of parting. The warmth of her lips captivated him, however, and flowed like a balm through his veins. He lingered, and the melancholy that had suffused him for days pitched high with nostalgia.

He pulled away. "You must excuse me now. I have a speech to give tomorrow, and I need to decide what I will say."

"Speak against reform, Adrian. Even if you believe otherwise now, it will make no difference. The bill will pass no matter what you do."

"It is not that simple. My patron's last command was to vote my conscience. It is time to decide what that is."

He kissed her hand and went to the door.

"Please come and find me. After. I would like to tell you about Marleigh, and what happened there," she said.

He could not promise that he would. That kiss left him thinking that he dare not.

He opened the door. "There is one thing that I need to know now. Tell me it will not be Stidolph."

"It will not be Gerald. I would kill myself first."

He did not return to his chambers. He walked the city, watching the people at their work, not thinking much about anything.

His feet took him through rich neighborhoods and

poor ones, along lanes of fine shops and market streets full of smells. He tried to walk off his feelings for Sophia, but that didn't happen. He struggled to weigh his options about the bill, but his thoughts remained scrambled and incoherent.

Somehow, despite the lack of rational argument, he decided what to do. After two hours he turned on his heel and headed back. He did not return to Sophia. Instead he visited another square, seeking out the home of a man who had already faced the choice that he confronted now.

A footman admitted him and accepted his card. "The family is about to sit down to dinner, sir. Perhaps tomorrow afternoon..."

A door opened off the hall and a tall man emerged. He saw Adrian and approached.

"Burchard, it is good to see you."

"Laclere. My apologies. I know it is an odd hour to call, but..."

The viscount waved his explanation silent and turned to the footman. "Mister Burchard will be joining us."

"I do not want to intrude."

"Nonsense. We are informal here. Bianca's bad influence, I am often told." He guided him toward the dining room. "Besides, now that you have finally come, I do not intend to let you get away."

"I only came for advice, but I would be honored to join you for dinner. And as for women and their influence, I have recently learned that they can exert it so subtly that a man does not even know it is happening."

Laclere's blue eyes pierced him. "If you take the step that I think you are contemplating, there will be no protecting you. Wellington will see that you spend your career in Parliament on the back benches."

"I know that."

"We will talk of it after dinner. Now come and eat. I warn you that Bianca insists that the children dine with us when there are no guests, and you were not expected. You have a good hand with animals, though. Perhaps you can get them to behave."

The next afternoon Adrian gave the speech of his life, supporting moderate reform. Since he was Wellington's protégé, and since everyone knew that his stand was on principle and would not affect the outcome, it caused a stir. The newspaper scribes did not miss a word.

While he spoke, his gaze swept the gallery. It stopped on a broad pink bonnet plumed with blue feathers. Its owner's green eyes never left him while she listened intently.

When he finished, the third son of the Earl of Dincaster moved his seat to join the dissenting members of his party, treading a short path that effectively ended his political significance.

It might have been a lonely path as well, but nine of Everdon's other M.P.'s rose and joined him.

After the session adjourned that afternoon, he went looking for Sophia Raughley.

chapter 24

As Adrian rode his gelding along the river, another horse fell into pace beside him.

Gerald Stidolph smiled over with malicious glee. "A remarkable performance, Burchard. Like a soliloquy in a Greek tragedy."

"And here I thought it was the most English speech that I have ever given."

"Douglas told me what transpired yesterday with the duchess. You made a mess of it, didn't you? Wellington would have had your head. Did you decide to fall on your sword instead?"

"The Commons is not debating whether to raise a tariff by three pennies, Stidolph. I decided to do the right thing. I do not expect you to understand that."

"What I understand is that I will not have to waste my time breaking you as I intended. You have done it for me. I overestimated you."

"Your estimation of me has always been irrelevant.

However, your opinion of Sophia is also off the mark. That is why you will fail."

"Do not force me to finish the job that you started today. Fifty well-placed pounds and your borough will vote you out. Fifty well-placed words about your true blood and no decent house will receive you. Without the protection of Dincaster or the patronage of Wellington, you are nobody but a half-breed bastard with no family and no fortune. Have anything more to do with Sophia and I will reduce you to the nonentity that you were born to be." Gerald turned his horse and trotted off.

Adrian rode on to Everdon House where Charles grimaced his regrets that the duchess was not at home.

"Is she truly not here, or is she refusing to receive me?"

"Not here, sir. She has gone to the shops. It is not uncommon for her to do that when she is out of sorts, as you know. She went to the other house and got the artists to accompany her, I believe. They have been living there since we returned here."

Adrian already knew that. The Ensemble was making free with the love nest. One more decision by the Duchess of Everdon that he didn't much like.

Charles assumed a doleful expression. "She took the grand coach. She had that look in her eyes, sir. I think that this may be a very expensive afternoon."

"Then I should stop her before she has to mortgage the estate. It will be easier if I walk. Have my horse dealt with."

It wasn't hard to find her. Everdon's coach stood on Regent Street, already bursting with packages. Adrian imagined the bonnets and gloves and jewelry they contained. The visit to Marleigh had not changed everything.

Sophia still buried her strongest emotions beneath a mountain of extravagance.

He discovered her in a tailor's shop, poring over fashion plates with Attila and Jacques. A blond English head bent with the two dark foreign ones. Hawkins had joined the Ensemble.

"These three waistcoats, I think. With gold buttons."

"You are too generous, *chéri*. Brass would be fine."

"They will look poor with the design. No, gold it must be."

The tailor nodded with professional agreement. "The lady is right. Only gold will do. And for the frock coats that you have ordered, as well. Now, gentlemen, may I show you some plates for riding coats?"

Adrian strolled up behind them and peered down at the fan of plates that displayed the Ensemble's expanding wardrobes.

Hawkins saw him first. The pup looked guilty as hell at being caught accepting a woman's support. As he should.

"Dressing up your dolls, Duchess?"

They all turned at his voice. Attila looked wounded and Jacques insulted. Sophia pursed her lips.

The artists prudently decided to go inspect the other designs.

Adrian sat beside Sophia.

She returned her attention to the plates. "I did not think that you would come. You did not say that you would."

"I expect that I will always come if you ask me to."

She flipped through the colored engravings, and stopped at one. "I can picture you in this, but you would never let me give it to you. You have never taken anything from me."

"That is not true. I took the most precious things that you had to give. I will always be grateful for your gifts. At least as much as Hawkins will be. What is he doing here?"

"He stays with a sister while in London. She has three children and he can never find the quiet he needs for his poetry. He has moved in for now with Attila and Jacques at the small house."

"Those sonnets needed more than silence to improve them. So you are giving him a home and today you are buying him new coats."

"I could hardly leave him out when I stopped by for the others."

"Does he understand how this works? That you purchase only friendship with these favors?"

"I can see that your mood is not much improved from yesterday."

"It was until five minutes ago."

She sighed heavily and threw the plates down. "I want to leave. This doesn't amuse me the way it used to."

"How unfortunate for our blond friend. To only catch the tail end of your fascination with collecting young men."

"Now you are getting insulting. Are you going to take me away from here or not?"

He went to the artists and informed them that the duchess was leaving. He collected Sophia and escorted her to the coach. He had to restack some packages, to make room for them both.

"Do not look like that and do not scold. I can afford it. I was astounded to learn how wealthy I am."

"I would never think of scolding. Since coming to London you have provided employment for countless seamstresses and milliners. The economy of England has grown dependent upon you. I trust that you ordered a dozen new gowns today, as well?"

Her eyes narrowed on the tower of luxuries. "I know what you are thinking. It is cowardly. Another diversion and distraction. Another means of running away."

"I thought that the reason for going to Marleigh was to put that behind you. What are you running from now?"

She regarded him with stark honesty. "You. Us. From the knowledge that you are all too aware of how pitiful those gifts were that I gave you. I am also running away from seeing the rest of it through. I am afraid."

Her bluntness stunned him. He had never expected to hear her admit that she had not given as much as he wanted.

Her regret moved him more than a declaration of love. He wanted to soothe her and say that it hadn't mattered. Except it had.

The coach still stood in front of the tailor's shop.

"Where do you want to go?"

"Take me to the park. Show me the black swan that you mentioned the day that Attila and Jacques arrived. I have heard others speak of it."

"There is no black swan. It is a tale men tell to lure women to a secluded spot."

"How secluded?"

Her gaze burned into him. The invitation surprised

him. It instantly fired the desire that he was still learning how to smother.

"Not that secluded."

"Then take me to your chambers."

"Another diversion, Sophia?"

"Yes. I want to run a little longer. Into your arms where I am beautiful and magnificent. I want to hide for a while before I learn if my life will be heaven or hell."

Memories of their lovemaking filled his mind. His blood craved to agree even though his heart knew he should not. For his own sake, if not for hers.

"Your coach will be recognized."

"You think my future consort will know about us? I do not care. In fact, if he does not, I will tell him. If I must marry some lord, he will be getting Everdon, not me. Never me." The determined line of her mouth trembled and her eyes grew moist. "Please. Before the Duchess of Everdon faces the reality that she will create for herself."

Her sadness and need touched him like it always had. He rapped the coach wall and gave directions. Then he closed the curtains and lifted her into his arms.

Her love cried for release, resenting its confinement. It screamed like a physical thing trapped in a box made of glass. Her spirit reached to free it, but the invisible panes intruded.

As she climbed in her passion, she beat against the barrier with her frenzy. The yearning became so painful that she begged for the sensual climax that would obliterate the emotional battle.

He did not give it to her. His mouth stopped its torture and he came up over her.

It was a joining drenched with emotions deep and unspoken. His embrace and movements told of his sadness and anger.

She sensed his resolve that this would be the last time. She could tell that he planned to keep her maddened and aching to the end. She tried to bare her heart so that he could brand it as he wanted to, but fire cannot penetrate glass.

He paused, leaving her tense with unbearable pleasure, one step from the highest peak that she had ever known. He rubbed his face against hers, as if he sought to inhale her essence.

"You will always be in my heart."

They were the parting words of a man who accepted the end.

He moved again. She clutched him frantically and soared with him, riding their desperate need to a moment of bliss.

For an exquisite instant she believed that there could never be loneliness again. His own beauty and magnificence saturated her. He filled all of her, all of the voids. The power of utter completeness suddenly cracked that glass, and the sweetest peace began dripping into her heart with a slow, cautious rhythm. *Trust. Believe. Give.*

She held him and listened and felt, overwhelmed by the fragile fulfillment. Was it real? Would it last after his embrace ended and she was left with herself? The glass had not totally shattered. The old hurts might yet repair the barrier.

He rolled off and gathered her into his arms. She rested

her cheek and hand on his chest and listened to his heart-beat, happier and more afraid than she had ever been in her life.

"Thank you for coming to the Commons today," he said.

"I could not stay away, especially after disrupting your life."

"Maybe I should thank you for that too."

"Why did you do it?"

"I realized how much I have permitted my birth to dictate who I am. I have always felt the need to be more English than most, in order to make up for the half of me that is not English at all. It molded me as surely as Everdon molded you. Maybe I thought that if I allied myself with England's great hero and supported the old traditions, no one would notice that I do not fit in."

"Does England's great hero know?"

"I met with him this morning. He does not like it, but he understands. He did not insult me by spelling out the cost, but of course that relationship cannot continue now. I find that I do not mind very much. I had renounced my independence in making my way more than I had real-ized. I despised Harvey Douglas, but I was no better. Worse, since I began being a player and not just a pawn."

"You said once that compromise is essential in govern-ment. Couldn't you have justified one more?"

"There are times when compromise is dishonorable. Every man knows when those moments arrive."

"What will you do now?"

"Maybe I will agree to manage one of those archeolog-ical expeditions. Some time away might be good."

A long time. Far away. From her.

"I made a mess of it, didn't I? I wanted you to be free to do what you thought best."

"Which is exactly what happened. You did not make a mess of it at all."

She nestled closer. The matching pulses of their hearts beat out the passing of their final hour together. The expectation of parting soaked their intimacy with heart-rending tenderness.

For three days she had put off learning how it would be. His restraint in coming to her had undermined the confidence that she had carried back from Marleigh. But she could not wait any longer.

"Adrian, you have never spoken of marriage to me. I have wondered why."

"You know why."

"Because of your birth?"

"It is an insurmountable barrier, but actually, I never contemplated that much where you were concerned."

"Then why? Did you never even consider it?"

He shifted abruptly, flipping her onto her back and bracing above her so he could look her in the eyes. "Do not imply that it was lack of honor on my part. If you want to run for a while, I will let you. I will even hide you. But not to endure insults afterwards. What if I had spoken of it? What would you have thought?"

"That you wanted to take care of me and protect me."

"I have never needed marriage to do that."

"That you loved me and wanted to stay with me."

"Would you have found my motives so pure? Nothing less than complete selflessness can win your trust, and no man proposing to the Duchess of Everdon can claim that."

"You sound bitter. You said yesterday that you do not blame me for being who I am, but you do."

"Who you are is one thing. How it stands between us is another."

"That is because of me, isn't it? Because of my suspicions. Because of how the past strangled my ability to believe, unless the selflessness was explicit. That is what you really mean."

He swung away angrily and landed on his back beside her. "Yes, damn it. Are you satisfied now? I do not know why you have forced this. Neither of us has learned anything that we did not already know."

"Haven't we? I have learned that you did consider proposing. You should not have assumed that I would know that you wanted me in that way. I am not nearly that self-confident. When you did not come to see me when I returned, I began imagining that I had misunderstood everything. We women have a tendency to do that at the slightest provocation."

"You may have imagined it, but I refuse to accept that you believed it. This has hardly been a casual affair, Sophia."

"It was enough to make me hesitate, and wonder, and worry about how you would react to the vote and the nominations and to the rest of it."

"Ah, yes, the rest of it. You wanted to tell me about that. If it refers to your plans to marry and execute your duties to Everdon, I must warn you that I will react badly. It would be best not to ruin our time together by speaking of it."

Our time. Our last time.

"I'm afraid that I must risk it. I want to tell you."

He exhaled with the exasperation of a man cornered by a woman who did not have the sense to sidestep a painful topic. It was not a very promising sound. She lay beside him, looking at the ceiling, frightfully aware that this was not how she had imagined it at all.

His arm rested beside hers. She sought his hand and entwined her fingers through his.

"I want you to work out the rest of it with me, Adrian. I want you to help me to see it all through."

"If you expect me to advise you on your marriage, you ask too much. Speak with Dot. She probably knows more about the suitable prospects than I do."

"I do not want your advice. I have decided on my own. I already know who I want it to be. All I need is for you to agree it was the right choice."

He turned so that he could see her. "What are you saying?"

She took a deep breath, and prayed that he wasn't completely selfless after all.

"Will you marry me, Adrian?"

She suffered the long minutes of silence, not daring to look at him. She could tell that he was surprised.

He cupped her chin and turned her head so that she could not avoid his gaze.

"Taking in another stray, Duchess?"

"That isn't fair. I decided this long before today. I knew I would ask even before I went to Marleigh. It is why I wanted to settle things with the past. If you had come that first night, I had planned to ask you then.

Although I am proud of your stand today, this has nothing to do with it."

"Then why? Are you so intent on destroying Everdon that you seek to pollute its bloodline?"

"You credit me with cruel motives. That was a harsh thing to say."

"No more harsh than what you will hear from others."

"I don't care what is said."

"You will. A marriage to me will be the scandal of the year. I know that your motives are not cruel, but I wonder what they are, nonetheless."

"I can trust you to take care of Marleigh and the other estates. To manage them well."

"A good employee can do that."

"I would have more confidence in you."

"Then hire me. At the moment I might accept, with my future being ambiguous."

"It isn't just that. I want my children to have a good father."

"There is no evidence that I will be one. I have no experience with children, or even with good fathers."

"You will be a wonderful father. There is the rest of it too. The seat in the House of Lords, for example. I know that you will use Everdon's place there well."

"Where I will speak in your name?"

"In Everdon's. We will discuss matters, but I would not expect to dictate to you. I would know better than to try."

She had not only been giving her reasons, but also enumerating the benefits and power. She could tell that he was waiting for more. She suddenly wished that he had compromised his political principles. It might have made him less obliged to adhere to others.

"I do not want to marry anyone else. You are my best friend, Adrian. In a way, my only friend."

"You have other friends. Attila and Jacques are true to you, and would be so even if the largesse ended today. However, you have created a habit of buying affection, Sophia, and I find myself stuck with the notion that you will now buy mine."

"I cannot help that Everdon comes with me."

"No, but you can help that duty to Everdon motivates this proposal. And I can wish that it did not."

Frustration made her eyes blur. "What more do you want from me, Adrian? I am offering you everything that I have."

"That is not true, damn it."

He was going to refuse her. The realization flooded her with desolation. She pictured the dry, formal, dead life she would be forced to lead. The thought of marrying some carefully chosen, appropriate man left her nauseous.

She closed her eyes to hold in the tears, but they dripped down her temples. She wished that she were half as impetuous and emotional as Alistair had always accused.

The cracks in the glass were still there. The perfect emotion dripped in, continuing its rhythm. How long before the trickle filled her and turned the love that she felt for Adrian into something free and peaceful and un-questioning?

Too long.

She wished that she could lie.

She wished that he did not know her so well that he could tell if she did.

She turned and embraced him desperately. "Listen to me. Please listen and believe me. It is not duty to Everdon that makes me ask this. It is not. It is keeping you with me. It is holding you like this, and being magnificent and not knowing the loneliness again. It is being loved, and loving as much as I am able, more than I ever thought I could. It is about tasting heaven and not wanting to find places to hide in hell."

His arm encircled her and pulled her closer, along his whole body. He kissed the tears on her temple, and then her mouth.

She ached for that complete intimacy again. She caressed him and deepened the kiss, urging his arousal while her heart cried with longing.

"I have never had much defense against your sadness, Sophia. But I need some time to think about this. I have to consider what you are offering, and whether we can be happy together."

His passion showed her again what that could mean, and why she dared not lose him.

chapter 25

The next morning Adrian met Colin at an auction called to sell the horses of a profligate lord whose gambling debts had gotten out of hand. He found his brother near a corral on a Kent estate, examining a tall chestnut gelding with handsome lines.

"There you are, Adrian. Hope I didn't drag you away too soon. I would have come in last evening instead of leaving the note, but I saw her carriage around the corner."

Adrian did not need Colin to remind him that it had been an indiscreet night. And an infuriating one.

He did not know why he was reacting to her proposal like this. Only a fool would hesitate. If a duchess in her own right was foolish enough, brave enough, to marry a man with his shadowed history and lack of fortune, that man would have to be an idiot not to agree.

Instead he kept viewing the proposal with caution. He did not doubt her affection, and his heart welcomed the chance to stay with her and take care of her. A simmering annoyance, however, would not permit much happiness with the other opportunities that she had offered him.

He could not shake the notion that this marriage would make him a more intimate and expensive version of Attila or Hawkins, and that she would actually be more comfortable with their relationship if it did. The power and wealth that she gave him would tip them back to her old way of managing men and interpreting their interest. The small, impossible distance still separating them might never be breached, and he would resent that gap every day of his life.

Perhaps he would view it differently in a few days. Right now, still heady with the liberation embraced in the Commons, he did not fancy looking in the mirror ever again and seeing an owned man.

"Your message made it very clear that we should meet here, Colin. Was there a reason for that besides your desire to bid on that gelding?"

Colin patted the chestnut's rump and then motioned Adrian aside. "Unfortunately, yes. I did not want you going to Dincaster House."

"I take it the earl is displeased with my speech."

"Displeased does not begin to cover his humor yesterday. He has given orders that you are not to be admitted. Ranted about your traitorous face never darkening his threshold again. He cursed himself for not having repudiated you at birth, and declared that he was disowning you."

"He essentially did that long ago."

"Dot is sick about it, and plans to work on him once things calm down."

"I will arrange to see Dot and reassure her that this is not the catastrophe it seems."

"He has ordered her to plan a ball as soon as possible. One to which you will pointedly not be invited. His way of declaring things to society at large."

"I have lived on the edge of society for so long that falling out will be a very small drop."

They began walking toward the auction circle. "If it means anything, I was very proud of you yesterday. I was out of town, but got back in time to hear you. I was in the gallery, but I doubt you noticed anyone but her."

"I noticed. Thank you."

"A damn fine speech. Everyone knew what it cost you. Even the conservatives were moved. When those other men rose and joined you...well, you will long be remembered for it."

How long? A year? Five? What was the name again of that promising young man who threw away his future on a matter of principle?

"I did not just rouse you to warn about the earl, Adrian. I've some news."

"What news?"

"I have found him. Captain Brutus."

The chestnut gelding was led into the auction circle just then, so Adrian had to wait impatiently until Colin finished bidding.

"I am feeling smug about how brilliant I have been," Colin explained while they walked to a tent to settle the bill of exchange. "I remembered how you said the duchess had described him as educated, so I took a chance and went to the universities. I found a don at Cambridge who remembered a student from about that time, blond-haired and radical, average build. Guess what his name was?"

"John Brutus."

"Damn, how did you know?"

"I have wondered if it could have been his real name."

"John Brutus Marsham, to be complete. Son of a clergyman from York. I rode to York and looked up the father and there he was, in the sitting room, as if he had been expecting me."

"The father?"

"Aren't you listening? Captain Brutus himself was there. I said that I found him."

"Did you warn him off? Tell him for me that it is worth his life to stay away from Sophia?"

"Well, that is where it starts getting confusing. Let me pay up and I will explain."

Adrian cooled his heels while Colin settled the bill and arranged for the gelding's move to Dincaster's stables. A quarter of an hour later they headed for their horses.

"He has been back in England almost a year," Colin said. "Came back a changed man."

"To be sure. Instead of burning threshing machines, he moved on to burning homes and threatening women. The hard life turned him into a hard man."

"It seems the opposite occurred. He studied for the Church at Cambridge and rediscovered the spiritual life while indentured. He has rejected all forms of violence. Still radical, but supports peaceful persuasion now."

"When confronted with the evidence against him, I do not doubt the scoundrel would claim that."

They stopped at the horses. Colin shrugged and ran his fingers through his blond hair. "I believed him."

Adrian had been indulging in a fantasy of beating Captain Brutus bloody. Colin's statement cut it short.

"I do not question your ability to judge a man, but events indicate he lied to you."

"Perhaps. It is not only my judgment, however. He swears he hasn't left York since he returned ten months ago, and his family supports him. He was troubled to learn that his name has been used on those broadsides, and that someone has threatened the duchess. If he is a liar, so is his father, and they both lie very well."

Adrian absorbed the implications. If Colin's impressions were correct, it cast a new light on what had been happening to Sophia the last few months.

"If not John Brutus, then someone else sent those letters and lit that fire, Colin."

His gaze met Colin's in a mutual acknowledgment of who that someone might be.

But it made no sense.

Of course it didn't.

His mind laid it out, and it all fit together like a cobblestone path winding into a dark maze. That path led to dangerous conclusions and sickening suspicions.

His blood chilled. If he was right about half of it, they were dealing with a monster.

He didn't have a dot of proof. Unless . . .

He swung up on his horse. "I have been blind, Colin. You have my heartfelt gratitude for discovering the truth."

"If you are going where I think, let me come with you."

If his ugliest suspicion was true, he would not want

Colin learning of it. Or anyone else. "Better if you are not involved."

"Damn it, if he is cornered he could be dangerous. Rats usually are. He almost killed you once. At least tell him that I know, too, so he doesn't think that removing you will solve it for him."

"I will not confront him until I have enough proof that nothing will solve it for him."

He turned his horse and went looking for the only person who might provide that proof.

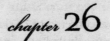

chapter 26

Attila's head flew back in a passionate swoon while his fingers evoked a flamboyant melody from the pianoforte. Jacques, who had provided the lyrics to the new song, watched anxiously while their collaboration unfolded in front of its first audience. The Viscountess Laclere warbled the love poem that the Ensemble had set to music.

The third verse veered into the rose metaphor. The viscountess blinked at the words on the sheet that she held, but did not miss a note.

Sophia reddened. Oh, dear. And at her first dinner party too. She should have demanded a rehearsal before she allowed Attila and Jacques to plan the entertainment. She had not realized that it was *that* poem.

The twenty guests listened attentively. Few reacted in a way to indicate they understood the symbolism. She glanced to her left. Three chairs away, Gerald Stidolph's tight lips barely held in his disapproval. His shock made her feel much better.

The song went on and on. The form and sensuality of the rose was described in amazing detail. The lovers in the song grew rapturous with their memories.

A few guests shifted uncomfortably. Several coughed.

Jacques beamed. Attila let the music transport him to a higher plane of existence. The viscountess persevered.

They got to the nectar-licking part.

The professional stance of the viscountess cracked. She shot a glance to the man sitting on Sophia's right and bit back a conspiratorial smile that only an idiot would not understand. Dozens of eyes followed her sensual acknowledgment. The Viscount Laclere, who had been maintaining an expression of cool passivity, closed his eyes and sighed at his wife's indiscretion.

"My apologies," Sophia whispered. "When I cajoled her to perform, I had no idea."

"It is an ancient metaphor with a long pedigree. There is a famous English medieval romance on the same topic. Should I tell Monsieur Delaroche that he digs well-tilled ground?"

"Maybe you shouldn't. He may decide to make his longer and more creative, as a form of competition."

"Heaven forbid."

The song finally ended. The guests could not get up fast enough. Conversations were initiated with determination. As Sophia strolled past Jacques, she heard two ladies inviting him to visit and advise them on their gardens' poor blooms.

Sophia thanked the performers. Laclere smiled at his wife in a way that suggested a loving scold was waiting for a private moment.

Hawkins joined them, breathless at the marvel he had just witnessed.

"A rose. Who would think a poet could get such a long and magnificent poem out about two lovers admiring a single flower? I am undone and humbled. An interesting problem, though. An inspiration. As an exercise, I may try it myself." He narrowed his eyes, an artist awaiting his muse. "Bluebells. Yes, I think so. There is a lot of soul in bluebells. At least forty lines worth, don't you agree?"

Laclere crooked his finger. "Come with me, Hawkins. All magnificent poems deserve serious analysis. Let us leave the ladies while we consider this one."

Sophia did her duty to her guests, but her heart was not in it. This dinner had been planned for a reason. Last night she had asked Adrian to attend and stay by her side. None of these peers and their ladies would have missed the significance of that.

When he had said that he needed to consider her offer, she had hoped that he would do so quickly. Right up to the moment when she had led the way down to the dining room this evening, she had prayed he would arrive. Evidently it took Adrian Burchard longer than one day to make up his mind.

Or not long at all. Maybe his absence announced his decision.

That possibility had been creeping into her mind all evening, making her listless. The party had become a chore.

Gerald Stidolph appeared at her side.

"You sent a letter that you wanted to speak with me," he said.

"Yes, I do. It is of some importance."

"Among all these people? I expect that it requires more privacy."

"It certainly does. Will you come with me to the study, where we can find some?"

"I would be delighted to, my dear."

She led him to the study. She had intended to inform him tonight about marrying Adrian. Doing so would have made this easier, and much more satisfying. *I have chosen the man whom I want, Gerald, and it is not you.* Now she was left with only half that declaration, and she doubted he would hear the same finality.

She sat behind the desk, in her father's chair. That left Gerald across from her, like a petitioner. She enjoyed that more than she ought.

"I visited Marleigh last week."

"So I was told when I called on you."

"It was a good visit. I had been avoiding Marleigh and what it meant. I am more at peace with it now."

"It is understandable that you avoided it. It is a heavy burden for a woman. As were those memories, and the duties required by them."

"You do not understand, but then you never did. I did not resist it because I am a woman. We are not nearly as stupid and helpless as men think. I am not nearly as use-less and frivolous as *you* think."

"I do not think—"

"It does not matter, Gerald. I went. I accept the title. All that it is and all that it means."

He smiled broadly. "I never doubted that you would, Sophia. Your dramatic decision about the M.P.'s showed the world that you do. An eloquent gesture, but perhaps an extravagant one. We will wait a year or two before reestablishing Everdon's power in those boroughs. Everyone will understand that with proper council you reconsidered."

"By proper council, you mean yourself."

"Of course, my dear. It has always been my only goal to help you."

He appeared very contented. Very pleased about the power that he assumed would now fall into his hands.

She remembered his expression that day after the fire, while he beat her heart with the cane of her guilt.

"It will not be you, Gerald. I accept all that it means, but I do not accept you. I will marry. I will give Everdon its next duke. But not with you."

A happy man one moment. A furious man the next.

"It is because of that interfering bastard, isn't it? He stole the affection that should have been mine."

"He stole nothing. He kindly accepted what little I gave him. He offered me comfort, while you only offered pain."

"I warned him. I'll destroy him, and if you have anything more to do with him, I will destroy you too. If you think for one moment that anyone will accept a marriage between you and that half-breed—"

"I did not say I was marrying Adrian. I merely said that I am not marrying you."

"I'll be damned before I accept this."

"Then be damned." She withdrew a folded paper from the desk and threw it across at him. "I only fulfill my father's wishes, as you always lectured me to do."

He scanned the letter that the late duke had written to him. "You read his private correspondence?"

"I read everything."

He gave her a blank stare. "Then you know all of it. That is why you repudiate me."

She understood neither his expression nor his words. He appeared defeated suddenly, like a man who knew he had lost. The depth of his vacancy made her uncomfortable.

"She does not know any of it. She repudiates you because she has always sensed what is inside you."

Sophia turned with a jolt. Adrian stood at the door. Absorbed in her confrontation with Gerald, she had not heard him enter.

"The game is over, Stidolph. Or should I address you as Captain Brutus?"

Gerald slowly turned to him.

"Captain Brutus?" she asked, completely perplexed.

"We found the real one, Sophia. Up in York. He never wrote those letters. It was Stidolph, counting on fear pushing you into his arms. He knew the route we would take to the boroughs, and went ahead, stirring up trouble. He was in the house when that fire started, too, ready to rescue you before it was too late. It would have been a dramatic, romantic gesture, if he hadn't turned coward."

"He is speaking nonsense."

"I am speaking the truth and she knows it. Look in her eyes and see who she really is. Not a woman easily duped. You always underestimated her."

"He is lying, to turn you against me. He wants you for himself."

"That is true. For herself. Not for Everdon. Not like you."

Adrian walked over and removed the letter from

Gerald's lax fingers and read it. "This explains much. After all your patience, I wondered why you killed him. Alistair could not foresee that in sending this he had signed his own death warrant."

The accusation stunned her. She turned in shock to Gerald. "Is it true? Did you kill him? Just because he no longer wanted you to have me?"

He did not flinch. He did not move or look at her. He watched Adrian with a soulless, empty face, like a man made of stone.

"Your admission of that is not necessary," Adrian said. "But she does need to hear about Brandon. She has a right to it, after carrying that burden all these years."

Her brother's name had her grasping the desk's edge. Something was happening here that she did not understand. The air in the study had grown cold and heavy and stale, like that in a tomb. The sensation sent chills through her.

Adrian regarded Gerald with a determined expression. Gerald reacted impassively, but deep in his eyes the coldest lights sparked and suggested the mind still worked, cunningly.

The horrible atmosphere came from him.

"What about Brandon?" she asked, barely getting the words out.

Adrian waited. Gerald watched him. He watched so hard that she wondered if he had heard her question.

"You did not kill your brother, Sophia," Adrian said. "Not even accidentally. He was pulling you to shore when Stidolph arrived in a boat to help. He saw his chance and took it. An oar to the head. A wound that looked later like the rocks had made it."

Shock paralyzed her for one eternal, terrible, cold minute.

Then hot outrage flared.

She went over to Gerald and stood where he could not ignore her. She wanted to bloody his cold face. Scratch out his eyes with her bare hands. All of those years and all of that guilt. Dear, kind Brandon...

Frustration and fury blinded her. "It is true, isn't it? My God, what are you? *Why?*"

He looked past her, through her, to where Adrian stood. He cocked one eyebrow.

"He already had your father's favor," Adrian said. "With Brandon gone, he could hope to get the power of Everdon through you."

"You would go to such lengths? You would kill for it?"

"I deserved it."

"Deserved it! Because you flattered Alistair? Brandon is the one who deserved Everdon. You killed him, and then my father, too, when you saw the plan going awry? You let my father believe it was my fault, and you let me live with that guilt. You even used Brandon's death against me. You are a madman!"

The stone of his face creased into a confident sneer. "Burchard's work as a clerk in foreign countries leads him to see intrigue everywhere. He is wrong. He has no proof."

"I have proof. Not for the duke, but for Brandon. You were not the only one watching while he saved his sister. Another saw you row out and take Sophia into the boat. Saw the oar go down. Sophia said the steward helped bring her around on the shore. You bought him off with money and a seat in the Commons, but he was an accomplice through his silence and does not want to swing with you. Harvey Douglas has told me everything."

Gerald shrugged. "It is his word against mine."

His reaction unhinged her. No remorse or guilt. No fear. He wasn't even flustered.

She flew at him.

With a smooth movement he rose, caught her clawing hands, and thrust her away. She landed in Adrian's arms.

He embraced her tightly and glared at Gerald. "His word will be enough. He has no reason to lie, and it will cost him dearly. He will be believed. You will not be the first criminal who thought he could outsmart justice, only to find the gallows' trapdoor open beneath him."

Gerald strolled around the desk. "You expect a trial? I think not. After all, if I find myself in the dock and things are going badly, I may be compelled to explain everything."

Adrian's arms tightened protectively. The two men eyed each other. A terrible tension arched between them, as if their locked gazes exchanged silent threats.

Adrian's hold relaxed. He set her away. "Go back to your guests, Sophia. I need to speak with Stidolph alone."

"I will not. They were my brother and my father. I have a right to hear everything."

"Trust me on this. You must go now."

"I will not be dismissed."

"*Go.*"

She stood her ground. Adrian tore his gaze from Gerald and pulled her across the room. Forcing her out of the chamber, he closed the door behind her.

Her mind red with indignation, she grabbed the latch to reenter.

It would not budge. He had locked her out.

Gerald sprawled in the chair behind the desk. Comfortable in Alistair's place. Smug. He surveyed the room with a possessive expression. Finally his gaze came to rest on Adrian.

"You don't want her to hear it. That means that you know."

"I suspected."

"If you deduced that part, you are very good."

"She commented frequently that you reminded her of Alistair. Then there was the way that he favored you. As you get older, the resemblance is there. It also gives those murders a clearer motive."

Stidolph ran his hand over the polished desk, looking more like Alistair by the minute. "Of course *you* would suspect quicker than most. It is a story you know well, isn't it? So here we are. Two men cut from similar cloth. Except, of course, that I am all English wool, and you are half-primitive weave. Two men fathered by men other than their mothers' husbands."

"Everdon knew?"

"Of course he knew. When my mother's first husband died, he threw his brother at her because of me. He knew how to take care of his blood, even if I was sired on the wrong side of another man's blanket. He saw to my education and bought me my commission. He saw himself in me, more than in his legitimate children."

Adrian fought his profound disgust. It was too much

to have hoped that Stidolph would lie, and have the decency to leave these secrets where they belonged.

"Whose idea was it? For you to marry your own half sister?"

"I think we both considered it separately. I certainly did. Otherwise, why do away with her brother? I sensed the duke would not be averse."

"So it was your plan. Your idea."

"It repulses you to think that our father suggested it? Sorry, but that is how it happened. He broached the subject after Brandon's death. He wanted Everdon to go to his son, and I was the one left. I would not get the title, but I would hold the power."

It did repulse him. It would sicken anyone. If Sophia ever learned that her father had planned this, if she ever suspected that Alistair had tried to force her into an incestuous marriage, it would be the final, horrible betrayal by a man who had given her little else. The wound might never heal.

"But he reconsidered. He remarried." Adrian tried to keep the hope for reassurance out of his voice.

"Ah, yes. Dear Celine. I reconsidered too. When no child came, I even tried to help out. If she had borne my son, I might have been satisfied. The title should have been mine. I was his blood. But if it went to my son . . . it might have been enough. But the bitch was barren. Wouldn't you know it. A sign, it seemed to me. Alistair thought so too. He revived the old plan. For a while."

"Then he reconsidered again, so you killed him."

"If you want to preserve your memory of him by thinking so, go ahead. It was not that way. He concluded that she could not be convinced, and that he was losing time.

He decided to accept another match so that he could at least secure the succession before he died. Stupid man. To think I would settle for nothing after having it all within my grasp. He never would have stood down. He should have known I would not either."

So there it was. All of it, including the most insidious part. If the world found out what Alistair had tried to do, it would be a smear on Everdon for generations. It would also destroy Sophia's fragile truce with the past.

"You should not have told her. About Brandon," Gerald said.

"She deserved to know."

"Now I have only one card left. I will tell her all of it, and threaten to let the world know what her father intended if she does not marry me. I don't fancy marrying her if she knows. Her awareness that I am her brother will make it very sordid. Still, you have left me no choice."

"Do you think that she will submit to such heinous blackmail? Accept incest in order to protect her father's name from the accusation of plotting incest?"

"Not to protect her father's name. I doubt she would do it for that. But to protect the prestige of Everdon, maybe. What do you think?"

"That she would let you do your worst. Play that card, breathe one word of this to her, and I will make you wish you had never been born. Do not doubt that."

"If I am tried for murder, I will have nothing to lose. If I find myself in the dock, I will speak of it. Don't *you* doubt *that*."

So there it was. The real blackmail. Not of Sophia, but of him.

She would never agree to keeping silent about Brandon,

especially if she did not know the reason. And her not knowing *was* the reason.

"It disgusts me to see you escape justice, but you have given her enough pain for one life. You have twenty-four hours to get out of Britain, Stidolph. I only make this concession for Sophia's sake."

"I have no intention of leaving. There is nothing for me on the Continent."

"Then flee to hell, where you belong. You have one day. Or I bring Harvey Douglas to the authorities and watch you hang."

Gerald drummed his fingers on the desk thoughtfully. "Without Douglas, you have nothing. Without you, Douglas has no coercion."

"Is that a threat?"

"It is an observation."

"Douglas is hidden where you will never find him."

"You are not."

"Others know."

"Not everything. If you offer me flight, they do not know about Douglas yet. Only Sophia does."

He spoke pleasantly, merely making another observation, but the conclusion was unmistakable. *I remove you and her and I am free.* Adrian's blood chilled as it had at the auction. A monster. Or, as Colin had said, a rat. Vicious when cornered.

Only, Adrian was cornered too. Bring Douglas forth, and Sophia would learn about her father's unnatural plans for her. Find a way to get Sophia to agree to keep silent, and Stidolph would one day try to remove the dangling threat of eventual disclosure.

He would risk his own safety. If Stidolph got to him, however, Sophia would be helpless.

"I have reconsidered. If you do not flee, I will not bring you to the authorities."

"I thought that you would see reason."

"Instead, I will kill you."

Gerald's smile froze. Then he laughed. "You don't have it in you."

Adrian placed both hands on the desk. He leaned forward, forcing Gerald back, and hovered while he looked him straight in the eyes. "I have it in me. Do you want the names of past ministers who can vouch for that? It was always self-defense before, but any one of the men I've killed had more right to live than you."

Gerald's face fell. Adrian swung away and strode to the door. "One day. After that, we begin an interesting game. Who will succeed in killing the other first? I think that the half of me that is a 'primitive weave,' as you put it, will give me the advantage. You will not even hear me coming."

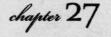

chapter 27

Sophia paced furiously in front of the study door, blinking back tears of scathing anger. Her heart filled her chest, pulsing painfully, strangling her breath.

Her scrambled thoughts veered between plans for delicious revenge and terrible pictures depicting Gerald's crimes.

She glared at the door separating her from her enemy. She raised her fists to pound on it and demand entry.

The door suddenly opened. Adrian stepped out and closed it behind him.

Her fists found a target on his chest. Her emotions poured out while she pummeled him.

"By what right do you throw me out of that chamber when what will be discussed is all about Everdon and me? You reject the marriage that would have given you that kind of authority, and then you exercise the authority anyway. I *will not* be managed, especially when it is a matter so important to my family and to *me*."

The words did not emerge with the indignation she

intended. Instead they wavered and broke and ended in a gasping sob that groaned out of her soul.

He pulled her into his arms.

He held her to his chest as he had at Staverly, keeping her together while the anger and grief engulfed her.

Slowly, within the security of his embrace, the tempest receded, leaving the profound calm that only comes after a dangerous storm.

Sounds of the pianoforte and conversation drifted and echoed. She looked to the music room.

"I cannot go back in there. I cannot spend the next hour speaking of stupid things after what I have just learned."

"You can send in word that you have taken ill."

She pressed her damp eyes against his shoulder. "I keep seeing Brandon. Over and over in my mind. All of the memories I blocked, have flooded into me all at once. It is breaking my heart. I can picture his face when Gerald came by in that boat. The relief, and then the shock. It is horribly vivid, as if I really witnessed it. I want to kill Gerald. If I had a weapon, I might have done so."

He caressed her hair with a soothing touch. A few distant footsteps intruded, then faded away. She jerked her head toward the sound.

"It was the viscountess. She will be discreet," Adrian said.

"I do not want to be discreet. I am sick to death of being discreet. Aren't you?"

"It has been a way of life for me, but, yes, sometimes I get sick to death of it too."

"Perhaps if it had been my way of life I would not find

it so stifling. I suspect that is what I will hate most about Everdon. Never having the freedom of Paris again."

"You are freer at this moment than you have been in eight long years, darling."

His words made her look inside herself. "I am, aren't I? Free of the guilt and the past. Despite the heartbreak of learning about Brandon and my father, there is a kind of peace at the center of my soul that I have never known before. Thank you for discovering the truth for me."

The study door opened and Gerald stepped out. Adrian pulled her closer and wrapped his arms around her protectively.

Gerald smirked. "Charming. Very touching." With the air of a man who has no care in the world, he ambled back to the other guests.

Sophia could not believe her eyes. "He thinks to stay. He shows no distress at all, Adrian. He expects me to play the hostess to the man who murdered my brother and father."

"Go to your chambers. I will have Charles bring an explanation in to them."

She narrowed her eyes. "I will not give Gerald that satisfaction. He has seen me weak and enjoyed making me so, for the last time. I will go back in. Gerald Stidolph will be damned before he makes me hide again." She turned her back on the waiting party so she could see only Adrian. "I would like you to stay."

"You have the strength to do it yourself. You do not need me holding you up."

"I will not let him see me weak, but I am not feeling very strong at all. He frightens me. His coldness, his own lack of fear, chills me as if I have been touched by the hand of death. I may not need you holding me up in there, but I would like to be with you later. Please stay with me tonight, even if it is for the last time."

"We seem to have a lot of last times."

"I would settle for one more, but would prefer a lifetime without any."

"Until matters are concluded with Stidolph, I cannot give you an answer about that. I promise that I will, as soon as this is finished."

"That should be soon, though, shouldn't it? You plan to take care of it tomorrow, don't you?"

"Yes. Soon. Probably tomorrow." He kissed her hand and looked into her eyes. "In truth, the man chills me too. I think that only your embrace will warm me."

Already she was warming. His touch and gaze, the lights burning deeply in his eyes, had her flushing. Anticipation of the comfort of his arms would carry her through the next few hours even more than her satisfaction in showing Gerald that he could not break her spirit.

She turned toward the music room.

Adrian released her hand. "We may both be sick of discretion, but this is not the night to abandon it. I will follow you in a few moments."

She had thought that he intended to wait in her chambers, but he was going to come in. He would be there, not holding her up, but helping her to find her own strength as he always had.

She walked down the corridor to where Gerald Stidolph waited among her guests.

She could do this. She could stare evil and death in the face, because later she would heal her heart in the arms of goodness and life.

The next night Adrian sat with Colin, St. John, and La-clere at a table in Gordon's gaming hall. Only half of his mind participated in their languid rounds of vingt-et-un.

Colin was winning, Laclere was breaking even, St. John was up a huge amount, and Adrian was down twenty pounds. Adrian decided it was a good thing he was not a superstitious man.

Normally.

"That chestnut promises to be a good runner. With some work he may be up to Ascot," Colin said, continuing the forced banter that he had employed all day while he doggedly trailed Adrian all over London. Colin did not know what had transpired in Sophia's study, but he was worried and had not let Adrian out of his sight.

"It won a race in Sussex last spring, didn't it?" Laclere asked, picking up the cue.

Gordon's was not one of Laclere's normal haunts. Adrian suspected that he had arrived tonight specifically to sit next to him. The news of Dincaster's decision to so-cially repudiate his youngest son had spread very quickly. Since Laclere was hardly a paragon of acceptability him-self, Adrian doubted that his display of support could break the fall much, but he was grateful for the effort.

Laclere may have come in friendship, but Daniel St. John had attended at Adrian's request. St. John made no attempt to enter the light conversation, and his eyes glowed with an internal distraction that echoed the ten-sion that Adrian himself felt.

St. John's glance caught Adrian's own and a silent message passed. Soon. Very soon. Stidolph must realize that there really wasn't any choice.

A ten showed faceup on the table in front of him. His hole card was a seven. Adrian debated calling for another card.

A chill shivered down his back. A shadow fell on the cards. Adrian did not turn but his companions did. St. John's body tensed in a way that announced who had arrived.

"Stidolph," Laclere acknowledged in greeting.

"Laclere. Odd finding you here."

"I am more particular about my company than my surroundings."

"It would appear that you are not very particular about your company at all."

Adrian turned in time to see Laclere's blue eyes harden into crystals. "I am most particular, which is why I must ask you to excuse us."

"That is not possible at the moment. I need to speak with your half-breed bastard friend."

The men at nearby tables heard the insult. An oasis of silence instantly formed.

Laclere shot a questioning glance at Adrian, who returned a quelling blink. Colin required more direct restraint. St. John reached for Colin's arm, to prevent him from rising.

"Insult one Burchard and you must deal with us all," Colin warned.

"The way I hear it, I do not insult a Burchard at all. The word is that Dincaster will finally make that official."

The oasis of silence spread. Their table became the

center of rapt attention. A few other gamers rose and sauntered closer.

Adrian met Stidolph's gaze with his own. "If you think to provoke me to a challenge, it will not happen. We will not do it quite that way."

"Then I must challenge you, although the evidence is that you do not have the honor to meet me."

Colin almost leapt out of his chair. St. John had to exert real strength to keep him in place.

Laclere summoned his best noble hauteur. "Unless there is good cause, there will be no excusing such a challenge, nor will any man here think badly of Burchard for refusing it."

"There is good cause, and he knows it. The best cause. The honor of a woman. The Duchess of Everdon."

"If the duchess believes that I have in any way harmed her, let her say so. It is not your place to interpret our friendship."

"Not that duchess, Burchard. The dowager duchess." Celine.

Adrian had wondered if Celine had been a player in Stidolph's plans. No doubt if she had borne Gerald's son, she would have married him after Alistair died.

She had probably even encouraged Stidolph's marriage to Sophia when she found herself barren. If Gerald got Everdon through Sophia, he would permit Celine to stay. A wife in one chamber, a mistress in another. Celine would accept that. Keeping the position that she had bought with her beauty was all that mattered.

Maybe not entirely. After all, she had agreed to have her name used now in this desperate bid to save her lover's skin.

"The dowager duchess has no argument with me," Adrian said.

"She has confided in me. She told me that you pursued her before her marriage, and continued to do so dishonorably after it. She let me know that on several occasions you importuned her, and the last time, just this summer, crossed a line that cannot be excused."

"That is absurd," Colin said. "Of all the women to claim such a thing, she is the last to be believed."

"Keep that up and I will need to issue two challenges."

"I beg you to do so. I will demand that you meet them in order of precedence. Me first."

"My brother forgets that we are no longer boys on the playing field, and that I do not need his protection."

"Will you give me satisfaction, or will the world know you for a coward as well as a bastard?"

"I will definitely give you satisfaction. I would not think of disappointing you."

The silence in the gaming hall broke as word of the duel spread like a wildfire. At their table, utter quiet reigned for a solid minute.

"I would be honored to serve as your second, Burchard," Laclere finally said.

"Thank you, but St. John will take care of it."

Laclere's eyebrows rose faintly in realization that much of this had been prearranged.

St. John assumed his role with steely calm. "I will meet with your second tomorrow, Stidolph."

"Tonight," Gerald said.

"Yes, tonight," Adrian agreed.

"Tonight, then."

Gerald strode across the room and out the door.

Dozens of astonished men watched, then directed their attention to Adrian.

He turned away, back to the cards.

"Damn the man," Colin muttered. "Whoever expected..."

"I expected."

"When you meet with his second you must seek to have the challenge withdrawn, St. John," Laclere said. "An hour or two and he will think better of it."

"I must insist that no one make any attempt to do that," Adrian said.

Laclere's brow furrowed. "May I assume, then, that this is about more than the dubious virtue of the dowager duchess."

"Yes."

"You are sure that it is necessary?"

"It is necessary, and the only way that I can see justice done."

Laclere called for a card. "I might remind you that it is illegal. Nor, after this public drama, will it be secret."

"Fifty men heard him challenge me in a way I could not ignore. No jury will convict me."

"Perhaps in France..."

"He will not agree to that either. It must be tomorrow, so it must be here."

Laclere turned his card with a troubled expression. "And if you fail in getting whatever justice you seek?"

"If I fail, there will still be justice. I am leaving a letter with Wellington, who will see to it. And if he cannot, another man will."

Laclere turned his head, suddenly very interested in the bland, calm presence of Daniel St. John.

"What weapons will you choose?" Colin asked, much subdued now. "You really are not a very good shot."

It was St. John who answered. "Sabres. Mounted."

Colin absorbed that. "At the risk of sounding like an older brother, may I point out that Stidolph was in the cavalry? He was trained by some of the finest swordsmen in England."

"A formidable man," St. John said. "Adrian, on the other hand, was trained by the greatest swordsman in Turkey."

Adrian gestured for a card.

It was a five. Twenty-two.

Hell.

She was dreaming about him one moment and awake in his presence the next. A swell of awareness gently raised her above the sea of sleep until she was alert to him.

It must have been the animals. They were silent now, as still as statues, but she could sense their eyes watching. They must have made a mild commotion when he entered, before he signaled them to behave.

She could not see him, but she knew he was in the dark corner by her bed, out of sight. His compelling aura filled the air.

"Adrian?"

"I am sorry. I did not intend to wake you."

"How did you get in?"

"This house has a garden door too."

"You have some experience with opening locked doors?" She had been wondering about those foreign missions ever since Jacques had suggested their purpose at Marleigh.

"Some."

"Will you tell me about it sometime?"

"Probably."

She turned on her side toward his voice. "Why are you here?"

"To see you. Just to look at you while you slept. To breathe the same air."

His quiet tone touched her more than his words. Something indefinable stretched and ached out of that shadow.

"Has something untoward happened?"

"No. Go back to sleep, darling."

She reached out her hand. "Come and sit with me. If you want to see me and breathe the same air, come closer."

He hesitated, then emerged from the corner. He shed his frock coat and sat beside her, his shoulders up against the board and his boots stretched atop her light coverlet.

She scooted up under his embracing arm. In the dim moonlight she imagined that she could see his serious expression, but in reality she only felt his deep, churning mood and could not see it at all.

"What is it, Adrian? Is it about Gerald? I understand that laying down information must have been difficult, no matter what his crimes."

"I will not regret Stidolph's death for one second, Sophia. I am not the sort to get sentimental about such a man. Justice will catch up with him tomorrow, and I will not regret it."

"Then what, Adrian? Your mood is troubling me. I have never seen you like this."

He nuzzled her hair. "A bad humor, is all. Too much thinking about the past and contemplating the future. Too much awareness of how fleeting life is, and how we waste it on insignificant concerns. I do not care to speak of it and infect you with my melancholy. Already it passes, as I knew it would if I came here."

That was not true. Whatever had brought him here in the night had not passed. She felt it in him like a dark, turbulent storm. He only contained it through his commanding strength of will.

It twisted her heart. This was Adrian. She had always assumed that he could snap his fingers and quell any inner turmoil as quickly as he did Yuri's rambunctious behavior.

It had been selfish and thoughtless of her to think that. He carried wounds as surely as she did. That he normally controlled whatever churned his depths and memories did not mean that those waters were placid.

Guilt pierced her. She had only learned about the parts of him that she needed to use. His strength. His passion. She had depended on him to fill her voids, but she had never thought that she might fill his. Maybe she should not blame herself too much for that, though. The Sophia Raughley that he had brought back from Paris would have laughed at the notion that she might have something such a man might want. Besides power and wealth, that is.

Well, she was not that woman any longer, thanks to Adrian. If he had come tonight just to breathe the same air, maybe she had more to offer him than she thought.

She turned and embraced him closer and let her heart reach out to his. Maybe she could hold him together a little, as he so often had done for her. Possibly she could soothe him like he comforted her.

He seemed to know what she was trying to do. He rested his cheek on her head. Invisibly, spiritually, without a word being said, he revealed his raw emotions.

They poured out of him and into her, creating a painful and poignant intimacy. Her heart both cringed from the dark onslaught and embraced it. She did not know what had provoked this in him, but she recognized the vulnerability too well. She tried to absorb it, hoping to make his burden a little lighter.

A long time passed silently. She felt him relaxing within her clinging embrace. The small sign that she was helping exhilarated her. He kissed her head gently, as if in gratitude.

A sweet, exquisite sensitivity bound them. Deep. Sacred. It suffused her with euphoria.

Easily, unexpectedly, love spread out from her heart through her whole being, and no barriers blocked its path.

It was her turn to give, and his to need. It had never been that way before. She had never known that the giving gave love its purpose and fulfillment. It obliterated the separateness and shattered the glass walls and created a world of perfect unity.

She trembled within the profound power of what she was experiencing. "I am so glad that you came," she whispered.

"I could not stay away. I knew that just being near you would make me feel alive."

Alive. Yes, that was what she felt. Totally alive, and

alert to the reality of the moment. A kind of living that had nothing to do with breathing and heartbeats.

She tilted her head and kissed his neck. With glossing touches she caressed his face, sensing his essence as surely as his skin.

Giving. She was new to it, and fascinated. She had gotten it all backwards, this thing between men and women. Love made it different. In love, the taking became giving. Without it, the giving became taking.

She moved so that she could kiss his mouth. She embraced his need, both physically and spiritually, and reveled in the opportunity to take care of him.

She unbuttoned his waistcoat, kissing his chest through his shirt as the fabric gaped open. A soulful arousal quivered through her.

"I did not come here to make love, Sophia."

She plucked at his cravat and whisked it away. "Are you going to stop me?" Her fingers went to work on his collar.

It was still in him, that dark turmoil. Binding them now because she shared it and took some of its confusion off of him.

"No."

"Just do not speak of final times tonight, Adrian. I do not want to think about that."

A peculiar emotion surged out of him, but it quickly retreated. "We will neither speak of it, nor think of it."

She got his shirt off. He remained unusually passive and did not help her much. She liked that.

"Take off your nightgown. I want to see you."

Rising on her knees, she slid it up. His warm palm caressed down to her breasts. "You are so beautiful. Like a white flower in this moonlight. Beautiful and magnificent."

Hearing the words from their first night together wrenched her heart. Even then there had been little giving on her part. She may have surrendered her virginity, but the generosity had been all his.

She splayed her fingers over his chest and traced the wonderful ridges of his muscles. "I am only beautiful and magnificent with you. Only for you."

They caressed each other slowly, as if their hands could print the forms on their memories. Their mutual pleasure became a language shared in silent conversation. Her breasts and skin were unusually sensitive to his touch. Her new depth of emotion imbued the pleasure with shared ecstasy.

She moved down to pull off his boots. His gaze on her body made her breathless. She unbuttoned and lowered the rest of his garments, caressing and kissing his hips and legs as they emerged.

Giving. It drenched her delight in his body with an amazing richness. It made the desire tether their hearts.

She bent to lick his nipples and then trail her tongue down his chest while her fingers slid to encase his phallus. His whole body flexed in response.

She laid her cheek on his hard stomach and watched her caresses and felt the tension of his passion climb. Her own rose with it, toward a determined, yearning level.

"I want to make love to you, Adrian. You have never asked it of me. Do you want me to?"

"Yes. But I want to be inside you before the end. I need to hold you to my heart this time."

She moved her kisses lower and licked. He tensed,

making her bolder. She explored more aggressively. A low affirmation escaped him.

Craving pleasure spread as his reactions absorbed her. Her own body began weeping with need. His hand warmed down her back and trailed her cleft to the spot that screamed for his touch.

They traveled a steep path of united sensuality. She kept expecting to shatter, only to pitch higher. Her consciousness blurred to everything except the release awaiting them.

Suddenly he reached for her. He flipped her on her back and bent her knees up to her breast. He lowered his head between her thighs and tortured her with intimate kisses that left her crying for him.

He rose up and came to her. The turmoil he had been carrying became a physical force. His thrusts left her gasping. She filled her arms with him, urging him to take whatever he needed.

At the end he rolled so that she straddled him. Arms wrapping her tightly, pressing her to his heart, he finally succumbed to a violent release. He brought her with him to that spot of heaven he had shown her before. Whatever drove him tonight simply disappeared in the peace of that special place.

He did not release her. Long after, he still embraced her. She grew drowsy in that contentment, and felt the relaxation that said he had fallen asleep.

Had he felt what was in her tonight? Did he know? She laid there and memorized every inch on his body against hers, focusing on the sensations bit by bit, the scent and texture and hardness of him.

"I love you, Adrian. You will always be in my heart."

His head turned slightly and he looked at her through the darkness. He was not asleep. He had heard her.

She woke to his presence again. He was standing beside the bed, looking down at her. His frock coat was slung over his shoulder, hooked on one finger.

She raised her hand and placed it flat on his chest. The first light of morning had turned his white shirt silver.

"Do you have to leave?"

"I have something that I must do this morning."

"Gerald?" She resented that seeing to Gerald's arrest would pull Adrian away before she could say what needed saying.

"Yes."

"Will you come back after?"

He kissed her hand and closed his eyes. "Of course. Now go back to sleep."

He lifted her chin and stroked her lips with his thumb, then bent and gently pressed his own to them. "I love all that you are. Hold me in your heart as you promised last night."

Turning abruptly, he strode from the chamber.

For some reason that she could not explain, that kiss shadowed her joy with a terrible foreboding.

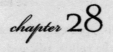

chapter 28

She carried the love inside her all morning, fascinated by its novelty. She turned it this way and that in her heart, examining all its facets with delight. It was so enchanting that she could ignore the tiny worry that still pricked at her because of the way Adrian had taken his leave.

It changed everything, unfettered love did. The sun looked golden and the air smelled pure. All of the servants smiled more. When Jenny pulled her into the wardrobe, determined to cull the old gowns to make way for the new, the onerous duty actually sounded like fun.

Her mood must have infected Jenny. The maid kept smiling, smiling. Talking, talking. Gown after gown emerged for consideration.

"Take that one for yourself," Sophia said when a lace-trimmed yellow silk faced judgment. "You always liked it."

"But it is almost new."

"Take it. It doesn't matter. None of it matters anymore."

Jenny's smile disappeared. "What an odd thing to say, my lady." She set the yellow silk aside and pulled out the next gown. "What about this?"

"That I will keep."

"To be honest, the shade of rose never suited you."

"I will keep it. It is the gown I was wearing the first time Adrian kissed me."

Jenny turned away quickly.

"Is something wrong, Jenny?"

"No, of course not." She turned back with the smile in place and became all business again.

At eleven o'clock they were surprised by the arrival of Dorothy Burchard. Bright-eyed and happy, she intruded on the dressing room unannounced.

"Forgive me, Sophia, but I was out for a walk and decided to stop for a little rest. You don't mind, do you? I told Charles to dispense with formalities. What are you doing? Wardrobe? I promise not to interfere."

She sat next to Sophia.

Was it her imagination, or did Jenny look relieved to see Dincaster's sister arrive? The two of them exchanged one quick look and then Jenny persevered.

Dot had promised not to interfere, but she did. Constantly. Questions about the French modistes who had made the gowns. Admiration of the details and fabrics. Judgments as to practicality. All the while she regaled Sophia with humorous stories about sartorial disasters witnessed at balls down through the years.

Smiling, smiling. Talking, talking.

A half hour later word came up that the Viscountess Laclere had come to call.

A peculiar silence stilled Dot's prattling for a five count. She and Jenny exchanged a quick glance.

"The viscountess? How wonderful," Dot said. "Will you receive her? Why don't we go down and call for some cocoa? The air has a cool bite to it today, and I think cocoa would be just the thing."

Dot smiled encouragingly. Jenny beamed with agreement.

Sophia recognized what was happening. They were managing her. But why? The tiny worry that she had been ignoring suddenly demanded more attention.

They found the viscountess in the drawing room, decked out in a sapphire riding habit. She approached Sophia with outstretched hands and a chagrined smile. "Do forgive me for the uncivilized hour. I was coming back from a ride in the park and thought I would stop to call and congratulate you on your dinner party. Promise that you won't tell Laclere, or he will scold his errant American wife for presuming. Dorothy, what a happy coincidence to find you here. I had a brilliant idea about creating a ministry to support the arts that I planned to confide in the duchess, but your wisdom regarding the matter will be welcome."

"It sounds fascinating. You must tell us all about it over some cocoa," Dot said.

"Cocoa would be wonderful. The morning holds more chill than it appears. I fear that the last of summer is gone."

The cocoa came. They sipped it while the viscountess described an outrageous plan to petition to establish an entire government ministry dedicated to supporting young artists. The scope of the patronage grew while she talked.

As if she was making it up as she went.

Dot asked lots of questions. Sophia watched the spirited exchange. Too spirited. Too earnest. Talking, talking. Smiling, smiling. Except the talk struck her as oddly forced, and the smiles as too determined. They chattered around her and through her, as if a pause would be disastrous.

More unexpected arrivals were announced. Jacques and Attila. Probably a coincidence. Maybe not.

Jacques appeared as smooth as always. Attila exuded an exaggerated joviality. They joined the conversation. The viscountess began explaining her idea all over again.

The relentless chatter grew unnerving. Sophia wanted to sit quietly and savor her love, not be distracted by all this talk.

Distracted. She peered at the viscountess and Dorothy. Something dark shimmered beneath their bright expressions. Jacques looked more solemn than smooth, now that she examined him. Attila's smile might have been painted below his mustache.

Charles entered and bent to her ear.

Sophia listened to him and nodded. "It appears that the Duke of Wellington has come to call," she announced. "Perhaps I will start a new fashion. Morning salons."

That cut short the relentless talk. Jacques remained blasé, but Attila shot Dorothy a worried glance. Dot's cloud of white hair ever so subtly shook a vague negative.

The duke paused at the threshold and took in the

collected visitors. "I feared that my calling so early might disturb you. I see that is not the case. Forgive my impertinence, but I was walking past and . . ."

"And the air was brisk and you thought some cocoa might be in order," Sophia said. "You are most welcome here. As you can see, this household is not rigid in its formalities."

She settled the duke down with Dorothy and the viscountess, and saw to his refreshment. A most awkward silence ensued, punctuated by small talk that only tightened the threads of tension weaving among the guests.

"Attila, I have been practicing that sonata that you gave me," Sophia said. "Come to the pianoforte so that I can show you my improvement."

Jacques did not want Attila to go off with her alone, that was evident. Neither did Dorothy. The viscountess leapt into the breach with a query to Wellington about the Battle of Waterloo. The duke grabbed the topic with gusto.

Sophia gestured for Attila nonetheless. Pasted smile wavering, Attila reluctantly joined her in the corner at the pianoforte.

"Wonderful. How you improve! Extraordinary, my lady," he said after she had tortured the first passage.

"Oh, nonsense. I am horrid, as I have always been."

"Not so. True, you miss a few notes still, and the hesitant tempo is a bit awkward, but your sympathy with the music touches my heart."

Her fingers persevered. The duke continued his stories. The viscountess wore an expression of rapt interest, but her gaze spent more time on Sophia than on Wellington.

"What is happening? Why are you all here?" Sophia demanded of Attila.

"To visit with you. Is that no longer permitted?"

"Attila, do not think me so stupid that I do not realize that this is most unusual. The Viscountess Laclere, with whom I am hardly intimate, has stopped by before noon. The Duke of Wellington is telling stories that must even bore him by now. You have agreed to listen to me play the pianoforte, when we both know that it pains you to do so. There is a shadow in this chamber, a dark shadow that everyone is trying to keep at bay with all this banter and amiability. Now, what is happening?"

He squirmed. "Nothing is happening. Jacques and I wanted to see you, that is all. We had no idea you would have other visitors. We came as friends. Is that so wrong? We did not want you to be alone."

Her gaze swept the little group. It *had* been a coincidence. They had not planned this. Each had come independently, because none of them wanted her to be alone. It was even why Wellington was here.

"Why didn't you want me to be alone, Attila?"

"Did I say that? I meant that we thought you might be lonely."

"It is something to do with Adrian, isn't it?"

She did not need to see his distraught expression to know the truth.

They did not want her to be alone in the event that bad news came.

The worry that she had been ignoring surged. The foreboding strangled her heart. She stopped playing and looked at her visitors. One by one they saw her expression. The talk drifted into silence. The careful smiles fell away.

She rose on trembling legs and rejoined the others.

She looked Wellington right in the eyes. "Where is Adrian?"

The duke's sharp expression donned a veil of sympathy.

Dorothy reached out and grasped her hand. "There was no choice. Colin assured me of that."

"Where is he?"

Wellington shook his head. "I do not know where the duel is happening. I received a letter from him this morning saying it would be done, but not where. The letter asked me to see to your protection if he did not survive. It also contained another, sealed letter, to be opened only in that event."

"A duel? He is meeting Gerald? Does everyone know except me?"

From their expressions she gathered that the whole city knew, except her. Even Jenny and the servants. It explained all those smiles this morning. That was the reason for the wardrobe duty. And for Dot's visit. And the rest. They had come to be with her in case bad news arrived, but also to make sure that she did not go out and learn what everyone else knew.

A duel. It was madness. Insanity. Gerald did not deserve the honor of it. He should be carried off in chains, not met one-on-one like a gentleman.

Adrian should have told her. Last night he should have shared it with her. Even if she would have argued to stop it. Even if she would have locked him in, to keep him from leaving. He should have told her.

Maybe he had. He had brought his fear to her, hadn't

he? He had sought to share a night of life before facing death.

Death. It could happen that way. Every person in this room recognized that possibility. Gerald would not escape justice in the end, but he might take one more person from her before he faced it.

"Who is with him?"

"His brother, St. John, and my husband," the viscountess said.

"And at least a dozen others whose names will never be known unless it is necessary," Wellington added.

"You can stop this. If the Duke of Wellington demands to know where this is occurring, someone will tell him. You can prevent it. Instead you sit here and wait to learn the result as if it is some stupid vote in Parliament."

"I sit here as if I wait to hear the result of some action on which I have sent my best soldiers. If Burchard chose this way of resolving whatever stands between him and Stidolph, he had his reasons. He would not welcome this unless he thought it necessary."

"Do you know why they are meeting?"

"Stidolph issued the challenge over the honor of the dowager duchess, but no one believes it is really about that. I think that you know the reasons better than I. I daresay that they have to do with you."

"Those reasons do not require such risky heroics. You must stop it."

"I will not. I cannot. It is already over." He reached out and patted the hand that Dot still clasped. "I suspect that you do not know the fullness of it, Duchess. God willing, he will triumph and none of us ever will. If not, I will open that other letter, and see it through for him." His chiseled face softened. "He is a brave man. I could have used him in the old days. If I had chosen your champion myself, I could not have done better."

Her champion. Fighting the battle she could not wage herself. Risking his life in a cause that had nothing to do with him.

She felt so helpless. So terrified. So grateful that he had come to her last night, and that she had finally been brave enough to let herself fully love him.

"So I must sit here and wait. I must simply endure it until word comes."

A hand touched her shoulder. She looked up into Attila's gentle face. "We will all endure it together, *kedvesem.*"

It was the worst hour of her life. A long hell of sickening anticipation. Her throat burned from swallowing back tears. Partway through, Dot entwined her arms around her so that they held each other, two women waiting to learn the fate of a man they loved.

A chill permeated the room. It had nothing to do with the brisk autumn air. Wellington called for a servant and had the fire built up in the hearth. They waited some more.

She thought that she heard a horse stop outside the house. She could not bring herself to run to the window to check. Nor could anyone else. They all froze, alert to the sound. It seemed as though everyone simply stopped breathing.

Boot steps approached. Charles opened the door and Laclere strode in.

He paused, taking in the group, surprised.

"Well?" the duke asked impatiently.

"I rode ahead. He is coming in a carriage, with his brother and St. John. He will be here shortly."

The wave of relief left her limp in Dot's arms. Her composure finally crumbled. Tears snuck down the sides of her face. "Was he hurt?"

"A gash on his thigh. Having it tended delayed us. I advised him to return home, but he insisted on coming here." He glanced pointedly around the chamber. "I do not think that he expects an assembly."

"Stidolph?" the duke asked.

Laclere said nothing, which said everything.

Wellington rose and bid his leave. He extracted a sealed letter from his coat. On his way to the door, he threw it in the fire. Jacques and Attila kissed her and departed in his wake.

"You must stay, Dot. You must see him," Sophia said.

"If you do not mind, just for a moment . . ." She wiped her eyes. "I never want to go through that again, let me tell you."

Laclere offered his hand to his wife. "Let us remove ourselves, my dear. I see that you have been riding. You rarely indulge in that pleasure when in the city. You used a sidesaddle, I trust."

"Really, Laclere. How can you be concerned about such silly little things on such a day? This has been about the great experiences. Life and death. Passions both grand and evil. Proper calling hours and proper saddles are of no account."

"In other words, no sidesaddle." He turned his attention to Sophia. "He may appear in a strange mood when he comes. It is not an easy thing, what has happened. Do not be surprised if he appears less than joyed with his victory."

"I understand. Thank you for everything that you have done for him today."

Sophia and Dot went to the library to wait for Adrian. Dot left the room as soon as the carriage sounded on the street. Whatever she said to her nephew was communicated privately in the reception hall.

Adrian entered the library slowly, carefully supporting some of his weight on a walking stick. He paused and faced her.

He wore no coats and his trousers stretched over the thick bandage that wrapped his thigh. His clothing was spotless, however. He must have traded with Colin in the carriage.

He looked at her with fiery eyes. Laclere had been right. No triumph. No joy. Just the stark awareness of what had occurred, and what might have. And deep lights of naked resolve.

Her heart ached with love and relief. She feasted her eyes on him, breathless with gratitude that he was alive.

He had never looked less English. His black eyes sizzled. His dark hair was disheveled. A thin, colorful sash belted his hips with its Eastern weave.

He carefully walked toward her. It gave him pain. A bad wound, then. He should have gone home, but she knew why he had come here instead. The reason showed in his eyes and the line of his mouth.

It had become a day for finalities. She prayed that she

could convince him that there was no need of one with her.

"Laclere told you?"

"I already knew."

"I had hoped you would not, until it was over."

"That was not fair. There are some things that you should not protect me from." She stepped the few paces that separated them, to embrace and kiss him. He winced slightly, and she felt another bandage on his shoulder. Not only his leg had been wounded. He had changed his clothes so she would not see the blood.

She gingerly rested her head on his chest and listened to the sound of his heart. He pressed a kiss to her hair.

"Won't you sit?"

He shook his head.

She lifted the end of the sash. "What is this?"

"My father gave it to me. He is still in England."

"Did he come?"

"He was there. He stayed in a closed carriage off a ways, but I recognized the coachman and went to him. He gave this to me for good fortune. It is his. He suggested that I stuff it in my shirt. I decided that its power might not work as well that way." He looked down at the band of color. "He has thirteen other sons, but he stayed in that carriage to the end and prayed that I was fated to live."

She fingered the woven patterns that he had displayed to the world. It had been a day for declarations as well as finalities.

"Why did you meet Gerald?"

"He challenged me. Fifty men will swear that it came from him. I did not provoke him."

Maybe not directly, but he had managed this. It had worked out the way he wanted it to.

She still tasted the torture of waiting to learn if he was dead. "Why, Adrian? Why risk so much? Why not just have him arrested?"

He laid his hand against her cheek. "Do you trust me? Do you trust me enough to believe me when I say that it was better to handle it this way?"

She gazed in his eyes and knew that he would not explain more than that. Not now, maybe not ever. Wellington had been right. The reasons had to do with her. Adrian had done this to protect her, and she might never know why.

"Yes, I trust you. Completely. I believe you. I believe *in* you."

She began to embrace him again, but he slowly paced away, distracted by emotions dark and deep. "I have killed before. Not like this, though. Those were like military skirmishes. Country against country. Laclere warned me that it would be different. He has stood to a man, and confided that the memory is a hard one."

She felt the rawness in him and it wrenched her heart. He might know that there had been no other choice, but he still wrestled with the deed.

"Laclere has been a good friend to you. I am glad that he was there."

He nodded absently and paced some more. "I dined with him the night before I gave my speech. His young children were there. I had never seen him with them before. He spoils them. They have a little joke that it is Bianca's American influence, but he can deny them nothing. All the discipline comes from her, not him. Seeing that domestic joy, sitting amidst that love, moved me so much that I wanted to weep." It came out in bits and phrases, as if he gave voice to random thoughts. "I would like to have that."

"I am sure that we can have it. We may not know what to do, but we certainly know what *not* to do."

He shook his head. "You will never be forgiven if you marry me. It will never be forgotten, who I am. What I am. Nor will I ever pretend otherwise again. Many will never accept that."

"I can think of a few who will never forgive me if I do *not* marry you. The people who matter."

"Do not think lightly of it, Sophia. Your title will not protect you. Half of the people who attended your dinner party will cut you as soon as a marriage to me is announced. I was tolerated as long as I stayed on the edges. I will never be accepted in the center."

"Then we will learn who our true friends are, and who the fools are. I said before that there are some things that you should not try to protect me from. This is one of them. I will not let you ruin the happiness that we might have, in the name of shielding me."

He stopped his thoughtful pacing and turned to her. His expression made her breath catch. Vividly alert. Ruthlessly focused.

"It is not about that, is it?" she said. "You know that I do not care about being cut. I spent eight years ignoring those people. Their opinions cannot wound me now, and you know it. This really has nothing to do with your birth."

"Maybe it doesn't. I suppose I never thought that mattered much with you. But I cannot bear to think of your being hurt because of me."

"Why don't we admit what it *is* about."

He evened his weight, standing tall. He might have arrived unscathed.

His gaze penetrated her. "Do you love me? Not only need me, or want me, or depend on me. I welcome all of that, but I want to know if you love me as I love you. There is nothing careful and contained in my feelings for you. It is rash and hot and saturating and perfect. Nothing else really matters. Nothing. Not Everdon and the past, not scandal and the future. Not the assumptions we will face that I use you, or that you buy me. I do not love what you are, I love who you are. That will make all the rest insignificant, but not if I only have your need and your passion."

"I love you. I have loved you a long time. It frightened me, so I kept it contained and hidden. I kept giving it other names and kept trying to turn it into something else. Perhaps I did not believe that I deserved the happiness. I have failed people whom I had loved before."

"You deserve every happiness. And if you feared it, you had cause."

"Not from you. Also, it was more than that. I did not trust myself to love well. Last night you gave me the chance to learn that I could. Now I know that I can love you very well. Better than any other woman in the world. If you will let me give to you and protect you as you have done for me. If you will bring me your burdens as you did last night, and have done again today."

His expression softened. His eyes glistened. Last

night's beautiful intimacy flowed across the ten feet of space that separated them.

She absorbed the emotions reaching her, afraid to move, lest she disturb them. She branded her memory with the sight of him. Strong despite his wounds. Mysterious in his dark, hybrid beauty. Brave and exciting.

In love with *her*. How astonishing.

"Didn't you feel it last night, Adrian? Didn't you know?"

"I felt it. I hoped. I carried that hope in me today. I came at once because I had to know that I had not misunderstood."

"You have always understood me. I do not think that you ever got it wrong. I only learned who I was by seeing my reflection in your eyes."

"The reflection of a beautiful woman, magnificent and strong. I am glad that you learned the truth of it."

His love made it true.

"I want us to fill each other's voids and end the loneliness forever, Adrian. I want us to make a happy family, where you can always sit amidst love."

His smile made the world sparkle. "If we are going to have a family, we should get married."

"Is that a proposal, Mister Burchard?"

He leaned his weight on the walking stick, and reached his free hand out to her. "We have both traveled alone for too long, darling. Will you complete the journey with me?"

Her happiness flew to him before her feet moved. She ran across the empty space and joined the man who had brought her home.

The man who valued and loved her, in her own right.

AUTHOR'S NOTE

In 1831–32, England came as close to open rebellion as it ever has since the seventeenth century. THE CHARMER uses that crisis as a backdrop to the love story of Sophia and Adrian. The conclusion of the episode may be of interest to some readers.

As Adrian anticipated, a Reform Bill passed the House of Commons in September of 1831. Although relatively moderate, it completely reapportioned the representation in the Commons according to population distribution. It gave new seats to the growing industrial regions in the north. It also abolished most "rotten boroughs," areas that had been sending representatives although they no longer had many voters. That seriously affected the lords, whose landholdings put those old, rural boroughs "in their pockets." The bill doubled the number of men eligible to vote to approximately one million (the right to vote was still contingent upon income, gender, and property).

The bill then went to the House of Lords, the very men who would see their power diminished if it became law. In October the Lords rejected it. Raucous debate in Parliament and massive demonstrations in the streets filled the next months.

In April 1832, the Lords passed a different reform bill, but they planned to severely modify the reform provisions in committee. Prime Minister Grey, a Whig, resigned his ministry. The population went wild and violence broke out. Hundreds died in rioting in several cities. King William asked Grey to return, and Grey agreed to do so only if the King agreed to a plan that Grey had concocted.

The true sentiments of the King known as "Silly Billy" are hard to pin down, but he accepted Grey's scheme. He threatened to create enough new peerages to pack the House of Lords with reform supporters.

Faced with the inevitable, in June 1832, the House of Lords passed the Reform Act that signaled the beginning of the end of aristocratic dominance in British politics.

The Duke of Wellington, who had been uncompromising in his opposition to reform, told the Tory lords who opposed the bill to either abstain or not attend. He abstained himself, a symbolic move that demonstrated his acceptance that the battle was lost.

ABOUT THE AUTHOR

Madeline Hunter has worked as a grocery clerk, office employee, art dealer, and freelance writer. She holds a Ph.D. in art history, which she currently teaches at an eastern university. She lives in Pennsylvania with her husband, her two teenage sons, a chubby, adorable mutt, and a black cat with a major attitude. She can be contacted through her web site, www.MadelineHunter.com.

Look for the two previous tales
of seduction and scandal . . .

Madeline Hunter's

THE SEDUCER

Daniel's story

and

THE SAINT

Vergil's story

On sale now

And watch for the glorious finale to
Madeline Hunter's "Seducer" series in

THE SINNER

Dante's story

in January 2004!

Read on for a preview . . .

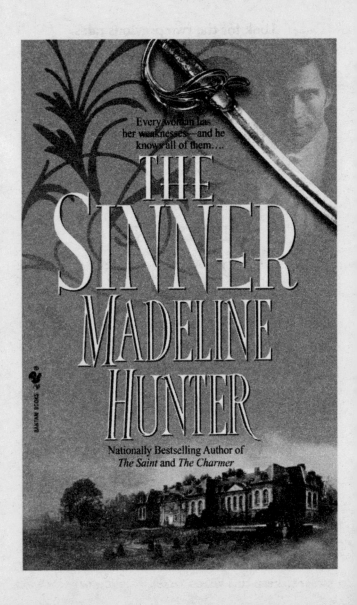

Every woman has
her weaknesses—and he
knows all of them....

THE SINNER

MADELINE HUNTER

Nationally Bestselling Author of
The Saint and *The Charmer*

THE SINNER

On sale January 2004

Utter ruin provokes soul-searching in even the least reflective of men.

Dante Duclairc was contemplating that unwelcome discovery when he heard the horse outside. He opened the cottage door to find one very annoyed physician standing in the moonlight at the threshold.

Morgan Wheeler peered severely over the top edge of his spectacles. "This had better be *very* serious, Duclairc. Your brother's land steward pulled me out of bed."

"It *is* very serious, and I am sorry that your sleep was interrupted."

"No one said you had come down to Laclere Park. Why haven't you called on me?"

"Only the steward knows I am here, so you must swear to keep this visit a secret. I should have sent for a surgeon, but you are the only medical man in the region I could trust to be discreet."

Morgan sighed heavily and stepped into the humble abode. "Why did you send for me?"

"There is a woman upstairs who needs your attention."

Morgan set down his bag and removed his frock coat. "She is alone here?"

"Except for me."

"Why does this woman require me?"

"The lady has been shot."

Morgan had been rolling up a sleeve. He stopped, arm outstretched and fingers engaged. "You have a lady visitor who has been shot?"

"Grazed, actually."

"Where was she shot? Excuse me, *grazed*?"

"In this cottage. Accidentally. We were playing a little game and—"

"I meant, where is the wound?"

"In the rear nether region of her trunk."

"Excuse me? Are you saying that you shot your lover in the buttock?"

"Yes. Come upstairs and—"

"One moment, my good friend. My dull life has feasted off the excitement of yours for years, but this is too much. You have secretly brought a woman, a *lady*, to a rustic cottage on your brother the viscount's estate, where you engaged in some orgiastic rite that resulted in her being shot in the buttock. Do I have the essential facts correct?"

"Her arm is hurt and she hit her head too."

"Not like you, Duclairc, getting rough like that. You surprise and disappoint me."

"I assure you that this was an accident. A little game gone awry."

"How? What? My imagination fails me. I try to picture it but . . . If I am going to debase myself by doing a surgeon's work, the price of my skill and silence is an explanation."

"As it happens, that is precisely what I can afford. Please come up now. The steward had some laudanum and we dosed her up so she is still out, and it would be best if you did this quickly."

"Details, Duclairc. I shall expect details."

As Dante led Wheeler up the stairs, he considered that details were exactly what his friend would never get. No one would. The woman awaiting Wheeler's attention had come to this cottage through bizarre circumstances. Dante knew in his gut that speaking of them to anyone would only cause him untimely trouble.

What had she been doing out there, dressed like a man and brandishing a pistol, on a night when the countryside was alive with a mob burning farming machines, and a posse on the chase? Dante had taken his own gun to the highest hill of Laclere Park, in a nostalgic effort to protect the estate on his last night in England. When he had been surprised by a trespasser he had returned fire, only to discover to his horror that he had not shot a radical but a woman.

As it happend, not just any woman.

Dante paused outside the bedchamber. "If you ever reveal what has occurred here, or that she was with me, she will be ruined."

"Discretion is a physician's second name. I never failed you in the past, did I?"

Wheeler became all business as soon as they passed into the chamber. He walked to the bed, took the patient's pulse, and felt her cheek. Ever so gently, he turned her head toward him.

He froze.

"Oh, my God."

"Exactly."

"Oh—my—God."

"Now you know why discretion is essential."

"It is Fleur Monley, Duclairc. *Fleur Monley*."

"So it is."

Wheeler collected his wits. Shaking his head, he proceeded to examine his patient. "*Fleur Monley*. Even I, who have seen women of highest repute faint at your smile, am thoroughly impressed. No one ever got Miss Monley to the altar let alone into bed, let alone playing games that get women shot in the buttocks. The closest was when your brother Laclere almost got engaged to her. . . ." The implications of *that* had Wheeler wide-eyed again. "He will probably kill you if he finds out."

"Another reason for discretion."

"Of course, of course. I promised silence and am bound by it, but it will be hell to honor my word. I will burst." He stripped away the bedclothes to reveal Fleur demurely dressed in one of Dante's nightshirts. "Charming, Duclairc, but why did you bother? She is drugged, I am a physician, and you are her lover."

He had bothered because he could hardly present her in those farm boy rags, and because it did not seem dignified to leave her naked despite her unconsciousness and the ribald story he was feeding Wheeler. No matter what a man's reasons for stripping off her clothes, even a scoundrel did not leave the Fleur Monleys of the world naked for someone to see.

Morgan touched her bare leg. "She is damp. Did you bathe her?"

"She felt warm, and I thought that I should." It was one more bold-faced lie. Upon removing the rags he had discovered a very dirty body and had washed off the worst of it.

"Of course. Next time, do not give laudanum if the patient has a head wound."

"It wasn't much, and we dosed her some time ago when she began to moan as she came to. I am concerned that it may wear off, so you should get busy."

Morgan was not to be rushed. He touched all around her scalp. "It does not seem too serious. Fell, did she? Went out? She will have a bad lump. She will have to rest quietly for a few days."

"Surely she can be moved."

"Best not. You will have to make some excuse if anyone is expecting her return. She should stay here at least two or three days, in bed. *Resting.* It will give this arm time to repair too. Bad sprain. I can only guess how *that* happened. Some exotic position for coitus that country boys like me never get to learn, no doubt. Hindu?"

Wheeler's grin invited explication. Dante ignored him. Fleur Monley was going to create problems. He could not keep her here for several days, because he had no intention of being here himself. In approximately ten hours he planned to meet a fishing boat on the coast that would spirit him over to France.

"Help me to turn her so I can see about this gunshot. Gently now."

Together they turned Fleur on her stomach. Morgan pulled up the nightshirt. Dante turned to leave.

"No you don't. She was only nicked but you were right, it needs to be sewn. Get over here and hold her. The laudanum made her sleep but she is not unconscious. If she wakens while I am at it, I want someone backing me up."

Dante truly did not want to stay. In his thirty-two years he had seen more women nude than he could count. He had long ago learned to release or suppress his sexual reactions at will, much like a canal lock controls water. Still, seeing Fleur like this was making him uncomfortable.

She was injured and needed care and he lied about being lovers only to protect her from the posse out there looking for blood. Having her in this bed, naked from the waist down and her face pressed in his pillow, appeared a desecration of sorts. All the same, he was annoyingly aware that stripping her and washing her and seeing her body had raised the lock's water level more than he would like.

That surprised him, because he had grown fairly jaded about such things. Furthermore, her reputation and condition made sexual reactions either ridiculous or despicable.

Then again, her very presence here indicated that the world may have gotten that business about her unblemished virtue very wrong. The woman Fleur Monley was supposed to be would never run through the countryside in boy's clothes on a night when the radical rabble were out committing crimes.

What the hell had she been doing out there? For that matter, where the hell had she come from? The last he heard, she was visiting France.

He sat beside her on the bed and carefully placed his palms on her back. Behind him Morgan prepared the needle, sloshed something over Fleur's bottom, and went to work.

She gritted her teeth and held in the tears. She wanted to scream. If she did, however, these men would know that she was awake. That would be too humiliating to bear, and possibly very dangerous.

Where was she? The bed seemed clean but she could smell earth and damp and she doubted that she had made it to Laclere Park. That man who shot her must have given her up. She was probably in a farmer's cottage, being tended before they carted her off to gaol.

Better that than Gregory, she supposed. Unless he learned about it and bribed them to get her back. In that case she would be right where she started.

The man holding her had not spoken much. She wished that he faced away. She would not have to swallow the pain so much if he were not looking at her. He was definitely doing that. She could feel his attention on her, despite his brief responses to the other's comments about horses and boxers.

A hand moved from her back to her head. She barely caught the cry of surprise that jumped to her throat. Fingertips gently brushed her hair back from the pillow and lightly stroked her head. She held her breath, cheek crushed against the down, and prayed that he had not seen her jaw clench or heard her shocked intake of breath.

That caressing hand should repel her. It implied

dangerous interest and she was horribly defenseless. Instead, she found the light touch comforting and sympathetic and not at all insinuating. Who was this man who bothered to reassure an unconscious woman?

"I don't remember her being so thin," the voice near her rump mused. A painful skewer by the needle accompanied the comment. She tasted blood as she bit down. "I can see her ribs plainly. Normally people gain weight on the Continent, not lose it. I hate to say that even so she has a nice, um, how did you so elegantly put it, rear nether region."

He spoke as if he knew her! If so, the night's risks had probably achieved nothing but more danger.

"Just sew," the man beside her muttered. "Aren't leeches supposed to be above noticing such things? Rather like artists?"

"I am a physician, a man of culture and learning, not a leech. If you think artists grow immune either, you are doubly a fool. All the same, I accept your correction. Although, coming from *you* . . ."

"I do not like my lady friends discussed by other men, that is all."

Her ears were half smothered in the pillow, but that voice sounded familiar. Why would he be claiming she was his lady friend? A dreadful possibility opened. Could this be the man she had heard speaking with Gregory last night?

"Considering how quickly you tire of your mistresses, I have always thought your reticence in talking about them a little priggish and ungenerous," the physician said. "Although it has never been the ladies who interested me but the strategies for winning and loving them. You could save yourself a lot of curious questions by writing a treatise as I suggested years ago."

"Maybe I will do that. I will have plenty of time in France, and it may pay my keep for a few years."

The rhythm of the needle stopped. "France? My good man, you are not! Has it come to that?"

"Afraid so."

"How bad?"

"Very bad. They are on my trail."

"Surely your brother—"

"I have been to that well far too often, and I will not go again. Once settled in France I will write and explain to him."

"Now I am distraught. You have ruined my humor completely."

"Well, finish up here, come downstairs, and I will tell you all, but it is such an old and tired story that I am sure you have heard it often before."

Efficient hands bound a bandage to her hip. More gentle ones slid the nightshirt down and carefully tucked bedclothes up around her shoulders.

They left. She exhaled the strain of keeping her composure and stillness. Her rump hurt badly now, even worse than when she had first woken in shock to that sewing needle. Still, the pain both existed and didn't, like something floating in part of her mind while the other parts daydreamed and slept. She did not know how long she drifted around the edges of consciousness.

She wondered if only the physician had recognized her or whether the other man had as well. He spoke in the cultured manner that said he moved in the sort of circles where she could have met him at some point over the years.

She clung to the hope that he was not anyone who had anything to do with Gregory, and certainly not the man who had spent last night bargaining for her like she was some four-hoofed animal.

A door below closed on mumbled farewells. Boot steps sounded on the stairs. Someone entered the chamber. She closed her eyes but she felt the warmth of the candle near her face.

"He is gone. Let us see if we can make you more comfortable now, Miss Monley."

She heard his voice plainly this time. Jolting up on her good arm, she twisted in shock.

And looked right into the resplendent brown eyes of the most charming wastrel in England.

The women of English society could bicker and argue with the best of them, but on one point they had always been in total agreement.

Dante Duclairc was a beautiful man.

That was the word they used. Beautiful. His luminous eyes, thick, lustrous brown hair, perfect face, and devilish smile had mesmerized any female he chose to conquer since he turned seventeen. Fleur knew three ladies who had committed adultery only once in their lives. With him.

The years had added some hardness to his countenance, but they had not dulled the heart-skipping effect that his attention provoked.

Even in her, and he wasn't even trying.

His expression bore curiosity and wry amusement. He smiled with warm familiarity, instantly bridging time back to that period ten years ago when his brother Vergil, the Viscount Laclere, had courted her. And yet underneath his cool, refined composure there shimmered a dangerous, exciting energy. With Dante it was always there.

Right now it frightened her speechless.

Somehow she knew without asking that they were alone. There was no female servant in this cottage, which meant that Dante had probably undressed her and put her in bed. What he had seen while the physician tended her had been the least of it.

"You are uncommonly brave," he said. "Wheeler never suspected that you were awake." His tone implied that he had known the exact moment when she had come to. He had caressed her head aware that she would feel him do it.

"It was my hope to avoid giving explanations to strangers."

"Since I am hardly that, you should not mind giving one to me. Let us get you comfortable first."

Her reaction the the Dante Duclaircs of the world had always been to run away, but she could not do that now. She suffered his lean strength hovering over her bed, propping pillows and arranging to her comfort. When he began to ease her onto her side she stopped his hands with a freezing gesture and managed it on her own.

That left he looking up at him and him looking down at her. He had removed his coat and collar, and his shirt gaped open above his waistcoat. As an unmarried woman, she never saw men this relaxed in their dress.

Her vulnerability hit her with force. She said a quick prayer of thanks that of all the libertines in England, she had been fortunate enough to fall into this one's hands.

After all, they had come close to being related. That should count for something. She hoped.

He crossed his arms and regarded her. For a man with a reputation for being good-natured, his scrutiny appeared more critical than one would expect. She tucked the bedclothes around her neck.

"This is a remarkably singular occurrence, Miss Monley. Finding you, of all women, in my bed."

He wasn't going to make this easy.

Memorable, magical stories from nationally bestselling author

MARY BALOGH

"A matchless storyteller."—*Romantic Times*

ONE NIGHT for LOVE
_____22600-7   **$6.50/$9.99 in Canada**

MORE THAN a MISTRESS
_____22601-5   **$6.50/$9.99 in Canada**

NO MAN'S MISTRESS
_____23657-6   **$6.50/$9.99 in Canada**

A SUMMER to REMEMBER
_____23663-0   **$5.99/$8.99 in Canada**

SLIGHTLY MARRIED
_____24104-9   **$5.99/$8.99 in Canada**

SLIGHTLY WICKED
_____24105-7   **$5.99/$8.99 in Canada**

SLIGHTLY SCANDALOUS
_____24111-1   **$5.99/$8.99 in Canada**

*Stories of passion and romance, adventure and intrigue,
from bestselling author*

Julia London

The Devil's Love
____22631-7 $5.99/$7.99 in Canada

Wicked Angel
____22632-5 $6.50/$9.99

The Secret Lover
____23694-0 $5.99/$8.99

The Rogues of Regent Street:
The Dangerous Gentleman
____23561-8 $6.50/$9.99

The Ruthless Charmer
____23562-6 $5.99/$8.99

The Beautiful Stranger
____23690-8 $5.99/$8.99

Bantam Dell Publishing Group, Inc.	TOTAL AMT	$_____
Attn: Customer Service	SHIPPING & HANDLING	$_____
400 Hahn Road	SALES TAX (NY, TN)	$_____
Westminster, MD 21157		
	TOTAL ENCLOSED	$_____

Name _____

Address _____

City/State/Zip _____

Daytime Phone (_____) _____

New York Times bestselling author

Josie Litton

takes you to a world of passion and intrigue....

Dream of Me
Believe in Me
___58436-7 $5.99/$8.99 in Canada

Come Back to Me
___57830-8 $5.99/$8.99

Dream Island
___58389-1 $5.99/$8.99

Kingdom of Moonlight
___58390-5 $5.99/$8.99

Castles in the Mist
___58391-3 $6.50/$9.99

Fountain of Dreams
___58583-5 $5.99/$8.99

Fountain of Secrets
___58584-3 $5.99/$8.99

Fountain of Fire
___58585-1 $5.99/$8.99

Spellbinding, intoxicating, riveting...

Elizabeth Thornton's

gift for romance is nothing less than addictive

~

DANGEROUS TO LOVE
___56787-X $6.50/$9.99 Canada

DANGEROUS TO KISS
___57372-1 $6.50/$9.99 Canada

DANGEROUS TO HOLD
___57479-5 $6.50/$9.99 Canada

THE BRIDE'S BODYGUARD
___57435-6 $6.50/$9.99 Canada

YOU ONLY LOVE TWICE
___57426-4 $5.99/$7.99 Canada

WHISPER HIS NAME
___57427-2 $6.50/$9.99 Canada

STRANGERS AT DAWN
___58117-1 $6.50/$9.99 Canada

PRINCESS CHARMING
___58120-1 $6.50/$9.99 Canada

THE PERFECT PRINCESS
___58123-6 $6.50/$9.99 Canada

ALMOST A PRINCESS
___58489-8 $6.50/$9.99 Canada

Please enclose check or money order only, no cash or CODs. Shipping & handling costs:
$5.50 U.S. mail, $7.50 UPS. New York and Tennessee residents must remit applicable
sales tax. Canadian residents must remit applicable GST and provincial taxes. Please
allow 4 - 6 weeks for delivery. All orders are subject to availability. This offer subject to
change without notice. Please call 1–800–726–0600 for further information.

Bantam Dell Publishing Group, Inc.
Attn: Customer Service
400 Hahn Road
Westminster, MD 21157

TOTAL AMT $_____
SHIPPING & HANDLING $_____
SALES TAX (NY, TN) $_____

TOTAL ENCLOSED $_____

Name _____

Address _____

City/State/Zip _____

Daytime Phone (_____) _____

FN 31 9/03

DON'T MISS ANY OF THESE BREATHTAKING HISTORICAL ROMANCES BY

ELIZABETH ELLIOTT

Betrothed ___57566-X $5.50/$7.50 Canada

"An exciting find for romance readers everywhere!"
—Amanda Quick, *New York Times* bestselling author

Scoundrel ___56911-2 $5.99/$8.99 Canada

"Sparkling, fast-paced...Elliott has crafted an exciting story filled
with dramatic tension and sexual fireworks."
—*Publishers Weekly*

The Warlord ___56910-4 $6.50/$9.99 Canada

"Elizabeth Elliott...weaves a wondrous
love story guaranteed to please."
—*Romantic Times*

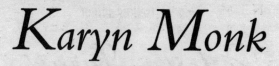